THE

wooing

OF

JANE GREY

THE

wooing

OF

JANE GREY

C.E. HILBERT

The Wooing of Jane Grey

© 2012 C.E. Hilbert

Published by
Deep River Books
Sisters, Oregon
http://www.deepriverbooks.com

ISBN-13: 9781937756017
ISBN-10: 1937756017

Library of Congress: 2012940041

Printed in the USA

Cover design by Jen Thomas

DEDICATION

To

My parents, Larry and Jean Ann, who have always believed in me,
even when I didn't believe in myself
My sister, Jennifer, who is the best cheerleader on the planet
And most especially, to God, who blessed me with the desire to tell stories
and a family of friends willing to listen to them.

Hope you enjoy
Jane's Story!
All the Best—

1 John 4:16

CHAPTER ONE

"GOOD MORNING," she said with a smile. "My name is Jane Grey."

"Jane Eleanor Grey. How are you today?"

Jane took in the length of her full five-foot-eight reflection as she continued with the mock introduction. "Me? Oh, I'm great, just great. I'm a complete idiot trying to change my entire life at the age of thirty-two, but other than that I'm awesome!" Jane let out a long sigh as she fell onto her bed.

Supported by her elbows, she appraised the full impact of her image. Her size-ten frame was forcibly mashed into the black size-eight pinstripe pants of her "interview suit." Bunching and creasing across her thighs, the pants fit like plastic wrap trying to corral a bucket of marshmallows. Her thick brown hair was scraped off her forehead in an absent-minded bun, and her rather unremarkable, slightly round face was devoid of any makeup. Ignoring her above-the-shoulders appearance masquerading as a piece of Cubist art, Jane focused on her immediate need for a pinch-hitter interview suit. The plastic wrap posing as pants was not going to make the cut for her interview the next day.

She wasn't too worried. Jane didn't need the job. She had a great job. She earned a fabulous salary, wore casual clothes every day, had a ton of responsibility, managed a great team of people, and had the respect of a pretty terrific boss. She had a good life. She didn't need the job—but she wanted the job.

Jane wanted to feel challenged, something she hadn't felt in longer than she cared to remember. She desperately needed a change. Something in the pit of her stomach wasn't allowing her simply to be satisfied with good.

Her life had become predictable. She promised herself, ten years ago when she received her diploma, that her life would never be predictable.

Safe and planned were okay; predictable was not. Death and taxes were predictable, and who wanted to be in the morgue or audited?

With the motivation of death and IRS agents, tomorrow at 10:30 a.m. she had an interview with the law offices of Miller, Wade & Jennings. They had an opening for an events coordination director, something Jane could master in her sleep. Who cared that her current job, and her entire résumé for that matter, had little to do with event planning? The interviewer would see past her lack of professional experience and take a chance on Jane. And Jane's apartment was located on the corner of Neverland Drive and Wonderland Boulevard, Columbus, Ohio, 43215.

"You are going to look like an idiot tomorrow," she said to her reflection. "Go ahead and order another two hundred business cards, because you're not going anywhere. You will die at DLT and your tombstone will read, 'Jane Grey: Dependable and Predictable; Always with a pen when you need one.' I guess death is better than the IRS."

Before she could order cheese at her table-for-one pity party, her phone rang.

"Hey, Janesie. It's Millie. Are you sitting down? I mean 'cause if you're not, you *totally* need to be."

"Yes, I'm sitting." Millie amazed Jane. At thirty-two, she still looked, and often acted, as if she were a twenty-one-year-old coed at Ohio State.

"Okay, so here's the deal—are you sure you are sitting down?" Millie had modeled professionally for nearly eight years, and at times the Runway Diva made her presence known.

Jane leaned into her elbows and stared at the small crack in her ceiling. "Yes, Millie, I am sitting down."

"Okay, so I was having lunch with a client today at Roscoe's—you know that yummy little Italian place near my office—when you will never guess who walks in."

"Lindy Barrett," Jane guessed, knowing that her favorite hockey player would never walk into the Dublin hole-in-the-wall.

"Yes!"

Jane jerked upright, and the sound of fabric tearing echoed off the walls. "Don't toy with me, Millie, I am not emotionally stable at the moment, and I just tore the seat out of my interview suit for tomorrow."

"I am drop-dead serious, Jane. There I am, chitchatting away with Tim "Balding Eagle" Booker, when in walks Lindy Barrett and sits down at the table next to us. My goodness, Jane, he's even better looking without his hockey gear."

"Tell me something I don't know, Mill. Was that it? He came in for a plate of carbohydrate goodness?" Jane tried hard to keep the dreamy tone hidden in her voice, but the thought of one Lindy Barrett set even her good-girl, Christian mind into fantasyland.

"Hardly. So there we were, the only other patrons in Roscoe's, sitting next to one of the best players in the NHL. I am in shocked silence. A thousand questions are running through my mind at warp speed, you know?"

"Uh huh . . ."

"I'm wondering, 'Why is he alone? Why is he at Roscoe's? Why isn't he with the rest of his hockey pals? Why am I at lunch with Tim Booker and not you?'"

Jane smiled at the continuity of Millie's all-out loyalty.

"All of these questions are running through my mind, when Tim leans across and taps Lindy's table. All I can think is, 'What a complete moron!' I mean, come on, is he going to ask for an autograph and embarrass me to high heaven? Not that I care about the jock type, but I was thinking about you, dearest."

"What did Lindy Barrett do?" Jane didn't feel she was worthy to refer to him by just his first name, despite the fact she'd been in the throes of a serious crush-affair with him since her junior year in college.

"He looked up from the menu and smiled. Man is he: gor-ge-ous. I don't normally go for the bigger-than-life, muscle-bound types, but Jane, he is an outstanding male specimen. Anyway, I'm digressing. So, he looks up, gives Tim a huge grin, and comes over to our table, chatting up Tim like they're old buds."

"Oh my gracious, are you kidding me? Your client knows Lindy Barrett? This is surreal," Jane said. With the phone suctioned to her ear, she began pacing the way she had in high school when a boy called to talk to her on the phone.

"It gets better. Not only does Tim know Lindy, he invited the hockey superhero to have lunch with us."

"No. Way! You had lunch with Lindy Barrett. I am the most envious person in the free world. My best friend shared pasta with Lindy Barrett."

"Don't pop another button. It wasn't quite *Lady and the Tramp* pasta sharing. Apparently, he and Tim went to prep school together and have stayed friends since."

"Bizarre . . . Lindy Barrett . . . You had lunch with Lindy Barrett. The Lindy Barrett . . . This has to be the coolest day in either of our lives. I mean, I know you modeled all over Europe, but come on, you had lunch with Lindy Barrett."

"Yes, I think we have established his name is Lindy Barrett. But you haven't let me get to the good part. Tim offered me two tickets for the game in his luxury box for tomorrow night, followed by a party benefiting the Children's Hospital. How would you like to be my date?"

"Sure, Mill that would be great, but how is that better than meeting Lindy Barrett? I mean, the tickets will be great, you know I love me some hockey. And I am sure the party will be fun, but come on, you met Lindy Barrett." As she spoke, Jane began to peel off her ruined pants. Once they made it to her knees, she used her socked feet to pull them the rest of the way down her legs as she continued to listen to Millie, envisioning sitting in the luxury box. She could almost see Lindy Barrett pointing to her as he celebrated his game-winning goal.

"No, Jane, the best part is that we'll be the guests of Lindy Barrett. We'll be sitting at his table for the event." Millie spoke slowly, obviously trying not to shock Jane. The effort was useless. With the news, Jane restarted pacing, and her pants, still around her ankles, caused her to fall face forward onto her bed. She bounced off the hard mattress and watched her phone take flight as she landed on the floor with a thud.

"Jane. Jane? Jane, are you okay?" Millie yelled.

Untangling herself from her pants, Jane stretched across the floor and retrieved her phone from the pile of discarded clothes. "I'm fine, just tripped. Now tell me again. We're going to be the guests of who at this charity brouhaha?"

"Of whom." . . .

"Of *whom* . . . whatever, Millie, don't tease me. Are you serious about Lindy Barrett?" Jane began to fan herself as her cheeks grew flushed.

"Yes. I take it you're free tomorrow night?"

"Uh, hello? This is Lindy Barrett. I'm free." Jane could feel her age drop as she pondered the prospect of dining with her decade-long crush.

"Great! The thing for the hospital sounds a little ritzy. Do you mind if I change at your place after the game?"

"Are you kidding me, Millie, you can change wherever and into whatever you'd like." Lindy Barrett, she thought. Lindy Barrett.

"Switching gears, are you ready for tomorrow?"

"Oh, the interview, I don't think I'm ready to leave DLT."

"'Oh, the interview . . .' Jane, for the last three months, all you've talked about is leaving your job. Getting a fresh start, new challenges, change, blah, blah, blah."

"I know. It's just that I'm really good at what I do now. Who knows if I'll be any good at this other thing? I don't know if it's worth the effort. I mean, come on, my interview suit pants ripped. That cannot be a good sign." She studied her rather pale, slightly cellulite-ridden bare thighs where her pants had been moments ago.

"Excuse me? Is this the same Jane Grey I've been listening to for the last three months? And I quote, 'My creativity is being stifled in this place. If I don't escape this myriad of green bars and flashing numbers, I will cease to exist. I will turn into one of those bitter old ladies who wears nothing but support hose and mid-calf-length skirts, always has a pen sticking out of her bun, and spouts statistics about the company like it's her single son she's trying to set up.' End quote."

"I know. I know. I just don't think I'm cut out for this job. I have practically zero event-planning experience. If you take out the political fundraisers and the sorority formals, I'm down to nothing. I have ideas, but no one is going to give this job to someone with ideas but no résumé. Even you aren't that charming, Mill. And let's face it: I need a job that pays at least as well as DLT in order to justify leaving."

"First, any company would be lucky to have you on its team. Second, organizing fundraisers for as many candidates as you have in the last six years should give you more than enough experience to set up a few cocktail parties for some loudmouth yuppies. Third, no amount of money is worth staying in a place that does not recognize your talent. Jane, they're using you for your business acumen at DLT. They don't give a hoot that you're a fabulous hostess, that you used to paint, or that you want to go back to school and study to be—what is it you want to be again?"

"I don't know . . . That's part of the problem. I shouldn't make any rash decisions in the state of mind I'm in today. Maybe I should make another list?"

"Honey, your state of mind hasn't changed in three months. Another day or another list is not going to give you some heavenly revelation as to what you want to be when you grow up. You need to step off the cliff. A list isn't going to give you a push. If you hate this job, then you quit and get another job. If you don't get this job, then you keep looking until you find the right job, but you should not stay at DLT to keep making good money. You like your job, but you don't want to be there forever. Jane, two years ago you were going to leave on principle, because you turned thirty, but what did they do? They promoted you to a director and sucked you right back into the whole mess, like Al Pacino in *The Godfather Part III*, 'Just when you think you're out, they pull you back in.'"

"I know you're right. I'm just not good at the whole changing-my-life thing. It's frightening."

"Of course it's frightening. It's change. Change is all about waking up the butterflies in your stomach and asking them to dance. You're nervous. They're nervous. And you're both moving about a million miles per second, generating moments of fear coupled with moments of great anticipation— definitely a whacked-out emotional roller coaster. Change is not for the weak of heart. Only the strong will survive. Will you take the challenge, my little buttercup, and fight for your freedom?"

"Okay, Braveheart, I'll go to the interview tomorrow." Jane mustered the enthusiasm of a teenager agreeing to clean her room. "By the way, you're doing an excellent job of being cheerleader of the month."

"I should think so. I must say that my pom-poms are getting a little overworked. When is it my turn to be glum again and you become the one woman pep squad that keeps me sane and bathing daily?"

Jane made her way back to her walk-in closet to search for something presentable for her interview. "Not until the end of the month, leaving me fifteen more days in October. And, lady, I won't be gypped like the last time when you broke up with that Italian folk singer who spoke zero English and drove a moped."

"Noted."

"Back to a much bigger issue, I don't know what I am going to wear tomorrow since I ruined my best, read that as 'only,' suit with my big, fat butt. And as DLT only cares that I come to work clothed, my closet is shockingly devoid of anything posing as traditional business attire."

"What time is your interview in the morning?"

"Ten thirty."

"Why don't you just swing by Taylor Longstrum's and pick up a new suit. The store opens at nine."

"Are you kidding? What if I don't find something? That is awfully risky, Millie."

"Hon, there is nothing risky about Longstrum's. They'll have a suit, and it'll fit like a dream."

"Millie, clothes only fit your body like a dream. The rest of us have to settle for presentable."

"Don't worry. They will have exactly what you need. It's the perfect plan." Millie's confident voice called up a distant memory of a dare she had presented to Jane in the eighth grade. The police still wondered how that manger scene ended up on the roof of the only restaurant in their tiny hometown.

"Call me tomorrow when you head into the office after your 'dentist appointment.' We can figure out times and such for the game then."

Jane dropped onto the pile of discarded clothing, absently rubbing her stomach, which suddenly wanted to reject her Lean Cuisine dinner. "Okay, but about the 'dentist appointment' idea, I still don't feel right lying about where I'm going."

"Get over it, Jane. What do you want to do? Take out an ad in the *Dispatch* that tells everybody you're going on an interview with another company?"

"No, but I don't feel right about being dishonest."

"Stop worrying. I'm hanging up the phone now. I'll talk to you tomorrow. Love you. Bye."

Jane pushed herself off of her mound of clothes and made her way back to her bed. Sitting on the edge, she caught another glimpse of her rather poor reflection and shook her head in disgust.

Not much I can do about the whole package tonight, she thought as she set her alarm for 6:00 a.m. and gave in to the temptation of snuggling into the comforting softness of her pillow. She promised herself she would only shut her eyes for a moment, but in that moment, she drifted off to sleep, with the fear of new clothes and hunky athletes floating on the edges of her mind.

CHAPTER TWO

HANDING HER WOOL TRENCH to the coat check girl at the Children's Cancer Research Institute benefit, Jane forcibly exhaled her breath in an effort to rid herself of the chaotic pieces of the last twelve hours. Today had made her feel she was the central figure in *A Tale of Two Janes*. "It was the best of times, it was the worst of times." From the interview this morning to her arrival at the hockey game tonight, Jane's day had taken twists and turns even the great plot master Dickens couldn't have developed.

The interview . . . Regardless of her attempts to let go of the nastiness of the experience, Jane's mind couldn't completely expel her morning spent at Miller, Wade & Jennings.

After waiting nearly forty-five minutes for her interview, Jane's nerves were spread as thin as the run in her nylons winding its way up the back of her thigh. And so, when the current director of events coordination at MWJ, Cara Jennings, a Neiman Marcus advertisement who was moonlighting as her interrogator—er, interviewer—asked her why she wanted to make a career switch, Jane's mouth moved faster than Millie at a sample sale.

"As you'll notice, I have extensive experience planning a variety of events and fundraisers for local politicians and for church. I enjoy making people happy and giving them an energetic and exciting place to have a party. I've had a great experience at DLT over the last seven years, but I really believe I'm ready to make a change and move on to a new opportunity in my life. This type of position is something I've always wanted to try full-time, but I've never found an opportunity that was available at the right time, until now. I know I can take events at Miller, Wade & Jennings to the next level."

Looking up from Jane's résumé, Ms. Jennings lifted a single, perfectly arched brow. "You're going to take our event planning to the next level?"

"Well . . . I didn't . . ."

"Not up to your standards, eh, Ms. Grey?"

"I really didn't mean to offend . . ."

"I will have you know, Miss Cambridge University, that under my direction the events at MW&J have made the cover of *Columbus Monthly* three times, been written up in the *New York Times Sunday Magazine*, and had a feature in *Town & Country*. Furthermore, I never had any intention of offering you the position. I was merely doing a favor for Millie Tandis, for all of the work she has done for our philanthropy over the years. I expect my successor to have at minimum the class and the style to fill this position at the standards to which I have set. I believe I fulfilled my obligation the minute I allowed you to give that egotistical, canned speech. You may now leave, Miss Grey." She stood and pulled the door open for Jane.

Stunned, Jane slunk through the doorway, feeling the breeze created by the heavy glass door's slow closure on her back. Jane turned and stared at the frosty entrance to the lioness's den. Swallowing audibly, she barely noticed her shaking hands as she searched her handbag for the comfort only candy could provide. Ripping the brown-and-white package, Jane sank her teeth into the chewy goodness, and her eyes slowly shut, welcoming the sweet calm that flowed from the chocolate in her mouth through her body. As she relaxed, her eyes flickered open, and her state of calm vanished as she caught her muted, yet gluttonous reflection in the glass.

Jane swiftly turned from the door, shoved the candy remnants into her bag, and frantically searched for her keys as she raced with her head down toward the sanctuary of the elevators with the single-minded focus of a wildebeest evading attack. She was startled, taking an involuntary step back, when her head rammed into an immovable object. Thinking she'd walked into a wall, as she had been known to do, she lifted her head and beheld one of the most attractive men she had ever seen, live and in full color.

Staring, unable to move, she watched the *GQ* model bend down and collect the extra copies of her résumé and files she didn't recognize, which must have flown on impact. He rose and sparkling white teeth peeked through his lips, as the blond Adonis handed Jane her papers.

"I think these are yours."

With her rapidly beating heart stuck in her throat, her voice took a brief vacation as she nodded, accepting the papers from his outstretched hands. Shoving them in her oversized bag, she gave him a quick, awkward grin before stepping around him to continue her speedy exit to the elevators.

Pressing the down button, she tried not to stare at the elevator doors which provided her with a muddled view of the gorgeous man. She wondered what his story was, but she would never be bold enough to turn around and ask. She wasn't Millie.

Her heart gained momentum as she watched the handsome stranger's reflection grow larger until he stood directly behind her and lightly tapped her shoulder. Turning, she looked up at his amused face.

The Adonis held out his left hand. "I think you may have dropped this."

In his open palm lay the small wooden cross her father had given her when he returned from Jerusalem seven years earlier. A soft smile tugged her lips as she reached for the token.

"Thank you. I would have been quite devastated when I discovered it was missing."

"You're welcome." His smile warmed Jane like a quilt on a cold winter's day. "I'm Paul Wade."

"Nice to meet you, Mr. Wade," she said, placing her hand in his.

"I'm assuming you have a name, or should I just call you pretty girl?"

Lowering her head slightly she tried to hide the blush she could feel rising in her cheeks. "More like clumsy girl, but most people call me Jane."

"It's delightful to meet you, Jane."

The *bing* announcing the elevator's arrival burst the fragile bubble that encased them.

Jane released Paul's hand and stepped toward the open door. "Well, I guess that's my cue." Turning, she entered the elevator. "It was nice meeting you, Paul."

She pressed the button for the lobby and leaned against the mirrored wall as the doors shut before her. Barry Manilow's woeful voice filled the elevator, allowing her mind to go pleasantly blank as she rode to the lobby. Grateful for the time to settle her heart and mind before driving the twenty minutes to her office, she pulled on her gloves and tightened the belt on her coat in anticipation of the cold wind tunnel of High Street. The elevator doors opened to the marble-and-glass foyer of the Huntington building, and Jane lowered her head as she stepped over the small opening leading to the elevator shaft; the click of her heels was the lone sound in the deserted lobby.

At the same moment she reached her right hand for the revolving door, she felt a gentle touch on her shoulder. Jane turned and took in the full length of Paul Wade.

His breath was coming in shallow spurts as he lowered his hand from her shoulder to her left hand. "I forgot to ask you."

Jane's breathing paced itself with Paul's as she waited for him to continue.

"I forgot to ask you," he repeated.

"You forgot to ask me what?" The feel of her hand in Paul's warm grasp sent a ripple of nervous waves through her stomach.

"I forgot to ask you"—he smiled as though inspiration were dawning— "if you would like to have lunch with me."

A giggle bubbled up through her. "You forgot to ask me to have lunch with you?"

He nodded. His slightly curling hair brushed the top of his starched collar, which lay partially inside his V-neck sweater, making Jane's hands itch to straighten him back to perfection.

"You forgot to ask me, who you just met, to have lunch with you?"

"I guess that doesn't make sense."

Jane smiled, reluctantly pulling her hand from his.

Relaxing, he shoved his hands in his pockets. "How about this—Jane, would you care to have lunch with me?"

"Umm, better." She glanced at her watch. If she could convince her boss that her dentist had run late, she probably could squeeze another hour out of her appointment. Millie would be so proud. "I think I can make it."

His grin stretched wide across his face, turning Jane's knees to Jell-O.

"Great," he said. "My car is parked down the street." Guiding her toward the side exit, Paul lowered his hand to the small of her back with a protective touch. In the distance, Jane was certain she heard the faint sounds of angels singing. All thoughts of calming candy, crazy interviews, and escape routes dissolved with one realization—Jane was having lunch with a hot guy.

Over lunch she discovered that beyond being beautiful, Paul was a successful attorney at the firm and a devout Christian. She was sure she could feel God nodding His head in approval throughout their meal. The hour flew by as Jane and Paul found they had nearly everything in common. Most important to her was Paul's easy conversation about his faith. For Jane, who often felt the lone Christian in the ultra-competitive dating world, meeting Paul lit a spark of hope about her romantic future, softening the disappointment of watching her career hopes fizzle like a wayward firework.

By the time she met Millie that evening for the hockey game, she'd stuffed the bad interview behind a door marked Do Not Ever Try Again and was flying on the high of New Boy Infatuation. She was so enthralled with the idea of a potential super-cute Christian man in her life that she'd nearly forgotten she was going to meet Lindy Barrett. For Jane, completely forgetting Lindy Barrett would normally require a lobotomy.

Mentally shaking the memory of her fairy tale of a day, complete with Prince Charming and the wicked queen, Jane surveyed the beauty of the elegant ballroom. She was slightly amused as dozens of eyes seemed drawn to the doorway where she and Millie stood.

Entering a room beside Millie was like being the basketball in Shaq's hand. People were so busy looking up that they occasionally missed the round object scoring the points. Millie was a hair's breadth under six feet tall with a mass of blonde hair that flowed perfectly down her back. With the exception of mascara and lip gloss, Millie had avoided makeup since she retired from modeling. Her face, in a single word: perfection. If Jane didn't love her so much, she would envy her to the point of sin.

Tonight was no different from any other night. Millie had draped her lithe body in a fire-engine-red cocktail dress and looked every inch the model that she used to be. Conversely, Jane exuded quiet elegance in her black crepe cocktail-length dress from the Macy's dress-up floor. When Jane paid $850.00 for the simple halter dress, which Millie insisted was the little black dress every woman needed, she nearly imploded. The dress might not be flashy, but Jane knew she looked good. She was thankful, because she knew she would need every ounce of confidence one little black dress could give her.

Jane still couldn't fully grasp the surrealistic situation in which she found herself. She had a realistic romantic thread of hope with Paul, and now she was living out a fantasy she'd held nearly all of her adult life. She was going to meet Lindy Barrett. She always knew God loved her, but this was beyond a bounty of blessing.

"Janesie, could this day get any better? Not only did you meet that dreamy lawyer at the awful interview, but you're going to sit next to your twelve-year fantasy while he eats his steak and potatoes." Millie spoke as she lifted one of the small place cards from the table.

"I've been so caught up in what happened this afternoon that the reality of Lindy Barrett being here wasn't really . . . real. I mean, I knew he was going to be here, but my brain kind of couldn't grasp the situation. He'll be sitting next to me for two hours while we have small talk and I worry about the spinach caught in my teeth."

"Well, get your babbly brain ready." Millie pointed behind Jane.

Leaning casually against the makeshift bar, urbane in a black three-button suit, hair still damp from his post-game shower, was six feet four inches of rugged masculinity named Lindy Barrett.

Embarrassed to be staring at him and fearful drool was dripping down her chin, Jane turned her back on the scene of fawning women and men. "Oh . . . my . . . goodness. Is he really that good looking?" She stole another glance over her shoulder. "Yep, he sure is."

Jane tried to pull Millie from the table. "We need to go to the powder room, immediately."

"Jane, number one: no one except my great-aunt Mabel calls the bathroom the powder room. Number two: you are not hiding in the bathroom all night like you did at the junior prom just to avoid Tuck Wilson's knowing that you ate and drank like a normal human being."

"I did not hide the whole night. I came out and danced two dances with Darby Strong, who also happened to be my date."

"Dancing with the class designated driver does not make you a woman who spits in the face of danger, Miss Grey. If I physically have to nail you to your chair tonight, you will have a conversation with Lindy Barrett. I did not throw myself at Tim "Balding" Booker so that you could have the chance to meet Mr. Wonderful, and then watch you toss the opportunity away."

Jane knew Millie was right; even if she didn't want to admit it. She wanted to run and hide, but she owed it to her friend to at least pretend she was above the age of sixteen.

She was probably worried about nothing. When Lindy came to their table, he wouldn't even see Plain Jane in the shadow of Magnificent Millie. If he noticed her, it would only be to discount her, as had most of the attractive, athletic, wealthy men with whom Millie had valiantly tried to set her up over the years. He would be entranced, as they all were, with Millie. All a man had to do was be in a room for thirty seconds with Millie and he was pulled with quantum force by her magnetism. It didn't take a rocket scientist to figure out that a healthy, red-blooded male would choose Millie over Jane. Heck, Jane would even recommend to most men the obvious choice; being chosen last for the boy-gets-girl team had been happening all of Jane's life.

While she listened to Millie rattle off the menu and the items up for auction, Jane gave herself a silent pep talk. *Get a hold of yourself, Jane. He's a normal man just like any other man. Pants: one leg at a time, etcetera.*

Breathing deeply, she glanced back toward the bar and watched as Lindy strode—not walked, but took long strides—toward their table.

Major correction: He wasn't even in the same league as normal. He was in the bottom-of-the-ninth-out-of-the-ballpark, penalty-shot-to-win-the-Stanley-Cup league, and she, her quite ordinary self, was going to sit beside him for two hours and eat. Food. Meat. Ugh! Lindy Barrett was going to know that she ate, on a regular basis, and in public no less.

Her legs felt like overcooked spaghetti, and she had the sneaking suspicion her body now included five extra worry pounds. Pulling her seat away from the table, she tried to sit gracefully while pretending to comprehend Millie's chatter. *Breathe. In and out. In and out. You can do this, Jane. You are Albert Puljous in the batter's box. Just another day at the office. No worries.*

"Are you a bit nervous, kiddo?"

"Not in the least. Why do you ask?"

"Because, my friend of over twenty years, your button nose is redder than Rudolph's on Christmas Eve," Millie said with a smile.

Jane's hand shot to her nose, and she could feel the heat emanating from its tip like a beacon in the night. "Mill, I have to go to the pow . . . ladies' room and fix it. I'll be right back."

"If you aren't back in ten minutes, I'm sending Lindy Barrett in after you."

Without pretense of grace or finesse, Jane bent at the waist to retrieve her handbag from under her chair. With bag in hand, she quickly stood and made her way toward the bathrooms in not quite a run, but definitely an exercise better suited for her Sauconeys than her Ferrigamos.

Whipping open the door, she scanned the spacious room designed with luxury in mind to see if she had any unwanted friends. Relieved to find that she had the ladies room to herself, and thus no need to be concerned with decorum, she made a beeline for the vanity area. Yanking her MAC compact from her bag, she immediately went to work repairing her nose.

Her nose, or rather her Achilles heel, was the first and best indicator when she was feeling any emotion other than calm. Angry or frustrated, sad or nervous, her nose, for no clinical reason, became a red flag for all to see. Her nose was her own built-in mood ring.

Covering the last of the scarlet, she closed her compact and pulled her nude-colored lipstick from her bag. She felt more in control as she smoothed the color across her lips. From her suit ripping at the seams through to her fifty-yard dash across the Hyatt ballroom, the last day had the makings of the best journal entry in her thirty-two years. And now she was only moments from meeting Lindy Barrett.

What did she really have to fear? Just because she'd been in a constant state of crush with Lindy Barrett for the last twelve years didn't mean she couldn't be her most charming, cocktail-party self, right? She'd come a long way from the girl who hid in the bathroom at parties. Even if she *was* currently in the bathroom.

She was successful, confident, and beautiful. Okay, maybe not beautiful, but definitely a step up from five years old, pudgy, and cute. She had shared meals with leaders of major corporations, senators, governors, and only six months ago, she'd sat on the dais with the former president of the United States. Why should she be scared of a little hockey player? He probably didn't even have all of his teeth.

Snapping the lipstick closed, she ran her fingers through her hair, gave it a toss, and winked at herself in the mirror. So what that he was *the* Lindy Barrett; she was *the* Jane Grey. *He* should be nervous eating dinner with *her*.

"Hah!" She laughed with a dramatic flip of her hair. Turning to the door, she pulled it open with a flourish.

Doing her best imitation of Rita Hayworth in *Gilda*, Jane sauntered across the room and back to her table. With each step, her confidence grew. She could feel eyes following her as she walked. They could sense her courage. They could tell she was not to be messed with, but to be admired and revered. As she drew closer to the table, pure feminine power oozed through her body like molten lava making its way down the side of a volcano, melting everything in its path.

Sparkling like Waterford crystal in sunlight, she addressed her dinner companions. "Good evening, gentlemen, my name is Jane. I believe I will be sitting with you this evening."

She was woman; hear her roar!

With her newfound confidence, Jane was barely flustered when Lindy—her Hayworth impression allowed her the freedom to call him by his first name—stood up and pulled her chair from the table. "Let me help you, Jane. My name is Lindy."

Looking into his deep, nearly navy-blue eyes, Jane felt her confidence waver for a moment as she mumbled a "nice to meet you" and "thanks" as she took her seat.

The remaining four occupants at the table introduced themselves with smiles and nods. To Lindy's left was Jason "Hooty" Horton, the best defenseman for the Jackets, who embodied every classic hockey stereotype, from a scar through his eyebrow to a scraggly blond mullet that would make Barry Melrose proud. To his left was Wilbur Macintosh, the chairman of the Children's Cancer Research Institute, the evening's benefactor. A completely entranced Tim Booker sat by Millie, barely looking away from her as he and Jane were re-introduced. The remaining two occupants were members of the Institute's board of directors and looked to be on the far side of eighty.

As Jane pulled her napkin from the table to her lap, Millie whispered in her ear, "Nice moves coming into the ballroom. So, Janesie, you just wowed a table of men worth more than a half a billion dollars combined. How do you feel?"

"Like I want to go to Disney World."

Turning to their table, Jane smiled. "I apologize for being tardy. What did I miss?"

Lindy moved close to Jane and spoke softly with a voice as smooth as velvet. "Hooty over there," he said, pointing to the defenseman, "was giving me a hard time for the three obstruction penalties I took tonight. Bookie has been drooling over your friend, the octogenarians in the corner are swapping war stories, which, I am pretty sure, are from World War I, and good old Wilbur has been racking his brain at how to get each of us to outbid ourselves in the silent auction."

"And what have you been doing?" Jane asked.

"Waiting with bated breath for you to return from the powder room, so I could have some decent conversation. I hope?"

His grin, full of God-made teeth, warmed her to her toes better than the best campfire ever built. "Well, we'll see what we can do about the conversation. Would you like to discuss applied statistical theory, or the rise and fall of communism in eastern Europe?"

"Definitely statistical theory. I can never find anyone to discuss p values with on the team bus."

Their salads were served, forcing a stop in conversation. Jane bowed her head and thanked God for the food, but mostly for gifting Lindy Barrett with an IQ as attractive as his physique. With an amen, she reached for her fork and knife and began to eat.

"She does that everywhere." Millie offered. "From Thanksgiving to a McDonald's Happy Meal, Jane gives thanks."

Stopping mid-bite, Jane looked from her salad to Lindy's gorgeous blue eyes, his handsome face marred by the slight crease in the middle of his forehead. She could feel her nose glowing. *Great! For five minutes of my life, Lindy Barrett thought I was cool, or at the very least, worth speaking to. Now I'm just weird. What ever happened to Andy Warhol's fifteen minutes?*

She laid down her fork and lifted her napkin to her mouth, dabbing invisible crumbs. "You caught me. I am a big, fat Christian."

Lindy continued to silently observe her without touching his salad. Peeking from the corners of her eyes at her other tablemates, Jane was relieved that they were not the subject of curious stares. Even Millie had gone back to flirting with Tim.

"Your salad is going to get cold."

Still, he stared. Death would be preferable to being the continued focus of his quizzical gaze, not only because Lindy Barrett—she was back to using his full name now; coolness had fallen out of her grasp like a hot potato—thought she was an oddball, but she was also missing the perfect opportunity to evangelize.

Please forgive me, Father, but this just isn't a good time for me. She felt God's disappointment flow over her as she returned her focus to her salad, pushing the blue cheese and croutons around her plate.

She sensed Lindy lean toward her, but she was too afraid to look into his eyes. "I think it's great," he whispered into her ear, squeezing her left hand under the table.

With a single touch of his hand, she felt her calm, her confidence, and her ability to chew return as she took a final bite of salad before the catering staff arrived with the main course.

As the tuxedo-clad servers descended upon the table, Lindy leaned back in his chair to allow the main course to replace his untouched salad. "Millie tells us that you're a bigwig at DLT. What is corporate America really like?"

"Millie tends to exaggerate. I am not exactly a bigwig."

"Don't let her kid you. That company would fold in two weeks without her, but she's looking for greener pastures. Aren't you, kiddo?"

Jane pinched Millie's arm under the table, but Millie wasn't one to take a subtle hint. Her mouth continued to run like a wheel with a gerbil inside.

"Janesie really wants to get into fundraising-slash-event-coordinating full-time. Don't you, kiddo? She throws a brilliant party. The best you'll ever attend. Trust me. I've attended more than all of our fair shares of parties, so I'm an excellent judge." She flipped her blonde tresses for impact.

"That's highly unlikely, Millie, but I would love to compare notes with you sometime," Jason interjected.

Jane chuckled to herself as she felt the revulsion Millie kept politely under wraps. Millie hated jocks. Jocks were Jane's type. Millie had never quite understood Jane's attraction to the bulky athletic type, but Millie also never needed a big man to make her hundred-and-ten-pound frame feel willowy. Millie preferred emaciated rock musicians and artists. Even hair-thinning Tim was preferable to Millie over thick-muscled, mullet-adorned Jason.

As if Jason hadn't spoken, Millie focused the attention back to Jane. "You really don't know what you're missing, Lindy. Jane's GOP fundraiser for the gubernatorial candidate raked in nearly two hundred thousand dollars for the chump. The event drew two retired senators, a top-forty recording artist, and a former president of the United States. Not too shabby for a research geek."

"Millie, I'm sure the gentlemen would like to discuss something other than politicians and fundraisers." Jane turned to Jason. "How about that game? You had your hand in some pretty spectacular blocked shots. I've always felt defensemen were underrated."

Millie ignored her and kept talking. "I'm sure you gentlemen of philanthropy can appreciate a woman who can throw a kick-butt party!"

"Millie, for goodness' sake. *Shut up*," Jane whispered through clenched teeth.

"I know I can!" Jason grabbed another roll from the breadbasket and ripped it apart with gusto.

"I think she was referring to a party to raise funds for our pet causes. Isn't that right, Millie?" Lindy asked, trying to defuse his teammate's enthusiasm.

"I just thought since most of you at this table have your own pet causes, you might want to solicit some advice from my very talented friend. Someone of Jane's experience and altruistic background is hard to come by. You have her cornered until dessert, gentlemen, you should pick her brain."

Memorizing the pattern of the tablecloth, Jane realized what her not-so-subtle friend was trying to accomplish. Despite Millie's best efforts, Jane would never be cool. No matter how hard Millie tried to make her a citizen of Cooltown, Jane was a life-long resident of Lameville. She occasionally had a visa to visit her friend, but a green card always eluded her.

"Well, Miss Grey, I for one would love to hear your ideas." Wilbur jumped into the conversation. "The Institute is always looking for new ways to raise funds and awareness."

The fifty-something, pudgy researcher looked like most of the men Jane knew through work, church, and politics. His glasses were slightly askew on his round face, and he had the gentle demeanor of a confirmed bachelor. He was safe, and Jane was thankful for the reprieve from Millie's cheerleading.

"Well, Dr. Macintosh, I think that if you're trying to gain awareness about children's cancer, you should come up with creative ways to integrate the people who would be most impacted if childhood cancer hit them. Your fundraisers should be kid and family centered, and they should be fun. Have a children's fair at the science center or a dance marathon with Ballet Met. Silent auctions are always good, but they just don't appeal to the common Joe. What you need is to focus on entry-level giving. Allow people to feel like they're part of the cure. Think about a thirty-dollar family ticket to a fair, which is tax deductible, rather than searching out your next thirty-thousand-dollar gift from one contributor. You can still benefit from those large contributors with programs like tonight's, but your reach through 'awareness giving' will generate a broader giving base. People will feel that they can help, even if just a little, and that makes people feel good. People want to be part of the solution."

Wilbur nodded his head as a smile stretched his chubby cheeks. "What a great concept, Miss Grey. Would you be willing to draw up some plans and show them to our board?"

Jane could feel her cheeks warm at his enthusiastic response. "I would love to, but there's probably someone more qualified to help you develop a fundraising campaign."

"No, no, Miss Grey. You're very creative. You're just what we need to spice things up a bit." With his emphatic speech, his native New England accent filled the space at the table.

Unsure she could speak, Jane nodded and gave Wilbur a soft smile, but under the table she squeezed Millie's hand in strained excitement.

"I'd love to hear what you could do for A Kid Again," Lindy said. "I sit on the board here in Columbus, and we're constantly in search of new blood to help with raising money for the kids."

"The research hospital isn't your pet cause? I just assumed this was your charity of choice, seeing as you're one of the guests of honor."

"Do you have to have just one?"

"I guess not," Jane said softly.

Over the main course, conversation at the table shifted to lighthearted quips and swift-moving stories. Jason regaled the table with a bawdy tale of how he and his teammates initiated the rookies. Millie, not one to be overshadowed, shared a story from her first runway show. The good-natured laughter continued throughout the meal, and as their dinner plates were cleared, and dessert served, Jane felt a twinge of sadness that her time as Lindy Barrett's dinner companion was rapidly drawing to a close.

Her will power forced her to keep sipping coffee, ignoring the beautifully appointed dessert in front of her. The cake, with its quarter inch of icing, was surely a little slice of heaven, but instead of digging into its delectable deliciousness, she pulled her eyes from the instant poundage masquerading as cake, and allowed her gaze to drift about the table.

Each of the occupants was in a varying state of completing the desserts. One of the two WWI veterans had fallen asleep, while Wilbur droned in his ear about the new developments in cancer treatments. Jason had devoured his piece of cake with the same enthusiasm he had shown through the meal, before heading back to the bar, opting for an after-dinner beer rather than coffee. Millie and Tim huddled as they ate, but Jane gave little care to the seemingly intimate scene. Had Norman Schwarzkopf been beside Millie at dinner, he too would have been huddled in close-quartered conversation with her by dessert and coffee.

Jane's gaze fell on the final table occupant, and she encountered deep blue eyes staring at her without the slightest subterfuge. Her blush, which had retreated, warmed her cheeks as she dropped her focus back to her coffee cup. Certain she would melt from the heat of his scrutiny, she sat her cup on the saucer with the intent to escape to her personal Eden, the ladies' room.

Before she could scurry away, the wall speakers threw out a squeal, drawing attention to the podium situated directly in front of their table, making a subtle exit impossible.

"Good evening, ladies and gentlemen. I hope all of you have had a pleasant dinner. My name is Dr. Toby Jenson. I'm a researcher with the CCRI. I would like to thank all of you for attending this evening. With your gracious ticket purchases, the Institute has raised close to fifty thousand dollars. We thank you. Your donations will help to move us a step closer to stopping cancer in our children."

His smile was broad as he waited for the applause to fade. "I am now pleased to share with you the items that generated the highest bids in tonight's silent auction." Looking down at his sheet, he slipped on small reading glasses.

"The item that drew the third-highest bid was for a hot-air balloon ride and champagne lunch over southern Ohio, donated by Lift-Us-Up. The lunch and ride will go to Colby Snyder with a bid of six hundred twenty-five dollars. Thank you, Lift-Us-Up and Mr. Snyder for your generous donations."

A gentleman in his mid-forties, presumably Colby Snyder, partially stood and nodded his head at the applauding dinner guests as an elegantly attired young woman wound her way through the tables and handed Mr. Snyder an envelope and a cluster of colorful balloons.

"The second-highest bid was for an hour hockey lesson with our own local hero, Lindy Barrett. The lesson went to Tyler Richardson for eight hundred fifty dollars. Thanks go out to Lindy and Mr. Richardson for your donations."

Applause greeted both Lindy and Richardson as they stood and shook hands.

As Lindy sat back down, Jane leaned over and whispered into his ear, "Congratulations. That's pretty impressive, being the 'item' that garnered the second-highest bid of the evening."

Throwing his arm over the back of her chair, he pulled her closer to him. "Kind of hurts my feelings. I never liked being second best." He leaned back in his chair, but his arm remained casually draped over Jane's shoulders. Butterflies the size of 747s took off in her stomach as she tried to refocus her attention on the podium and off the tremor that rippled through her body.

"The highest bid was for two tickets to this fall's Ohio State–Michigan game. The tickets are in A Deck and are the generous donation of the OSU Athletic Association. The tickets went to Don Watson for a donation of one thousand dollars. Thank you, Mr. Watson. Tonight, to give the tickets to the lucky bidder, is a legend who needs no introduction, Archie Griffin." With the announcement of the OSU football hero, the audience erupted in a thunderous ovation. The former halfback and current assistant athletic director handed a small envelope to the highest bidder before waving to his adoring public.

Clapping, Lindy leaned back to Jane and whispered, "Well, at least I was beaten by a worthy opponent. In this town, an hour on the ice with me isn't even in the same stratosphere as a handshake from the two-time Heisman winner and Ohio State v. Michigan tickets."

She shook her head. "I don't know about that. Even as a native, I've never been into the OSU-Michigan rivalry. Given a choice, I think I would definitely take an hour on the ice with you than sit through yet another mind-numbing football game in the freezing cold."

"I knew I liked you for a reason." Lindy drew her into a casual side hug.

Jane forcibly turned her attention back to the podium, but her mind was reeling with the information that Lindy Barrett liked her. The 747 butterflies transformed into fighter jets.

Assuming that the good doctor was finished, people began to move from their seats and into the ballroom for dancing. Some ventured over to shake Jason's and Lindy's hands, congratulating them on their win and showing their admiration for Lindy's donation, separating Jane from Lindy.

Jane picked up her handbag, when she noticed a buxom woman in a skin-tight royal-blue dress slither up to Lindy. Shaking her head, Jane turned to Millie. "I'm going to fix my nose. I'll be back in a bit."

Millie lifted her head and nodded to Jane just as the curvaceous redhead leaned into Lindy. Motioning Jane down to her level, Millie chuckled. "Do you think they gave her talcum powder with that dress to avoid chafing?"

Jane giggled. "Where are Stacy and Clinton when there's a true fashion emergency?"

Once she was blessedly ensconced in the quiet luxury of the ladies' room, she went about repairing her glow-in-the-dark nose and touching up the other slips caused by a combination of the warm banquet room and her nearness to Lindy. Feeling confident everything was securely in its place, she made her way back to the table.

With dinner now over, she assumed that Lindy and Jason, finished with their obligatory philanthropic event, would be off to other more lively activities. A soft pang of regret hit her heart at the thought of not speaking with Lindy again. The likelihood that the two of them would ever be in the same room, that was not Nationwide Arena, was about as high as the Kennedys voting Republican in the next presidential election.

When she saw not only Lindy, but Jason too, still lounging at the table, a gentle smile lifted her lips, until her eyes moved six centimeters to the right. "Annie," as Jane now dubbed the redhead reminiscent of the Susan Sarandon character in the baseball classic *Bull Durham*, had taken residence in Jane's seat. Draping herself over Lindy's shoulder, she was giving her best impression of wallpaper with the little room her skin-tight dress afforded.

Lightly tapping Annie's exposed shoulder Jane gained her attention, "Excuse me. I believe you are in my seat."

Tossing her mane of hair, she didn't bother to look at Jane as she spoke. "Oh, sorry, I thought dinner was over. I decided to come over and keep Lindy company. You won't mind finding a new seat, will ya, sweetie?"

Lindy quickly stood, taking Jane's hand in his. "Sweetheart, you've been gone so long."

Caught off guard, Jane played along, leaning into Lindy, who threw his arm around her shoulders and pulled her tight, kissing her lightly on the top of her head. The fighter-jet butterflies broke the sound barrier, and Jane tried diligently to suppress the giggles from their turbulence as Lindy introduced Annie to her.

"Darling, this is Cassidy. She was nice enough to visit with me while you were in the ladies' room."

Jane beamed at Cassidy, whose face was becoming an alarming shade of red as she twisted awkwardly to watch the cuddling couple. "How do you do, Cassidy?"

"I didn't realize that Lindy was dating anyone."

Lindy grinned at Jane, squeezing her closer to his side. "Janesie here likes to keep a low profile, but now she owes me a dance. Don't you, sweetheart?" Looking at the table he continued, "Please excuse us. It was nice meeting you, Cassidy."

Sliding his fingers through hers, Lindy led Jane through the dining room and into the ballroom. She was grateful for the anchor of his fingers for she was certain she would float away on the clouds under her feet.

CHAPTER THREE

AFRAID TO SPEAK, for fear she was actually dreaming, Jane stepped into Lindy's arms and they began to dance to the jazz band that was playing.

"Thanks for rescuing me." Lindy smiled down at her.

"I guess I'm a little confused. I didn't even expect you still to be here when I got back, let alone want to leave the dish in the dress."

"It doesn't matter what city or what bar, women like Cassidy are a dime a dozen, literally. When we get done with a game, or arrive in a new city, they're hanging around like vultures circling their prey. I guess I'm over being the fresh meat. You know?"

Jane nodded in agreement, not that she knew what he was talking about; no one had ever considered Jane a piece of meat, let alone circled her in an anticipation of a meal.

They continued to dance, enjoying the comfortable ease with which their bodies moved in time to the music. She could feel her whole body relax as she looked into his eyes. His gaze was intense, causing an effect similar to that of warm tea on a cold winter's night, soothing and hot, all at the same time.

As the band picked up the beat, Lindy twirled her around the dance floor with the effortlessness of a *Dancing with the Stars* star in the making. The naturalness with which they moved allowed Jane the freedom simply to be in the moment, reveling in the safety and security of his strong arms. Yet, somewhere, deep in her subconscious, she began to grapple with the question of why this gorgeous man had decided to pay attention to her. She pushed her self-doubt and the overweight teenager back into the Pandora's Box from which they'd escaped and pulled a Scarlett O'Hara: she would think about it tomorrow.

The music slowed again, and Lindy began to leisurely move Jane across the dance floor. She laid her head lightly on his broad shoulder, comfortably at ease in his quiet embrace. A winding stream of memories flowed through Jane's mind as she swayed to the music. She could see herself at twenty or twenty-one, staring for hours at the images of Lindy wallpapering her dorm room. How many times had she dreamt about a moment like this, and now it was real. Whoever said that God didn't answer prayers?

"So, Miss Jane Grey, why don't you tell me a little about yourself?"

His question was like ice water in her face. Why in the world would he want to know about her?

"Umm . . . It's n-not that interesting of a t-topic." Seriously. She was going to start stuttering now? Stupid Pandora's Box of tricks. "Gee, umm . . . How about we discuss the upcoming election or the World Series? I must say I'm p-pretty much over the stranglehold the Yankees seem to have on the playoff picture, but who knows, some people like dynasties. I was particularly fond of Alexis C-C-Carrington in the mid-eighties. Heck of a woman. How about we talk about her?"

"Nope. Spill it. I want to hear all of your deep, dark secrets."

The box burst open and teen angst spewed out of Jane, treating her like a ventriloquist's dummy. "Well, I hate to disappoint you, but there really isn't m-much to tell. I'm five foot eight. Thirty-two years old. I'm a native of Columbus, and with the exception of a few years of college, I have . . . umm . . . lived here my whole life. And now, I'm d-dancing with you. Although I must warn you, I do tend to trip a lot, so if for some odd reason I f-fall over some invisible object, please pretend like you didn't see me tumble. Umm, and yeah, I'm pretty involved in my church. I'm a fanatical movie buff. That about sums me all up in a t-teeny-t-tiny nutshell. Umm, yep, that sh-should do it. Like I said, not that interesting. Why don't we t-talk about you? I am sure your life can f-fill more than a double-spaced index card." Why did her parents ever her teach her to talk? *Really, Jane, five foot eight, really? Who rattles off her height with her biography?*

"That's all I get?"

"That's pretty much all there is to give."

"I guess I'll have to be satisfied . . . for the moment. But I'm warning you, eventually I'll know all there is to know about you, Janesie."

He pulled her tighter in his embrace. She once again laid her cheek, now burning what she was sure was a bright shade of red, against his shoulder. Moving slowly to the music, her embarrassment melted into the dance floor as her long ago boxed up hedonist emerged. Here she was, an upright, morally astute citizen who prided herself in her Christian ethics, and all this gorgeous hunk had to do was smile at her, ask a few questions, and she was draped over him like her Grandma Garrett's favorite shawl. She was, to her most distraught consternation, a typical female.

———

After nearly an hour of dancing, Lindy led Jane by the hand back to their table before returning to the bar to fetch her a diet soda. At the table, Jane was surprised to find Millie in a heated debate with Jason, while Tim nursed whatever brown liquid resided in his glass.

"You're crazy if you believe that Miles Davis is not one of the best, if not the best, jazz musician in the modern era," Millie said, leaning toward him.

"I'm just saying that he's awfully commercial." Jason propped his chair back on two legs. "True fans of the art know the underground musicians, the ones who only play in holes-in-the-wall and dingy nightclubs."

"Did you hear that, Janesie, he thinks I am not a *real* aficionado of jazz, simply because I like popular music. Fans are what create popularity." Millie matched Jason's casual posture and shot him a cold look. "Translation: *aficionado* means *fan*, hockey boy."

This was serious. Millie never got nasty with men. She preferred to have them eating out of her hand, saving the sharp side of her tongue for catfights in ladies' rooms. *Very interesting.*

"Thanks, O Blonde One." Jason saluted her, dropping his chair to the floor. "I must have missed the day at Harvard when they taught multisyllabic words to us dumb jocks, or is it just hockey players you believe to be illiterate?"

"Did you really go to Harvard?" Jane asked.

"Not only did the genius go, but he graduated with honors," Lindy said as he placed Jane's soda in front of her and slid into his chair. "Not an easy feat for an athlete. What was that brainiac major you had, Hooty?"

All eyes moved to the defenseman, best known for brain-rattling checks and late-night parties. "Molecular Biology," he answered.

"Didn't you apply for medical school?" Lindy sipped his drink.

Jason focused his attention on tearing the label from his bottle. "It was my backup plan. Can we talk about something else?"

"Your backup plan for what?" Jane asked.

"In case I didn't make it in the draft. I was accepted to Duke when I was selected in the second round by Detroit. I decided to give it a try. I figured if I didn't make it out of the AHL in two seasons, I'd give up hockey and go to school. I was traded the following summer to Columbus and called up when one of the starting defenseman was injured. The rest is history." Relaxing in his chair, Jason acted as if the information he had shared was not counterintuitive to his long-standing dumb-jock image.

"You mean you could be a doctor right now instead of some, some . . . some . . . some jock?" Millie exclaimed.

"Give me a break, lady! What do you care? You're not my mother who's still after me, ten years later, to quit this stupid hobby and go to med school. What's your deal? Are you always this much of a witch to everyone you meet, or am I special?" Draining his bottle, he glanced at Lindy. "I'm outta here. You coming?"

Lindy shook his head in the negative.

Jason shoved back from the table and pulled on his suit jacket. "It was nice meeting most of you," he said, pointedly ignoring Millie. "I'll see you at practice, LB."

Jane turned to Millie, who, perhaps for the first time in her life, had to be feeling what commoners refer to as a serious case of rejection. She appeared composed, but the lively color that usually brushed her cheeks had faded, replaced by a ghostly white.

Jane reached her hand to Millie. "Are you okay, Mill?"

Unable to break her gaze from Jason's retreating form, she simply nodded her head.

"Sorry about that. Hooty's sensitive about being a smarty," Lindy shared. "He has it somewhere in his thick skull that his intelligence is a weapon that can be used against him on the ice, so he acts how he thinks everyone expects a big NHL star to act. I never should have goaded him. I hope you're not too offended, Millie."

Millie shrugged her shoulders. "No it's not your fault. This entire evening, I implied I was superior in both intelligence and class, and he took it. Apparently, I'm neither. I'm simply a snob." Turning to Jane she said, "I'm really not feeling too well. Do you mind if I leave?"

Jane's mind began a private war. She knew she should leave with Millie, do the whole best-friend thing, but she wanted to be Cinderella for a little while longer. However, she owed her best friend more than ditching her in her hour of humiliation. "I'll just go and get our coats."

Millie put her hand atop Jane's. "I wouldn't hear of you leaving. I'm sure Lindy wouldn't mind dropping you off at your apartment. Would you?"

With a wide grin, Lindy leaned forward and possessively draped his arm across Jane's shoulders. "It would be my pleasure."

"Are you sure, Millie?"

"I wouldn't dream of asking you to leave simply because I've been a horse's behind and need to wallow a bit."

As Millie stood, Tim followed suit, lightly placing his hand on the small of her back. "I guess I'll be on my way as well. Millie, would you mind if I walked you to your car?"

"That would be lovely. Thank you, Tim." Turning toward Lindy, she smiled. "It was nice meeting you again, Lindy. Hopefully the next time we meet I'll be more Princess Charming and less Wicked Witch of the West."

She leaned down and kissed Jane on the cheek. "I want the complete romance novel details in the a.m."

Lindy and Jane watched as Tim and Millie gracefully made their way through the tables before disappearing out the side exit. Cradling his chin in his palm, Lindy returned his focus to Jane. "And then there were two."

Jane turned and mirrored his position, a slight smile on her lips.

Lindy's gaze made Jane feel like he was studying her for a midterm. "Well, Miss Grey, in what can I interest you? More dancing, perhaps? A nightcap? Or would you really like to ditch the hockey player and call your friend to grumble about what a horrible evening you had entertaining this dumb jock who wouldn't leave you alone?"

Jane couldn't help but chuckle at the irony. The more likely scenario would have her gushing over Lindy for hours upon days to the point of Millie pulling a *Moonstruck* Cher and hitting Jane upside the head, yelling at her to snap out of it.

Taking a quick look at her watch, Jane was shocked that it was after one. She couldn't remember the last time she'd stayed out past midnight. "I didn't realize it was so late."

"It's not too late." Lindy pulled her left hand to his, reading the time on her watch. "I haven't turned back into a frog, yet."

Unable to resist the temptation, Jane boldly played her fingers through his as they rested on the table, indulging in the warmth spreading through her with the simple touch of their hands. "We should probably go." Her protest sounded weak, even to her own ears, but the rule-following Christian girl always took over the controls when the least amount of passion was involved. "I don't want to be the reason you're grouchy at practice tomorrow." Although she secretly wanted to be the reason he was anything tomorrow.

"You're probably right. For as whacked as our schedule is, I'm not much of a night owl. I'm surprised I made it this long." Standing, he kept his hand linked with hers and pulled her to him. "It must be the company. How about a quick walk along the river?"

Longing to embrace every moment of the fantastical night, Jane readily agreed. Lindy led her through the ballroom as Jane followed, her feet a good two inches off the ground.

———

Wrapped in her full-length black evening coat against the brisk October air, Jane linked her arm through Lindy's as they stepped onto the quiet streets of downtown. She could have sworn she heard an orchestra playing in the background, and she was quite certain that if she looked at her hand it might be the gray of a classic 1930s romantic comedy come to life. As they walked, their discussion remained firmly rooted in whimsical topics from movies to sports. Nothing deep or monumental, just conversation among new acquaintances: safe, non-emotional, and lighthearted.

Sometime between their introduction and their walk along the riverfront, Jane forgot he was *the* Lindy Barrett. He was Lindy. Not the hockey player. Not the dream man of her life. Not the guy on the Wheaties box. Just Lindy.

Nearing the Firefighters Memorial, Lindy stopped to silently read the inscription on the memorial marker. Giving him a private moment, Jane walked to the low wall leading to the water, searching the murky depths of the Scioto.

"This is a pretty amazing monument," he said. "The eternal flame and all. I've never seen it before."

She turned to face him. "You've lived here, for what, four years now, and you've never seen the Firefighters Memorial?"

Walking to her side, he leaned against the wall and focused his attention on the moonlit river. "I drive by it nearly every day leaving the arena, but I guess it never registered. After 9/11, everyone sees firefighters in a different light. They run into buildings when everyone else is running out. They risk their lives so other people can live." He rubbed his hands together against the cold. "It's a little overwhelming to think about, you know?"

She nodded her head and joined him in shared silence, allowing the sounds of the river to wash over them. The fog was lifting off the water and made their surroundings seem more primitive and less industrial. A sudden gust of wind chilled Jane, and she pulled her coat tighter across her chest. Noticing her movements, Lindy put his arm around her shoulders and drew her to his side. He kissed her head and spoke softly. "I should probably get you home."

"You're probably right."

Turning, they walked in a couple's embrace, pacing their steps with reluctance and contentment as they retreated to his car.

The serenity she had enjoyed on their walk degenerated in the two-minute car ride to her apartment. The soft sounds of the radio tempered the silence but did little to quiet Jane's hyperdrive mind. Would he walk her to her door? Would he want to come in? Would he simply drop her off and wave good-bye? Her hibernating nerves awoke with the near scream of her internal sixteen-year-old.

Pulling into her parking lot, Lindy turned off the ignition. The silence was deafening as each second clicked by without either Lindy or Jane moving. He flexed his hands on the leather-encased steering wheel, a muscle in his jaw dancing to an unheard melody as Jane waited for a sign, desperately trying to keep the teenager at bay. It was not everyday that the object of a girl's fantasy dropped her at home after the most spectacular evening of her life. At least it wasn't everyday in Jane's life.

"Well, I suppose I should go up."

Lindy nodded.

Her inner teenager erupted with the reverted hormonal frenzy of awkward insecurity. "It's been great, Lindy. We'll have to get together sometime when you're in town. It was very nice meeting you. Good luck with the season and all. Umm . . . yeah . . . well . . . bye."

As she reached for the door handle, Lindy brushed her arm with the lightest of touches. "Wait," he said with a brief breath of a voice.

Her heart beat quicker, pushing down the uncertain teenager and reasserting a glimmer of hope in the woman. Seconds ticked by like hours on an unseen clock in Jane's head as Lindy's hand lightly slid down her arm to clasp her hand.

The single parking light shone in behind him, partially veiling his face in darkness. He toyed with her fingers, slowly stroking them in his grasp, simultaneously calming her and stoking the fire building deep in her soul.

"I don't really know what to say, Jane." His voice was soft and broken. "You're an amazing woman, and I guess I didn't believe women like you still existed."

Jane's face warmed with his compliment.

He lifted his head. "I can't believe I'm saying this, but I feel like I know you already, and I think you'll understand."

Oh no . . . "You'll understand" is never a good statement from a man.

"About five months ago, I split up with the woman I'd been dating for nearly four years. We weren't right for each other, but on paper we made sense. Tess figured it out long before I did, and she went about finding someone else, someone who was right on paper and off. It was a pretty nasty break-up, and to be quite honest, I'm not over it."

Ugh. Here it comes . . . I just want to be friends.

"You're fantastic, and I'd really like to get to know you better, but I'm not looking for a girlfriend right now, or even a casual date. I'd really like to be friends, if that's okay with you."

"Let's be friends." Ladies and gentlemen . . . we have a bingo! Masking the war between desire and rejection in her heart, she squeezed his hand

and smiled. She knew this routine better than most. Her male friends out-numbered most people's Facebook friends.

"That would be great," she said, with a smile that was the product of her sorority years. "I'm not really looking to date anyone now either. I can always use a new friend, especially one with access to free hockey tickets," Jane awkwardly joked. "It'll be great. Give me a call when you're in town, and we can get together, go for a walk, or a dance, or if you really want to be just one of the girls, we can sit up late, paint each other's toenails, eat chocolate ice cream, watch old movies, and cry."

Making his way around the outside of his car, he opened her door and offered her his hand. "You're too much. I *will* give you a call. I don't know about the toenails, but the rest sounds great."

With what she hoped was grace, and not her usual clumsy movements, Jane took his hand and stepped from the car. Unsure of where their new relationship status left them, Jane withdrew her hand from his but kept in stride with him to the back entrance. With each step, she pushed down her dejected teenager who was trying to escape her box.

Unlocking her back door, she turned slightly to Lindy and smiled. "It's been really great meeting you, Lindy."

"Hey, Janesie, you're talking like we'll never see each other again."

And with that innocent statement, Teenage Jane burst through her mouth like a scene from *Alien*. "Come on, Lindy. Let's be honest with each other. You say you want to be friends and that you want to get to know me, but deep down you know I'm the last person you want to be around. Little, plain Jane Grey is okay for a dinner party, but not for anything else. 'Don't want to hurt her feelings, so I'll throw her the line about "Let's just be friends." That ought to do it.'"

Unable to take his reaction, Jane turned back to the door, fumbling with her keys as she tried to pull them from the lock. *I will not cry, I will not cry. I didn't cry when I got stood up for the winter formal, and I will not cry over some dumb hockey player.*

Lindy slid his hand over her shoulder, tenderly turning her back to face him. "Jane, I don't know what makes you think I don't want to get to know you better, but I do. I just can't be anything more than friends with anyone . . . right now." He lifted her chin and forced her to look him in the eye. "I really could use a good friend. A friend who wants me for me . . . not because of the hockey or for the money or for what I can do for her, but simply because she cares about me. I think you could be that kind of friend, Jane. I know I want to try and be that kind of friend to you. I'm really sorry if I came off sounding like an insincere jock, but I'm not the most eloquent of guys. You'll need to talk to Hooty if you want smart. Me, I'm only good for a few slap shots and some laughs."

She felt Teenage Jane slip back into Pandora's box, firmly closing the lid. "Did I forget to mention that I can be a bit of a drama queen?"

"I told you earlier I want to know everything about you. It didn't take me to long to discover your dramatic flair. Give me time, and I'll know all of your deep, dark secrets."

She smiled. If only he knew her biggest secret was her reawakened crush standing six inches in front of her.

CHAPTER FOUR

A DISTANT RING WOKE Jane from peaceful sleep. The self-indulgent, slothful imp on her shoulder convinced her sleep was more important than any emergency her mother, her sisters, or Millie might have. Ignoring the phone, she snuggled under a mound of blankets.

She prayed it was a telemarketer, which meant no message and no annoying beep signaling a message waiting to be heard from the well-worn answering machine she'd had since college. She waited and then, as if God Himself decided to kick her imp to the curb, the beeping began with its ridiculous regularity, proving to her that the acceptance of the modern convenience of voicemail had more to do with annoyance than with a desire to be a more evolved species.

Unable to return to her blissful state, Jane looked at her clock: 8:03 a.m. She knew it would be justifiable homicide when she went Michael Corleone on the inventor of the answering machine for denying her an extra hour's sleep.

While she devised different forms of torture worthy of *The Godfather Part IV*, the distinct sounds of her cell phone penetrated her criminal thoughts. Obviously someone, likely Millie, was desperately trying to get in touch with her.

Pushing back her covers, Jane scrambled to reach the elusive cell phone. She flipped it open and began to talk without looking at the number. "Listen, lady, it is still too early to have a coherent conversation. Meet me at the Bean Scene in an hour. You're buying."

Not waiting for a response, she snapped the phone closed and dropped it back into her bag,

An hour later, she stepped onto High Street, looking fairly chic for an early Saturday morning, in a white T-shirt, a black V-neck sweater, dreadfully hip jeans, supple leather boots, and a buttery-soft cashmere scarf. Something about the possibility of cute men in the general vicinity had her wanting to spruce up a bit, and after two encounters in one day, Jane thought sprucing up was definitely in order. Her mother would be so proud.

She made the short walk to the local coffee shop in mere minutes. After ordering her double-shot skinny cappuccino from a teenager with enough piercings to qualify as a water sprinkler, she stepped aside to wait for her coffee. Couples cuddled in corners and students pounded on laptops. Two dark-haired young men, not much older than nineteen, hunched over a laptop, as one's fingers rapidly typed away plans for the future. Near the window, a man sat neatly dressed in a Mister Rogers sweater and a button-down plaid shirt, seemingly content to sip his coffee and simply be with other people. The activity in the coffee shop was nothing extraordinary, just another Saturday in the WonderBread City of Columbus, but Jane felt like Jane Goodall as she surveyed the scene.

With a secret smile, she pulled her focus from the societal study to the stationary line in front of her and began tapping her foot to a rhythm only she could hear, willing the rather tall blond man in front of her to take one tiny step forward. Something about him was familiar; his hair, maybe? Perhaps she knew him from church? Or maybe he was a client? It was useless. Without caffeine, the mystery would have to wait. Her brain wouldn't function without the pressed little glory that was a gift from God, and she would never be so bold as to tap on his shoulder and ask him how she knew him. She wasn't her mother.

As she reached the front of the line, she watched the two baristas do more chitchatting than actual milk steaming and espresso pressing. At the pace the two were working, she'd be lucky to have her coffee by the time her first child entered elementary school. Between her dance routine and the line's advancement, she kept a peripheral eye on the entrance, watching for Millie, who seemed to be running inordinately late, even for her.

At the sound of her name, Jane greedily grabbed her coffee from the latte lady, took a long drink from her cup, and let out a sigh of relief. Taking a second drink, she glanced down at her watch and registered that nearly an hour and a half had passed since she'd spoken with Millie. With her brain now fortified, her worry kicked into gear.

Standing by the window near Mr. Rogers, Jane shifted her gaze between her watch and the door. With her eyes working like a metronome, her concern over Millie's absence developed into a Terror Level Red panic attack. Millie was not a punctual person, but it was uncharacteristic for her to be this late when she was desperate for details about Jane's nocturnal activities.

Jane punched *1 on her phone and waited for Millie to answer with, "I'm still looking for parking, Miss Antsy Pants." Or "Got pulled over by a state highway patrolman and now he's trying to get me to go on a date with him."

After four rings, a slightly groggy Millie answered her cell phone. "Hello?"

"Where are you? I'm freaking out that you're on the side of the road, left there for dead by wandering gypsies who make their cash by posing as scary carnies at the state fair!"

"Okay, um, crazy girl said what?"

"Where are you, Millie? You're now officially twenty minutes late."

"Late for what? You do realize I'm not the best morning person, so if you could back up a few chapters and give me the *Reader's Digest* version, I might be able to follow your psychotic interlude."

Feeling a slight nudge on her shoulder, she stepped to the side, assuming she was blocking the flow of traffic in the minute locale, and slid into a tall chair by the window. "Amelia, I realize it's quite early in the morning, and you of all people know I empathize with your lack of early morning chipper, but you called me at something-after eight this morning, remember?"

"Dearest Jane, you must be mistaken, because this Amelia has been deep in decadent dreams, until two minutes ago, enjoying the reprieve from remembering my abhorrent behavior of last night and the rather insistent headache gathering at the base of my skull. You must have spoken with another of your age-old friends who will forgive your rudeness and will continue to love you despite your hyper-paranoia."

"But you called this morning."

"Jane, did I actually speak to you?"

Biting her lip, Jane thought for a moment. "Well, no, not exactly."

"What exactly happened?"

Jane tried to relay the play-by-play of the phone call. "My home phone began ringing before eight this morning, and you know how I hate any calls before nine, so I didn't answer it out of principle, thinking it was a telemarketer or my mother. Then the stinking answering machine started its annoying beep, beep, beeping that really pushes me over the edge."

"Jane, darling, the point you were getting to, do you think you might want to share it before lunch?"

Jane sighed. "A few minutes into the beeping, my cell phone started to ring. I figured someone must be pretty desperate to get in touch with me, which I translated to be you. I answered the phone and said, 'Meet me at Bean Scene in an hour,' and hung up the phone."

"Jane that could have been anyone."

"But it wasn't anyone, it was you."

"We've already established it wasn't me. Who else could it be?"

"I have no idea." Thoughts of her mother stranded on the side of the road or her father lying under his tractor raced through Jane's mind, turning the coffee in her stomach like the spin cycle in a washing machine and causing her to barely notice the renewed soft tap on her shoulder.

"It could be anyone," Millie said.

Jane's mind was in warp speed worry, her nose surely flaming, as she turned in her seat to give the nudger a good excuse-me look when she came red nose to perfect nose with Paul Wade, hottie Christian lawyer from the horrid interview. The washer in her stomach shifted to delicate with a subtle flutter. "Uh, Mill, I know who called. I have to go."

Before Millie could ask a question, Jane shut the phone, rubbing her nose to try and wipe away the Rudolph. "Hi."

"Do you mind if I sit down?"

"No, not at all . . . You must think I'm a horrible person. I thought you were my friend Millie when you called this morning. I reserve rudeness for my closest friends and family."

Smiling a deliciously sweet smile, Paul winked. "Well, then I'm glad I received that greeting this morning. I hope to be a very close friend in the near future."

Jane warmed from her temples to her collarbones, and she knew the effervescent glow of her nose could light up Times Square. No amount of wiping was going to help. "I'm so sorry about how things started this morning. I wish we could just restart the day with a do-over."

"Okay." Picking up his coffee, Paul left the coffee shop by the back door. Jane watched through the large expanse of windows as he walked up the sidewalk toward the main entrance.

He breezed through the front door, looking windswept and rugged in his lightweight North Face jacket, worn jeans, and cotton sweater. Glancing around the shop, he appeared to be nervously in search of a familiar face, until his eyes fell on Jane, and a welcoming smile spread across his cheeks—the kind of smile that says, "I am so happy to see you," and does wonderful things to the inside of the recipient's heart.

"Good morning, Jane. I'm so glad we could get together today." Paul greeted her with a light peck on the cheek before sliding into the seat across from her.

After a half hour of smiles and casual conversation, they decided to take their to-go cups of now-cold coffee and wander through the Short North art district where they both lived. The morning spilled over into early afternoon as Jane and Paul explored the unique shops and galleries. Their conversation flowed easily, like that of old friends whose rhythm was seamless from years of practice. Jane didn't feel any of the nauseating 747 butterflies or moments of insecurity she'd experienced the night before; Paul was just a man, not a legend.

When they were ready for lunch, Paul suggested an impromptu picnic along the river. Jane readily agreed, feeling herself sliding deeper into the dreamy haze of the afternoon. Opting for pizza from the North Market, Paul offered Jane the crook of his arm as they walked the short distance between the market and the river. Jane couldn't help herself as she snuggled into his side, reveling in the idyllic picture they made on their walk: boy and girl "in like."

Paul dusted off a bench in the deserted little park. He set the pizza between them as Jane settled onto her end of the bench, pulling her right leg to her chest and wrapping a single arm around it to ward off the cold October afternoon. Sitting on the opposite end of the bench, he angled himself toward her as he handed her a napkin and a slice of pizza.

A sudden wave of timidity washed over Jane as she reached for the pizza and the awkwardness of a food date reared its ugly head with the arrival of Teenage Jane. She mumbled a thank-you, laying the napkin and the pizza in the small space between her and the box. She could feel the awakening butterflies. Not quite 747s, but definitely not sweet little fluttering butterflies. She hated being sixteen.

Paul tore into his slice of pizza like a man who hadn't eaten in, well, four hours. He was on his second piece when he noticed Jane hadn't touched her slice. "Do you not like pizza? I can go back and get you something else." He pointed behind him in the direction of the North Market with his half-eaten slice.

"No. I'm fine." Jane picked up the pizza and took what she hoped was a dainty bite. She chewed with deliberate slowness, willing the butterflies to not reject the pizza. A picnic by the river had sounded so romantic, but as Jane sank her teeth into a second bite of pizza, her fear of eating in front of boys, umm, men, made her favorite food taste like castor oil.

Paul's watchful gaze took in Jane's pained expression. "Jane, you don't have to eat it if you don't want. Are you not feeling well, or do you just not like pizza?"

Jane looked into Paul's questioning green eyes, and her thirty-two-year-old self made a play for power. *This is ridiculous. You need to learn how to eat in front of men you think are handsome. You've been lucky up to this point that most of the men you have dinner with are icky.*

"I'm really fine, Paul. I'm just taking in the moment." Jane took a larger bite and smiled, forcing her sixteen-year-old-girl nerves down with a swallow.

"I was hoping you weren't one of those girls who eats salads and picks at her food because she's afraid she's going to get fat or talk with her mouth full."

Jane took another bite of pizza to stifle the giggle over the accuracy of his description.

Paul reached across the back of the bench and laid his hand on Jane's shoulder. "Because I think you're pretty amazing, and I would hate to think you didn't believe the same about yourself."

Jane couldn't move as he withdrew his hand, the warmth of the imprint seeping through her body. From the corner of her eye, she watched him pull a third slice from the box and focus his gaze on the river. He thought she was *amazing*. She should probably correct him, but her mouth was full of pizza, and she was enjoying the puddly feeling of her melting heart.

They ate in companionable silence for a few minutes, the distant sounds of cars on Broad Street and the flow of the river encapsulating them from the outside world. Jane stealthily watched Paul take the last bite of his pizza slice.

Crumpling his napkin in his fist, Paul lifted his gaze to Jane. "I don't mean to be presumptuous, but do you have plans for this evening?"

"What, aren't you sick of me yet?"

"I wasn't asking for myself. I have this friend, and since you've been such a good date, I thought I would share the love."

"Nice."

"So are you?"

"Am I?"

"Free tonight?"

"Um, yeah, I think so. What did you have in mind?"

"Well, let me think." He shifted his gaze to the riverfront, deep in thought. "I see candles, maybe a little nice jazz music. Nice dinner."

Great. More eating. "Hmm . . . you used *nice* twice in the same sentence, so either you have a pitiful vocabulary, or this must be my signal that a dress-up dress is in order."

"That might be a good idea."

"Well in that case, I'll need some time to primp and be a bit girlie."

"I don't know. You look pretty darn good to me right now."

Survey says: good answer.

Jane smiled. "Although I hate to argue with your educated and enlightened opinion, I still feel the need to go home and be the girl my mother always wished I would be. Besides, I like to get gussied up every now and again. Please, don't tell Bitsy Grey. My mother might implode in a fit of ecstasy at the mere thought of my taking more than thirty minutes to get ready for anything."

"Deal. How about I pick you up at seven?"

Jane glanced at her watch. Four o'clock had come and gone. She was going to be pretty tight on girlie time, but she could swing it. "Sounds like a plan. I should probably head back so I can wow you with the other me that only comes out for fancy parties."

He laughed as he cleaned up the remainder of their makeshift picnic. Watching him as he threw the trash in the waste can, she was amazed that such a sweet, smart, gorgeous man could still be single. She suppressed her innate urge to ask him if he was a psycho killer or a recently released mental patient. God would not do that to her. He loved her too much—although He did tend to have a fairly ironic sense of humor when it came to Jane's love life.

After dusting the remnants of crumbs from his hands, Paul gallantly extended his hand to help her stand, but respectfully released her hand as they began to walk.

They made their way up Marconi Boulevard toward the arena in companionable silence. Jane used the quiet to try and mentally google her closet and her sorry excuse of a makeup bag, wondering how she was going to make herself into Millie in less than three hours.

The cold suddenly whipped off the river, reminding them it was October in Ohio. She snuggled deeper into herself, wrapping her arms tighter across her center, trying to conserve her body heat. When she had left her apartment in the morning, she had not anticipated a lovely afternoon of sweet guy wrapped up in fabulous conversation, or wandering the Short North and the Arena District without a coat. Her body was near frigid in her simple sweater and scarf, but she did look good.

Slipping her hands deep into her jeans, she glanced up at the arena as they crossed the street, and she was hit head first by the train of Lindy Barrett and his a billboard size image plastered on the side of Nationwide Arena. Her sixteen-year-old self rose to the bait.

How could one man be that beautiful? The events from the previous night floated through her mind like a taunting ballet. She could feel Lindy embracing her as they danced and the warmth of his arm around her as they walked along the river.

"Jane, are you okay?" Paul placed his hand lightly on her shoulder.

His worry was etched in his forehead and she knew she needed to reassure him, but she was having a hard time remembering his name or in fact, where she was. She was too lost in the black-and-white magic of the night gone by.

"Jane?"

"I'm fine, got a bit lightheaded. It happens sometimes."

Guilt over her lie of omission returned the heat to her face. But what should she have said? *"Oh, sorry, I got all gooey and gushy over the big billboard of the hot hockey player I've been in lust with since I was twenty and who I fell all over last night, but who thinks I'm good friend material?" Umm, not likely.*

"Do you want to get a cab? We still have a mile to walk back. I don't want you to get sick."

He was so concerned that Jane could feel her nose starting to glow like a lighthouse on a stormy night. "No, really. I'm fine. It happens all the time. I just need a little sugar. I'll eat a cookie when I get home."

"Okay, but I'm walking you all the way to your front door. No arguments."

Extending his support, he slid his arm around her as they continued past the arena. She was thankful for his warmth, helping to shut out the memory of Lindy's face.

The brief walk to her apartment led them through the parking lot of the North Market and by the beautiful Greek Orthodox Church, the unofficial gateway of the art-filled community of the Short North. At the High Street entrance to her apartment, Jane turned and smiled up into Paul's face. "I'll see you in a little bit."

"Are you sure you'll be up to it?"

"I'm feeling better already. Seriously, I'll be fine. Just a little low blood sugar—an excellent excuse for a few Oreos."

"Well, if you're sure. I'll see you at seven."

"That sounds wonderful. Until later?"

"Until later."

He leaned in and kissed her softly on the cheek. The gesture was sweet, just like him. *Lindy, schmindy.*

She waited until he disappeared down a side alley before sprinting up the three flights of stairs to her apartment in less than thirty seconds. Pulling open her cell phone and her door simultaneously, she punched *1 and proceeded to her closet.

"Yes, O Rude and Nearly Ex-Friend," Millie said.

"I'm so sorry, Mil, but you'll never believe the day I've had, let alone the last twenty-four hours. I feel like I'm in Jane Austen's England, not in Plain Jane Grey's Columbus, Ohio."

"Okay, I'm desperate for the gossip, so I'll accept that measly excuse for an apology, but the story better be good, and I mean *New York Times* Top Ten list good, Jane Eleanor."

"It is. But before I give you the details . . . what are you doing for the next hour?"

"Plopping down on my couch for an evening of sappy love stories and Ben & Jerry's, why?"

"Could you bring over your essential Millie Gear and get me sassied up for a date?"

"Wait a minute? Is this my friend Jane using the words *sassied* and *date* in the same sentence? Since when do you have a date for which you must become sassy? Be honest with me—you have connections with the Big Man Upstairs—is this the Apocalypse?"

Jane laughed. "No it isn't the official Apocalypse, I don't think. But I know if you don't haul your little bottom over here, this night might be the apocalypse of my dating life."

"I'm on my way."

Jane closed her phone and slumped against the wall beside her closet. Millie was the Superwoman of friends. Able to leap make-up catastrophes and anxiety-laced dates in a single bound.

CHAPTER FIVE

"OKAY, DETAILS. And you'd better give them to me fast—in order—or you're not even going to get to look into the essential gear case," Millie said, breezing past Jane.

Shutting the door behind her friend, Jane sighed. "Where do I even begin?"

Millie headed straight for the bedroom and began efficiently preparing the emergency makeover kit, known since high school as Millie's Essential Gear. "Well, why don't you start by telling me who's the date?"

"Paul." Jane collapsed into her overstuffed chair across from Millie, who had turned her bed into a Lancôme counter.

"Paul?"

"Christian-hottie-from-the-horror-interview-yesterday Paul?"

"Oooh. When did you talk to him?"

"Today. He was the person I thought was you, rudely calling me this morning. He's who I met at the Bean Scene. And he's who I spent the entire afternoon with, meandering through the Short and along the river."

Millie lifted her head and raised a single inquisitive eyebrow. "Why, Jane, you little minx. You meandered in public?"

Jane rolled her eyes. "Millie, stop it. It was sweet. He is very sweet."

Millie winked at Jane. "Okay, so we're getting you all sassified for Mr. Sweet-and-Hunky Christian," she said, refocusing her attention on the project before her, selecting and rejecting a variety of eye shadow and lipstick shades.

"Good." Jane pushed herself out of her chair and leaned over the edge of her bed to review the rejection pile.

"Now, question number two . . ."

"Yes?"

"What happened with the McHottie Hockey Stud last night?"

Jane looked up from the makeup rejects, as her stomach did a complete three-hundred-and-sixty-degree flip. "We danced a little bit then went for a walk along the river. We talked . . . about nothing, really . . . and then he brought me home."

"Man, I need to spend more time by the river. Sounds like quite the hot spot for some smooching."

"Get your mind out of the gutter, Tandis. There has been no smooching. Both of them were perfect gentlemen." Jane bit her bottom lip, willing her flushed cheeks to cool as a ten-second trailer of her time with Lindy rolled in her mind. Lindy had kissed her on her cheek and her head, but that wasn't *technically* smooching.

"Of course they were. They were trapped in the aura of Saint Jane, patron saint of all single virgins over thirty."

Jane rolled her eyes. "We're not going to get into my life decisions right now, Millie. I have less than an hour to make myself look like something other than myself."

"Darling, that's why I am here. Now sit your cute butt down and tell me the rest of the details on the hockey player. I know you, Jane, that blush did not come from walking along the stinky river and casual conversation."

Pushing through the cosmetics, Jane sat cross-legged in front of Millie on the bed and closed her eyes, thankful for the excuse of a makeover not to have mind reader Millie searching her eyes as she recounted the previous evening. "I don't know what to tell you. We had a great time, or at least I did. And, of course, my mind jumped ahead to babies and growing old on the front porch at about the same time he told me he wanted to be friends because he just broke up with his girlfriend of forever. He said he liked me, but he wasn't ready to jump back into any type of commitment. I then became a just-add-water instant drama queen, thinking he was blowing me off—I mean, after all, we had fantasy kids and rocking chairs together. I was quite devastated."

Millie provided a comforting murmur as she brushed eye shadow across Jane's right eyelid.

"Anyway," Jane continued, "once he calmed me down, he told me he genuinely wanted to be friends. He said he needed people in his life who were interested in him beyond hockey. I think he's serious. I told him to call, and we could watch sappy movies and paint each other's toenails. I left out the part about my twelve-year infatuation with him. It seemed a little too creepy."

"I think it wise to avoid revealing anything to a man that could result in restraining orders," Millie offered.

"I feel bad for him. Never knowing if people like him for himself or for what he can do for them," Jane said, trying to ignore the pull on her heart.

"I know how he feels. Ultimately, that kind of isolation is why I quit modeling. That and the fact I couldn't eat chocolate cake on a regular basis," Millie added, smoothing foundation across Jane's cheek.

Peeping open one eye, Jane smiled at her friend. "I'm so glad you quit. I was getting sick of calling New York, or Paris, or Milan, or wherever, when I had a crisis. I like it so much better now that you can drop by and cheer me up whenever I need it."

"Close, I need a smooth canvas."

Jane obediently closed her eyes and remained silent as Millie continued to create her masterpiece.

"I'm glad I quit, too. I hated every minute I couldn't share with you."

Contentment from a lifetime of friendship hugged Jane's heart. "I love you, too."

⁓

"Well, will I do?" Jane asked forty-five minutes later as she turned from her full-length mirror.

With eyes squinted and lips pursed, Millie took on the air of a high-end art collector trying to assess the value of a new piece. She lifted her eyes back to Jane's and nodded her head. "Friend, if I were a guy, I would ravage you on the spot."

Jane laughed, dusting invisible lint from her lightweight black wool pants and cashmere sweater. "I'll remember that for future reference." Walking into the spare bedroom, she pulled a tiny snakeskin bag in an ombre of greens off the beautifully orchestrated shelves, specifically built to hold her ridiculous handbag collection. She opened the clutch and dropped in a lipstick, a compact, her ID, a key, and twenty dollars. Her crazy mother had taught her a vital thing in life: just because the bag is small does not mean one should skimp on the necessities.

Her front door buzzer sounded with the closing *snap* of her bag, as if orchestrated by an unseen movie director. In response, Jane sighed dreamily, causing a reflexive roll of Millie's eyes.

"Janesie, he may want to come upstairs," Millie said.

"I guess so," she said without moving.

"Jane, snap out of it! It's just a date. You spent all day with him. Remember?"

"I know." Jane shook her head as she unlocked the street door with the panel buzzer. She could hear Paul's feet on the bottom stairs as he made his ascent. Taking a deep breath, she stepped into the hallway and leaned over the banister, greeting him with a quick hi.

He grinned. "Do you live at the top of Everest?"

"Hey, the top floor is always the best." Jane leaned against the railing and watched as he scaled the final stairs.

"Whew, I guess I didn't need to run this morning." He took in the length of her as he handed her a small bouquet of flowers. "Wow. You look incredible."

She lifted the flowers to her face and breathed in their delicate fragrance. The scent drew the corners of her lips. "I believe you've earned the award-winning tour of apartment 3D."

She linked her arm through his, leading him through her doorway. They turned down the hall, and she gave him the grand tour of her apartment in thirty seconds. "And this is the living room. The attachment to my favorite chair is my best friend. Amelia Tandis . . . Paul Wade."

Millie extended her hand to Paul as she stood. "Please call me Millie. I must say it's nice to see that Janesie didn't exaggerate. You *are* fine."

"Millie!" Jane yelled from the kitchen as she placed the flowers in a vase.

"I guess a thank-you is in order." He chuckled.

"I just call 'em like I see 'em."

"Millie, I think it's time for you to go now." Jane said with a gentle push to her friend.

"Gotcha," she said with a wink. "You don't need to drop an anvil on my head. Nice meeting you, Paul."

"And you, Millie."

Jane walked Millie to the door. "I can't believe you," she hissed.

"Sweetie, it needed to be said. He *is* fine, and now you can relax because you're more worried about me than you are about being with him." She kissed Jane on the cheek. "Have a great night, Cinderella. And since you're having such a great month, I voted—it's your turn to be the cheerleader."

"Duly noted."

Jane closed the door before straightening her pants and sweater as she returned to Paul.

"She's quite a character," Paul said, shaking his head.

"Yep. We've been friends since we were in elementary school. I don't know what I would do without her, even when she does embarrass me."

Pulling on a short, black, heavily lined trench coat, Jane tied the belt snugly at her waist as she walked to Paul.

"So, where are we going?"

"This little place around the corner, nothing too special, but I like it."

"What's the name of the restaurant? I have to admit I've lived in this neighborhood for six years and only go to a handful of places. Creature of habit, I guess."

"It's a reservations only place. And it's relatively new, so I doubt if you've been there before," Paul said as he closed the door behind them.

———

"Well," Jane said, reaching for her cup of coffee three hours later. "I can definitely say I've never eaten in this restaurant before."

"You enjoyed the meal?" Paul leaned across his apartment-sized, well-worn antique table and cleared Jane's plate along with his.

"Five-star for sure—the best food I've had in months. I love a good steak."

"Well, I pretty much know how to make the meal you just ate and Kraft Macaroni and Cheese. Would you like a little more coffee?" he asked from the kitchen as he loaded the dishwasher.

"No, I'm good. Can I help you?"

"No. Go ahead and enjoy your coffee. The balcony has a nice view of the park, and the city to the south. I don't think it's too chilly."

Taking advantage of the time to regroup, Jane slipped from the expansive main room of the loft through the modern French doors to the corner balcony. Up eight stories, she could see above the trees in Goodale Park and make out the curves of the river. The night air was brisk, but bearable for a few minutes. Resting her forearms on the railing, she took in the God-painted beauty of the few visible stars shining brighter than the city lights. The evening had been better than she could have imagined. They'd shared their family histories, delving into the tense and tenuous topics of religion and politics. The more they talked, the more they found in common. It was as if God had taken her imaginary list and formed Paul out of the dust of the earth and her requests.

Thank You, God, for such a special evening. This is reality, not fancy hockey players and dancing. But is he too perfect, Lord? I mean, this isn't some sort of test, is it? You wouldn't send a serial killer to me as some sort of evangelistic outreach, would You? No, You wouldn't do that. I'm sorry even for the thought. Thank You, Father, for allowing me always to feel Your presence. I love You. Thank You for loving me first.'

"Penny for your thoughts," Paul said, resting his arms beside hers on the balustrade.

"So cheap?"

"Well, I guess inflation could take my offer as high as a quarter. . . ."

She laughed, turning to take in the full length of him. His slightly long blond hair fell across his forehead with the breeze, shadowing his deep-set green eyes. He wore his GQ-casual ensemble with the ease of a man who was comfortable in any environment.

"What had you so engrossed?" he pressed.

"Oh, I was talking to God about you and asking how you could possibly be so perfect. You can tell me the truth, are you a closet serial killer or something? Do you have mental illness in your family? Do you wear black and navy blue together?"

"Umm, definitely no to the first, although I do have an occasional murderous thought from time to time. In regards to the second, there is some question about my father's stability, but as it stands today, he's legally sane.

And I must admit that from time to time I do have some color blindness, and the navy and black socks get a bit mixed up."

"Whew, I feel better. It's kind of intimidating with all of this perfection surrounding me."

"I'm far from perfect," he said, brushing a wandering wisp of hair from Jane's face. "But I suspect you might be."

His statement so startled her, she snorted, spitting haphazardly in his face. "Oh my goodness, I am so sorry."

Moving upright slowly, he brushed the droplets from his face and chuckled. "Well, that's an unusual response."

"Sorry." Jane felt her remaining nerves blow away in the night breeze.

"No apologies needed. I think I rather like the unusual." His smile was soft as he took her hands in his and pulled her gently into his embrace. His hug was light, not pressing any boundaries, but close enough to allow his warmth to flow through her from the tips of her toes to the ends of her hair.

This is nice. She rested her face on the soothing roughness of his sweater. She fit her arms neatly around his waist, her heart slow and steady. She was completely at ease; all butterflies but a few still idling and ready for emergency flight, were asleep for the night.

CHAPTER SIX

AFTER SUCCUMBING TO THE TEMPTATION of her snooze button a third time, Jane willed herself to slide out of bed onto the cold hardwood floor beneath her feet. Padding toward the bathroom, she caught sight of the flowers Paul had brought to her apartment the previous evening, and a sheepish grin curved her lips. She'd met a boy. No, she'd met a man. She met a cute, Christian man. *God is good.*

Her normal morning routine went surprisingly speedily, and she was able to linger over a strong cup of coffee and the latest copy of *In Style*. She had some guilt about not using her extra thirty minutes to read Scripture or a devotional before she left for church, but her mind wasn't prepared to absorb more than the latest fashions on the "It" girl as her morning church duties loomed before her.

Signing up to work in the nursery room for the three- and four-year-olds, who purportedly were potty trained, had come about when the senior pastor implored the congregation to give those few faithful volunteer servants a break. Jane, in the midst of her pre-mid-life-I-don't-know-what-I-want-to-do-with-my-life crisis, volunteered for one month in the nursery, thinking that this would be a good way to see if she had in fact missed her calling to be an elementary school teacher. Thirty minutes into her one-month tour of duty, Jane came to the realization that she in fact had not missed her calling to be a teacher, nor had she missed her calling to change the diapers of the so-called potty-trained three- and four-year-olds. In two weeks, she would be released from her nursery purgatory and would honestly be able to say to future askers that nursery was not her ministry.

Glancing at her watch, Jane drained the remainder of her coffee and made her way down the steps to her car. Jars of Clay barreled out of her car speakers as she turned the key in the ignition. Singing along with the woeful tunes, she was unable to suppress the grin on her face.

She kept replaying the previous day's and evening's events. Both dates had been perfect. She could not have fashioned more idyllic scenes in her own overactive imagination. Sighing at the movie reel in her head, she glanced down at her cell phone, which, out of habit, she'd pulled from her purse and laid on her lap for the drive. She'd left her phone on vibrate for the evening, so she wasn't surprised to see the message screen scroll with: 3 New Voicemails, October 17 8:06 a.m.

She pushed in her voicemail code as she pulled out onto High Street and listened as the strangely annoying, yet deliciously intoxicating voice repeated the familiar phrase, "You have three new messages. First Message . . ."

"Jane, it's Millie. Girl, you better so call me when you get home from your date with Mr. Cutie Christian. You totally understated his assets. He is completely fall-on-the-bed-dreamy. Can't wait to hear all the juicy, or in your case, less-than-juicy, details. Kisses."

Jane shook her head and pressed 7 to delete Millie's message. She was automatically advanced to the next voicemail as she continued the familiar route to church.

"Lady, where are you? It is like ten fifteen p.m. and you have yet to call me. Are you snuggling on his couch and blowing me off or are you lying in a ditch, because Mr. Perfect Pants is not quite as perfect as we thought? Okay, now I'm worried. I know you're probably fine, and enjoying some long overdue male attention, but it's so unlike you to not call. Call me. That is not a request. It's an order from your dearest and bestest friend on the planet. Oh, and if you call me, I can tell you about the odd phone call I received from a certain defenseman. I guess I didn't offend him sufficiently last night, because he asked me out for drinks after the game Sunday. I don't think I'll go. I mean, come on, he's a jock . . . I don't do jocks. He is so not my type. Anyway, call me. Kisses."

She deleted the message, making a mental note to call Millie back as she parked her car. Walking into the church, she listened to her third and final message.

"Hi, Janesie, it's ten thirty, so I hope you aren't sleeping. Umm, this is Lindy. You remember . . . long walk, cold river . . . Anyway, I have two tickets for tomorrow's game, that's Sunday afternoon, and I thought you and your friend might like to come. No need to call me back, I'll just leave them for you at will call. Don't worry if you can't make it. I thought you might be free and I did promise free tickets. Hope you can make it. Bye."

Jane ripped the phone from her ear and stared at it as she continued into the church, tripping over the threshold as she tried to grasp that Lindy Barrett, her hockey icon and ultimate crush, had left her a voicemail message. On autopilot, she continued down the main hall, ignoring dozens of people who waved and smiled as she replayed Lindy's message. Lindy Barrett wanted her to use his tickets for tonight's game.

"Oh, my goodness! Oh, my goodness! Oh, my goodness!" she muttered, channeling Punky Brewster.

Walking into the nursery classroom, she listened to the message a third time and saved it to her archives. Was this even her life? She wanted to look in the closet to see if Ashton Kutcher was punking her.

Despite the fact that she and Lindy had sparked on Friday, she was stunned that he'd called. Lindy Barrett, *the* Lindy Barrett, had phoned her and left her a voicemail. She sat down slowly in a chair designed for a three-year-old bottom, continuing to listen to the automated voice of the voicemail. Two different classroom volunteers greeted her. She nodded hello, remaining superhumanly attached to her cell phone.

Instinctively, she dialed Millie, whose cell went straight to voicemail, forcing Jane to dial Millie's home phone number. When the answering machine picked up, Jane began to yell into the receiver, drawing horrified looks from the parents and volunteers.

"Amelia Tandis, wakeup this instant!" she shouted. "I must, must talk to you! Call me back the instant, I repeat, the instant, you get this message."

Jane flipped shut her phone, leaned back in the plastic red chair, and promptly somersaulted backward onto the floor. Most of the children laughed, yelling, "Again, again."

"Aun' Dane, you wook tilly."

Jane sat up and looked into the face of her own three-year-old niece, Eliza, who was dressed to perfection in mounds of ruffles and bows. "Well, little Lizzie, we all have our ups and our downs. Today appears to be a bit of a downer for me."

Her towheaded niece tilted her perfectly coiffed head, shrugged her shoulders, and strutted off to play in the fake kitchen inside the fake plastic house.

Jane watched her youngest niece play and wondered if her brother-in-law, Jake, had dropped little Lizzie off in the class, or if her oldest sister, Molly, had deposited her youngest daughter without Jane being aware.

Molly and Jane were fighting. Not that fighting was a new thing. They had been in one fight or another every eight to twelve months since Molly was seven and Jane was three and Molly had taken to running Jane's life as her hobby. Their current fight was ridiculous and had unfortunately risen to epic proportions.

Three months earlier, Molly had invited Jane over for a girls' lunch, promising gossip, finger sandwiches, and a respite from the self-reflection triggering Jane's quarter-life crisis. Molly failed to mention that the girls' lunch had evolved into a group of Molly's couple friends, and instead of gossip and finger sandwiches, the afternoon menu became hamburgers, hotdogs, and manly grilling.

Jane felt foolish in her full-skirted summer swing dress and Sabrina sling backs, intended to be oohed and awed over by the fashionable ladies, when she walked into the backyard, which was swimming with couples in khaki shorts and polo shirts. As an added bonus, Jake invited the new guy from his office, Bill, aka Stud-du-Jour.

Upon first introduction to the SDJ, with his shiny blond good looks, buff tanned body, and six-foot-three frame, Jane had the most obvious of reactions. She hauled Molly into the back bedroom for a sister-to-sister showdown.

"What is this, Molly? I thought this was going to be all girls. I thought we were going to paint our toenails and watch stupid Meg Ryan and Tom Hanks movies while we ate chocolate in between going through boxes of Kleenex?"

"Jane," Molly began in her I-am-your-older-sister voice, "I knew if I told you that Jake had a friend he wanted to introduce you to, you wouldn't have stepped through the front door. You and your romantic sensibilities would have protested and remained locked up in your apartment watching sappy romantic comedies and wondering why you never meet anyone."

Jane stopped pacing and turned to face her sister sitting sweetly on the end of the guest bed. The three steps that represented the chasm between the two sisters were closed with the echo of Jane's heels clicking against the glossy floor. Stopping directly in front of Molly, Jane crossed her arms, but her sister continued her speech.

"I'm sick of hearing you gripe about being single. Despite your disappointment with your current status, you won't let anyone help you find Mister Right. No, not the mighty, beautiful Jane, you couldn't possibly need help. You insist that God will send you your version of Cary Grant in *An Affair to Remember* by tracking you down via the phonebook—in which, by the way, you're simply listed as J. Grey—knock on your door, and sweep you off your feet."

Jane focused her attention on the floor. "Well, except for the whole Deborah Kerr paralyzed thing."

Molly rolled her eyes as she stood and placed her hands on Jane's shoulders. "The point is, my dear romantic sister, you want to be married. We all want you to be married."

Jane's head popped up. "Who does *we* consist of?"

Molly ignored her. "Sweetie, we love you and we want you to be happy. I want you to be happy. I want you to have someone you love the way I love Jake. I want you to have the joy of being a mommy."

As if on some perfectly choreographed cue, Molly's oldest daughter, Chelsea, bopped into the room to ask her mother a question. "Not now, Chessie, Mommy and Aunt Janie are having a grown-up conversation. Go ask Daddy to help you. Go on, now."

Chelsea's little shoulders dropped, and her curly pigtails seemed to deflate as she left the bedroom.

Molly waited until her daughter closed the door. "Now, what was I saying?"

Jane lifted a single eyebrow, uncrossing her arms. "You were saying you wanted me to experience the joys of being a mommy."

Molly shook her head. "Oh, yes. Being a mother is the most life-affirming thing a woman can do. No amount of career success can replicate the joy you feel when you first hold your child, or hear her first words or watch her take her first steps." She sighed. "Jane, we just want you to have a full life. We don't want you to wind up an old-maid spinster with one hundred and one cats all named Boo-Boo Kitty."

At the mention of Boo-Boo Kitties, Jane resumed her pacing. Molly crossed her arms and watched her sister move like a caged animal in four-hundred-dollar shoes for about thirty seconds before Jane's temper reared its rather ugly face.

"First, thank you for caring about my happiness, in whatever sick and twisted form your caring comes. Second, you could have told me you wanted to fix me up. I might actually have said yes, or perhaps I would have handled the proposition with a bit more maturity than I did today. I am thirty-two years old, Molly. You don't need to trick me into doing things like I'm a five-year-old who refuses to eat green beans. Third, although I want the traditional *Leave It to Beaver/Ozzie and Harriet* life, I will not cease to exist if that doesn't happen. I know I'm ridiculous to want the Ali McGraw *Love Story* kind of toe-curling, once-and-only-love-that-lasts-a-lifetime experience, but that's who I am. The notion that I'm somehow less of a person, simply because I'm single and not the mom of many rug rats, is an archaic belief. The fact that you said it makes me believe you've spent a little too much time in the self-help aisle at the Barnes and Noble."

Jane expelled a final breath and turned to look at her sister. Although Jane took in Molly's hurt expression, she was on a roll, and like a snowball becoming an avalanche, she found it impossible to stop regardless of the destruction that would follow in her wake. "You have a good life, Molly, but I don't want your life, especially if it's a slightly smudged facsimile. I want my own life—one where I feel free to be more than just a mom, but to be a whole, well-rounded person. Your life is pooping in the potty and rounds of dance lessons. The only friends you see are the ones who have the same potty-centric life you do. What happened to your girlfriends from college or grad school? Most of them are fulfilled, successful women, but you wrote them off because they didn't achieve the ultimate goal of wifedom and motherhood."

Stopping her pacing, she sat down next to Molly, who had taken a seat sometime in the middle of the avalanche. Softening her voice, she finished.

"Molly, I love you, but I don't want to be you. I have tried, for thirty-two years, not to be you."

Tears began streaming down Molly's beautiful, angelic face. Jane's heart broke for her sister, and she began to console her by apologizing for what she said, when Jake walked in to ask a question. He saw Molly's tear-streaked face and went into protection mode.

Grabbing Molly away from Jane he said, "Jane, what did you do this time?"

Standing, Jane tried to explain, "I . . . just . . ." But she couldn't come up with an adequate response, and she felt her own bout of tears trickle down her cheeks.

Jake sighed at the two sisters as he pulled his wife into his arms and she turned his polo shirt into a giant tissue. Sighing at Jane, he said, "You'd better go. Your mom just got here. If she sees both of you crying, she'll want to be the peacemaker and taskmaster all at the same time. You can probably miss her if you slide out the back door."

Jane nodded before rushing to her car in a fit of tears. She drove home, watched three Cary Grant movies, finished a box of Godiva chocolates, and emptied a brand-new container of Kleenex.

Since that afternoon, she and Molly had exchanged only a handful of civil words.

Jane was sick of the fight and wanted to apologize to her sister for being such a jerk, but every time she picked up the phone to make amends, her pride generated meaningless conversations. *But not today.* Today would be different. Today was going to be the day that her world would come completely in line. Why not? Everything else in her life, with the exception of the interview, was going freakishly her way. She'd had two great dates in one day. She was now friends, or at least semifriends, with Lindy Barrett. Today was the day to have the perfect reconciliation with her sister, too.

Resolved, Jane slipped her cell phone into her pocket and threw herself into her nursery duties, which included a vicious game of Simon Says and a scary *Desperate Housewives*–laced version of playing house before children's time in the worship service.

She and the other nursery volunteers herded children from the education wing to the front of the sanctuary as the organist played a somber version of "Jesus Loves the Little Children" while the thousand or so congregants mumbled along. Jane watched the youth pastor, Brad, her last serious boyfriend who had blissfully transitioned to a dear friend in the let's-do-coffee category, kneel to eye level with sixty little ones near the front altar.

He launched into a funny story that was intended more for the adults than for the children, when Lizzie yanked on Brad's trousers. Lizzie notoriously did not pay attention to the children's message and often pulled Brad's attention when she would invariably say something inappropriate and generally quite funny like "Mommy tries at *Dabes ob Our Libes.*" (Translation: "Mommy cries at *Days of Our Lives.*") Or "An Danie is deporate por a man. What does deporate mean?" (Translation: "Aunt Janie is desperate for a man. What does desperate mean?) Lovely little girl, that Lizzie.

"Pattor Brad," Lizzie started as she tried to gain Brad's full attention. "An Danie fell down on hor tushie. She wooked weally tilly." Lizzie covered her mouth in a fit of giggles as all eyes in the church shifted to Jane.

Brad smiled and quickly moved on with his pseudo children's message, ignoring Lizzie's story. Jane thought she was out of the embarrassment woods as Brad had the children bow their collective heads to pray, when her forgotten cell phone shrilled in the relative silence of the sanctuary. Heat bolted from Jane's toes to her head at the speed of light, as the ever-helpful Lizzie shouted, "Dat's An Danie's pone."

One thousand heads, previously bowed in prayer, snapped up and focused on Jane, while one of the three spotlights illumining the enormous cross at the front of the worship center seemed to turn and bathe her in a circle of light.

Jane looked imploringly at Grace, another nursery volunteer, and swiftly vacated the worship center. Trailing in the distance, she could hear Brad continuing to pray amidst muffled chuckles and choked laughter.

When Jane was safely ensconced in the bathroom, she looked at the caller ID. As expected, the call was from her loyal ally with bad timing, Millie. She dialed her voicemail and listened to the message.

"My darling girl, I can imagine one of two scenarios in which you would call this early on a Sunday morning. A: You had such a fabulous time last night that your time of calling was actually your time of arrival home, in which case, I am exceedingly proud of you, girlie. And thus, obviously you skipped making the rest of us look bad to God by attending church on no sleep. Option two: You continue to make the lot of us look like wretched heathens and called me on your way to church, in which case you are dying of embarrassment because your cell phone rang in the middle of service. The embarrassment should be punishment enough for waking me at this unearthly hour on a Sunday. Dear, you do know that God intended today to be a day of rest, don't you? Whether A or two, meet me at Spagio's for brunch at one. You can fill me in on all of the delicious and not-so-delicious details then. Kisses!"

Jane deleted the message and shut the power off to avoid any further mortification as she returned to the nursery room and her duties. Thankfully the next two services were without incident and as she bundled her last three- to-four-year-old into her fashionable shearling lined coat, she caught a glimpse of her sister leaving her Sunday-morning Bible study. Jane knew that Jake had already picked up their two girls and trotted them off to McDonald's for their post-church lunch. Jane wouldn't have the easy opportunity to talk to Molly she desired. She was going to have to go in for the kill the hard way.

Jane hurried behind her sister, reaching her as she was ready to step into the cold October morning. "Mol," she said. "Can I talk to you for a sec?"

"Umm, Jake was going to let the kids play in the playland at McDonald's before I met them for lunch. I'm sure he is wondering where I am. We have a busy afternoon. We have to buy new shoes for the girls, but I guess that seems pointless and trivial to you."

Good one.

"I really need to talk to you, Molly. I want to clear the air." Jane gently guided Molly away from the doorway. "I feel horrible about what's going on between us, and I don't know how best to repair the damage I've done. You are my very best friend. Don't tell Millie. I'm truly sorry. I said hateful, cruel things to you. I wish I could take them all back."

Molly burst into tears as she dropped onto an old love seat. "Wh-what do you have to be s-sorry for?" she stuttered through her tears. "I started everything w-with the whole Bill thing. It's just that you'd been so sad since you broke up with Brad. And I know somewhere inside you think the t-two of you will get back together, but Janie, it's been two years! I just want you to be h-happy."

Jane sat next to her older sister, placed a hand on her knee, and felt an unseen weight lift from her heart. "I know Mol. I know you want me to be happy. Let's call it even and forgive each other. And forgive ourselves, too."

Molly lifted red-rimmed, smiling green eyes to Jane and nodded her head in agreement. The sisters hugged and reverted back to four and eight years old, when a simple "I'm sorry" and a hug made everything better. *Maybe that's the answer to world peace? Maybe the UN should be notified of this hug-and-sorry tactic?*

Each sister wiped away tears as they settled into the love seat. "I have a great idea," Jane said. "I'm meeting Millie for brunch at Spagio's today. Why don't you join us?"

"I don't want to barge in on your afternoon."

"Who's barging? You're invited. Millie will be so pleased. She's been after me for weeks to mend our broken fence. She's sick of hearing me mope."

"Well, that might be nice. Let me call Jake to make sure he'll be okay with the girls."

As Molly walked to make her call, Jane leaned back, closed her eyes, and smiled the smile of satisfaction and relief. *Thank you, God. You're on a serious roll with all of these answered prayers!*

Sitting alone, she reveled in her peace for about fifteen seconds before Brad settled into Molly's empty seat, "So, Cheshire, why the grin?"

She opened her eyes and focused on her former sweetheart. Brad was cute in a Santa-Claus-meets-Joey-from-*Friends* kind of way. At a time, not too long ago, she had worked quite diligently at creating romantic feelings for Brad. Those feelings were now locked away deep in her heart, allowing her the safety of a dear friend.

"Molly and I made up."

"I'm glad." He sat silent for a moment. "That niece of yours is a trip."

"Everyone says she's just like me at that age."

"I can see it."

She responded with a love hit to his bicep.

"Hey!" He rubbed his arm. "So, who was on the phone?"

"You deserved that, and it was Millie. I called her in a panic this morning. She was returning the call."

"What was the big emergency? Anything a silly old pastor can help solve?"

Jane thought for a moment about telling Brad everything that had transpired over the last forty-eight hours, but she decided it was best to keep the details to girlfriends until something came to fruition, or the bubble of romantic bliss in which she found herself at the moment burst.

"Nothing major, just girl stuff. You know me—always a crisis."

"If you say so . . ."

The two chatted about nothing, and Jane couldn't help but feel safe and happy with Brad. He was so easy to be with, and their long history lent itself to a wistful desire to simply enjoy his company. Their quiet conversation was interrupted when Molly returned and announced that she was allowed to go and play.

"Sorry it took me so long. Ethel stopped me and asked for a recipe. Her hearing aid battery is nearly out of juice, so I needed to write it down for her. Jake said to have a good time. He said that Lizzie and Chelsea already have plans for their afternoon that include Barbie saving GI Joe, who's locked inside a pillow fort. Jake's ecstatic."

"Sounds good. Ready?" Jane stood and pulled on her coat. "Millie is probably wondering where we are." Turning, she smiled. "See you later, Brad."

"Have a good lunch, ladies."

———

Millie was on her second mimosa by the time Jane and Molly arrived.

"Hey, girls," she said with a tilt of her glass as the sisters slid into their seats. "Glad to see you two kissed and made up. And speaking of kisses, did anyone at the table get any last night?"

Jane rolled her eyes at Millie but was unable to berate her due to the prompt arrival of their waiter. He took Molly and Jane's coffee orders and left the three ladies to their gossip.

"Ladies." Millie looked directly at Molly. "I am highly disappointed that I will be the only one who will be partaking in sparkling beverages this afternoon."

"Mills, the strongest thing I want this afternoon is some coffee and a sizable portion of eggs Benedict. Besides, when have I ever had a sparkling additive to my juice?" Jane began to peruse her menu.

"And, well, I think I might be pregnant." Molly dropped the sentence like she was commenting on the weather.

Jane's and Millie's heads simultaneously jerked upward as they let out in unison. "What?"

Molly blushed as she carefully laid her menu in front of her. "It's very early, only a couple of weeks, days really, but I don't want to take any chances just in case. Jake and I have been trying for six months. I even started hormone supplements."

Jane reached her hand to her sister's and squeezed gently. "But I thought you were happy with the two girls? 'No Jan Brady syndrome in my house,' you always said."

"We are, but we both wanted to try for a little boy. I know it's trite, and I love the girls and so does Jake, but in his heart of hearts he wants a boy so bad, he goes into a funk whenever the *Sports Center* intro comes on the TV. He's already trying to turn Lizzie into his missing son. Now all she does is run around in circles at dance class saying, 'Who da man?' while she pretends to spike the football in the end zone. First position in ballet has officially become 'stupid and boring' and 'not what football guys do,'" Molly concluded with a shake of her head.

The waiter placed their drink orders in front of Jane and Molly, allowing Jane to cover her grin with a deep drink of her coffee. She sighed. "I'm going to be an auntie."

Millie quickly corrected her. "You already are an auntie."

"Yes, but not to a nephew. A nephew I can take to hockey games and teach how to properly score a baseball game. This deserves chocolate." She made eye contact with their waiter and motioned him to the table.

"Andre," Jane said, reading his name badge. "A round of chocolate crème brûlée and that marvelous brownie sundae."

"Would you like to order breakfast first?" he asked.

"Nope, we'll get around to healthy after we celebrate." She raised her water glass. "To my possible new nephew or niece: I can't wait to meet you."

The three ladies clinked glasses and drank heartily as they settled back into their seats.

"So, Miss Auntie Jane, are we still pure as the proverbial driven snow?"

Dreamy about the possibility of a new addition to her family, Jane was blindsided by Millie's question and began choking on her celebratory water.

Molly pounced on Millie's question. "Jane Eleanor Grey, what in the world is Millie talking about?"

Before Jane could answer her older sister, her soon-to-be-ex-best friend jumped to fill in the details of Jane's miraculous forty-eight-plus hours.

Molly sagged against the back of her chair. "Well . . . oh my . . . Jane . . . It's like you're living out the best Cary Grant movie ever made. Please don't keep us in suspense, sweetie. What happened last night with the dreamy lawyer?" Molly asked with all the enthusiasm of a five-year-old on Christmas morning.

"Well, after he picked me up, we went back to his house and he made a lovely dinner."

Millie choked on her drink. "Hold up, Mr. Wonderful Cutie-Pants Christian cooks, too?"

Jane leaned her elbows on the table, resting her chin in the palm of her hand. "We had dinner, which was followed by coffee on his balcony. He has an amazing view of the city. He lives in one of those lofts by the park," she added for Molly's benefit.

"Well, that's nice that he lives in your neighborhood, isn't it?" Molly added.

"Yes, well anyway, we stood on the balcony and talked for a bit. You know me—I could only take the cold so long. So, we went back inside, sat on the couch, and chatted. Then he drove me home to save my feet from my sickness of a shoe obsession. End scene." She finished with a dramatic tilt of her head. Pushing away from the table, she picked up her coffee cup. She took a small sip as her sister and her friend sighed like teenagers, their eyes glossing over in what could only be described as a state of gush.

Jane held her cup close to her lips, steadying herself for the inevitable onslaught of questions and commentary bound to break free from the two women closest to her.

"Oh my, Jane, he sounds just perfect. And he is a Christian, too?"

Jane nodded to her sister.

"Oh, that's just wonderful. But didn't Millie say you had dinner with Lindy Barrett, too? I'm confused."

"Well, I guess when it rains in the desert, it pours." Jane turned to Millie. "I almost forgot. Lindy left me a message last night. He's leaving me two tickets for tonight's game at will call. He thought we might want to go. What do you think, Mill?"

The truth was, she really hadn't "almost forgotten," but she wanted to play it cool. Even though she was talking to her sister and to her best friend, Jane worried that too much emphasis on Lindy Barrett might make her appear to be a groupie or worse yet, a puck bunny. With Paul now in her life, if she could really think of him as in her life, she needed to be very clear in her mind that the Lindy Barrett situation was a friends-only scenario and nothing else—regardless of any ill-conceived fantasy from her early twenties . . . and thirties. The teenager would have to just stay in her box.

"Gracious, Jane, you've become quite the popular princess, haven't you?" Her sister said with a smile.

"I know!"

As all three ladies fell into a series of adolescent giggles, their server placed a chocolate crème brûlée in front of each of them and centered a beautifully decadent brownie sundae, dripping with sin, in the middle of the table with three spoons.

"Oh, where to start?" Millie sighed.

Lifting a spoon to her sister, Jane toasted the occasion. "To my soon-to-be-nephew: we can't wait to welcome you to this wonderful world of wackos!"

"And to my little sister." Molly lifted her spoon. "May her turn of luck with the gents—and her blessings—continue to overwhelm."

"And to my speedy metabolism," Millie added. "Oh, that it may continue to reign supreme over brownie sundaes, crème brûlée, and french fries!"

"Here, here!" they said in unison. Clinking spoons, they broke the candied glaze on their desserts and dug greedily into their respective calorie fests.

CHAPTER SEVEN

BRUNCH WAS A DELIGHT, Jane thought as she slipped into a pair of jeans and a black cashmere sweater later that afternoon. The three friends eventually ate semi-grown-up food in the form of pancakes and eggs, but for the day, worries of cholesterol and calories flew out the window.

Jane checked her watch and realized it was much later than she'd thought. She swiped lip gloss across her bottom lip, then pulled on her soft down jacket and wrapped a black scarf around her neck before she closed her door and skipped down the stairs on her way to the arena.

Jane and Millie had agreed to meet at 4:45 p.m. at will call. With a 5:30 p.m. start time, Jane would be able to watch the pregame warm-up, and it would give Millie an opportunity to ogle her new infatuation. After much mental debate, Jane had decided that going to the hockey game was not disloyal to Paul. First, she and Paul had known each other for only two days. Although, it must be noted that they were the two best days she had experienced in years, commented the angel on her shoulder. Second, Lindy made himself very clear on Friday night—he was looking for a friend. Thus, Jane's little imp on her opposite shoulder argued, there was no conflict between her budding romance with Paul and her budding friendship with Lindy. Her little angel would just have to settle down and stop making her stomach flip over like a rowboat in the middle of the perfect storm.

Besides, if this really was even a pretend date, I wouldn't be wearing a turtleneck and sensible shoes, would I? Justification was a skill she should really add to her ever-growing résumé.

She glanced up at the arena in the near distance and was struck again at how the building resembled a large glowing anthill on game nights, with all of the fans marching toward the entrance from various directions. Approaching the arena from the east, she walked up Nationwide Boulevard, smiling as she took in the kids bopping excitedly up the walk, sporting foam pucks on their heads; an occasional foam finger mingled in the crowd. She breathed deeply, pushing down a wave of nostalgic tears as she remembered the countless times she'd held her daddy's hand and chattered as they made their way to minor league baseball and OSU football games. *They still believe that those guys are heroes. They believe in the purity of the game. They just want to play and believe.*

She dabbed the corners of her eyes as she turned at the edge of the arena and approached from the south side. Pulling open the glass door, she found her place in a short line and took in the larger-than-life action images of various players, including Lindy, who was captured in his trademark shooting motion with his left leg raised on his follow-through and his tongue curled around his upper lip. Jane sighed and forced herself to look away from the wall. *He is only a man.* She stole another glance. *A gorgeous man, but still a man.*

Jane focused on the glass window as the ticketing agent motioned her forward.

"Jane Grey," she said through the speaker box.

The agent behind the glass looked through a shallow box and pulled out a white envelope. "Here we are, Miss Grey. I'll just need to see your ID while you sign this paper." She slid the envelope through the ticket slot with a pen and a small form.

Jane pulled her ID out of her pocket and exchanged the envelope for her hideous driver's license. Short hair hadn't been a good look for her chubby-cheeked face.

She signed the release and slid the paper and the pen through the slot as the attendant returned her ID. "Enjoy the game, miss."

"Thanks." Jane smiled. As she turned away from the ticket window, she saw Millie arrive.

She was dressed head to toe in black, her long blonde hair flowing loosely over her cropped leather jacket. Jane could almost feel a gust of wind from the whiplash suffered by two-thirds of the male population in the ticket area for the opportunity to look at Millie's beauty as she walked across the lobby, flipping her hair back over her shoulder.

"Hey, Janesie," she said with a smile.

"It's official. All the men are jealous because I have the best-looking date in the arena."

They both laughed. Jane opened the sealed envelope as the two friends wound their way around the large oval building, pulling out two season tickets wrapped in a small piece of white paper.

Jane unfolded the paper and handed Millie one of the tickets as she noticed the words written on the sheet: "I'm glad you're here, friend. I bet you'll be my good luck charm L.B."

Biting her lower lip, she reread the short note. *He called me friend.* Her heart did a little flip, which she quickly squelched before it could flop. *You're reacting to a decade-old crush, Grey. Nothing else.*

Millie entered their row first and sidled her way to her seat. "I told Jason I was sitting with you tonight and that we could meet up after the game. Do you think I'm nuts? He is totally not my type. He's a jock, a hockey player, for goodness' sake. I hate jocks. You know me, Janes. I like skinny artists and guys in bands with tattooed arms who look like they haven't showered for the better part of their cross-country tour."

Jane was so lost in her own mental pep talk as she settled into her seat that it took her a moment to realize that Millie was in need of her own cheering squad. Her nearly flawless former-model best friend was displaying signs of doubt with a guy. Maybe Millie was right. Maybe this was the Apocalypse.

"Millie." Jane turned her full focus on her friend. "Am I hearing you correctly? Are you worried about a guy? What happened to my friend the man-eater, the one-woman wrecking crew to men's hearts around the globe?"

Millie began twisting a piece of long blond hair through her fingers. "I don't know. He's used to a certain type of girl—girls—who don't ask questions; girls who fawn all over him and expect very little in return. He probably isn't used to a smart-mouthed female who is overly opinionated. Jane, what if he was only attracted to me on Friday because I looked fabulous?"

Jane's draw literally dropped. "Are you serious?"

In Millie's sea-green eyes, Jane saw something she had never seen reflected in their mysterious depths: self-doubt. Millie was definitely serious.

Jane rubbed her temples to ease her sudden headache. "Amelia Tandis, first, who cares what you look like? Your looks are not important. When are you going to see what the rest of us see? You're one of the most amazing women I've ever known. You're smart and witty and one heck of a poker player. Any man who can't see you for the amazing, wonderful woman you are, without seeing your face, is a moron." Jane rested her hand on Millie's leg. "Second, do you see the same face and body in the mirror that I see? I know you know the affect you have on men. Millie, you have been using your feminine wiles on the entire male gender since you were twelve years old."

"I know, but Jason is different. He's used to women throwing themselves at him, while I'm used to having men throwing themselves at me. How does this work, having two beautiful people in one relationship?"

"I guess I wouldn't know," Jane mumbled as she pulled her hand away. She leaned against her seat back and watched Millie's typical overconfidence bubble and dissolve like Alka-Seltzer.

"Nope, it simply can't work," Millie said with finality. "That's it. Drinks tonight and then I'll ignore him. Two overly desirable people can't be together. There must be some sort of cosmic law about it. I mean, really, I simply can't afford to be dumped, or worse, to have to chase a guy." She shuddered, and her face took on what could only be described as an odd shade of ashen gray generally reserved for severe illness and hospital stays.

Jane rolled her eyes, choosing to skip attendance at her friend's neurotic pity party, and focused on the team as the players took the ice, led by Jason. From the corner of her eye, she stole a quick glance at Millie, whose face bloomed with color, a spontaneous smile gracing her full lips as she watched the tough defenseman skate to the far face-off circle. *Oh, she has it, but good!*

"Jane, look at him," Millie mooned. "He is simply amazing."

"Yes, so you mentioned."

"I know, but he's not just cute, in the breathtakingly rugged, I-can-chop-wood-with-my-bare-hands kind of way; he's really smart, too. Let's face it. I might have the face, but I'm usually the keenly intelligent and witty one in my relationships," she said with seriousness. "I'm the one who can draw on a wide range of topics, from current affairs to fashion magazines, while my emaciated artist of choice stares at me, adoringly overwhelmed by wonderfulness."

Jane took her focus off the ice, staring at her friend to see whether she was being sarcastic or she really believed the conceited drivel. "Millie, what are you talking about?"

"Oh, you know, Jane. How guys are always staring at me with those puppy-dog eyes filled with wonderment at how such a pretty package can contain such unbelievable brains too," Millie said with a knowing flip of her hand as if to acknowledge an unseen group of men.

Jane sat in silent disbelief.

"Anyway, I think in all reality, Jason might not only be more beautiful than I am, he might be smarter than me too."

Jane realized the sincerity of her friend's speech. Although it was misguided and terribly self-involved, Jane knew it was the signal for her to put on her best cheerleader face and prop up her dearest friend. "Well, sweetie, did you ever think that maybe the whole dating thing has been too easy for you? That maybe the reason you breakup with every guy is because you're the superior one in the relationship?"

Millie came to attention, sitting straighter in her seat as she cocked her head. "I never thought of it that way."

"Maybe it'll be a good thing for you to date, your, uh . . . equal." Jane struggled to keep a straight face. "I've always had a sneaking suspicion that the reason you date the skinny artists and brooding band members is because you so outclass them that they worship at the Temple of Millie. But let me tell you something, you'll never be satisfied with the kind of guy who's more interested in being your lap dog than in being your warrior hero. You may think you like having men you can lead around by the nose, but you don't. The only reason you keep going for the same type of guy is so that you never run the risk of losing control. Friend-o-mine, you want—no, you need—a man who will stimulate you not only physically, but also mentally. At the end of the day, you want a guy who'll be courageous enough to protect you and strong enough not to take any of your ridiculousness."

Millie slumped back into her seat, letting out a heavy sigh. "I know you're right. And it stinks. I really do like being the prettiest and smartest one in the room, even when the room only has two people."

"Millie you're a piece of work." Jane said, shifting her focus from the topic of their bizarre conversation to her longtime crush on skates. As she watched him stretch and chat with his teammates, she gave herself a mental warning regarding falling back into a state of lust over Lindy; a warning that she'd been reciting practically all weekend—well, at least since her world tilted on its axis and she had two dates with an amazing guy and was officially on her way to a friendship with one Lindy Barrett. Somehow, before she knew him, the lusting after him hadn't seemed quite as sinful as it did now that she'd ridden in his car and knew his personal cell phone number. Of course, she knew that God didn't see a difference between one form of lust and the other, but her conscience had varying levels of guilt for different sins; and lusting after one's friend, especially when one had a potential boyfriend waiting in the wings, was definitely high on the guilt ladder. Jane wanted to be guilt free for a little while, or at least until her mother phoned again.

She watched the players swirling around in circles, taking shots at the goalie between the pipes, alternating sides and passers. Following the line off of the right point, Lindy shot high to the goalie's glove side, rocketing the puck in the upper left corner of the net. His movements were measured and succinct from years of practice and repetition. Shadowing the shot, he skated around the back of the net and moved to center ice to continue stretching with a smaller group of players. Jane had watched this same scene unfold dozens of times, but tonight Lindy was more than a hockey hero set to win a game, he was her friend. The 747's resumed their flight.

———

At center ice, Lindy stretched in a butterfly pose as he casually scanned the arena seats. He made eye contact with Jane, gave her a brief smile, and lifted his gloved hand toward her in a quick salute. She mimicked the action, and amazingly the small recognition left Lindy unsettled.

He was shocked by the relief he felt when he saw her in the stands. He was so entrenched in his own thoughts that he didn't register a word the team captain was saying to him. He nodded at moments when it seemed appropriate, without taking his eyes off Jane when she wasn't watching him. She turned to say something to her friend whom Hooty was hung up on, when she covered her face with her hands. He could almost hear her laugh, and he chuckled at the inaudible joke.

Snap out of it, Barrett. He jumped to his skated feet and swirled into a series of pregame drills.

After taking a shot on goal, he skated to the back of the line and leaned lightly against the shaft of his stick as he watched his teammates take their own shots. Hooty deftly flipped a wrist shot up and over the glove side of the backup goalie before skating to Lindy.

The mullet-haired defenseman drank deeply from a green water bottle, letting the liquid slide down his chin. Without looking, he said, "They're both here."

Lindy nodded.

Hooty looked toward the new object of his affection. "Man, I think I'm in love. She's gorgeous. Don't you think?"

"Definitely," Lindy responded, but he didn't know if he was referring to Jane's friend or Jane.

"You'll meet up with us after the game. Help keep the friend occupied?"

"Let's win the game, lover boy. Then we'll worry about how to celebrate the victory." Lindy skated back toward center ice, but not before good-naturedly hitting the top of Jason's head.

He heard the buzzer announcing one minute remaining in the warm-up, and his teammates slowly made their way to the locker room. Only a few remained as the final seconds wound down on the jumbotron clock. When the final buzzer sounded, Lindy pulled a puck from behind his skate and made his way smoothly toward the net. As was his ritual, Lindy took the final shot on the goalie before the game, and then he and Hooty skated together off the ice. Lindy was the last member of the team off the ice, following a long-standing habit from his mini-mite days. "Always be the last one in the barn," his dad had told him. "That way they know your level of dedication."

He made his way down the hallway, following Hooty. He knew his friend wouldn't talk to him or anyone else, with the exception of a surly insult earmarked for one of their opponents, until after the game for fear of breaking his concentration. Lindy liked trailing his moody friend. He didn't feel much like talking tonight and felt distinct comfort in Hooty's brooding silence.

CHAPTER EIGHT

THE GAME WAS A KNUCKLE-BITER. Jane didn't think she took a breath in the last five minutes of play. The score was tied 1–1 going into the third period. The Jackets and the Wings battled toe to toe in the boards and they skated stride for stride up and down the ice. Tomorrow morning when each city opened its paper, neither would be able to complain about a lack of effort from their hometown favorites.

In the waning moments of the final period, sudden-death overtime loomed like a two-headed dragon. With each tick of the clock, extra minutes looked like a certainty. Then the lead scorer for the Red Wings broke away in the neutral zone, avoiding a hip check as he veered to the left when the Jackets' rookie defenseman veered to the right, and he skated hard toward the boards at the Jackets' blue line. The forward continued into the offensive zone, barreling at the goalie with the speed of a runaway train. The much-lauded all-star ripped off a ninety-mile-an-hour slap shot, top-shelf, to the goalie's glove side, which the goalie swatted away like an annoying mosquito. In Jane's opinion, the save was definitely *Sports Center* "Top 10" material, but just as she was ready to send the clip to Barry Melrose, the goalie deftly directed the save from the tip of his stick to a waiting Lindy.

Lindy skated with impressive speed through the neutral zone, literally jumping out of the way of a solid hit from a seemingly ageless veteran defenseman, before releasing a shot from the top of the point, through the five-hole of the Red Wings' goalie with less than five seconds remaining in regulation.

Jane was mentally enjoying an instant replay as she and Millie waited for the heroes of the night to finish up their postgame interviews and showers.

"Can you believe that game?" Millie said.

Jane stared at her friend, who generally counted every minute of a sporting event as one in her plus column for getting out of purgatory early.

"Wasn't that an amazing finish? Jason was on fire!" Millie hadn't been this excited when *Project Runway* asked her to be a guest judge.

Jane bit the side of her cheek, allowing Millie to continue with her overzealous gushing. Her best friend was done, finished, down for the count. Millie was in full-on crush mode. She was talking like a kid on Christmas about the new toy she had just received. Her cheeks flared a soft pink, and her voice could only be described as giggly. She had reverted to her childhood habit of pulling on a lock of hair and twirling, all the while dancing from one foot to the other in anticipation as she spoke. All she was missing was the clicking of chewing gum between each word.

Jane watched the unusual interpretive dance her best friend was inadvertently presenting. She knew Millie would be horrified by her own reaction to a male. In a normal male-female setting, Millie was the picture of cool confidence and sexy sophistication, but when she truly got her crush on, she regressed to the gawky, overly tall, skinny thirteen-year-old she once was. Only four times in the entirety of their twenty-five-year friendship could Jane remember Millie in full-on crush mode. Unfortunately, the guy had decimated her heart each time, sending her into a predictable rebound relationship where the XY worshipped Millie, and she, in turn, treated him with the respect one shows toward the gum on the bottom of one's shoe.

Jane continued to nod at appropriate intervals as Millie babbled. The possibility of having a coherent two-way conversation wasn't likely. Only half listening, Jane began rummaging through her three-by-five-inch handbag, not quite sure what she was expecting to find, but she needed something to squelch the onslaught of nervous energy, and as it appeared that Millie had assumed the role of speed-talker, Jane's only option was to search for candy.

Lindy and Jason emerged from the locker room at the same time. Each had a mixture of sticks, pucks, and pictures thrust into their hands by eager

fans wanting a piece of the legends to take home with them. Taking the
Sharpie offered by one of the Community Relations staff who guarded the
locker room, Lindy signed the items with little care. His focus wasn't on the
fans, or on their memorabilia, but on the pretty brunette intently searching
her diminutive handbag and the stunning blonde whose mouth was moving faster than the motor on his speedboat.

His heart softened at the picture the two friends made. They were comfortable together, speaking an unspoken language of head nods and hand
gestures, all while dancing a creative waltz, passing various items, from lipstick to mints to the beat of an unheard rhythm known only to the two of
them. Despite three sisters, a few overprotective aunts, and a mother, who
he could still feel watching him from the stands, women remained a mystery to him, and yet Jane made the mystery worth trying to solve. Shaking
his head, Lindy pulled his focus from the ladies to the waiting fans.

He signed a picture for a boy of about ten, whose mother was making
not-too-subtle overtures to Lindy's disgust, when Jane looked up and he
caught her eye. She smiled at him with genuine warmth. He mumbled
something to the eager young boy about flicking his wrist at the end of
his shot then tapped Hooty on the shoulder, and the two extricated themselves from the autograph seekers as they were pulled by the magnet of
two smiles.

———

"Hi," Millie said to Jason as he approached.

"Hey."

Jane rolled her eyes at the disintegration of the two highly intelligent
individuals to nearly mute preteens meeting at a middle-school dance.
She half expected them to start moving with their arms stiffly laid on each
other's shoulders, shuffling from one side to the other, out of sync, with a
bad 80s ballad playing in the background. In the midst of her thought, she
caught Lindy approaching her, his face alight with amusement.

He threw his arm around her shoulders, pulling her to his side as he
said to Jason, "Come on, Hooty, you can make goo-goo eyes at the lovely
Millie over dinner."

The foursome chose a small Italian eatery a block from the arena and after they placed their orders, Millie took center stage.

"When we were in junior high, Jane had this terrible crush on a ninth-grade football player," Millie said with a conspiratorial smile at Lindy. "She was always into the jocks."

"What about you, blondie?" Jason interrupted. "Did you have a crush on any of the football players?"

"Not on your life. I always fell for the tortured artists."

"She means the artists she could torture," Jane quipped.

Jason leaned into Millie's side and in a stage whisper said, "Babe, you can torture me anytime."

"Just for calling me babe, you can forget about it." Millie pushed him away. "Anyway, Jane was desperate to get this football player, Stacy Lorry, to notice her."

"Wait, you were in love with a boy named Stacy Lorry? What kind of self-respecting jock has two girl names?" Lindy grinned at Jane, who could feel her embarrassment rise by the millisecond.

Millie snorted. "What kind of name is Lindy anyway? It sounds kind of girlie to me."

All three sets of eyes shifted to Lindy's face. He leaned back in his chair. "Well, my mom wanted another daughter named Rose to round out her Lily, Flora, and Jasmine. She'd read this book about this tree the Linden Rose or something like that. When I was a dude rather than a dudette, she couldn't name me Rose so she convinced my dad that the name Linden sounded very stately. My dad knew no self-respecting hockey player, or guy for that matter, could walk around with a name like Linden, so he shortened it to Lindy. Not that Lindy was much better. People assume that because I'm the youngest child in a family full of sisters, my parents just messed up and wanted a Linda. I was teased a great deal when I was in primary school—at least until I was bigger than the rest of the kids. But, hey, thanks for bringing up painful childhood memories."

"Join the club," Jane said with a smile.

Lindy reached under the table and gently squeezed her hand, in an innocent gesture of support that left Jane warm and jittery. Putting needed distance between herself and Lindy, she slowly pulled her hand away and forced her complete attention on Millie.

"Anyway, so Jane was desperate for Stacy's affections, and I, her very best friend in the whole world, with only her best interests at heart, came up with the perfect plan to gain one silly little jock's attention." Millie leaned into the table for dramatic affect.

"Well, please don't keep us in suspense." Lindy winked at Jane as Millie launched into an in-depth account of Jane's teenage misadventures that made her want to sink under the table to keep Teenage Jane firmly locked in her box.

"Tonight was fun." Jane said. "Thanks again for the tickets. I would never have believed Millie would stay for an entire hockey game without whining if I hadn't seen it for myself."

"I'm glad you were there. Clearly you were my good luck charm." Lindy's broad smile spread across his chiseled face.

"Oh, I don't know about that. I'm not much for luck or charms."

"Well, I'm a hockey player, and I know a thing or two about good luck charms. You're definitely in the running."

"Thanks."

"And besides, it was worth having the two of you at the game, if for no other reason than to hear all about your teenage antics with one Miss Amelia Tandis in tow."

"Just what I need, more people who think I caused the trouble we always found ourselves in and not the other way around. I was definitely Ethel to her Lucy."

"Well, it did all start with one Stacy Lorrey," he said.

"Okay, Rosey."

"Nice. Maybe I'll have to rock it old school on you. Take you out back behind the schoolhouse and teach you some respect for such a stately name." Lindy took an imposing stance.

Trying to play along, Jane stared him down with her hands on her hips and her best tough-guy face, but the act was short-lived and they both broke out in laughter on the middle of High Street, causing a few passersby to stare at the crazy people.

"Thanks for dropping me home," Jane said, breathless. "It wasn't necessary, but it's much appreciated."

"No problem. I'd hate to think of you walking around down here after dark. It can't be safe."

Jane roughly pushed her hand through her long hair. "Now you sound like my dad. You'd think I was twelve and not thirty-two the way everyone worries about my safety. I mean for goodness' sake, I live in one of the safest neighborhoods in the city. And it's not like Columbus is New York or LA. It's not exactly hopping with crazy homicidal freaks."

"Whoa, didn't mean to hit a nerve." Lindy took a step back from Jane and her unprovoked rant.

She sighed, leaning against the doorway of her building. She felt her ire vanish as quickly as it had mounted. "Sorry to jump you like that. I guess I have a short fuse on this particular topic. It was the only thing my old boyfriend and I ever argued about."

"Old boyfriend?" Lindy perked up, obviously curious.

"I've had a few, not probably as many as you, but I'm not completely repulsive," she mumbled, feeling a blush rise to her cheeks.

Lindy leaned against the opposite side of the doorway and studied her. Looking her up and down slowly like an artist set to paint a portrait, he nodded in agreement. "Nope, not completely repulsive."

Jane punched him in the shoulder before she could think about what she was doing or to whom she was doing it.

"Ow!" He grabbed his arm and rubbed it.

Jane's hands flew to her mouth. "Oh my goodness, I'm so sorry. I tend to be a hitter. Just reflex . . . my sisters still sport a few scars from our childhood."

"I may never be able to shoot with this arm again."

Jane stepped closer and touched his arm with a light caress. "I'm so, so sorry. I didn't really hurt you, did I?"

"The fact that I get hit by two-hundred-pound men, nearly every day, nine months a year, coupled with the fact that I actually felt that punch, crushed my pride at the very least."

His wounded expression exonerated Jane from any residual guilt. "Ugh! Men!" She reestablished her distance with a tone of genuine disgust.

"Hey, pride is as important for a hockey player as any pad he puts on his body or the sweater he pulls over his chest for a game. Let me tell you that pride is more difficult to heal than a torn ACL or rotator cuff."

"Aw," Jane said, drawing on her best baby-talk voice. "Poor baby, what can Janesie do to make it all better?"

"Well, smart-butt, I think at the very least I deserve to hear about the old boyfriend," he countered.

Jane's dinner began to rumble in her stomach at the thought of discussing Brad with Lindy. "You want to know about Brad?"

"Yep."

"Well, umm . . . there's really not much to tell." She started twirling her hair. Shifting from one foot to the other to avoid pacing, she could feel her nose growing warm. "We met about four years ago at a conference in Indianapolis. At the time, he was finishing up school in Kentucky. After graduation, he got a job here. We talked about the future, but once we were in the same city we realized we were better buddies than we were a couple. He decided we should break up before we lost the friendship. He was right that we're better friends. No broken hearts or boiled rabbits. Sorry the story isn't too interesting."

"So, do you still see each other?" Lindy asked, lifting his water bottle to his lips and swallowing deeply.

"Sure. He's one of my pastors at church."

Lindy began to choke on his water. He leaned forward at the waist and clutched his thighs as water spurted out of his nose.

Jane leaned over him and pounded on his back. "Are you okay?"

Shaking his head in the affirmative, he pushed himself up and placed a hand between the two of them to stop her next hit. "I'm fine," He panted.

"That was weird. I don't know if I've ever seen anyone choke so violently on water." She picked up the bottle from the ground and examined it. "This *is* just water, isn't it?"

"Yes. It's water." Looking to the side, Lindy said, "I must have swallowed a bug or something. Just went down the wrong pipe." A few moments of silence sat between them as his breathing returned to normal.

"So, your ex-boyfriend is a priest, eh?" he asked.

Jane laughed. "Not a, um, priest, he's a pastor. Actually, he's the youth and children's pastor at my church. I left my old church when Brad was offered the job at another church in the area. I figured if I was going to be the pastor's wife, I should probably attend his church. The wife thing didn't come true, but I do love the church. It really is my home in a way my old church never was."

Lindy merely nodded his head.

"Well, I should go in. Some of us have to work early in the morning." Her keys jingled as they played between her fingers. She stared up at Lindy's face, waiting for him to say something. Unable to take the tense quiet, she turned and unlocked the door to her building. Pushing the door open, she rested her arm against the open door as she turned back to face him.

"Thanks again for the walk home," she said, to which he merely nodded.

His gaze held hers and grew more intense, drawing her into the unreadable depths of his deep blue eyes. Confused by the rapid change in his mood, Jane dropped her eyes from his. "Well, goodnight, then."

Lindy lifted her chin with a single finger and reestablished the intensity of their connection. Standing in the force of his invisible embrace, Jane was helpless to move or speak and could barely breathe. After seconds, which extended into what she was sure were hours, Lindy dropped his hand from her face and held open the door for her escape. "Good night Jane," he said, gently guiding her through the entrance.

When she was halfway up the stairs, she gave into temptation and turned around, partly expecting to be turned into a pillar of salt, as she took in his silhouetted frame still standing in the doorway. She drew in a breath to say something, but she didn't know what. She shook her head, smiled, and ran up the rest of the stairs to safety.

Lindy leaned against the door frame, staring at the space left empty by Jane for several moments after she disappeared around the corner. He tried to think of what he needed to do next, but his mind had gone completely blank.

After a few minutes, he shook his head and stepped away from her apartment entryway, realizing that he was behaving like a slightly demented stalker. He turned and walked back toward the arena. Something just shifted in his world. He wasn't sure what, but his feet definitely didn't feel as steady.

Jane could hear the beeping of her answering machine through her front door as she unlocked it and entered her apartment. Dropping her coat and keys on the hallway floor, she walked to the answering machine and pressed play.

"Jane, this is your mother." Jane was always amazed that her mom thought she would not recognize her voice. "It would have been nice if you would have stopped by to see your father today after church. You know how he misses you." That was mom code for "I heard you had a date. You didn't call me with all of the details. I'm hurt and disappointed in you."

Her mother's sweet, cultured voice continued to echo throughout Jane's small apartment. "Well, I called to give you some exciting news. Emory phoned us this afternoon, and Baylor finally proposed." The punch that her younger sister was getting married felt like the right hook Marilyn Benter delivered when she thought Jane had looked at her boyfriend in the seventh grade.

Her mother's message continued, "They're planning a July wedding for the year after next, after they both finish law school. Isn't that exciting, dear? Oh, do call your sister and congratulate her! We have so very much to plan and only a year and a half to do it." Jane didn't make out the remainder of the message, because the bile that was rising from her stomach somehow had blocked the sound from processing into audible communication in her brain.

Her mother's voice broke through her despair. "Well, do call us soon, Jane, dear. For all we know, you have fallen in a ditch and forgotten your name, or God forbid have been kidnapped by some burly truck driver who is holding you captive with his sawed-off shotgun. Love you."

Jane vaguely heard the machine beep as it clicked off while her mind completely shut down and she fell into the pillowy comfort of her favorite living room chair. Her twenty-four-year-old baby sister was engaged. Her baby sister was going to become Mrs. Baby Sister, and she, Jane, would be officially reduced to the crazy spinster aunt. Her mind flashed forward forty years, and she could see a forty-something Lizzie coming to pick Jane up at the nursing home, where she was allowed to keep her seventy-six cats, two birds, and seven years' worth of old newspapers neatly stacked in the corner.

As she readied to board the first-class section on the plane to self-pity land, trying to decide between the doors marked Godiva Dark or Thin Mint Girl Scout cookies, her phone rang. Fearing that her mother had once again decided to hunt her down to share the blessed news, or worse, that Emory herself had decided to call and spew her joy all over Jane's pity party, she allowed the machine to pick up the call.

She heard her own familiar words, "You know the drill," followed by the harsh beep of her machine.

"Um . . . Hi, Jane . . . this is Paul. I know I'm breaking every man code on the planet by calling you so soon, but I wanted you to know what a great time I had last night and well, umm . . ."

Jane picked up the receiver, mid-umm. "Hello."

"Oh, you're home."

"Yes. Sorry about not answering. I was screening my calls in an effort to avoid my mother."

"Oh . . ."

"It's not what you think. My mom is great, most of the time. But she could win a gold medal if guilt and meddling were Olympic sports. I made the mistake of going out to brunch with my best friends, Millie and my sister Molly, instead of going to see my dad and her after church today."

"Oh, okay."

"I'm really not a whacko, although I do sound like it right now." Jane rushed her words, fearing that this moment would be the one she would be discussing in therapy when she was fifty and couldn't figure out why she was still single. "I think it's a mother-daughter thing. Guilt is a pre-requisite. You'll never please them regardless of your achievements, even if you're doing exactly what they want you to do. It's an endless cycle of guilt and disappointment. My mother goes through it with her own mother, and I've already seen my sister Molly drop the guilt bomb on my nieces. It's nature."

"Okay, I see."

"I guess it does sound a bit crazy."

"Just a little bit . . . it's okay. We all have our family baggage we carry around. Why do you think I'm a lawyer?"

"Your dad," she guessed.

"Yep, he's a US district court judge appointed under Bush, Sr."

"Wow! That's a lot to live up to. And I thought being the only single daughter was bad."

"Your life always looks better through the lenses of someone else's."

"That's good. Who said it?"

"Me. I just made it up."

Jane felt the tension ease from her shoulders as she sank deeper into her chair.

An hour later, she looked at her watch and realized her alarm would be screeching sooner than she would like to think. She said as much to Paul.

"I hate to get off the phone," he said. "I can't believe it's been an hour."

"I know, but if I don't hit my bed soon, I'll regret every minute of lost sleep during the Monday meeting. Especially when they dim the lights to review last week's results. I'll be out like a champ, and it's never fun to have your boss nudge you awake so you can wipe the drool from your chin before you make your weekly presentation to the CEO."

"I gotcha."

"But I have to thank you. You were an excellent diversion from the choc-olate coma I was planning for myself over the news of Emory's impending wedding."

"I'm not quite sure I fully understand, but I'm glad I could be of help."

"I'll explain sibling rivalry to you sometime, only child."

"How about over dinner on Tuesday? I promise we'll go to a real restau-rant this time."

"I don't know. I liked Chez Paul."

"I'll pick you up around 7:30. Is that okay?"

"Sure." Jane said.

"Good night, Jane. Have sweet dreams."

She nestled the phone back in the cradle then leaned against the back of her chair and let out a satisfied sigh. "Well, God, I can't say I wasn't selfishly upset by the news over Em and Baylor, but I have to say, as usual, You continue to amaze and delight me. I have a potential boyfriend and have now spent two evenings in less than seventy-two hours with Lindy Barrett. Anyone who doesn't believe that You love us with an unconditional grace and benevolence only needs to look at my life for one day to realize how amazing You are. Of course, the whole eye-locking moment with Lindy out front is something that I'm sure does not fall into the 'friend' category in Your handbook, but can we shelve the guilt over that situation for a moment, or like, ever? This month is awesome, and I just want to enjoy it, okay? I love You. I love You more than anyone or anything. Thank You so very much for loving me. Amen."

Jane pushed herself out of the comfortable chair and floated down her hallway. Stepping across the threshold of her bedroom, she glanced heavenward. "Oh, I'm not going to lie. The Emory-getting-married-before-me situation will probably make me a touch bitter, but October as a whole is making this pill go down just a little easier."

CHAPTER NINE

"HOW WAS DINNER LAST NIGHT?" Millie asked through the earpiece of Jane's mobile phone.

On her way to work on Wednesday morning, Jane had called Millie under the guise of confirming Pilates class the next evening.

"Well, since you asked," Jane began sheepishly.

"Since I asked? You called me because you wanted to talk about your date."

"I didn't. I needed to know about Pilates." Jane could almost taste the lie on her tongue.

"Whatever, this is the same kind of ploy you used when you wanted to talk about your date with Jesse Monroe in high school." Millie responded. "So, how was the date with Super-Stud Christian?"

As Jane exited I-670 East toward her office, she recounted the details of the evening. "Well, we went to that new Italian restaurant in the neighborhood. I never realized how nice it would be to date someone who lived a block away."

"Well, how would you? You did waste over two years on the Moron, constantly schlepping yourself out to the suburbs three-plus times a week." To Millie, *suburbs* was a four-letter word.

"He's not a moron and I wish you wouldn't keep calling him one. Brad and I are still friends, and he's one of my pastors. And while we're on the subject of name calling, I wish you wouldn't keep referring to Paul as the Christian stud or hottie or any other clever name you invent. I'm afraid you'll slip up when you see him again. You didn't exactly come off smelling like a non-crazy with your first impression."

"Hey, I'm the Best Friend, so I get all name-calling, nickname-invention privileges as it states clearly on page six of the Best Friend Contract that we signed in the seventh grade."

"Are you ever going to stop relying on a twenty-year-old document as an excuse for all of your crude behavior? Millie, we're considered adults by federal and state law. We should probably start acting like ones."

"Okay, I'm ignoring that snippy little remark as I'm sure you're still too caffeine deprived to know what you're saying. Back to the CSM, aka Christian Stud Muffin, when am I going to get to meet him for real, not just some fly-by in the apartment hallway?"

Jane pulled into her parking spot and reached across the console to pick up her shoulder bag, while delicately balancing her aforementioned caffeine addiction. "Let's get through another few dates before I scare him off with my gorgeous yet not-so-closeted psychotic friend."

"Whatever, you know all boys love me. Even the Moron loved me."

"Millie . . ."

"Okay, no more names. So, tell me, how was the rest of the date?"

With a smile plastered across her face, Jane walked down the wooded path to the sleek gray and chrome building she called home fifty hours a week. "Dinner was wonderful. The conversation didn't miss a beat. You know how there are supposed to be those awkward silences every seven minutes?"

"No . . . I didn't."

"Well, I read about it in some magazine on a flight somewhere. Anyway, it's been clinically proven that every seven minutes there's a natural lull in conversation, also known as the 'awkward pause' where everyone gets a little uncomfortable, and my nose turns into a beacon better suited for a snowy night in December."

"Jane. Focus. The date, what happened on the date?"

"Sorry. Conversation was great and when dinner was over, he walked me back to my place. He was very sweet. He even held my hand a little."

"Ugh! Stop blushing, Janie. You're going into work. Jasper will think you have a fever and you're trying to avoid going to the doctor again. So did you make out?"

Jane forgot to pick up her feet and tripped across the threshold, dropping her bag and scattering her paperwork ten feet. Blessedly, she was able to save her coffee.

"Millie! What is wrong with you? I just dropped everything in the middle of the lobby."

"I know, I know. You're a Christian and Christians don't do that kind of thing. Yadda, yadda, yadda."

"Amelia Tandis, it's not simply a yadda-yadda thing. And no, not that it's any of your business, we didn't make out. He kissed my cheek at the door. End of story."

"That's way faster than the preacher boy. What did it take him, like ten dates and one hundred-plus hours on the phone to work up the courage to even call you his girlfriend? How long did it take for the lip lock to actually occur? I'm having a hard time recalling."

"You're not. You kept track of it on a calendar like you were trying to determine the optimal time to bet in Vegas. And it wasn't that bad. He kissed me when he was ready and he *thought* I was ready. I just wasn't clear that I was ready earlier. But that isn't important anymore. Let's change the subject. I want the dish on you and the defenseman you don't want to talk about."

Jane could sense the exact moment that Millie's eyes glazed over in a haze of infatuation and puppy-dog love. "This is crazy. When have I ever even looked twice at a jock? And Tommy Mitchell doesn't count, because we were in like, the fifth grade, and the only thing he showed athletic prowess in was Field Day. Who knew that he would graduate to the NFL as a quarterback?"

"Well, Mill, maybe that's why you like him? Maybe you like him because he's different from every other guy you know." Jane felt like a broken record, repeating the same argument she'd given Millie each time she wavered on her budding relationship with Jason.

"Maybe? I don't know. He doesn't take my stuff, which I'm totally not used to." Jane smiled at Millie's effort to respect her wishes and not use foul language, even when it was just the two of them.

Millie sighed. "Usually, I take the first few dates to see what guys will do for me. You know? Will he get my drink when I ask, or will he already have it there for me? Will he hold my purse when I'm shopping? Will he pull the car around? Will he defer to my choices for dinner, movies, etc? And he hasn't done any of the things guys usually do for me. In fact, I seem to be doing all of those same things for him. Crazy?"

"Well," Jane said as she opened the heavy wooden door to her office. "It sounds like you've finally met your match."

"You know, Jane, you might be right. Who would've thought? He asked me to come to the game on Friday. Do you want to go? I need someone to explain everything to me. And in all honesty, I've never really listened when you've prattled on incessantly about the details of the sport. I don't want to seem stupid and congratulate him on his field goal or something."

"Well, I don't know." She deposited her bag in the corner. Setting her coffee on the glass-top desk, she glanced over the messages that were already stacked in a neat pile.

"Please, Jane."

"Paul asked me out for Friday."

"You're going to bail on a silver anniversary's worth of friendship for a guy you've known for a handful of days?"

Jane dropped into the oversized black leather chair and swiveled to look out her office window. She kneaded her forehead. "Millie, don't be dramatic. Let me see what I can work out. We'll talk about it after class tomorrow. Mill, I have to go. I have a mountain of work to push through."

"Okay. Bye."

"Bye."

She wasn't off the phone for fifteen minutes when her office phone rang. As she glanced at the caller ID, Jane's stomach dropped. Her mother was calling.

Jane had been blatantly ignoring her phone calls since Sunday when the announcement of Emory's engagement had become front-page news in the *Grey Daily Telegraph*. She was trying to be happy for her sister, but the thought of spending the next year and a half talking about dresses, place settings, and how Jane was hopeless in the love-and-relationship category made her head ache.

Accepting her penance, she took a deep breath, pressed the speakerphone button, and answered the phone with a pleasant "Jane Grey."

"Jane Eleanor Grey, where have you been? Your father and I have been worried sick about you!" Her mother's voice came through the speaker like fingernails on a chalkboard.

She swiveled to face the window. "I'm sorry, Mom. I've been very busy the past few days. I did call Em and congratulated her and Bay on the engagement. It's great. Just great." Even to Jane, her voice sounded less than enthusiastic, but she hoped that her mother was too angry too actually notice.

"Jane, you know that you're never too busy for your sisters or your parents. Unless you've lost an arm, a leg, or your memory, you should always return a call from family."

"Yes. I'll remember that, Mom. Must call home in all cases, unless amnesiac or loss of a major appendage. I'm assuming a finger or a toe doesn't count?"

"Don't be flippant, Jane. Now, ask me for my forgiveness and we can move onto discussing your sister's delightful news."

Jane felt like she was six years old again and being blamed for breaking a vase, which Molly had actually knocked to its death. "Will you please forgive me, Mom?"

"Well, with that tone, I should say no, but for the sake of familial harmony I will ignore your runaway mouth. You are forgiven."

"Thank you."

"Now, on to more exciting things: Your sister's engagement. Her ring is simply amazing. She sent us a picture over the e-mail. The stone was apparently Baylor's great-grandmother's and must be at least three karats."

"And we all know that the Bible says that the key to a beautiful marriage is the strength of the three-corded braid: God, the couple, and Tiffany's."

"Jane, just because you could care less about jewelry does not make it sinful, nor does it make appreciating beautiful things a sin. A big ring does not make your sister's impending nuptials a heathen binding. Emory loves the Lord . . . in her own way."

"Yes, Mother. In the everything-works-out-for-me-so-I'll-thank-the-Lord-just-to-be-safe way."

Her mother let out the same exasperated sigh she had been passing on to Jane since Jane hit puberty. "I understand you might be a little bitter about your sister's good fortune, so I will ignore that last statement, but I do not want to hear even a single complaint, or the slightest bit of an attitude, in the next twenty months. You will not only act like you are the supporting, caring, older sister that I know you are, you will also be the supporting, caring sister."

Jane rolled her eyes. "Yes, Mother."

"Okay. Well, now that we have that settled, you will need to put the kids' engagement party on your calendar."

"You're already planning a party? They've been engaged for, like, ninety-six hours."

"Jane . . ."

"Sorry."

"The party will be here at the farm on the Saturday before Christmas. We have to wait so long because Emory and Baylor have class until the twelfth, and then his mother wants to throw her own party. Of course, ours should be first, but logistics are not in our favor."

Jane listened as her mother told her who would be invited, where the invitations would be printed, but as the details wore on, Jane's mind began reformatting her upcoming presentation, outlining the afternoon's agenda, and contemplating what she was going to eat for lunch, so when her mother began to complain about dresses, Jane was beyond disinterested and simply responded with, "That's nice."

After twenty minutes, Jane's mother seemed to sense her lack of conversational participation. "Jane, you haven't been listening to a word I have said."

"That isn't true. You said it's not fair of Mrs. Boudreaux to throw the first party, but you would never utter a word, because you don't want to cause a family squabble. Oh, and you're thinking of using Jan Phillips's daughter to do the catering, since she just graduated from culinary school and should be good and cheap."

"I said inexpensive and up on the latest techniques." Her mother's voice reflected her obvious surprise over Jane's conversational recap.

Jane silently chuckled at her mother's reaction. She knew her mother was unaware of her middle child's one true talent: to hear and not really listen to anything. "Sorry, I tend to paraphrase."

"Darling, I've been babbling on about all of these arrangements. Is there anything new with you?"

Jane stopped typing the e-mail to her team about the Johnson meeting the following week, at the insinuation in her mother's voice. Could her mother know? Had Molly inadvertently told her parents about Paul? She did get space cadet-ish when she was pregnant.

"No, Mom, nothing is new. I'm sorry to cut you off, but I have to rework a presentation for this afternoon, and I'm kind of under the gun. I'll call you later today, when I'm on my way home. Maybe you and Daddy can come into the city for brunch on Saturday."

"Oh, sweetie, I'm sorry to have kept you on the phone when you should have been working. Saturday would be lovely. I love you, dear."

"I love you, too, Mom."

Jane pushed off the speakerphone button and laid her head on the desk with a sigh. After a moment of peace, a knock clicked lightly against her door, and she sat up. "What now?" she said softly before calling, "Please come in."

"Hi, Jane. I saw your light go off on your phone and I couldn't wait any longer."

"What's up, Sarah?" Jane asked the department administrative assistant.

"You received a delivery earlier, when you were on the phone, and I have a phone message for you."

The delivery would be the shipment of test product from the Johnson group for next week's meeting; Jane asked her to keep the package at her desk. "Could you also save the message until after the Baker meeting? I really need to finish things up, and if I don't just hammer down and focus, I'm going to be up a creek without a paddle this afternoon."

"Whatever."

"Sorry, Sarah," Jane called out after her, as the door clicked back in place. The Baker Boys were calling and she dove into her work.

———

Nearly seven hours later, Jane walked out of the main boardroom with the clients from the Baker account. Her face hurt from smiling for nearly four consecutive hours. The last time she had experienced this much facial pain had been when her dentist removed all four of her wisdom teeth.

"John and Matt, it was great seeing you again. I look forward to wrapping this up in a couple of weeks with your complete satisfaction," she said, shaking each of the suits' extended right hands.

"I would expect nothing less," said either Matt or John. Jane couldn't really keep the two Brooks brothers suits straight.

"Boys, I'll see you out," Jasper said as he started to follow the suits to the elevator, before he turned back to Jane.

"Out of the ballpark, Jane! As always, great job! Really great job. Have a good night." With that vote of confidence, he jogged after the Baker "Brooks Brothers" boys.

Jane leaned against the doorjamb and let out a long sigh of relief. She lifted her eyes heavenward. *Thanks. Couldn't have done it without You.*

After taking one brief moment of rest, she pushed away from the door and padded down the hall to her office. The area was quiet, but she noticed that Sarah, who was usually one of the first to leave, was still seated behind her tall, round centralized desk, flipping through a copy of the latest *ELLE* magazine.

"Sarah, what are you still doing here?" Jane asked as she leaned against the desk.

"I've been waiting for you to get out of your meeting. I have some messages for you, and that delivery you didn't pick up at lunch," Sarah said without looking up from her magazine.

"Sorry I didn't pick up the delivery. I was really focused on the presentation and didn't even stop to get lunch. You didn't need to wait for me. I appreciate your thoughtfulness, but you could've left the delivery in my office and the messages on my desk. I hate for you to have waited all of this time."

"I know I could have left the messages, but I wanted to see your face when you got your delivery. And, I wanted to personally give you your messages."

Jane took the pink slips of paper from her and turned slightly away from Sarah's view. As she read, she began to understand why Sarah was so willing to sacrifice her own time: gossip. She wanted to know what was behind the messages, and by the look on her face she must have thought the potential for juice was pretty good.

The first message was time-stamped at 9:35 a.m. The message was from Lindy, and as Jane read the note, she could feel heat spreading to her nose that was likely as bright and shiny as a Clark Griswold's Christmas tree. He wanted to know if she would like to join him for dinner that evening.

She moved on to the second slip of paper, which had been left at 10:02 a.m. Paul had called to say he had a great time the night before and could she call him about Friday evening.

The third note was left at 1:37 p.m. The message was also from Lindy, saying he'd save a seat for her at Mitchell's. The reservations were for 6:30 p.m., and he hoped she could make it.

The fourth was from her dentist, reminding her of her real appointment at noon on Friday.

Feeling slightly lightheaded from all of the unprecedented attention, Jane leaned on the tall desk as she looked at Sarah, whose smile had shifted from warm to sly.

"Anything else, Sarah?" Jane asked.

"Your delivery . . ."

"Oh, that. Sorry. I'm just a little frazzled. Is the package still here or did you take it into my office?"

Sarah turned from Jane and bent low behind her tall desk. As she rose, she held a wide square-cut glass vase, which held nearly two dozen yellow roses of various hues, and a single white rose, sitting softly in the center of the arrangement.

"Are those for me?"

"No, silly. I just wanted to taunt you with the hundred-and-fifty-dollar arrangement my secret admirer sent to me."

Jane's nose burned as she reached forward and pulled the tiny envelope tucked neatly in the blooms. The card was handwritten and read: "To the new light in my life. Paul."

"These are lovely, aren't they?"

"And the note is so romantic."

"Sarah, you read the note?"

"Hey, lady, possession is nine-tenths of the law. If you leave your stuff at my desk all day, I can't be held responsible for my nosy tendencies."

"Remind me never to leave my diary at your desk."

"Oh, I've already read through that notebook you leave in your office. You really should lock things in your desk drawer. That's why the company gives us keys."

Jane was left with little rebuttal but made a mental note to take all of her personal effects home over the weekend. "I guess I should call Paul and thank him for the flowers. They really are thoughtful."

"So . . . no dinner with the hot hockey player?"

"Umm . . . well . . . Lindy and are just friends. Dinner with a friend isn't a big deal, right?"

"Sure," Sarah said, appearing unconvinced.

Jane looked at her watch and mentally calculated the time she had to drive home, change clothes, and fix her makeup. If she left in the next five minutes, she would only be about ten minutes late. She could recap the meeting in the morning.

As Jane turned toward her office to pick up her coat and bag, she heard Sarah call from behind. "Jane, a man who considers you 'just a friend' does not call twice to invite you to dinner at the nicest steak house in Columbus, on the off chance that you might be free. Men who want to date you do."

"Sarah, don't be ridiculous. He knows about Paul, not that there's that much to know, but he does know. Lindy is a bit lonely and needs a friend. I enjoy his company. Please don't make anything more of it than it is."

"Honey, don't fool yourself. The Lindy Barretts of the world are not lonely. That man is not only the most eligible bachelor in this city, but he was also named as one of the Top 25 Bachelors in *People* magazine last year. No, he definitely isn't lonely."

"Believe what you want Sarah, but I prefer to keep an open mind. I believe women and men can be friends. I believe that they can support each other without needing to resort to romantic entanglements."

"Girl, did you not see *When Harry Met Sally*?"

"Good night, Sarah," Jane said with finality. She placed her flowers on her desk, picked up her coat and bag, and headed toward the door for her just-friends evening.

CHAPTER TEN

DINNER WAS UNEVENTFUL AND NATURAL, as uneventful and natural as dinner with one of the most famous men in the city can be. The conversation was comfortable and the food was delicious. Men and women could just be friends. Who cared what Harry or Sally said?

The next few weeks took on a fairly common pattern. She went out two nights a week with Paul, who was now kissing her good night and holding her hand everywhere they went, and she talked to Lindy nearly every day. A part of her felt guilty about her burgeoning friendship with Lindy, but Paul encouraged her. He told her it was an excellent opportunity to witness and be the Body of Christ to a lost person. Jane agreed, although her motivation didn't always feel so altruistic.

October gave way to November, and as the weather turned colder, Millie's newfound fling grew hotter and into a serious commitment for the once commitment-phobic duo. Both she and Jason seemed like teenagers in love for the first time. Jane now knew all of his vital and less-than-vital statistics. With the information she had amassed, she could start a whole new fan page devoted solely to the Harvard hockey wunderkind.

Millie called on Jane to give her tutorials during most home hockey games. On occasion, Lindy would leave her tickets, and Paul would come from time to time, but most nights, it was she and Millie sitting among the hockey wives and girlfriends. Jane explained everything from cross-checking to icing, and as Thanksgiving approached, Millie was yelling at the refs with the best of the unruly hockey masses.

The Tuesday before Thanksgiving, Lindy left a message with Sarah offering Jane tickets that night for her and Paul. He also extended a dinner invitation for the couple following the game. As she was about to call Paul and pass along the invitation, her phone rang.

"Good afternoon, Jane Grey."

"Hi, Jane." Paul's familiar smooth tone came across the line.

"Well, isn't this a coincidence? I was just picking up the phone to call you."

"I don't believe in coincidence," he said. "I believe in God-incidence."

"Do you use that to pick up the girls at the Single Mingle, at the Naz?"

He laughed, "Only the super-cute brunettes."

"Noted. So, what's up?"

"Well, I need to apologize. I know I was supposed to go to your family's place for Thanksgiving dinner, but I was assigned a case today, and I have to leave for Juneau this afternoon."

"Is that Juneau, as in Juneau, Alaska: home of Sarah Palin and the big moose?"

"One and the same. I'm sorry to bail on you last minute. I was really looking forward to meeting your family for the first time."

"No worries, Paul. There'll be plenty of time to torture you in the future. Christmas is right around the corner."

"Are you sure?" When she confirmed that she was sure, he let out a relieved-sounding sigh. "This is a pretty big case. I'm surprised my Dad and the other partners trust me enough to take it."

Paul briefly explained what he could about the case involving environmental rights and restrictions. The descriptions were a bit over Jane's head, so she responded with what she hoped were appropriate *reallys* and *that's wonderfuls* at measured intervals.

"Needless to say, I'll have my hands pretty full for the next few weeks or possibly months, but I'm excited to get started."

"Paul, I'm so happy for you. Will you need to be in Juneau long?"

"Probably the next two or three weeks, but I'll be home for Christmas and the New Year. I imagine it'll be a lot of back-and-forth until we get things settled. The initial phase of research and taking depositions is always the lengthiest."

"Three weeks, huh?"

"I know. Your sister's engagement party is in three weeks. I should be back before then. It'll be okay. You'll have a boyfriend in tow. I promise."

What a perfect boyfriend. He knew exactly what I would be worrying about. Wait . . . boyfriend?

"Did you just say boyfriend?"

"Umm . . . yeah? I'm sorry. I guess I jumped the gun a little. Things are just going so well, and I feel so close to you. . . ."

"No it's okay. It's better than okay. I think I like it."

"Really?"

Jane turned from her desk and looked out her window to the cold winter's day outside. Twirling her phone cord through her fingers, she was unable to suppress her sixteen-year-old grin. "Yeah, really. So, Boyfriend, I guess this case is your tough luck, since we were offered prime seats at tonight's matchup against the Penguins."

"Bummer. I guess you'll have to console yourself over my absence, Girlfriend, with some bloody fights and trash-talking fans. I'll be mid-flight when the puck is dropped."

"You really have to leave so soon?"

"I'm afraid so, but I'll call you when I get to Alaska."

"Okay." Jane turned from the window and began drawing imageless circles on her desk, trying to ignore the waves of sadness and loneliness threatening to pull her under.

"It'll be late when we touch down, so I'll leave a message. Enjoy the game, but no consoling any broken hockey players."

"I wish you were going to be there, but I really am excited for you."

"Thanks, Jane."

Her forced enthusiasm was waning, and she knew she would need several closed-door minutes to wallow. "Have a safe flight."

"And Jane . . ."

"Yes, Paul?"

"This probably isn't the best way to tell you, but I won't have a better one before I get back. I'm falling in love with you, Jane Eleanor Grey. I know it's fast, and I know you're too practical to probably feel the same, but I wanted to tell you anyway."

All she could do was stare at the phone.

"Well, I guess that was too much sharing. Don't worry, Jane. I don't expect you to feel the same, so soon, I just wanted you to know how I felt."

Jane sat with perfect posture in her seat regressing to six years old when Grandmother Garrett had tried to teach her to be a lady. Her ladylike self only revealed herself when Jane was placed in positions of extreme awkwardness. "Thank you, Paul. I appreciate your sharing with me."

"Okay, well then . . . I probably should get off the phone and go home to pack. I'll call you from Alaska."

"Have a safe trip. I'll talk to you later. Good-bye, Paul."

"Bye."

Jane slipped the phone into its cradle and swiveled back around to look out into the gray Columbus sky.

Paul was in love with her. Her mind tried to wrap itself around the conversation, but she couldn't quite understand how he could know he was in love with her. Sure, they got along well. He made her laugh. They had marathon conversations and seemed to finish each other's thoughts, but they'd known each other for only a little over six weeks. Six weeks was hardly enough time to know if you liked a new television program, let alone to know if you were in love with someone.

She definitely loved him in the agape, unconditional, Christian connotation of love, but was she truly in boy-meets-girl, toe-curling, Cary-Grant-on-top-of-the-Empire-State-Building kind of love?

And then there's Lindy . . . Where had that thought come from? She and Lindy were just friends, nothing more. Sure, most of her romantic fantasies in college and early adulthood, revolved around said hockey player and his ruggedly masculine good looks, but that was all behind her. They were friends. They were, in fact, on their way to becoming the best of friends . . . just friends.

A soft knock interrupted her reverie, and she turned with thanksgiving for the reprieve, seeing Sarah's smiling face peek through the door.

"Jane, Jasper wants to see you in the boardroom and he wanted to remind you that you have the final Baker presentation today."

"Thanks, Sarah. I'll be right down."

Jane began retrieving files from her desk, thankful for the distraction from her own thoughts. "Thanks, God. I really couldn't deal with that much self-discovery right now. Can we shelve it to later?"

Thank heaven for the distraction of the Baker Boys in their Brooks Brothers suits.

CHAPTER ELEVEN

THANKSGIVING CAME AND WENT with relatively little drama, as the entire dinner discussion was focused on the upcoming engagement parties. Baylor had decided to go to Charleston and have dinner with his family, but Emory had deigned to lend her presence to the Grey clan.

As the conversation between her sisters and mother turned from the engagement parties to cake, flowers, and train length, Jane, Jake and her father left the table for a healthy dose of football and napping.

On her way out the door later that evening, she thought she was going to be able to escape without any in-depth questions about her relationship with Paul, when her father broke the code of silence.

"Jane," he said as he held her coat open for her to pull on over her bulky sweater. "Your mother and I would like to meet this young man of yours sometime before you get married and give us a grandchild."

She looked at her tall, silver-haired father, who had the air of a distinguished Marlboro man with his slightly thick mustache and weathered, dimpled cheeks. "Daddy, when did you become . . . Mom?"

"I don't know what you mean."

"Dad, Mom is always the one who gives me the guilt trip about not including you guys in every detail of my life. Did she put you up to this?"

"Peanut, you know your mother worries about you. She just wants to be a part of your life. She thought that maybe, if I asked you about Paul, you might be more willing to give in and bring him by the house. She's afraid you're embarrassed by her."

She linked her arm with her dad's, leading him through the front door of the stately farmhouse and down the path toward her BMW. "Dad, I explained that Paul has a big case he was just assigned otherwise he would have been here. I'm not embarrassed by Mom, at least not on most days. And I'm not keeping you from meeting Paul or him from meeting you."

Well, at least not now that he's officially my boyfriend. . . . Paul is my boyfriend. . . . I have a boyfriend. Her queasiness rose again.

"That's what I told Bits, but she just wouldn't believe me."

"When he's back in Columbus, I'll bring him out to the farm, and Mom can treat him to her famous cherry pie and endless hours of interrogation. Will that make her happy?"

"Immensely," he said, kissing her forehead as he opened her car door.

Sliding behind the wheel, she turned on the ignition. He gently closed the driver's door and tapped the top to signal his good-bye, and she rolled down the window to callout her own before driving away.

Jane thought back to the conversation with her dad as she pulled into the parking lot of her apartment building. She knew she should feel guilty about not bringing Paul to meet her parents sooner, but she was afraid that if she did, the bubble of their relationship might burst.

She walked up the three flights to her apartment and as she unlocked her door, she could hear the faint beeping of her answering machine. After dropping her keys and bag at the front entrance, she pushed the button to play back the messages and continued on to the kitchen to make some tea.

From the kitchen she heard the now-familiar, smooth voice, "Hi, Jane, it's Paul. I hope you had a happy Thanksgiving and that you didn't pass out in your mashed potatoes with the talk of the engagement party."

Smiling, Jane pulled the tea bag out of the container and dropped it into her waiting cup. They had known each other for less than two months and yet, he knew her so well.

"I celebrated Thanksgiving with a few locals at the hotel restaurant. Who knew that the Alaskan pilgrims ate moose and salmon instead of turkey and stuffing? Anyway, I do hope your day was a good one. I'll talk to you tomorrow. I should have a break in the afternoon. Oh, and Jane, I love you. Hope you're getting used to hearing it. Bye."

Jane's hand froze in mid-pour as she tilted the steaming teakettle toward her cup. "I love you." Shouldn't that phrase be warming her ears, not freaking out her stomach?

A shot of water scalded her foot, snapping her back into reality. She'd forgotten that her hand held a container of boiling water and had proceeded to allow the cup to overflow onto her granite countertop and waterfall over the edge onto the hardwood floor.

"Ugh!" Jane slammed the kettle back on the stove and grabbed a dish-towel to mop up the water.

Throwing the wet towel into the laundry room, she proceeded to her comfy yellow chair. The chair sat in a small alcove, which overlooked the typically busy High Street, but tonight the area was peacefully quiet, leaving Jane distraction free and alone with her thoughts.

Why can't I say the words back? He was a great guy who met all of her basic requirements: Christian, tall, employed. They enjoyed each other's company. He made her laugh and got her jokes. She was attracted to him. What was the problem?

Pondering the question, she debated the pros and cons, when her thoughts were interrupted by her ringing phone. "Hello."

"Hey, Beautiful," Lindy said. "What are you doing?"

"Just sitting here thinking. Not something a big, old, dumb hockey player would know anything about."

"Ouch! Did you just call me old?" he asked.

"*Old* is what bothered you in that phrase?"

"Hey, I make my living defying the odds of my age. We can't have it slip out that I'm on the downside of my expiration date."

"Noted."

"What's causing that pretty little brow of yours to furrow? Maybe an old, dumb hockey player can help you out."

She sighed and quickly weighed the need for advice against asking Lindy instead of Millie. A male point of view might be what she needed.

"It's just something Paul said to me before he left for Alaska."

"Sounds pretty serious. Did he break up with you?"

She chuckled as she swung her legs over the arm of her chair. "No, he didn't break up with me, although it's nice to see you know me so well as to be able to predict the longevity of the majority of my relationships."

"See, we *are* soul buddies."

"Interesting. . . ." She muttered, ignoring the flutter of butterfly wings in her tummy.

"So what did the lawyer say to you?"

"Well, he called me his girlfriend."

Lindy cleared his throat. "That's a good thing, right?"

"Yeah, it's a good thing. He's a great guy and I enjoy his company. Defining the relationship is not the problem. He also said that he loved me."

Lindy let out a low whistle. "Whoa."

"I know, right? We haven't even known each other two months. How can he possibly be in love with me? He doesn't even know what I look like when I wake up, or how I talk to myself, or that I once had the ambition to become a tightrope walker after going to the circus, when I was eleven. He hasn't met my parents or my sisters or any of the other crazy relatives that pop out of the woodwork on various holidays." She continued on her tear through the reasons he couldn't know he was truly in love with her, including the fact that she'd gone to fat camp when she was thirteen and that she'd lost the horse queen contest to a girl who looked like a horse, until her pent-up fear was completely spent.

Silence hung between them and Jane wondered if she had showed too many of the neurosis cards in her hand.

As Jane was ready to give Lindy the out she assumed he wanted, he spoke. "Okay, killer. That's a pretty lengthy list. I don't think Paulie took all of that into consideration. Maybe I should call the dude up and warn him to stay in Alaska."

Jane sighed. "I know. I'm a complete disaster. Why would anyone think he's in love with me? Paul should run for the hills, but I guess he's in Alaska, so he should run for Mount McKinley and never look back."

"Okay, drama. Are you finished?"

Leaning back in the chair, she rested her head against the opposite arm rest and shrugged her shoulders. "Yep. Sometimes my mouth runs away with my mind, and then neither is worth much more than a pound of mushy spaghetti."

Lindy chuckled. "Now, that's an image. Why do you think Paul's telling you he loves you bothers you?"

"I don't know. Don't you think it's all too quick?"

"You're asking the wrong dumb hockey player. Tess and I dated for over a year before I said the three words. Then it was only out of guilt. Eventually, it became more of a habit. I'm not really an expert on love."

"Me either. I guess it just kind of freaked me out."

"You think?"

"Okay, so I'm really freaked. I like Paul, but I'm not sure I'm in love with him, you know? It's so early in the thing, and for all of my romantic notions, I'm a pretty practical girl. I like order and a plan. I like checklists and weighing the pros and the cons. I like rules and steps and black-and-white scenarios. This is moving too fast. It's all a little too gray area and squishy for me."

"There's another stunning visual."

"I'm serious, Lindy. I don't want to screw this up. Paul is the best guy I've met in a really long time, present company excluded, and I don't want to miss out on what I could have because I'm afraid to jump off of the pro-verbial cliff."

"I get it, Beautiful. But I don't know what to tell you. If you don't know whether you're in love, then you probably aren't. But that doesn't mean you won't fall in love with him eventually." Lindy choked as he spoke. Jane could hear him take a drink of water, likely to soothe his throat.

Poor guy is probably coming down with something.

"You're probably right. I just feel bad that I can't say the words back, you know?"

"I know, but don't let guilt lead you to do something you will later regret."

"Thanks, Dr. Phil, I'll cherish that advice."

"No problem. So, the tightrope thing . . . I'm trying to imagine you in tights, balancing on a wire skinnier than my skate. Quite a picture." Lindy's laugh lifted the mood of the conversation, and Jane could feel him perking up. Laughter was good medicine.

Sighing with relief, Jane filled in the blanks of her long-ago dream and put the gray future lying before her in a box to be dealt with tomorrow. What was good enough for Scarlett would be, once again, good enough for Jane.

CHAPTER TWELVE

LINDY'S ADVICE ROLLED THROUGH Jane's mind the next morning as she shopped with Molly for Black Friday deals. The two friends talked for about an hour, with the conversation ending more lightheartedly than it began, but something Lindy had said weighed particularly heavy on Jane's heart: *Don't let guilt lead you.*

Not letting guilt act as her guide in life was an interesting notion. Most of her decisions had been motivated by guilt or responsibility. From the college she chose to where she looked for a job after graduation, almost all of her decisions had been based on the expectations she and her family had for her life. Even dating Brad, and now Paul, fit nicely into her life expectation model. But was she really doing what she wanted?

"Earth to Jane." Molly poked Jane in the shoulder with tremendous force.

"Sorry, what's up?"

"I've asked you three times whether you thought Lizzie would like this dress, and you haven't even looked up from the rack in front of you."

Jane took in the black-and-white polka-dot dress with its wide red sash before looking at her sister. "Sorry. My mind must be somewhere else."

"I understand. You miss Paul. What about the dress?"

"Well, it's a dress, which means she will not like it out of principle." Jane ignored the casual mention of Paul.

"I know, but she can't wear jeans and a T-shirt to Christmas Eve service. This is the least frilly one they have, and I can find one that is complementary for Chelsea so they look right in the pictures."

"Are you really worried about your kids color coordinating so they don't mess up the Christmas picture?"

"Jane these are memories we'll cherish forever. I won't be able to forgive myself if I look back in twenty years and my daughters looked like ragamuffins on Christmas."

"Okay, Bitsy. The dress is cute. I'm sure Lizzie will tolerate it long enough for a picture."

"Thank you, and there's no need to call me Mom. You'll understand better when you have kids someday."

Someday kids in her someday house with... Paul? Why could she only envision miniature hockey skates by the back door?

Jane mentally shook the image from her head. "Molls, let's not go down that road today."

Molly sighed, turning back to the rack. "Whatever. It seems to me that Paul is pretty interested in you, and he does meet the requirements on your list, so I thought . . ."

"Well, corral those thoughts, Annie Oakley. Paul and I've only been dating for a few weeks. There's no need to run to Macy's and pick out china patterns and baby name books."

"Okay, but you can't be mad that I've daydreamed a little."

"Why are you daydreaming about me? Don't you have enough on your plate with Em and Bay's engagement party and wedding? Why fantasize about the possibility of a future when you have the reality of a one filled with flowing wedding dresses and cute christening gowns with Emory and Baylor?"

"Well, they're no fun, are they? They followed all of the prerequisites, just like Jake and I. Meet in college. Fall in love. Get engaged. Get married. Have two point five children. I mean it's nice, even if it did take law school for Emory to make Baylor propose. But the whole scenario is all a little bit boring. Your life, on the other hand, is so exciting, what with Paul, and Lindy Barrett, and how we all thought you would be married to your career. Who knew that my little sister would live such an exciting, *Days-of-Our-Lives*-worthy life?"

"First of all, I'm no Marlena. Second, Lindy is my friend, so please do not put him in the same classification as Paul. And third, please don't build any expectation for Paul and me. I don't want to disappoint everyone if things don't work out. Think how depressed Mom was after Brad and I broke up. I might end up married to that comforting career of mine."

"Okay, Pessimist Patty. But can't you dream a little? Paul is a really wonderful guy."

"Molly, you met him once."

"I know, but I looked into those green eyes and knew he would be a great husband and father."

"All from one look into his eyes?"

"Don't be mean, Jane. People's eyes do not lie. He was so nice to the girls at church, and Jake really liked him. You know Jake doesn't like just anyone."

"Really, that is why your postman comes to your Christmas party every year, and the new stock boy at the Kroger came for dinner last week, at Jake's insistence."

"You know what I mean. They're both nice men and so is Paul. Jake only likes nice people."

"Yes, Jake only likes nice people. Can we get back to shopping?"

"Well, who put the bitter pill in your coffee this morning?"

"I'm sorry. I didn't sleep much last night."

"Up late talking to a particular guy?" Molly asked pointedly.

"Something like that. So are you good with the dresses? Do we need to pick up anything else?"

"I did want to take a turn through Brookstone to look for something for Jake for Christmas. He wants one of those putter thingies. But if you're too tired, I can take you back home."

"I wouldn't dream of you losing that 5:00 a.m. parking spot. I can drag my tired old body a little longer. What I don't understand is that you're three months pregnant and you don't seem fatigued at all."

"I know. Maybe it's the thrill of shopping, or maybe God is too good to me and I'm going to have a boy this time. I feel so different, Jane. I'm not sick or tired or any of the stuff I was with the girls. I feel like I could take on the world," Molly said with a Mary Tyler Moore spin in the aisle.

"Whoa, there, Mary, Rhoda here isn't so energetic. How about I treat us to some smoothies before we brave the crowded frontier of the north end of the mall?"

"Sounds good, Rho."

"Okay, Mar, let's go." Jane linked her arm through her sister's and led her to the Smoothie King.

Twenty minutes later, Jane wandered through Brookstone, slurping the remnants of her strawberry-blueberry Bonanza Blitz, but her thoughts were on Paul. Why was she struggling with his declaration of his affections? For her whole life, especially the two years she spent with Brad, she had been waiting for the right guy to tell her he loved her. From her first reading of *Cinderella*, she had envisioned her Prince Charming right down to his bulging biceps and soft, adoring eyes. And here she was, over a quarter of a century later, and her Prince Charming was real and offering his love and affection. What was her problem?

Picking up a battery-operated five-day weather forecaster, Jane flipped the box over to read the directions, but her mind tilted with her problemless problem. Molly was right: Paul was a great guy. He would make a terrific husband and father. He fit all of her criteria.

And he wanted to be with her. Was that the problem?

Was she struggling with his love simply because he was giving her that love?

"Whoa," she said with a slight exhale.

In that moment Jane realized what the problem was: she wasn't loveable, so how could anyone as great as Paul love her?

Well, that's a trip down a pretty obvious Jan Brady psychotherapy session.

Who knew she was such a typical middle child? Well, if she thought about it, she did know. And Millie knew. And Molly knew, which probably meant that her mom and dad both knew she was a middle-child head case. Paul and Lindy probably knew. The only person who likely didn't know was Emory, and she was unaware simply because Jane's insecurities didn't directly affect her. Anything that didn't fall into the orbit of Planet Emory wasn't of her concern.

She laid the weather gadget back in the stack of thirty similar boxes and turned to find her sister, who was in the back of the store intently listening to a twenty-year-old sales boy describe the details of the Putt Master. Jane made her way toward Molly and could hear the eager young man try to sell her sister on the contraption.

"The Putt Master has several built-in features. The extra-tacky grip is crucial for those hot, you know, Columbus summers. Just feel this handle, ma'am." He handed the clueless Molly the putter. "Isn't it wonderful?"

"Uh, sure. It's great."

"The total kit also includes a, you know, scope and a practice target to ensure, you know, complete success on the green."

"Are you buying a putter, or, a, 'you know,' sniper's rifle, Molly?" Jane asked.

"Jane . . ." Molly said.

"Sorry," Jane muttered, loudly slurping her smoothie.

"Todd, I'll take the putter. Can you have it wrapped?"

"That's great!" Todd's eyes lit up, and he crushed the putter to his chest like his favorite stuffed animal. "I can have it wrapped for you next week. Unfortunately, with today being such a, you know, busy day I can't, you know, have someone wrap it."

"No worries about the wrapping. I can do it at home. I was being lazy."

He loosened his hold on the putter as his shoulders drooped. "Oh, okay. Do you want anything else? We have never-lost golf balls that glow under water and beep for twenty-four hours until they're, you know, retrieved. I'm sure your husband would like a set of those too."

"No, the putter will be fine."

"Okay, if you're sure. I'll just take this up to the register and Mikey can, you know, ring you up. Thanks again, ma'am."

"Sure."

Molly watched him rush toward the wrap desk. "If that little kid called me ma'am one more time, I was going to, you know, hit him over the head with that stupid, you know, putter. Jake better know how much I love him."

"Huh."

"What?"

"Well, I've not seen a sales guy get under your skin like that. You're usually the calm, rational one. I'm usually the ranter."

"I think I'm tired," Molly said, rubbing her temples.

"Well, let's go buy the 'stupid, you know, putter' and head home. I'm tired, too."

They walked to the end of the long line, and Molly linked her arm through Jane's. "So, what revelation hit you a few minutes ago?"

"What do you mean?"

"Sister dear, you would be the worst poker player on the planet. You had some internal revelation that was either something about meteorology as you stared at those silly wall weather machines, or it was about that man who has consumed your thoughts all morning."

"Am I that obvious?"

"Jane, you couldn't be easier to read if you were a picture book."

"Gee, thanks."

"Janie, it's not a bad thing. It's just that every emotion you feel is pretty much written on your face. What did you unearth in that brain of yours about Mr. Obviously Wonderful Paul?"

"Paul told me he loved me."

Molly uttered a loud, mildly offensive word, causing all the people in the store—and some idle window shoppers—to focus their entire attention on Jane.

"Nothing to see here, folks. . . ." Jane waved them away. "My sister has mild Tourette's, that's all."

"Sorry," Molly whispered. "Paul told you he loves you? But you've only known him for two months."

"I know. It's a little overwhelming and unexpected, right?"

"Overwhelming, yes. Unexpected, no. Jane, you're an amazing woman. I personally don't understand why every single male, and some not-so-single ones, in the tri-state area haven't already declared their undying love for you."

"Yeah, right."

"I'm serious."

"I know you're serious, Molly. You're my sister who cannot see my faults, but let's be realistic. I'm cute-pretty at best. I'm slightly involved with my work. I'm committed to God as my number one, which puts every guy as number two. Most guys do not appreciate being second on even the shortest of lists—they're very competitive, even with God. And if you haven't noticed, those fifteen pounds everyone is supposed to gain in college stuck with me like Grandma's mashed potatoes, and they have made friends. I'm not exactly Millie material."

"Millie? Who was talking about Millie?"

"Millie is every guy's ideal. All you have to do is walk into one room with her to realize how less than perfect you really are."

"Jane, that's your biggest problem. You're always comparing yourself to everyone else. You judge yourself on what you think you're missing, rather than seeing how much you are. Jane, you're a beautiful, intelligent woman. You've accomplished every goal you've set for yourself your entire life, but when it comes to men and relationships, you have a twisted sense of reality."

Jane's heartbeat quickened. "What do you mean?"

"When you were two or three years old, I read you *Sleeping Beauty*. Do you remember?"

"Did you really read it, or did you just turn the pages when the record player beeped as the Disney record read the story?"

"Whatever. Do you remember the story?"

"Yes. It was my favorite, until Emory was born and Mom used to call her the 'Little Sleeping Beauty.' It kind of ruined the story for me."

"Jane, please focus. In the story, Aurora waits for her true love, Phillip, to fight through a ton of obstacles to rescue her. She's completely passive, allowing all of these bad things to happen in her life before she's ready to fall in love with her Prince."

Jane crossed her arms. She could feel her lips tighten into a straight line. *How much longer is this line going to take to move?* "I remember the story, Molly. Chelsea makes me watch it every time I babysit the girls. What's your point?"

"My point is, when it comes to relationships, you're Aurora. You wait for all of the bad stuff to happen to you in life. You sit passively by, wondering when your prince will come to rescue you. In what other part of your life are you passive?"

Jane's heart went into fifth gear. She could feel her cheeks burning like a flare gun in the middle of the highway screaming, *disaster this way.*

"Jane, the reason you're so inert with men is because you're afraid you're going to get hurt. You've been friends with Millie for so long that you don't understand that men aren't supposed to simply fall into your lap like an errant crumb from a dinner roll. You see Millie's physical perfection and men's response to that beauty, and somewhere in your mind you have convinced yourself that pretty is all men want. In reality, Millie feels the same way or she wouldn't dump every guy she ever dated. She doesn't want to feel like she's an object. Whereas you cannot see beyond the fact that most men do not want an object, they want a breathing, laughing, wonderful woman. Jane, my dearly delusional sister, you're that woman. So the thought that Paul could be in love with you in less than two months is to be expected. I understand it may be hard for you to trust, but you're definitely worthy of that love. Paul sees in you what we all see in you—you're wonderful."

"I guess I'm pretty messed up."

"No more than the rest of us."

"Do you think Emory ever feels inferior?"

"Do you think Emory ever feels anything more than sorrow at the loss of a good sale on shoes at Nordstrom?"

"Molly, she's our baby sister."

"I know, but really, did the girl ever have a thought that didn't originate between the pages of *Vogue* or *SELF*?"

"As Mother says, 'Emory loves the Lord in her own special way.'"

"I'm sure somewhere underneath the Gucci and the Prada, Emory loves God very much. He's been awfully good to her."

"Thankfully, He has. Can you imagine what she would have been like if Baylor hadn't proposed this fall?"

"She was pretty much ready to self-destruct at commencement last spring when he didn't get down on one knee as he crossed over the dais," Molly confirmed as they inched closer to the front of the line.

"We truly are horrible people. Emory is our little sister and we should be protecting her, even if she did come bouncing into the world seven years into my comfort zone of being the baby. Not that I'm bitter."

"Clearly," Molly said. She pulled her credit card from her wallet in anticipation of being the next in line. "So, Jane, if Paul loves you, how do you feel about him?"

"He's really a great guy. He's everything, and more than what I've prayed to God to find in my life. I always dreamed that a man would come in and sweep me off my feet. I know . . . too many Cary Grant movies. But a girl can dream."

"What is the problem?" Molly asked as Mikey took her card.

Jane shrugged her shoulders. She felt like she had run a marathon in the last five minutes. "I really don't know."

"Well, Sister," Molly said as she signed the cashier slip. "You'd better figure out whether you love this man. He's too fine, both physically and spiritually, for you to dangle on a thread. You both deserve better than half-way commitment."

"I know. Maybe when I see him in a few weeks, it will all be different. Maybe it was just the shock of the thing. You know I'm not very good with surprises."

"I know, but Jane, I want you to think long and hard about this. If Paul really loves you and he wants to share his life with you, please give him a chance. Guys like him do not grow on trees."

Jane nodded but remained quiet as they left the store. Everything Molly had said was right. Jane was competitive, borderline aggressive, in most areas of her life. She was valedictorian in high school. She graduated magna cum laude from college and summa cum laude from graduate school. She sat on several fundraising boards in the city and was one of the recognized and relied-upon leaders at church. *Passive* was definitely not a word with which most would label Jane. And yet, when it came to dating and guys, she was a relative snail.

She prayed that God would grant her the calm reassurance to let her know that Paul was The One, or at the very least a nudge off of the cliff.

CHAPTER THIRTEEN

THE HOLIDAYS SHIFTED INTO high gear following Thanksgiving weekend. She talked to Paul every day, although their conversations were rather limited by the time zone differences. She had yet to respond to his declaration of love, despite the fact that he ended every call with a simple "I love you." The best she could come up with was "Talk to you tomorrow." It wasn't exactly romance-novel worthy, but she figured it was better than "Thanks."

As the cold of December bore down on the city, Jane's workload tapered to a near standstill. Most of her clients were preparing for Christmas parties and closed holiday offices, so when Millie invited Jane to join her at an away game in Chicago, she quickly accepted.

As she was changing lanes on I-670 West toward downtown, her phone rang. Slipping the earpiece into her ear, she answered. "Hello."

"Hello, sweetheart."

"Hi, Paul, what time is it in Juneau?"

"Just about two in the afternoon, not that I can tell since it's pretty much been dark since I woke up this morning. I thought I might catch you in the car on the way home."

"Do you have a GPS on me or something?"

"You caught me. I'm not your boyfriend. I'm actually an inspired stalker who is only posing as your boyfriend to convince you that you love me. Naturally, I would have placed a GPS on your car. How else would I know how to track your every move?"

"Funny."

"I thought so."

"It's a good thing you're so pretty."

"Wow, I'm pretty. I almost feel like Natalie Wood."

"Okay, Maria. You have officially been hanging out with me too much when you start referencing *Westside Story*. What's new in the frozen tundra?"

"Same as yesterday—more depositions. But I'm starting to get used to the cold. I really connected with the front desk man, and he offered to take me on a dog sled ride after church on Sunday. It should be an interesting adventure."

"I think I'm jealous, except for the freezing-cold-and-no-sunlight thing."

"Yeah, the sunlight thing is killing me. I never thought I would miss the sun so much. Growing up in Columbus, it's pretty much gray central. But C-bus definitely gets more rays than Alaska, at least midwinter."

"Less sunlight than Columbus, that *is* depressing."

"Tell me about it. That's why I need to talk to you every day. You're my dose of vitamin D."

Jane's stomach twisted at the obvious compliment. Too embarrassed to respond, she waited for Paul to continue the conversation as she pulled into her parking lot.

"What do you have on the docket for this weekend? Do you have more party planning with your mom and sisters?"

"Thankfully, no."

"How are you avoiding the engagement party plans?"

"Millie invited me to Chicago. I haven't broken the news to my mom or Molly. My mother will act like I'm going AWOL and Molly will treat me like I've led her into the lion's den and left her without prayer access to God. I can't thank Millie enough for the invitation. Getting out of Columbus when Mom is this far into party plans is a welcome relief. I probably should extend an invitation to my Dad, but that would put a crinkle in Millie's third-wheel plan she has for me."

"Third wheel?" Paul asked.

"Yep." As she unlocked her back door and started up the three-flight trek, Jane explained. "Millie has it in her mind that Jason invited her for this weekend to make some, umm . . . romantic moves on her."

"I see," Paul said, as if he was twisting the end of his imaginary mustache.

"Paul!"

For Jane, it was an unwritten rule that sex before marriage wasn't done, and not really discussed among the opposite gender, but she had found that not all Christians held the same standard. She had assumed Paul felt the same way she did, but maybe she was wrong.

"Why are you yelling at me, Jane?" Paul asked.

"Well, what was that tone?"

"What tone?"

"You know what tone. 'I see.' What do you see, Paul?"

"I don't know. . . ." Paul said hesitantly. "I just assumed that Jason and Millie were—"

"You assumed Jason and Millie were *what*?"

"I assumed that they were together in the intimate sense."

"Why would you assume that?"

"Well, they're both adults, and they're dating each other. He invited her away for the weekend. One would make the assumption that there was more to their relationship than holding hands. That's all."

"That's all? If you invited me away for the weekend, would you assume that I was going to . . . umm . . . you know?" Jane whispered as she opened her front door, slipped inside and quickly shut it.

"No, of course not," Paul said.

"But you assume that because Jason and Millie are going away together for the weekend that they will be . . . umm . . . intimate?"

"I guess so."

"That's being pretty judgmental, don't you think?"

"Uh, I guess, but you have to admit, based on the information at hand, the case for that assumption is fairly valid."

"Don't get all lawyerly on me." Jane tossed her coat on her couch and paced across her living room floor.

"I'm sorry. I didn't realize this was such a touchy topic."

Jane dropped onto her favorite chair, a feeling of numbness sweeping her body. "I'm sorry, too. I shouldn't have jumped on you. It's a pretty sensitive subject with me. I really am sorry."

"It's okay. But please remind me, if you ever change careers and become a lawyer, that I do not want to be your opposing counsel."

"Okay."

"Not to broach an obviously sensitive topic unwarned, why is relational intimacy such a touchy topic?"

"Wow, you actually made sex sound like a clinical topic."

"It's a skill. Like your avoidance is a skill, Miss Grey. Please answer the question." His lawyer voice had the effect of Sodium Pentothal on Jane.

"I guess it's a weird discussion topic for me. Most guys, heck, most women, don't understand why I chose to wait until I'm married. And I guess I've always felt a little bit on the outside looking in when the topic is brought up. I know I've made the right decision, it's just that a lot of people, even seemingly devout Christians, make me feel like I'm an idiot for the choice I've made." Sharing the weighty revelation with Paul broke down one of the final discussion barriers for Jane. Her mind flashed to a documentary she watched about the day they tore down the Berlin Wall. Tear down that wall, Mr. Gorbachev, er, Mr. Wade.

"Well, I'm sorry to bring up something that appears to bother you so much, but I'm glad to know how you feel. I appreciate your being honest with me."

"Paul, I love you." The words tumbled from her lips before she even knew they were coming. Did she mean them? She checked herself. How could she not love a man who seemed to accept her, completely, for who she was? Yes, she loved him.

"Wow! Remind me to fight with you more often. Now I really wish I were with you in Columbus."

"It feels good to say it. I love you, Paul."

"I love you, Jane."

The simple exchange of words calmed her spirit more than any of the crazed mental conversations she'd had with herself over the days since Paul first dropped the love bombshell. Loving Paul was right. Jane knew that in her core. She was sure the slight twinge of uneasiness in her stomach was the result of a few errant butterflies swarming in her belly, not doubt.

She snuggled into her chair. "Gosh, I don't know what else to say. I'm pretty spent."

"I know. I don't want to get off of the phone, but I have another deposition in a few minutes, and I have to review the notes before my next witness gets here. I'll call you tomorrow."

"Sounds great. Good night, Paul."

"Good night, Jane. I love you."

"I love you, too." And her mind knew that they were the right words to say. Her gut would eventually catch up.

CHAPTER FOURTEEN

ON FRIDAY AFTERNOON, Jane boarded a fifty-seat jet to Chicago, gliding to her assigned place on the airplane on the light wings of her newfound love. She, Jane Eleanor Grey, was in love.

She was excited to share her love-life update with Millie. Millie's excitement for Jane's news would be short lived, as she would be calculating her romantic chess moves to one-up Jason. Jane shook her head at her friend's antics. In all the years she'd known Millie, Jane hadn't seen her this twisted up over a guy. Jane was convinced that Jason was Millie's match. It was now up to best friend Jane to make sure Millie understood this fact and didn't mess up her chance at happy couple-hood.

Jane absently listened to the flight attendant's various safety instructions, but her mind paid little attention to where the emergency exits were or what to do in case of a water landing; they were flying over Indiana, for goodness' sake. Rather, she focused on the future she could now almost touch.

She could see herself in five years, married to Paul, maybe with a baby or even two in tow, flying to Chicago to watch her dear friend Lindy play hockey. The trio would go out for a nice dinner after the game, reminiscing over filets and cheesecake. Jane smiled at the thought of the three of them together doing a variety of things. She knew that their lives would always be intertwined. Perhaps Millie and Jason would marry, and the five some would be able to vacation to exotic places together.

Over the fifty-five-minute flight, Jane planned a range of adventures for her little posse of five, but in the midst of her joyful planning, a tiny nudge of doubt crept in to her mind. Her perfect group of friends included two couples and one single. What if Lindy met another woman? What if Lindy married?

The smile, which had been a fixture on her lips for twenty-four hours, faded abruptly as the pilot landed with the grace of an overweight ballet dancer, shocking Jane back to reality. What if Lindy married? Who would she be? Would Jane like her? Would this mystery lady like Jane?

Questions swirled around her head in pace with the pilot circling the airport toward their gate. How could Jane be so blissfully ignorant as to think that someone as fantastic as Lindy would stay single? Of course he would get married. The thought made Jane a little queasy.

It must be the rocky landing. I need to pick up a soda on the way to the hotel.

As she deplaned with her fellow travelers, her once lighthearted and love-filled mood had been twisted into an internal reflection of the windy, damp, and cold surroundings of Chicago in December. Exiting the gangway, she turned toward the arrival screens, to the left of her gate, scanning the computer images for Millie's flight. She watched as the arrival information changed from "on time" to "delayed." Millie's new anticipated arrival time was 7:15 p.m., only fifteen minutes before the puck dropped.

Looking at her watch, she pulled out her phone to call Millie. It was only 4:45 p.m. local time. Jane had plenty of time to get to the hotel, check in, and arrive at the arena for the pregame skate. She just didn't have any tickets.

"This is Millie."

"Thank goodness. Millie, it's Jane. Your flight is delayed."

"Thank you, Captain Obvious, for telling me something I do not know."

"Sorry." Jane put money in a vending machine, selecting a lemon-lime soda to calm her stomach. "Do they think you'll be able to take off any sooner?"

"They really aren't telling us much. I guess this is what I deserve for trying to play games with Jason. That God of yours isn't always a funny guy with this irony stuff He pulls."

"I'm sorry your flight is delayed. What happened? I didn't think the weather was bad in Denver."

"It isn't. There's some mechanical problem with the plane, and I must say that I'm glad they found it out while we're still on the ground, rather than mid-flight."

"Agreed . . ."

"Jason was supposed to leave his player tickets at the front desk under my name. I'm not sure I'll even make it for the first period, but you should go ahead and go. Just leave me a ticket at will call. I'll take a cab directly to the arena."

"What about your luggage?" Jane wasn't foolish enough to think that Millie would have packed similarly to her one smallish carry-on bag.

"Don't you worry your pretty little head about my suitcases. Getting luggage to its appropriate destination has never been an issue for me."

"Spoken like the best friend I've known and loved all of these years."

"Well, Jane, my oldest and dearest, it's like I've said since I was fifteen years old—bend the world to you, or you'll find you're facedown in a pile of mud."

"It still isn't any prettier an image than it was when we were in high school and you were jetting all over the world being gorgeous."

"Hey, you're the eloquent one, lovey. Speaking of love, have you told the hunky Christian that you have the total hots for him yet?"

"Millie, do you always need to embarrass me?"

"Dude, I'm not even with you. How can I embarrass you?"

"You're gifted."

"You're stalling. You told the hottie you have a thing for him, didn't you?"

"Well, if you mean did I tell him I love him, then yes, I did." Jane whispered.

"You told him you loved him? Oh my! This is serious. What did Lindy say when you told him?"

"That's an odd question, don't you think? Why would I tell Lindy?"

"Well, for starters, you two have been attached at the Bluetooth since you met. I'm starting to get jealous of a hairy hockey player. And you have to admit you have the teensiest of crushes on the man. Aren't you curious to see if he'll declare his love for you and try and win you away from the upright lawyer?"

Jane handed the cabdriver her bag and a card with the address of the hotel and then slipped into the backseat of the car. "Amelia, I've nothing but friendship in mind with Mr. Barrett. And the feeling is mutual. We set very specific ground rules. Please, do not try and read anything more into our friendship."

"What you're telling me is you haven't told Lindy about your love fest with Mr. Cutie Christian?"

"Is it really too hard for you to simply call him Paul? And I've sort of told Lindy about the love thing with Paul."

"What do you mean, you 'sort of told him'?"

"Well, he called me on Thanksgiving, you know, after Paul told me he loved me and I had my freak-out."

"Yes, I know that part."

"Well, so he knows that Paul told me he loved me. I just haven't, you know, told Lindy that I told Paul I, you know, love him." Heaven help her, but Jane was starting to sound like the sales associate from Brookstone.

"Please wait until I'm there to watch his face."

"Millie, you're so weird. Why do you want to see his face when I tell him?"

"Don't worry about why, just promise me you'll wait until I'm present."

"Okay."

"They're starting to board my flight. I might make it to the game sooner than the second period after all. Don't forget to leave my ticket at will call."

"It will be there in a perfumed envelope with your name embossed on the outside."

"It better be, smarty pants. I only accept the best. See you in a few."

"Bye, Millie."

Five hours and one hockey game later, Jane put the finishing touches on her hastily applied makeup before she rushed to meet Jason and Lindy in the lobby of the hotel for a postgame dinner. She brushed blush across her cheekbones as she reflected on the end of the game.

Millie had arrived at the game fifteen minutes into the third period. Her flight had been delayed another hour after she boarded, and she nearly missed Jason's fifth goal of the season.

At almost the exact moment Millie took her seat beside Jane, Lindy checked a Blackhawks' rookie hard into the boards and was called for a double minor penalty due to the blood drawn on the eighteen-year-old's chin. The hockey veteran balked at the call but took his seat in the sin-bin with only a minor ruckus. He then watched as his teammates, particularly Jason, fended off swirling 'Hawks who seemed to multiply throughout the penalty kill. Jason was able to make a clean break-away down the ice to score a short-handed goal to tie the game, but the effort was futile as the

Blackhawks' captain scored off the point in the waning moments of regulation to secure the win. When the final horn sounded, Jane watched Lindy leave the ice. Tonight would not be a lighthearted occasion. She hoped God would help her find the words to comfort Lindy.

Jane glanced at the clock. The game had finished over an hour earlier, and the guys likely were impatiently waiting on her and Millie. She snapped closed her tiny imitation-pearl-encrusted handbag, barely glancing at her reflection in the mirror hanging above the desk in the room she shared with Millie. "Fashionista, are you ready?"

"Almost," Millie called through the echo of the tiled bathroom walls. "Why don't you head down to the lobby and pacify the boys. I need five more minutes."

"I'll go down to the lobby, but five minutes better be five minutes in mortal time, not five Millie minutes. Those guys are hungry and shouldn't have to wait another twenty minutes to leave for the restaurant because you're trying to improve on God's perfection."

"Whatever. I'll be down in five minutes."

Jane grabbed her full-length black wool trench coat and headed toward the elevator. Catching her reflection in the doors, she was surprised she actually liked what she saw. Maybe it was the fuzzy elevator doors, but the winter-white off-the-shoulder full-skirted cocktail-length dress made her figure seem like, well, a figure, and not a large block.

Jane emerged from the metal cocoon and spotted the guys through the glass partition as they waited for her and Millie.

Both Lindy and Jason had still damp hair from their postgame showers and wore simple wool suits. Lindy's was black and Jason's was a deep gray. They each wore crisp white button-down shirts under their tailored jackets, but only one wore a smile, while the other grimaced as he swirled the ice in his small bourbon glass.

Jane approached the two friends and tried to gauge how best to broach the duo. "Hi, boys," she said. *Yep, that's clever and comforting.*

"Hey, Janesie. Where's my girl? She couldn't possibly need more time to get beautiful, considering the package God gave her in the checkout line."

"Please tell her that, will you, Jason? And I like your checkout theology. I might have to steal that line."

"Steal away. You forget I went to Harvard. Genius lines fall out of my mouth all night long. I can't help myself."

"Be careful where you stand, Jane. It's getting pretty deep in here." Lindy stood and pulled out the chair that sat between him and Jason.

She nodded and slid onto the high barstool as gracefully as she could, but her wool dress wasn't cooperating with the fabric-covered seat. Jane could feel the back of her skirt pushing up her hind end, which translated to wrinkle butt.

Great! The first night in weeks I feel particularly pretty, and the furniture is out to get me.

Jane's nose had to be a dark shade of pink as she shifted on the seat cushion, trying to extricate her skirt fabric from the chair, but she only made the situation worse as she felt the rough, industrial fabric through the delicate textile of her silk stockings. *Please, no runs tonight. My extra pair of hose is stored away in my suitcase, and I'm fairly certain it has a run that's mended in the toe.*

"Are you okay, Jane?" Lindy asked.

"Yep, I'm fine. I'm just trying to find the best spot to enjoy these comfortable bar stools."

"Okay." He said with a shrug of his shoulders and the slightest squint of his eyes. "Do you want something to drink?"

"No, Millie said she'd be down in five minutes."

"You'd better order another drink, L.B.," Jason said. "Millie minutes are like five for every one, and the more time she gives herself, the more time each minute represents. We probably have another twenty-five minutes to kill. Right, Jane?"

"She'd better not be that late. I warned her she's on mortal time tonight, not Millie time."

Jason smiled and nodded to the bartender with the universal sign for another round, looking at Jane expectantly.

"Well, I guess I'll have a club soda with a lime."

Jason nodded to the bartender. "You heard the lady." Turning to Jane, a grin stretched across his face. "Although I thought you might get a little crazy on us tonight, by the look of that dress."

Jane looked down at her dress and then back up at her companions. "What's wrong with my dress?" Other than the obvious full-backside view she was in danger of showing the entire bar.

"Well, Janesie, honey," Lindy began as he trailed a finger across her shoulder. "You have to admit that this dress is a little more daring than your typical attire."

Jane's shoulder felt as though a path of lava flowed behind Lindy's fingers. She was too embarrassed by the guys' turn of topic to focus her attention on anything other than the drink that was placed in front of her.

"Cat got your tongue, Jane? No comment? Are your cheeks pink? Your nose red? Did we embarrass you?" Lindy said with a smirk in his voice.

"What is wrong with you?" she asked.

"Nothing, Beautiful. I've just been sitting here waiting on you ladies with nothing to do but kill the better part of that bottle of Macallan."

"Lindy, are you drunk?"

"Well, darlin', I guess I am. Are you going to call that pastor boyfriend of yours and have me reprimanded?"

Jane turned her back to Lindy and spoke to Jason. "I think you should take him up to your room, and we should forget about dinner tonight."

"Janesie, Lindy's a big boy, and besides, Millie just walked in." He stood to welcome the beautiful blonde draped in a dolman-sleeved backless top in black matte jersey that caressed the waistline of her black pencil skirt with effortless ease.

"Hey, gorgeous."

"Hi, handsome." Millie gently pressed her lips to his.

Facing Jane, Millie smiled. "Take a look at your watch, friend. I'm only five minutes late. Are you impressed?"

"I know I am." Lindy slurred his words as he raised his glass in a mock toast, simultaneously sloshing brown liquid down Jane's white sleeve.

Startled, she stood up quickly, ripping a hole in her stocking. "Oh my goodness!"

Lindy picked up a handful of cocktail napkins and began swiping them down Jane's sleeve. "Janie, honey I'm sorry."

Looking at her with sorrow-filled, glassy eyes, Jane saw an indefinable pain flash deep in their navy depths that threw off warning signals in her mind, simultaneously crushing the barrier to her heart.

She touched her hand to his, forcing herself to ignore the ripple of tingles that rolled from her fingers to her stomach as she took the torn napkins from his grip. "It's okay."

Lindy nodded and ran his now empty hand through his hair as he leaned back against the bar. Jane was thankful for his retreat. With the distance, she could feel the oxygen returning to her lungs. Clasping her hands in her lap, she fought against the growing need to console Lindy as she turned to Millie. "Mills, I'm sorry, but I think I need to call it a night."

"Oh, Janes, go up and change really quick. Be like Superman in the phone booth. We won't even know you're gone."

"No, I think both Lindy and I need to skip tonight's festivities. Don't you agree, Lindy?"

A slow smile pulled across Lindy's face. "Janesie, you want to spend the night alone with me? All you had to do was ask."

Millie looked at Jason as confusion marred her perfectly arched brows. "What is wrong with Lindy?"

Turning his back to his friend, Jason tried to explain Lindy's unusual behavior to Millie and Jane. "L.B. found out that the little chin music he laid on the rookie tonight was worse than we originally thought. When the doctor checked him out, he diagnosed a pretty severe concussion. They had no idea it was that bad until they were stitching him up in the locker room and the kid started vomiting like a three-year-old stuffed with cotton candy, riding the Tea Cups for the first time."

"Thanks, Hooty," Lindy muttered from behind the trio, his attention on his empty glass. "Pete, fill me up," he said with a motion of his wrist toward the bartender.

Jane reached around Jason and put her hand on top of Lindy's glass. "No, Pete, I think Mr. Barrett is done for the evening."

As Pete pulled the glass from Lindy, Jane slid off the chair and lightly pulled Millie to the side. "Why don't you and Jason go on to dinner? I'll get Lindy settled up in the guys' room."

"But what are you going to do tonight?" Millie asked.

"Don't worry about me. I will read a book or watch a movie. I could use a night of nothing." She pulled Millie into a quick hug.

Before Jane could release her, Millie spoke directly into her ear. "Don't forget. You promised you wouldn't tell Lindy about you and Paul until I'm there."

Jane instantly stepped back from Millie and spoke through clenched teeth to avoid yelling. "Are you serious, Millie? The man is clearly torn up about that young boy's injury, and you're worried about whether or not I'll tell him that I told Paul that I loved him?"

Millie tilted her head to the side. "Well, yeah. Don't forget your promise."

Jane let out a sigh. "I won't forget."

Beaming as if she had just won a one-year contract with Cover Girl, Millie turned back to Jason and linked her arm through his. "Have a good night, you two."

"L.B., make sure to get some decent sleep. We have practice at ten tomorrow and then a flight to the West Coast at five," Jason said over his shoulder before leading Millie through the double glass doors and out into the cold night air.

Jane looked to the man who had become such a dear friend, and she felt her heart breaking for his pain. "Let's get you up to bed."

"Why, Miss Grey, I thought you were a virtuous woman. But if you insist."

Jane rolled her eyes and extended her hand to him to help him stand before leading him to the bank of elevators.

After stepping inside, she turned to the panel of numbered buttons and asked for his room key.

"I don't have one." He shrugged his shoulders.

"What do you mean you don't have a room key?"

Leaning closer to Jane inside the elevator, Lindy used the wall to balance. "I mean: I do not have a room key."

"But where is it?"

"It's in Hooty's coat pocket."

"Why is it there?"

"Because I didn't want to carry it."

"But why didn't you want to carry it?"

"Because it was heavy."

"Lindy, it's the size of a credit card. You're the size of a Zamboni. How could it be too heavy?"

"Don't know, just is."

Jane pushed the button to her floor. "Well, I guess you can sleep on Millie's bed until they get back from dinner."

"Aww, why can't I sleep in your bed until Hooty and the hottie get back from dinner? Huh, huh, that's funny . . . Hooty and the hottie. They could be a music group." Lindy chuckled to himself as a goofy fifth-grader grin lifted his lips.

Jane began tapping her foot, watching each floor pass on the digital screen above the double doors. "You really need to sober up, Lindy. I don't know how to deal with drunk people. Millie has only been drunk once, and our friend Lynn from high school was there. I don't do drunk, Lindy."

"Snap out of it, Jane! I'm only a little drunk. It's not like when I busted up my knee and couldn't play for a year or even when Tess dumped me for that stupid what's-his-name weenie. I'm going to be otay," he said, trying to snap his fingers in front of her face. His eyes opened wide in astonishment when his fingers didn't make any noise.

Jane pushed his hand away as the doors smoothly opened to her floor. "Let's go. Hopefully, no one will see you go into our room. I would hate for rumors to be spread about you."

Lindy leaned against the wall as Jane unlocked her door. "Beautiful, a rumor about you and me would make my day."

Jane pursed her lips, forcing her biting retort to remain in her mouth, as she held open the door. Her need to console Lindy had fallen down the elevator shaft somewhere between the lobby and the second floor. Lindy stumbled into the room and bounced onto the nearest bed. The six-foot-plus hockey player seemed to fall asleep in an instant, completely dressed from his crisp white shirt to his perfectly shined shoes.

Jane followed him into the room and closed the door. She dropped her coat on the nearest chair and slipped out of her ridiculously high heels.

In the bathroom she tried to right the damage of the scotch to her beautiful dress. Looking in the mirror, she sighed, "Jane, old girl, you were never intended to be a stunner.

Peeling out of the dress, she walked in her slip to retrieve her pajamas from her carry-on.

"So, Jane," Lindy said from behind her. "Do all Christian girls look like you under their pretty white dresses? If so, I really have been missing out."

"Lindy, close your eyes." she shrieked, pulling her flannel pajamas tight across her chest. She could feel the heat of a blush rising from her toes to the tip of her head. Peeking over her shoulder, she saw Lindy casually propped up on his elbow. "You're supposed to be asleep."

"Sorry." He threw a pillow over his face, allowing her to sprint to the bathroom to change.

Closing the door with a loud click, she rapidly replaced her slip with her pajamas and deposited her ruined stockings in the trash can. As she was brushing her teeth, her phone rang. It was well after eleven o'clock central time. Millie was likely calling to check to make sure that Jane had deposited Lindy safely in his room.

"Tell Millie I'll be right out," she yelled through the door when she heard Lindy loudly answer the call.

When she emerged from the bathroom a moment later, her hair was tied on top of her head and her face scrubbed clean of makeup. Any romantic notions Lindy had earlier professed would surely be put to the side, Jane concluded as she reached for the phone Lindy had left open on the nightstand before falling asleep.

"Hey, Mill."

"It's Paul." His voice had the sharp edge of lawyer.

Jane's legs went weak, and she sat on the second bed in the room, afraid she could no longer support herself. Could this night get any worse? "Oh, hi, Paul, I looked at the clock and assumed it must be Millie."

"Well, I guess you assumed wrong."

Her heart hammered to the rhythm of *The Flight of the Bumblebee*. "I guess."

"Do you want to keep going back and forth like this, or do you want to tell me why Lindy Barrett is answering your phone at well after eleven o'clock at night."

She bit her lip, not sure of how to tell Paul everything without telling him everything. "Well, it's kind of a long story."

"Give me the short version." Paul's voice dropped an octave and became exceedingly steady, too calm for Jane.

"Millie and I were supposed to go to dinner with Lindy and Jason after the game. You remember Millie's plan to foil Jason's plan, right?"

"Go on, Jane," Paul said with his best *Law and Order* voice.

"Well, I went down to the lobby to meet the guys, and they'd been drinking. A player Lindy hit tonight has a severe concussion. Lindy took the news hard, and I guess he decided to drown his sorrows. I told Millie and

Jason to go on to dinner and that I would get Lindy to his room. And then I stepped into the bathroom for a minute and you called and Lindy answered. That's pretty much the whole story."

"That's the whole story, Jane?"

"Pretty much." A wave of guilt washed over her for omitting the fact that they weren't in Lindy's room, but hers, and that he had seen her in her slip. Other than those tiny transgressions, she really had been totally honest. *God, please forgive me.*

"Well, if that's what you say happened, then I believe you. I don't like this jealousy thing, Jane. It's not the person I want to be." Paul sighed.

"I know. I'm sorry I made you worry."

"It's okay. I like to worry about you. However, I don't want to have to worry about you with other men."

Jane could feel her blush return with his words. "You definitely do not have to worry about me with other guys. I told you before, Lindy and I are just friends."

"I know. He's pretty messed up over that kid?" Jane could hear the lawyer retreat with the return of the Paul she loved.

"It seems like it. I don't understand why he got so upset. Hockey players hit hockey players every day. That's what they do. I guess maybe tomorrow, when he's more coherent, I can ask him what caused him to go over the edge like this. But tonight I just need to support him." *Regardless of how much he frustrates me.*

"You're good person, Jane Grey."

"I don't know about that. Most people would do the same thing."

"I disagree. I just wanted to call you when the time difference was only three hours instead of four. Call me tomorrow when you get a chance. I love you."

"Love you, too. Good night."

"Good night, Jane."

Jane heard his phone click. She sighed and could feel the tension from the phone conversation ease. Snapping her own phone closed, she lifted her gaze toward the two-hundred-and-thirty-five-pound problem lying in Millie's bed. The sight of his sleeping form, his face buried in a pillow, softened Jane's heart, washing away her guilt over her white lies to Paul. Lindy seemed overly upset about hurting the rookie. Not that she wouldn't feel bad if she had hurt someone herself, but Lindy was a hockey player. Hockey players hurt people. It was a job requirement, but somehow, it seemed this injury opened an unseen wound in Lindy, and she wanted to understand why. He had been an idiot tonight, but he was still her friend, and she wanted to help him. But he was out like a champ after a prize-winning knockout punch. Any healing she wanted to help push along was going to have to wait until tomorrow.

CHAPTER FIFTEEN

THE NEXT MORNING, Jane sat in the lobby, sipping her coffee and looking through her travel-size Bible as she waited for Millie to start their sightseeing. Jane had difficulty focusing on the Scripture in front of her. With her thoughts replaying the bizarre movie of the previous evening, she turned to the comfort of prayer, knowing that only God could help her forgive Lindy and hopefully He would help her understand her friend's actions.

Thank you, Father. Thank You for this day and for all of the blessings You have put into my life, starting first with the gift of salvation and the sacrifice of Your Son. Lord, please help my friend Lindy. He needs You more than he realizes. Please, if it's Your will, please allow me the opportunity to share Your love with him. Holy God, he could be such a wonderful man after Your own heart, if he would just open his eyes to You. Please, help him find his way. I love You so much. Thank You for loving me more. Amen.

"All done?"

Jane turned at the sound of Millie's voice, startled by her friend's presence.

"Had your little talk with Jesus? Did you him tell all about your troubles?" Millie's singsong voice lifted Jane's spirit.

"Yes, I did . . . and when did you get into gospel music?"

"Sista, my grandma dragged me to church every time she could. She was afraid of those demon model people."

"She was trying to help you know someone bigger and more beautiful than even you, Mills."

"Yep. That's probably why I'm so prickly about the Big Guy. He's way prettier than I am, and smarter too. You know I don't like it when men have the upper hand."

Shaking her head, Jane stood and pulled on her coat. "Well, my dear lovely friend, are you ready to brave the cold, busy streets of Chicago? Are you still willing to forgo shopping for a morning tooling around the Art Institute?"

"Do we have to go and be all cultural? Can't we just pick up a coffee-table book and pretend we went? If we do that, we'll definitely have enough time to shop at the Barney's CO-OP. It's right around the corner."

"Millie, are you serious? You shop on every business trip you take. I can't even believe you have room in your suitcase for more clothes."

"That is why God invented shipping."

"Now you want to call on God?"

"Lady, you're the one always professing His miracles. Well, clearly overnight shipping is one of them."

In awe of her rationale, Jane had no response as she followed her friend through the glass doors.

Hours later, as they shared a piece of cheesecake, Jane listened to Millie recount the debate she and Jason had the evening before.

"He doesn't believe in government-sponsored medicine, even though he was going to go to medical school. How can that be? Everyone knows we have the most messed-up system of making people well in this country."

"What did he say to that decisive argument point?"

"He said if we didn't live under a free-market medical system, the poor in other countries would never experience advances in medicine the rich pay for here."

"He does have a point."

"I know," Millie said as she dug into her half of the cheesecake. "Where does he get off changing my opinion? No one ever changes my opinion."

"I'm well aware."

Millie dropped her fork on the plate and rested her chin in her hand. Her eyes reflected astonishment and mild confusion. "He did it in such a civilized, honest way. He didn't talk down to me or try and act like I wasn't as smart as he clearly is. He was rational and said that I had the right to believe what I wanted to believe, but here's why he believes his point of view is correct. Men are way too logical for words."

"I guess so." Jane's phone rang, and she pulled open her handbag to retrieve it. "Hello?"

"Jane Grey? This is Scott, the Jackets trainer. I got your number off of L.B.'s phone."

A feeling of uneasiness settled in Jane's stomach alongside the cheese-cake. "What can I do for you, Scott?" Jane covered the phone to mouth to Millie who the caller was.

At the mention of the trainer's name, Millie lifted her eyebrows and drew a question mark in the space between them. Jane shrugged her shoulders and focused on the call.

"I'm sorry to bother you, but Lindy mentioned that you were in town, and we're in a bit of a bind here. Lindy was hurt this morning during practice. He reinjured his knee and compounded that with a mild concussion. Neither of the injuries is life threatening, but we hate to put him on a plane with the con-cussion symptoms, and the team leaves in a few hours for a ten-day West Coast road trip. His best alternative is to have someone drive him back to Columbus. I would do it or send one of the assistants, but we really need all hands on deck with as many injuries as we have. We could hire a service, but I remembered that you were Lindy's friend and thought maybe you wouldn't mind taking the long way back to Columbus."

"Umm, I guess that would be okay. Are you sure he's okay to travel, even by car?" Jane covered the mouthpiece and quickly told Millie that Lindy was injured and needed to be driven home. The shock Jane was trying to process reflected in Millie's stunned expression.

"Definitely. He'll just need a pretty roomy automobile to ride in so he can prop his leg up. We can have a car dropped off at the hotel for you, if that works?"

"That will be fine, Scott."

"I know this is rather unorthodox, and I wouldn't ask you if Lindy didn't speak so highly of you."

"Thanks. And Scott . . ."

"Yes."

"You're sure he's going to be okay, right?"

"He'll be fine. He needs rest. He'll need to see the team orthopedist and the neurologist tomorrow. Tonight would have been better, but even if you left in the next twenty minutes, it would be pretty late by the time you get back to Columbus."

"Are you sure he shouldn't see someone here? Maybe he should stay at the hospital?"

"No, the team physician released him to travel, and we would prefer he see our specialists back in Columbus rather than here in Chicago."

"Well, I guess that makes sense."

"We really appreciate this. The team should have a car for you shortly."

"Okay. We'll see you at the hotel in a half hour." Jane slowly pulled her phone from her ear. Lifting her hand, she signaled their waiter to bring their check. She needed to get back to the hotel as soon as possible. Lindy was hurt and he needed her. She refused to acknowledge the squeeze of her heart, but she felt compelled to get to him as quickly as possible. Lindy needed her and that was all she needed to know.

CHAPTER SIXTEEN

JANE PULLED THE RENTED SUV into the drive of Lindy's exclusive apartment building and turned the ignition off. Her traveling companion was still asleep, which allowed her a moment to settle down after the six-hour drive. Resting her cheek on the top of the steering wheel, she focused on the gleam of the building against the rich night sky and the watery outline of a shadow it made in the muck and mire of the still waters of the Scioto River. She wanted to concentrate on anything but the motionless figure in her backseat.

In the silence of the long drive home, Jane had plenty of time to review Lindy's actions from the previous night and talk them over with God. Although she had read stories about his erratic behavior early in his career, she was having a hard time aligning the man from last night with the friend she had come to care about and respect over the past few months. Something dark and painful must be hiding under the surface for him to have fallen so deeply, and quickly, into despair. She needed to uncover what motivated Lindy's excessive drinking and character 180, but the discovery process would be impossible until he woke up.

Lindy was so different from Paul. Paul was safe and secure. With Paul she felt like she was eating a bowl of vanilla ice cream—smooth and consistent. With every date and phone call he was more grounded, more real, and more godly. He was the man she'd always wanted. Paul was the man she had prayed to God to send to her. She was sure of it.

Then why was she with Lindy?

If she was honest with herself, her friendship with Lindy brought with it an edge of excitement. He was a good guy with a huge heart, but under the surface he had an intangible, almost dangerous quality. When she was with him, she always felt a twinge of nervous energy. In ice-cream terms, Lindy was Cookies & Cream—soft and smooth with a few rough, surprising spots.

Unwilling to delve any deeper into her feelings, Jane slowly pushed herself to an upright sitting position as she tried to solve the problem of moving the motionless Lindy from the backseat to his penthouse.

Before she could tackle the issue, there was a light tap at her window. She turned and faced the doorman. Of course this place would have a doorman.

The round-faced man looked to be in his early sixties and was a person who had the appearance of one who had lived a love-filled life. His smile was warm and inviting as Jane rolled down the window to talk with him.

"Miss, can I help you? You've been sitting here for a while. I wasn't sure if you knew where you were."

"Oh, I'm sorry. This is a friend's building, and I was dropping him off. Unfortunately, he's hurt and will need some help getting up to his place. I was trying to figure out how to make that happen."

"Who is your friend?" He tried to peer through the tinted window.

"Lindy Barrett."

The doorman stood up quickly, and his face turned from curiosity to concern in an instant. "What can I do? What did he hurt? Hopefully it isn't his knee again. Mr. Barrett had such a time of it before."

Jane hoped that the doorman's fear was unfounded and that Lindy's injuries were not like before, but the reality of her motionless friend in the backseat argued with the optimism of her heart. "It's his knee and his head, Mr. . . . ?"

"O'Connor, just O'Connor, Miss . . . ?"

"Grey. Jane Grey."

"Nice to meet you, Miss Grey. Let me help you get him up to his place. I have a wheelchair in the maintenance closet. We have to use it every once in a while when residents come home via . . . umm . . . hired transportation. If you give me a moment, I can fetch it for you."

"That would help immensely."

Jane stepped out of the driver's seat, opened the rear door, and looked at Lindy. He was sound asleep. He hadn't even twitched the whole drive home. His drugs must potent.

She walked to the back of the SUV, released the hatchback, and pulled out both their bags. Thankfully, his hockey equipment would travel with the team. She wasn't sure she was up to maneuvering a thirty-plus-pound bag of pads, sticks, and skates in an elevator.

Closing the back hatch, she hoisted Lindy's garment bag onto her shoulder and unlatched the handle for her roller-bag. She hustled as quickly as the cumbersome bags allowed into the lobby. She placed her bag near the security desk, hoping that would keep it safe while she got Lindy situated. Since the team was sending someone in the morning to pick up the rental, she planned to call a cab for the short ride home.

Within moments, O'Connor appeared, pushing a small black-and-steel wheelchair through the lobby.

"Will that be big enough for Lindy?" Jane asked as she readjusted his garment bag up on her shoulder.

"Should do. It's supposed to hold up to three hundred and fifty pounds. Based on the media guide, Mr. Barrett is well within that range," he said with a twinkle in his eye.

O'Connor wheeled the chair through the main doors, and as Jane watched, Lindy slowly pushed himself out of the car and slid into the wheelchair. By the time they reentered the lobby, Lindy's eyes were once again closed, and his leg was propped up on the leg extension of the chair.

The trio rode in silence to Lindy's penthouse, allowing the quiet drone of the unidentifiable music track to fill in the spaces. The elevator opened to a small hallway containing only three doors. With the ease of one who had maneuvered the chair on countless occasions, O'Connor deftly turned the wheelchair to the right.

Jane followed slowly behind. Burdened by the uncomfortable heaviness of Lindy's bag, she focused her attention on the smooth, marble floor to avoid slipping in her wet boots.

She wiped her boots on the doormat before entering the four-thousand-square-foot apartment. At first sight of the large expanse of windows overlooking the city and the river below, Jane was speechless. She dropped the heavy bag on the floor and took two steps into the grand home, before she heard gentle female tones coming from the far corner of the apartment.

The female voice stopped Jane's advance. Lindy had someone, a female someone, waiting for him. She stood in the foyer, afraid to intrude, and waited for O'Connor to come back so she could tell him about the rental car. She remained rooted just inside the entryway for fifteen minutes hearing only muffled tones in conversation. As the voices grew closer, she tried to stand tall and relaxed, hoping she looked cool and casual, and that her naughty nose would remain neutral.

"Mr. O'Connor, thank you for bringing Linden up."

"Oh, it was nothing, ma'am. Miss Grey did all the heavy work, driving Mr. Barrett back from Chicago, and all."

"Where is this Miss Grey? I would like to thank her." The voices grew closer, and dread mingled with curiosity filled Jane like a water balloon ready to burst.

The portly Mr. O'Connor turned the corner into the foyer, followed by an elegantly dressed, petite woman in her mid-sixties.

"This is Miss Grey, ma'am." O'Connor extended his hand toward Jane.

The tiny woman walked to Jane with her hands outstretched and a sweet-natured smile across her lips. "Miss Grey, how can I thank you for driving all that way with Linden in tow? He has spoken highly of you, but I believe you went above and beyond the mere call of friendship today."

Jane shrugged her shoulders while embarrassment fought curiosity for control of her mind. "It was the very least I could do, but I should be on my way." She glanced at her watch, hoping to give herself an easy exit.

"Do you have to go just now? Linden has spoken often of you over these past few months. I would love to have a bit of time to get to know you."

"Umm . . . well," she mumbled.

O'Connor quickly filled in the missing piece. "Miss Grey, this is Mrs. Barrett, Mr. Barrett's mother."

Jane felt curiosity slingshot past embarrassment. "You're Lindy's mom?"

"Guilty. My name is Annabelle Barrett, but my friends just call me Anna."

"It's very nice to meet you, Mrs. Barrett. Lindy has told me so much about you." Jane said.

"Please, call me Anna. Won't you let me fix you some coffee to warm you up while Mr. O'Connor calls a car for you?"

"Sure."

"Good. Mr. O'Connor, please call a car for Miss Grey and give us a buzz when it arrives." Turning to Jane, she continued, "I'm assuming you have a rental car from the team. Why don't you give Mr. O'Connor the keys, and he will make sure to return it."

"Oh, but my bag is still in the lobby. I thought I would be right back down. Are you sure I can't do something?" She handed the keys to the doorman.

"Consider it all taken care of," he said with a smile. "I'll ring up when the car arrives."

"Thank you." Anna followed him to the door and closed it softly after him. Turning, she faced Jane and smiled.

"Well now, Jane. We'll have a bit of time to get to know each other. Why don't you make yourself at home? You can place your coat and your boats on that bench and then wander around. The coffee should be ready in a few minutes."

"Okay."

"Jane." Anna smiled up at her. "Don't look so frightened, dear. Lindy is home now and resting. The doctors will look at him tomorrow. I'm sure he'll be back in one piece in no time. Have a seat in the living room and I'll be right with you."

"Do you mind if I use the powder room?"

"Oh my, no! I should have thought of that myself. My mother just rolled over in her grave at the thought of me being so inconsiderate." She laughed.

Jane smiled at the lilting sound of her voice and felt embarrassment slink back into its corner. "Don't worry. My mother just woke up from a dead sleep because I admitted I needed to use the facilities."

"We mothers are a strange lot," she said. "There's a bathroom on the other side of the living room. Take all the time you need."

Jane removed her snow-covered boots and coat before padding quietly across the darkly stained hickory floors through the living room, toward the bathroom.

Searching for a light, she lightly ran her hand along the right wall, when she heard soft snoring. She had walked into Lindy's room. She hastily turned to leave before she disturbed him when she caught sight of his large form under the blankets. The light of the moon shone through the expanse of windows and bathed him in an ethereal glow. Her heart melted her, a little, for the man who looked so like an angelic child in his sleep.

His arm was angled above his head, and even with a day's growth of beard he looked soft and innocent. The pain, both physical and mental, was hiding on the distant edges of the medication, and she was thankful for the peace it provided. She watched him for a few more moments, wondering, once again, what caused his dramatic change the night before. The man sleeping was the man she knew. The man she encountered last night had demons she wasn't sure she could handle. Not wanting to encroach on his sanctuary any further, she retreated from the room and found the bathroom.

She tidied herself and applied a fresh coat of lipstick, taking in her full appearance. She was a bit pale and her hair was windblown, but her clothes were free of wrinkles, and the dark circles under her eyes were easily concealed with a little additional powder.

"Well, Miss Grey," she said quietly to her mirrored self. "You're going to have to do."

She closed her purse and returned to the living room to wait for Anna Barrett. Anna Barrett. Never in her wildest imagination would she have thought that she would be having coffee with Lindy Barrett's mother.

Lindy's mom juggled two steaming cups of coffee and sat down on the couch with Jane. "Milk and sweetener?" she said, extending a cup to Jane.

"That's right. How did you know?" Jane took a long, deep drink.

"Just a guess."

They sipped their coffees in companionable silence, watching the still night through the frosty glass. Time ticked by, and Jane could feel her muscles finally relax from the tension of the day. The quiet helped her mind erase the merry-go-round of conversations she'd had with God over the six-hour drive. Jane let out a soft sigh, releasing the burden of her thoughts before taking another long drink, appreciating the simple pleasure of the creamy coffee goodness warming her from the inside.

"So, Jane, are you in love with my son?"

Coffee burned a hole through her nasal cavity as she tried to stop choking. Was the woman omniscient? Had she somehow heard Jane's pleading prayers in the car about her conflicted feelings for Lindy and Paul? Had Mrs. Barrett somehow captured Jane's sigh and read her hidden thoughts?

"Oh dear, I'm sorry to have given you a start," Anna said as she took Jane's coffee cup from her and placed it on the oversized ottoman. "Are you okay?"

She patted Jane's back. "I guess I have a tendency to be blunt and straightforward. My daughters are constantly telling me I need to hold my tongue, but I figure there's no reason to tiptoe around if there's a pink elephant in the room. You might as well point him out so you can figure a way to get him back to the zoo," Anna explained.

Jane's labored breathing slowed, and she tentatively reached for her cup. "That's okay, really. Please, just give me a little forewarning next time so that my mouth isn't full of hot liquid before pointing out the pink elephant."

"All righty. So back to my question: are you in love with my son?"

"Mrs. Barrett . . ."

"Anna."

"Anna, I care very much for your son. In a very short time, Lindy has become quite a dear friend of mine, but I have a boyfriend whom I love. Lindy and I are just friends." Jane sounded convincing, even to herself.

"Are you sure he feels the same way?"

"Yes. We talked about it. Actually, Lindy was the one who wanted to be friends."

"Well, I guess feelings can change," his mother challenged.

"They can, but I don't believe your son has changed his feelings toward me." Jane could not believe the conversation. Forget surreal, this was borderline *Twilight Zone*.

"No?"

"No, ma'am. Lindy is a great guy. I love having him for a friend and a confidant, but I have a man who loves me and whom I love," Jane said with an emphatic nod of her head.

"So, how did you end up driving Lindy all the way back from Chicago today?"

"The trainer called and said they needed someone to drive him back."

"And no one from the team could do it?"

"That's what he said."

"And they couldn't get him a flight?"

"Scott, the trainer, he said that Lindy couldn't fly because of his concussion. But it kind of confused me that he could take such strong medicine for his knee, if he had a concussion. Who knows? I'm not a doctor. I just watch a lot of medical television."

"Jane, dear, I'm a hockey mom. I've spent more than my fair share of time in a variety of doctor's offices and emergency waiting rooms. I've picked up a thing or two. If Lindy had a concussion, they would have kept him under observation for twenty-four hours. A trainer or a doctor would have stayed with him the whole time. He would not have been put in the back of the car, with an unknown, or at least relatively unknown, woman driving. My son has two things wrong with him. First, he reinjured his knee, which is bad, but hopefully they can fix it. And second, he's trying to figure out how to heal his relationship with you."

"Heal his relationship with me? Is it broken?"

"I heard he treated you poorly last night."

"He wasn't himself." Jane wondered how this woman knew so much. Was she Super Mom, able to read minds in a single bound?

"And I heard that he hasn't told you why he was the way he was last night."

"I'm sure, if he feels it's appropriate, he'll tell me."

Anna leaned forward and placed her small hand over Jane's long fingers. "Dear, Lindy is going to have a hard time telling you why he was an idiot last night. To do so, he would have to tell you about the accident."

"The accident?" Would Anna fill in the blanks for Jane?

"Many years ago, when Lindy was still in Juniors, he and another player collided hard against the boards. Lindy's shoulder came up as the other player's chin came down. It was a freak collision, and at the time the other player seemed fine. Later that night, he went into his housemother's room and told her his head hurt. She called the team trainer, who told her to give him a couple aspirins. When she went in the next morning to wake him up, he wouldn't budge."

Jane felt as if her heart stopped as she tried to fully grasp what Anna was telling her. "Was he dead?"

"No, but he had slipped into a coma in the middle of the night. This was well over a decade ago, back when we knew next to nothing about the impact of concussions, not that we know a lot today. She called an ambulance, and he was taken to the hospital, but by then it was too late. He died three days later, after his parents arrived."

Jane could almost see the young man's parents as their pain rushed over her like an icy waterfall. "That is horrible."

"It is. And it has taken Lindy years to get beyond that night. He was drafted that summer, but by the time he made his NHL debut, he wasn't the same powerhouse everyone expected. He still scored, but he seemed to be afraid to hit anyone, or even go into the boards for that matter."

"What changed?" Lindy was anything but gentle when it came to checking his opponents.

"He spent his rookie and sophomore seasons playing under a veteran captain, who made Lindy his pet project. He razzed him and made him carry his drinks at every bar. He stuck him for every bill and made full contact during practice, until one day, about six months into his rookie season, Lindy's temper exploded. He went after his captain in the middle of practice and the two fought like animals, or so I've been told. His captain knew why Lindy was afraid to hit anyone and was trying to get him mad enough to rely on his instincts rather than stay hidden in his guilt, and it worked."

"So when the kid from Chicago got hurt . . ." Jane's heart wept for Lindy. The thought that he was relieving his past, because of a simple hit, made her ache.

"It brought back all of those horrible memories. Lindy's a good man. He's not the best person in the world, but in his heart, he's good. He's a little selfish and rough around the edges, but the right girl will straighten that out."

"Or God will," Jane said before she could stop herself.

"Oh, that's right. You're the religious one." Anna smiled, leaning back in the couch and drinking deeply from her cup of coffee.

"I prefer *faithful*, but yes, some might call me the religious one."

"Oh dear, don't be offended. I love God as much as anyone, but my son is a . . . what would be the term . . . lapsed churchgoer. Not that I haven't tried to get him to go, but sermons and worship music don't seem to keep his attention like *SportsCenter*."

"Sorry, I guess I'm used to people judging me because I'm a Christian. I tend to get pretty defensive."

"That's okay, dear. We all have our weak spots." She reached her hand to Jane. "But I want to make something clear. I told you about the accident because I believe you do care for my son. I know he cares for you. I believe that the knowledge, the knowledge of what is weighing him down, will help you understand him a bit better. He needs someone like you, Jane. The women my son usually surrounds himself with are more interested in his athleticism or his bank account. They don't care about helping him to heal. I was hoping he was over the accident, but I guess some things can be buried pretty deep and still find a way to burn you."

Jane squeezed Anna's hand. *Even Lindy Barrett has a box.* "Yes, they can, Anna."

"He needs a friend who can help him find his way. Someone who will help him to move beyond his guilt and see that his life does not need to be a perpetual state of penance. My son needs to learn that he's loved, regardless of the mistakes he makes. The Lord knows that I've tried, but sometimes family members are the worst messengers. And you're right, he needs to know God. But my dear, the only way that hardheaded, beautiful son of mine will ever come to personally know the Son of God is through the love and dedication of a friend. My knees are relatively flat from praying for such a friend. Maybe God has finally answered my prayer with you."

Jane didn't have a response for Anna's soliloquy. She wanted to say that she could be that friend for Lindy. She wanted to say that God could do anything and that her son would be free from the guilt of that poor boy's death, and the laundry list of other guilts he carried with him. She wanted to say so much, but she couldn't promise Anna anything, because she wasn't sure her heart could survive helping to save Lindy and then having to walk away.

She knew she loved Lindy, but she loved Paul, too. That is what she had been struggling with in prayer. Paul had made a commitment to her, and she to him. Once Jane made a commitment, there was no turning back. But with the feelings raging inside of her, she knew she needed to put some new boundaries on her friendship with Lindy. She needed to figure out how to share the love of God with Lindy without giving in to the desires she could feel crowding her heart.

God help her, she needed to help Lindy fall in love with Jesus without falling in love with Lindy herself.

CHAPTER SEVENTEEN

PREPARING FOR ONE of Bitsy Grey's parties was akin to enduring the rigors of marine boot camp, sixteen weeks of marathon training, and a twelve-week etiquette course given by Emily Post. Jane's mother prided herself on making every detail of a party both seamless and memorable. In order to accomplish her lofty goals, she made her daughters' lives completely miserable for weeks leading up to an event. As the date for the engagement party hastened, Bitsy was in full General Patton mode, demanding complete dedication from her troops, er, daughters.

Sitting at the breakfast table the morning of the party, Jane stared into her cup of coffee, simultaneously trying to forget the happenings of the last week and to fire up her energy for her sister's big night. She was failing.

The conversation with Lindy's mom had turned over in her head nearly a thousand times in the last seven days. She hadn't given Anna an answer regarding her feelings for Lindy, but the woman had sensed she had pushed Jane far enough and changed the conversation as they waited for a cab to arrive. On Sunday, she talked through the whole conversation with Paul, skipping the part where Anna asked Jane if she was in love with her son. His compassion for Lindy's pain renewed his desire for Jane to be a witness to her friend and compounded her guilt for not sharing the whole story with Paul.

Their conversation lasted an hour or so, with both trying to decide how best to reach out to Lindy spiritually. Before he hung up, he assured her that he would be home Friday night, in plenty of time for Emory's party. But as of early this morning, his flight out of Juneau was grounded, due to a significant snowstorm. She feared she'd have to face the family without a boyfriend, yet again.

Staring into her coffee cup, Jane was vaguely aware that Molly had slipped into the kitchen and was sitting across from her. "I think you might have a mental condition, Jane. Is staring-into-space-phobia a diagnosed condition?"

Jane looked up to the beautiful, glowing face of her older sister and returned the soft smile. "How long have you been sitting there?"

"Not too long, but if you don't buck up, little buttercup, you're going to experience the wrath of not just the general, but also her little protégé."

"Has Mom been in here already?" Jane asked as the fear of being caught by her mother sitting, aka being lazy, welled up in her belly. Flashbacks from her childhood, when she had been caught in such a position on the day of a party, bombarded her like she was a war veteran suffering from post-traumatic stress disorder.

"No. You can relax. She called me about forty-five minutes ago, waking me up mind you, tsking about the fact that she was putting this whole party on by herself."

"Yeah, and the fifty hours of manual labor we've put in this week have accounted for nothing," Jane snorted.

"I think Mom figures, if she has to tell you to do something, then she pretty much did it herself." Molly leaned back into the soft cushion of the built-in breakfast nook bench.

"I should have known that."

"So, you haven't seen the general, or the Little Princess, this morning?"

"No. Dad was leaving when I arrived. Somehow, he convinced Mom that he should take Baylor and Mr. Boudreaux out for a manly breakfast. He was meeting the other men downtown. I'm sure Daddy has the timing perfect and he won't arrive back at the house until after the caterers have arrived, when Mom can no longer yell at him."

"That Daddy is a sly one," Molly agreed.

Jane took a long drag of her lukewarm coffee and looked around the remodeled kitchen of her childhood. Gone were the yellow cabinets and rooster-covered walls. In their place, her mother had created a kitchen masterpiece.

"You have to give Mom credit on this kitchen," she said, breaking the silence. "It really is stunning."

"Mom definitely knows how to make pretty work."

As if on cue, Elizabeth "Bitsy" Grey wafted into the spacious room on a cloud of perfume and hairspray. Jane's sixty-two-year-old mother's short, artificially white-blonde hair framed her seemingly ageless and perfectly made-up face. She was as beautiful today as she was in the pictures from her stint as the Ohio Fair Queen. Even in what Bitsy called her work clothes—a black velour Juicy Couture track suit with a classic white bateau-neck tee—she looked every inch the lady of leisure and elegance. Jane almost envied her mother's innate sense of style and grace. Bitsy knew exactly what looked beautiful on her petite five-foot-three-inch frame, and she never made a poor fashion choice. Her eldest and youngest daughters had inherited her stature, her coloring, and even her simple yet elegant looks, but Jane had taken completely after the Grey clan. She was, as Grandma Garrett liked to say, "a robust and hearty young woman who would one day grow into her looks," which, in non-Grandma language, translated into "fat and homely."

"Good morning, my dears. Thank you so much for coming over to help with our little party for your sister," she said as she kissed each of her daughters on the cheek.

"No problem, Mom. Where do you want us to get started? You sounded in a bit of a panic this morning," Molly said.

"Oh, Molly, sweetie, I'm sorry I called you in a state. You know how I get when I start to feel things are out of control. Your father had the nerve to insist on taking Baylor and his father to breakfast this morning. I think it's a ruse to avoid doing any of the heavy lifting, but it was so nice of him to think of our guests that I couldn't say no. Hopefully, Mrs. Boudreaux will stay at the hotel until the party. God love that woman, but her Southern slowness is enough to drive a saint to violence."

Jane giggled at her mother's frustration. She'd heard all week about Mrs. Boudreaux and the party she threw for the kids. Her mother wasn't going to be outdone by anyone, let alone a Southern belle. "Mom, I'm sure she isn't that bad, but I agree it would be better if we Grey soldiers take care of the last details of the party. We've done it enough, we're nearly able to anticipate your every need."

"Nearly, Jane, nearly," Bitsy said as she patted Jane's shoulder.

"So, Mom, where's Em? Shouldn't she be down here ready to schlep tables and chairs and arrange artful bouquets of flowers?" Molly asked as she accepted the glass of water from her mother, who had silently noticed her older daughter's lack of beverage.

Settling down next to Jane, Bitsy shook her head in the you-ought-to-know-better fashion for which she was infamous. "Now, Molly, when we had your engagement party, did you have to do any of that nonsense?"

"Well, actually, yes, and if I remember correctly, Emory had a cold and stayed in her room until just before the first guests arrived."

"Molly, I'm sure that isn't true, but you believe what you want to believe. Emory needs her rest. She had a big weekend, and after all of those horrible finals and now this party. You want your sister to be her shining best for her big night with all of our friends and relatives, don't you?"

Jane smiled at her sister over her coffee cup. "How can you argue with that, Molly?"

Molly drank deeply, filling her mouth with water instead of allowing her real opinion of their sister to filter out.

"Mom, where do you want us to start?" Jane asked, determined to keep the peace among the family. The role was typically Molly's, except when she was pregnant and her hormones couldn't be counted on to remain in check.

"Aren't you my good little helper, Jane?" Bitsy gave Jane a smile and a slight hug around her shoulders.

The rest of the morning and early afternoon went relatively smoothly with Bitsy directing her troops, which expanded to include the caterer, Jane's father, Baylor and his dad, and even a well-rested Emory, who conveniently was given the job of arranging the candles on the mantel, which were already artfully displayed. Jane was so intent on completing her assigned tasks that she missed a phone call from Paul.

An hour after he called, Jane noticed she had a message on her cell phone. She sat in the kitchen eating a sample plate of the appetizers when she heard the news she had dreaded.

"Jane, this is Paul. Sweetie, I'm so sorry, but my flight has been delayed again, and I'm not sure we're even going to take off today. Please forgive me. I should have taken a flight earlier in the week, but the case is becoming exponentially more difficult each day, and I thought getting a few more interviews completed would allow me to stay in Columbus through New Year's. I'm so sorry I'll miss your sister's party. Please tell your mother and father I look forward to meeting them over Christmas, because even if I have to hire a dogsled to come home, I'll be there to celebrate the holidays with you. I love you. Call me if you get a chance."

Jane rested her forehead on her crossed arms. *Why does this always happen to me? I can never be the normal girl with a normal boyfriend at one of Mom's parties. I always have to be the spinster.*

She looked at the plate in front of her and bit into the hearty portion of a beef Wellington puff, choosing to drown her angst in fattening food. She was chewing a mouthful of the macaroni-and-cheese Big Bite when her phone rang.

"Hey, Lindy," she said with her mouth still full.

"Hey, Beautiful, what're ya eating?"

"Just some of the appetizers for the party," she mumbled.

"They sound good. Has the lawyer made it back from the frozen north yet?" The two friends had slowly been getting back to their conversational rhythm since the events in Chicago. He had apologized for his antics, but hadn't explained where the behavior was rooted. Jane felt guilty that Anna had supplied the needed filler, but she figured when Lindy trusted her enough, he would share.

"No, and it doesn't sound like he'll make it out of Alaska anytime soon."

"That stinks. Have you prepared your mom?"

"No. I'm kind of afraid she will think that Paul is my Snuffleupagus. You know the mastodon that only Big Bird could see on *Sesame Street*?" Apparently she'd been watching too much television selected by her nieces.

"I think I remember. Would you be up for a one-legged stand-in?"

"What do you mean?"

"Well, if you don't mind having a gimpy hockey player as an escort, I would love to fill in for Mr. Wonderful."

Jane sat up quickly in her seat. "Are you serious? But your mom is still in town. Don't you want to spend the evening with her?"

"She's having dinner with some friends and asked me to go along, but I would much rather spend the evening with you, if you want me."

"Of course I want you to come. I would have invited you in the first place, but Emory can be peculiar about inviting people she hasn't deemed necessary. I can't really explain my sister. She's an experience, kind of like going through a hurricane. One you always remember, but don't really want to repeat."

"Okay, well, I definitely enjoy a good natural disaster. Is a suit good enough, or do I need to wear a tie too?"

"No, a suit will do. Lindy, are you sure this won't be too much on your knee?"

"Naw, I'll take some good pain killers and have the driver the team hired for me bring me out to the farm. If I have a tall stool to sit on, all will be fine."

"Oh, I can't thank you enough. And don't worry, I'll make sure everyone knows you're here to fill in." As the words fell from Jane's lips, she could feel her heart drop a tiny bit. She refused to think about how it would feel to have Lindy coming as more than just a friend.

"Don't fret so much, Beautiful. It'll give you frown lines. Now, what time do you want me there?"

"Could you be here a little before seven? The rest of the guests are supposed to be here around seven thirty, but I'd like to introduce you to my folks and the rest of my family before we're inundated by the crush my mother has artfully planned."

"Seven it is. See you tonight."

"See you." She hung up the phone and could feel her entire mood shift from self-pity to anticipation at the thought of Lindy attending the party tonight as her escort. She knew they were just friends, and that he was filling in for her perfect boyfriend, but the part of her that was twenty years old and was still in a mad crush over the guy who had once graced her dorm room walls, was pretty excited to be fulfilling a longtime fantasy.

The guilt butterflies fluttered. She pressed her hand over her stomach and had another bite of the beef Wellington. It wasn't *that* wrong to feel this way.

CHAPTER EIGHTEEN

JANE SIPPED THE TALL GLASS of lime-splashed soda as she took in another of her mother's masterpieces. Nearly two hundred of her family's closest, and not-so-close, friends filled up every space in her childhood home and spilled out like champagne bubbles onto the back lawn, under the heated tents. Bitsy had outdone herself with the setting; every candle, flower, and tablecloth was perfect. The caterer exceeded everyone's expectations. Several of her mother's friends were asking for Kate's card and trying to snag her for future events.

Jane took another sip, before balancing Lindy's iced tea in her other hand as she wove her way through the crowded party. What a lifesaver her friend had turned out to be. Bitsy and her father were highly perturbed with Paul for not making it back for Emory's party. They were, as her mother put it, "Simply dying to meet him. That young man should know better than to stay in that awful frozen place longer than he needed to." Her dad was a bit more sympathetic, but he was definitely disappointed he was going to miss another opportunity to meet Paul.

After her mother's mini-rant over Paul's delayed flight, she made an about-face with the news that Columbus's very own superstar hockey player would be gracing the party. "Oh, my, Jane. Do you think we have the appropriate food to feed a hockey player? What do they eat?"

"Mom, he's not some tribal mystery from another continent. He doesn't eat raw beef or cut the heads off of wild boars for dinner. He's a normal man, just like Daddy. He'll be happy with whatever Kate has prepared," Jane reassured her mother. "The party will be perfect, Mom."

And it was. Her mother had surpassed even Emory's demands for the event. Jane caught sight of her sister's smiling face as she talked quietly with her future mother-in-law. All of the work and nagging she and Molly had endured over the past week were worth it to know that Emory and their mother were pleased with the result. At the end of the day, familial happiness was a great feeling.

She maneuvered her way back to the stool where she had left Lindy, who was now being monopolized by her brother-in-law, Jake, and his buddies. "Did you know you were going to make that shot at the last minute, or were you just shooting and expecting the game to go into overtime?" Jake asked him as she approached.

"Well, you always hope the shot goes in, Jake. That night, my hope must have been a little stronger than the others'." Lindy grinned.

"Okay, boys, break it up. Let me give this poor injured man his drink." Jane tilted her head to the glass of iced tea for Lindy.

He took the glass from her outstretched hand and melted her heart as his TV grin gentled to a smile filled with warmth and welcome. "Thank you."

"No problem. Gentlemen, I think Lindy has entertained you enough this evening. Why don't you all go find your wives and play the doting husbands I know you can be."

Taking the not-so-subtle clue, Jake and his friends dispersed in a mumble of *nice to meet you*s and went in search of their wives. Jane stepped closer to Lindy, filling some of the vacated space, and leaned against a wall.

"Thanks, Beautiful. Your brother-in-law and his friends are great, but it gets a little old reliving the same five plays." Lindy chuckled as he gingerly readjusted his seating to better accommodate his injured leg.

"No problem. It must be horrible hearing how wonderful and amazing you are."

"Funny."

"But seriously, are you feeling okay?"

"Yeah, the leg is a bit tender. Nothing to worry your pretty little head about. Have I told you tonight how great you look? You put every other woman to shame."

Jane looked down at her deep burgundy A-line cocktail dress of heavy silk and caressed the folds with a smile. "I'm sure that's not true, but I appreciate the compliment."

"Your little sister is an, umm, interesting woman," Lindy said, appearing to try and grasp the right words to describe Emory.

"Well, that is definitely a true statement." Jane shifted her gaze to her stunning younger sister. "Don't get me wrong. I love my sister, but she's a bit much to take sometimes." Jane lifted her hand slightly in response to Emory, who smiled and waved before turning back to her friends.

Emory looked every bit the Southern belle in a full-length midnight-blue velvet dress. Her blonde curls were tamed into a beautiful twist that ended in a tight bun at her nape. She stood in the circle of Baylor's arms as they chatted with Emory's friends from high school.

They are happy.

"Baylor is good for Em," she said to Lindy. "He's the strong, silent type who plays against Emory's chatterbox tendencies. I think they'll be very happy together. And that makes me glad."

"Really." Lindy lifted a single eyebrow as he took a drink of tea.

"Really. She's my little sister, and I want her to be happy. I'm rather ashamed of the way I've behaved about this whole engagement and party. Despite our differences, I love Emory very much and only want the very best for her."

"Now that sounds like the Jane I know and love," a familiar voice said from behind her.

Jane felt a tremor of excitement laced with a twinge of guilt race up her spine as she quickly turned at the sound of her travel-weary boyfriend. "Oh my goodness, Paul! You made it." She stepped into his open arms. Jane squeezed her eyes tightly shut, willing the feelings of delight to overwhelm her as Paul wrapped his strong arms around her, but they vanished as swiftly as they had come.

Jane was the first to remember Lindy. She turned out of Paul's embrace and faced her friend with hot, embarrassment-stained cheeks.

"Paul, you remember Lindy?"

Paul extended his hand with a smile that didn't reach his eyes. "Lindy."

"Paul," Lindy said as he shook his hand. He took a long, deep drink of his iced tea and looked like he wished there were something stronger in his glass.

Paul stepped back and possessively put his arm around Jane's waist, dragging her awkwardly to his side. Unnerved by Paul's overt attentions, Jane tried to regain a semblance of her own equilibrium by taking a slight step away. "Lindy rescued me from being minus a plus one. Wasn't that nice?"

"Quite." Paul once again eliminated the personal space Jane had tried to establish.

"Well, I felt so bad for Janesie," Lindy said with a drink of his tea. "I didn't want her to have to face all of her relatives alone, again."

"I appreciate the stand-in," Paul said, pulling Jane so tight she could barely breathe. "What with that big case, and of course, there was the blizzard I flew through to get here."

"Yep, the blizzard and the case. It's a good thing I messed up my knee, or I'd be out in Vancouver right now playing a game—probably would have been stuck in a snowstorm myself."

"How is the knee? I heard about that night in Chicago. Must have been pretty hard for you?"

Jane felt like she was watching a bizarre tennis match, and she was the ball. She was afraid Lindy was ready to serve an ace to win the match. "All righty, then . . . let me see if I can find my parents. They're dying to meet you, Paul."

"Yes, Paul, you must meet Bitsy and Hank. They're truly wonderful people. I'm sure you'll love them, and they'll love you," Lindy said with a tone that spoke of a long history with Jane's parents rather than the reality of their two-hour relationship.

"Will you excuse us, Lindy?" Jane said.

"I'll be waiting right here for you, Beautiful." Lindy grinned.

Jane linked her arm through Paul's and pulled him in the direction she had last seen her parents.

"I know that guy is your friend, but he really gets under my skin," Paul admitted through clenched teeth as they walked toward the tent-covered backyard.

"I was wondering about that testosterone tournament back there."

"I guess I feel a little inferior to him, what with him being a professional athlete and all. That's kind of like being a crusader during the Middle Ages."

"If he's a crusader, what does that make you?" Jane asked as they approached her parents.

"The town squire, fighting with a pen rather than a sword." Paul's smile warmed his green eyes, sending a tremor of tingles down her spine.

Now that's more like it.

"Well, I believe Shakespeare said that the pen is mightier than the sword. And more people have read *Romeo and Juliet* than the *Morte d'Arthur*," she said as the stepped up to the foursome including her parents.

"Yeah, but wasn't Thomas Marlow, Shakespeare's rival, stabbed to death in a bar fight? Makes one think that the pen is not so mighty after all?" he said with a wink.

"Touché, Mr. Barrister," Jane whispered before she interrupted her parents' conversation with a tap to her mother's shoulder. "Mom . . . Dad . . . There's someone I would like you to meet. This is Paul Wade . . . my boyfriend," Jane said slowly to help ease her mother's shock. She was unsuccessful.

"Oh my gracious! Why he's gorgeous, isn't he?" She exclaimed in an octave reserved for only bats and dogs.

"Calm down, dear, we don't want to scare the poor man off," Henry said with a slight tug on Bitsy's arm.

"Paul, these are my parents, Bitsy and Henry Grey. And their longtime friends, Kathryn and Jack Willow." Jane proceeded with the introductions, in a calm, gentle voice, ignoring her mother's overzealous reaction and her father's weak attempt at trying to control his wife.

Paul put out his hand toward Jane's father, but Bitsy could not be contained.

"We don't shake hands here, Paul. We're huggers. You just step into Momma's arms and give her a nice big hug." Bitsy yanked Paul to her small frame before he could respond.

The image of Paul's lanky six-foot-three-inch body hunched over to accommodate Bitsy's five feet three inches was comedic. Pushing down the laughter, Jane looked at her father, who shook his head at his wife's behavior.

"Mother, please let Paul up for air. You're squeezing all of the oxygen from his lungs."

"Oh, stop fussing, Jane." Bitsy released Paul from her death grip but remained attached to him like Velcro as she slid her right arm through his left. "I'm so glad to finally meet your young man. I was beginning to think you were a myth."

"No, I'm definitely not mythical," Paul chuckled.

"I thought you were stuck in Alaska, son." Henry stepped in to try to help diffuse his wife's excited behavior.

"The flight was able to take off. However, not many were adventurous enough to climb aboard."

"But you just had to get back here to our little Janie?" Bitsy beamed at Paul, her eyes glazing over like melted candy as she hung on his arm and his every word. Jane's mother was officially in love with her boyfriend.

Paul extricated himself from Bitsy and stepped closer to Jane. Drawing her to his side, he kissed the top of her head. "I would go through anything to be with this lady."

"Aww, Katy, did you hear him?" Bitsy put her hand to her mouth. Jane watched her mother dissolve into a pool of gush at their feet.

"Yep, Bits. He's a keeper," Kathryn said.

"Well." Jane cleared her throat. "We'd better get moving. I want to introduce Paul to Emory and Baylor."

"Of course, dear. Has he met your friend Lindy, yet?" Bitsy innocently asked.

Jane could feel Paul's entire body stiffen at the mention of Lindy. "We've met before."

"Hmm," her father coughed as he reached forward and shook Paul's hand. "It's very nice to meet you. I hope you'll make it out for the Christmas festivities this week. Maybe we can pull you away from that church you go to, and you can come to our little country church."

"You don't go to church with Jane?" Paul asked.

"No. We have three generations of tradition at our old church right here in town. I know Molly and Jane love their big corporate church, but there's something special about sitting in the same pews your grandparents sat in," Henry said pointedly to Jane.

"Yes, Dad. Do we *have* to revisit your disappointment over my leaving the church?"

"No disappointment, sweetie. I just miss having my kids and grandkids at church with me. And you too."

"I love you, Daddy." Jane stepped forward and gave her father a kiss on the check. "We really do need to get moving if we're going to meet Em and Bay. She said earlier that they were thinking about driving into the city to meet up with some friends who couldn't make the party."

"She'd better not leave," Bitsy said. "She and Baylor are the guests of honor. What will Mr. and Mrs. Boudreaux think?"

"I'm sure they'll wait until everyone has left, Mother. Please don't worry about it." Jane mentally kicked herself for sharing Emory's plans.

"Well, you tell her she cannot leave," Bitsy insisted.

"I'll try, Mom. It was nice seeing you again," Jane said to her parents' friends. Turning back to her parents, she added, "I'll find you both later."

"Yes, dear. It was very nice to meet you, Paul. We look forward to getting to know you better." Bitsy stood on her tiptoes and kissed Paul on the cheek before allowing her husband to pull her to his side.

"Yes ma'am. The feeling is mutual." Paul's eyes shined with genuine affection. *Bitsy didn't scare him. Oh, he makes it easy to love him.*

Jane guided Paul from her parents and their friends. Taking the long way around to the front of the house, she led him through the side entrance of the tent. After the ordeal with her mother's reaction to Paul, she needed a breather before she introduced him to Bitsy, Jr.

Braving the cold, they walked in companionable silence. Jane let her head fall back as she searched the silky black sky, speckled with a vast array of stars, and as her eyes caught a shooting star in the eastern sky, she quickly turned to Paul. "Make a wish."

"Okay, but I don't think it comes true unless I actually see the star fall from the sky." He stopped, turning toward Jane.

Her eyes were closed tight as she tried to make her wish, but she couldn't think of one. Her brow was furrowed in confusion as she opened her eyes and looked into Paul's.

"You look confused. Haven't you been making wishes since you first blew out the candles on your birthday cake? Don't you remember how?" He drew her closer to help ward off the chilly night air.

"I know how to make a wish, silly. I didn't have anything to wish for."

"Nothing?"

"Nope. I'm clean out of wishes." She sighed.

"No wishes should be a good thing."

"Why is that, Mr. Pollyanna? Wait, what do they call guys who always look at the bright-side, glass-half-full, rose-colored-glasses version of life? Has any guy ever been the rose-colored-glasses aficionado?"

Paul answered her first question. "If you have nothing to wish for, you must be pretty happy with your life."

Jane stepped deeper into his embrace, tilting up her chin to look him in the eye. "I guess I am."

Paul lowered his mouth and caressed her lips with his. His touch was feather light. He pulled her tighter, deepening the kiss, when Jane placed her hands on his chest.

"Paul," she whispered, dragging her lips from his. "We need to be careful."

He rested his forehead against hers, lowering his arms and linking his hands at the small of her back. "I don't think anyone can see us, Jane."

"God can." Her words were like a bucket of cold water on the tender heat growing between them.

Paul stepped away and roughly ran his fingers through his tousled locks, leaving Jane to face the brunt of the icy December night without his embrace.

She took a small step toward him and lightly touched his shoulder, unsure of what to say to soothe him. "I'm sorry, Paul. I shouldn't have said anything."

He turned to face her, and the shame that flickered in his eyes caused Jane to drop her hand and take an involuntary step backward. He gave her a weak, almost broken smile. "You're right. God is always watching. You don't need to apologize. I'm the one who should be sorry. I'm sorry if I offended you."

Relief flooded Jane's spirit. She closed the gap between them and tenderly placed her hand in his. "Paul, please don't be sorry. You went through such an ordeal to get here, and I haven't even offered you a drink, let alone asked you about your trip. And the first moment we are alone, you're being sweet, and I have to get all churchy on you. I'm the one who should be sorry."

He took her other hand in his. "No, you're right. It's just that we're out here in this beautifully starlit night, and you look absolutely breathtaking. I couldn't help myself. I love you. All of you. And because of that, I need to be especially cautious when we're alone, because I just want to jump headfirst into kissing that incorrigible smile off of your face. And that is not appropriate. I should be more respectful. I'm sorry."

He brought her fingers to his lips, lightly kissing the tips. "Please forgive me."

She gave him her brightest smile. "No forgiveness necessary."

"I guess I lose my head when I'm around you." Paul laced the fingers of his left hand with her right, and they started back toward the house.

"Yeah, me too," Jane said, but the words rang hollow in her heart.

CHAPTER NINETEEN

AS JANE AND PAUL made their way through the house, she introduced him to her sister and Baylor. The normally quiet Baylor perked up at the mention of Paul's law firm and his current case, peppering him with a variety of questions and excluding Emory and Jane from their conversation.

Before the two sisters could begin even a superficial chat, three of Emory's sorority sisters swooped in and dragged the bride-to-be off to another corner to discuss bridesmaid dresses and possible groomsman, leaving Jane alone. She caught Paul's eye and mouthed that she was going to the bathroom. He nodded but quickly resumed his legalese conversation with her soon-to-be brother-in-law.

Jane avoided the congested main-floor bathrooms, opting instead for the childhood bathroom she had shared with Molly. The Jack-and-Jill style bathroom connected their two rooms. Her mother had updated the decor to classic whites with only a hint of its former pink glory with accents in the towels and on the bathroom rugs.

She washed her hands and checked her face in the mirror. Considering it was almost eleven o'clock and she'd dealt with her mother, an errant boyfriend, a testosterone contest, and the general shenanigans of a Bitsy Grey affair, she looked pretty good.

The thought of the testosterone war reminded her that she had left Lindy on his own for well over an hour, and she needed to rescue her friend before any more adoring fans or *Bull Durham*-esque Annies in training found their way to his corner.

Opening the adjoining door to her childhood bedroom, she stepped onto the refinished hardwood. Her cherry canopy bed remained the focal point with its mosquito netting draped to the floor and overstuffed pillows propped against the headboard. However, a new, much longer pillow appeared to have been added to the bed.

"Lindy," Jane whispered.

"Hey, Beautiful, I needed to rest my knee. I didn't think you'd mind if I stretched out on your bed." He pulled himself to a sitting position, leaning against the mountain of pillows.

Lindy was lying on her bed. Discovering him there was strangely creepy—yet exhilarating. "No, I don't mind at all."

"The pain pills finally wore off and made me sore and tired, and bam, I was toast." Lindy gave Jane a sleepy, heavy-lidded smile, causing sixteen-year-old Jane to make a nervous giggle appearance.

"Sorry," she said, pushing the teenager back into her box. "I shouldn't have left you alone for so long. This is the first time most people have met Paul, and well . . . they're curious."

With adult Jane fully in control, she walked forward and sat on the edge of the mattress. She lifted her gaze to Lindy, frighteningly aware of the intimate coziness her enclosed childhood bed created.

"No worries, Janesie," he said in a low, deep, gravelly voice. "I'm a patient man."

Jane's voice matched his quiet tone. "Well, I'm not a very good hostess, to leave you to the sycophants and the leeches."

"I survived. Although I did miss your witty repartee. I guess that's what I get for being number two on your men-in-waiting list. Or maybe I'm number three?" He smiled slyly.

"Number three?"

"Jesus, then Paul, and then me. Maybe I'm way off and there's another guy, maybe the pastor, waiting in the wings to sweep Miss Jane Grey off of her lovely feet." He winked.

"Lindy, have you been drinking again?" Jane asked as she started to push away from the bed.

"Just sweet tea. I'm committed to an on-the-wagon lifestyle after that last wheels-off experience in Chicago. Jane, I'm clearheaded. I know what I'm saying."

Jane could feel the hairs on the back of her neck stand at attention. "What are you saying, Lindy? I'm a little confused. We agreed to be friends.

Friends don't make comments like that. You're the one who wanted to be friends, remember?"

Lindy's eyes closed, and his head dropped into the mountain of pillows. "Trust me, I remember."

Jane slid across the bed until she was nearly beside him. "Lindy," she said, reaching for his hand. "Please don't be hurt. I know you're a little messed up right now, what with the medicine, and the rookie, and everything. I know you don't mean what you're saying. In a few weeks, when you're playing again, things will get back to normal, and you'll be happy we're still buddies. I love your friendship. I can't believe how important you've become to me in such a short time. Let's not make things awkward."

Opening his dark blue eyes, he stared deeply into hers, causing liquid fire to pour through her body and her breath to quicken, but strangely, she could feel her heart steady.

Without breaking his gaze, Lindy turned his hand over and laced his fingers through hers, barely gliding his thumb over hers. With that slight touch, Jane's heart went from a fifteen mile-per-hour pace to running the Indy 500 in a butterfly breath.

"Jane." He dropped his focus to their joined fingers as he began softly, stroking her hand and sending chilling tremors chasing after the liquid fire. "I have a lot to apologize for and a lot to explain to you. I'm not used to explaining myself, or even wanting to explain, but I want to with you. I know now isn't the right time, but I want you to know that last weekend, when I was the worst version of me, the fact that you still showed me compassion was amazing. Even though I was a drunken jerk, even though I manipulated you into driving me all the way back to Columbus so that I could try and apologize to you, and never did, you still forgave me. You forgave me without even a halfway, decent apology. Why?" He lifted his eyes to hers, his voice barely a whisper.

Jane swallowed deeply. Her breath was coming in shallow waves. Her gaze locked with his. "Because you're my friend."

"That's all? That's the only reason?"

"Why do I need another one?"

"Jane, tell me, why are you in love with Paul?" Lindy continued to tease her fingers with his own.

She tried to follow Lindy's rapid conversational turn. Her mind was growing foggy with the seemingly innocent, yet highly intimate, connection between them.

"Why do I love Paul?"

He nodded. As he waited for her answer, he dropped his eyes to their hands, giving Jane a welcome relief from the intensity of their deep blue depth.

"Why do I love Paul?" she absently repeated as she tried to think of her well-laid-out list of reasons, but at the moment, she couldn't remember even one. Her mind, her heart, and her body were lost in a muddled haze of unspoken feelings evoked by the simple touch of Lindy's fingers. The two sat on Jane's bed, silently holding hands. The only sounds in the room were their breaths moving in time with each other and the hollow echo of the voices of the partygoers below. Jane stared at Lindy, his gaze still intently focused on their hands.

What am I doing? I have an awesome boyfriend who is downstairs, right now, giving my future brother-in-law advice for becoming an attorney, and here I am fulfilling a college fantasy. I'm disgusting! But she couldn't bear to pull her hand from his.

"No answer, Janesie?" His eyes locked with hers.

Jane yanked her hand from his, breaking the cherished connection. She pushed herself off the bed and began to pace the floor. "Of course I have an answer."

Lindy stacked his hands behind his head and leaned back into the pillows on the bed as he watched her pace. "Well?" His voice remained low and sultry.

"Well," she started, grasping for the right words, or any words, to express the love she knew she had for Paul. "He's honest and hardworking. He loves God more than he loves me. He's funny. He keeps me honest. I don't know. I guess . . . we're compatible?"

"Jane, other than the loving-God part, you just described a really great dog."

"Oh, shut up! I'm trying to think." She stopped pacing and crossed her arms in front her chest and faced Lindy. "What do you know about loving someone? Those are great reasons to love Paul, and I do love Paul."

"I've no doubt that you love him, Beautiful."

Relaxing, she dropped her arms. "Thank you."

"But I didn't ask you why you love him. I asked you why you're *in* love with him."

"What's the difference?" she asked.

"Jane, you're one of the most freely loving people I've ever met. You're kind and considerate. You show compassion to almost everyone you meet whether he deserves it or not. You naturally love people. I have no doubt that you love Paul. But loving someone and being in love with someone are two completely different things."

"Oh." Her mind began to grapple with the true meaning behind his question.

"Jane Eleanor Grey, are you in love with Paul?" The question fell between them like a white glove dropping a challenge for a duel.

Before she could respond, there was a knock on the door. "Come in," she said in a strained voice.

"Sweetheart?"

Jane heard Paul's concerned voice before she saw his sinewy frame fill the doorway.

Paul's glance moved from her face, burning with self-imposed guilt, to Lindy, sprawled out on the bed like a sultan waiting for his harem to arrive, and his face quickly turned from questioning concern to the blank, hardened stare of a well-trained litigator.

"Jane, your mother was looking for you. We didn't know where you were."

Stepping forward, she clasped Paul's hand in hers, trying to infuse him, and herself, with physical reassurance. "I'm sorry. I used this bathroom to avoid the chaos downstairs. Lindy was tired from all of the standing on his injured leg and came up while we were outside, to get away from everyone. I didn't even know he was up here, resting, until I walked through the room to leave. We were just talking." *Stop babbling, Jane.*

"Yeah," Lindy added, not moving from his position of repose on the bed. "We were just talking."

The two combatants stared each other down, ready once again to do battle. Paul tugged Jane closer to his side, blatantly establishing his territory, as Lindy pushed himself up to a seated position.

Jane squeezed Paul's hand. "What did my mother want?"

Breaking the staring contest with Lindy, he looked to Jane's upturned face and gave her a half smile. "People were starting to leave, and she wanted us to get on the road home. She said she's worried about the country roads and something about driving at night. Your mom is a bit of a worrier."

"You may just have made the understatement of the year," she said. "Mr. Barrett, I do believe we have been summoned back to the party in an effort to kick us out."

"I wouldn't want to cause Bitsy worry." He pushed himself off the bed and lurched forward in an attempt to reach his crutches. Failing, he began to topple, causing Jane to break from Paul's embrace and rush to Lindy's side to keep him from falling.

She bent down, allowing him to drape his left arm over her shoulders. Using her as a makeshift support, Lindy pulled her close, a little too close for Jane's comfort, as he reached for the metal crutches. "Thanks, Beautiful. You're always there when I need you," he said softly.

As soon as he had his crutches in hand, she stepped back to Paul, putting breathing distance between her and the feelings she didn't want to process. "Well," she said. "Are we all ready to go?"

Paul hauled her tightly to his side and kissed her on the forehead, leaving Jane feeling like a steer who had just been branded. "You okay to get down the stairs by yourself, Barrett?" Paul asked. Without waiting for a response, he turned and dragged Jane through the door.

"I'm golden, friend," Lindy called to their backs.

Jane had to walk quickly to stay by Paul's side, making it impossible to assure herself that Lindy made it down the long staircase safely. They approached Molly and Jake, putting on their coats to leave, forcing Jane to push all thoughts of the conversation in her bedroom into Pandora's box. Her box was becoming quite full.

"Are you two leaving?" she asked Molly.

"Yeah, the babysitter was supposed to be home by twelve thirty, and we'll barely make it to our house by then. I wish we could stay longer. Mom really knows how to throw a party," Molly said with a fading smile. "Are you okay, Jane?"

"I'm fine. I think I'm a little tired, what with all of the party planning and order following today. I probably should get going, too." Jane watched her sister's face and knew Molly didn't believe her answer, but the intuitive older sister kept her concerns to herself.

"Molly, I'm truly amazed at your stamina," Paul commented. "Here you are, pregnant, and you're outdoing all of us."

"Well, I'm sure I'll be asleep before we pull out of the drive, leaving my poor husband alone with the quiet of a Suburban."

"After tonight, I relish the thought of some quiet. It was good seeing you again, Paul." Jake shook Paul's hand. "Glad you could make it after all. You had our Janesie a little out of sorts."

"Thanks, Jake," Jane mumbled.

"Hey, I kind of like the idea of keeping you off balance." Paul drew Jane closer to his side.

"Will you be at church tomorrow?" Molly asked.

Jane knew her sister wanted to know if she would be able to ask her a litany of questions and was subtly telling her she would wait until church to do so. "Yes."

"We'll see you tomorrow, then." Molly hugged Jane. Releasing her, she turned to Paul. "Will you be joining us for Christmas Eve or Christmas?"

"Your father passed along an invitation to attend service on Christmas Eve. I'll need to see what my dad is doing. It's been just the two of us for the past few years, and he usually attempts to go to Christmas Eve service. He pretty much stopped attending church after my Mom died. Hopefully, I'll be able to join you on either Christmas or Christmas Eve."

"You should bring your dad with you. We can be a little loud and overwhelming, but we're pretty fun."

"I'll pass along the invitation and see what he wants to do. Thank you."

"Good night, you guys. Be careful going home," Molly said as she turned toward the door.

"Same to you. Be safe." Jane held open the door. Jake gave her a brotherly peck on the cheek as he followed his wife over the threshold.

She stood with Paul, watching them make their way down the long sidewalk, before fading into the distance in search of their car. Stepping out of the chilly air, Jane closed the door with a click.

"Are you about ready to leave, too?" Paul rested his hands on her shoulders and kissed the top of her head.

She turned in his arms, shoving the uncomfortable awkwardness their closeness created into her box, and wrapped her arms around his waist. "Definitely. I'm exhausted, but I can't imagine how you must feel. Traveling halfway across the continent and then driving the long, winding roads out to the farm."

"It was all worth it, to see you." He smiled as he leaned down and brushed his lips to hers.

Jane felt a tiny flutter in her belly and tried to ignore the little imp on her shoulder who reminded her that the kiss didn't come close to the sensation she had holding hands with Lindy.

The imp wouldn't be ignored, because he began coughing at the bottom of the steps. She turned at the sound of the fake cough and wasn't surprised to see Lindy leaning against the banister. She tried to step free of Paul's embrace, but his arm became like a vise squeezing her tightly to his side.

"Sorry to interrupt. My driver should be here any minute. I want to thank you for a wonderful evening, Jane," Lindy said as he hobbled closer to them.

"I should be thanking you. You really came through for me. You're a great *friend*, Lindy."

Breaking free from Paul, she extended her hand forward to shake his, but instead he pulled her into a hug. "We'll finish our conversation soon," Lindy murmured into her ear. He released Jane and nodded his head to Paul. "You make sure she gets home safe."

Paul laced his arms across his chest, while a small muscle flexed in his jaw. "That's my job."

"Janesie, please tell your parents thank you for the party. I felt right at home."

"I will. Thanks again," she said as she held the front door open for him.

He clicked slowly through the doorway on his crutches. From the front step, he turned and looked over his shoulder. "Let Bitsy know I'll extend the Christmas invitation to my mom. I'm sure she'd love to be around family for the holiday. Have a good night." Jane's stomach dropped as she felt Paul tense behind her at Lindy's implied reference to being part of her family.

With the parting blow, Lindy made his way down the front walk to the waiting town car with the natural ease and agility of an athlete, making Jane wonder if his earlier stumbles were real or for her benefit.

CHAPTER TWENTY

NEW YEAR'S WAS HERE and gone before Jane had time to relish having an actual date for the second biggest date holiday of the year. Paul took the latest flight available on New Year's Day to Juneau, but he still needed to leave by 4:00 p.m. The couple ate a late lunch at the restaurant just outside the main terminal, but spoke little as both were drained from the week of holiday celebration.

She waved him through security before heading back to the short-term parking lot to retrieve her car. Saying good-bye left her with a mixture of emptiness and relief that the constant tension between him and Lindy would be alleviated for awhile.

On the drive home, her mind traveled over the last week and the time she'd spent with Paul. Part of her felt they'd grown closer, but she knew she was holding back a piece of herself from the relationship. They had a great deal in common and could talk for endless hours, but she had a growing sense she was on a tightrope during every conversation. She wanted to make him happy, but she feared she was headed down the same path she had traveled with Brad.

With Brad, she'd become a regular contortionist trying to make herself into his ideal mate and in the process lost who she really was; eventually losing him. She didn't want the same thing to happen with Paul, but she wasn't sure how to avoid it.

He seemed to like her quirky sense of humor and unique outlook on life, but the pieces of her life that weren't Christian-centric didn't seem to settle well with him. Whenever she mentioned hanging out with Millie or grabbing dinner with friends from work, he subtly asked if she was able to share God's love with them. He asked unassumingly and without judgment, but still she could feel his disappointment in her actions when she answered with the excuse of not wanting to push away her friends. She knew he expected more from her, as he should.

As the week progressed, she shared less about her friends and listened more to what he had been doing in Alaska. Paul had come to enjoy the open wilderness. In the midst of nearly endless night, he could see God's beauty and was in awe of the majesty. He spoke of the friends he made, who were also living in the hotel. Her guilt deepened as he shared with her about the Bible study he started with some of the kitchen staff. He was working sixty to seventy hours a week, and yet he found time to organize a Bible study. She couldn't even get the nerve to talk to Lindy about their friendship, let alone his relationship with Jesus.

Trudging up the three flights of stairs to her apartment, she could hear the beep on her answering machine. Out of habit she dropped her keys as she entered and stepped out of her wet boots, leaving them by the door. She pushed the button on the machine and grabbed water from her fridge.

"Hey, Beautiful." Lindy's voice bounced off the walls of her apartment. "I thought you might be lonely after the lawyer left and didn't know if you wanted to have some pizza with me and Mom tonight. Just give me a call."

Her machine clicked off after the offer. She was tempted to pick up the phone and lose herself in hours of mindless conversation and gooey cheese, but she knew she would only be avoiding loneliness. She didn't want to use Lindy as a crutch, which was exactly what she had been doing.

Since their first meeting in October, Jane had talked with Lindy almost more than she had with Paul, which was evident during the Christmas festivities, fueling the hostility between the two men. Lindy knew her better than Paul did, and they both could sense it. With Lindy, she was her complete self, except for the overtly faith stuff. With Paul she was her complete self, except for the overt worldly stuff. Who was the real Jane? Was she the Christian she thought she was? Or was she more interested in being a part of the in-crowd of this world? Honestly? She wanted both.

She was selfish. She wanted to keep her feet planted in both worlds. She wanted her résumé-perfect Christian boyfriend and her exciting, little-bit-crazy friend, who happened to be a boy. Staring out onto High Street, quiet in the midst of the holiday break, she debated calling Lindy. She should call and tell him she wasn't coming, but she was afraid that when she heard his voice, she'd give into her own pitiful loneliness and warring feelings and agree to go over.

Closing her eyes, she rested her head on the back of the chair. With puddles of tears threatening to pour down her face, she prayed. "What am I supposed to do, Lord? I know You don't want me to tie myself to someone who hasn't accepted You, and this shouldn't even be an issue, but . . ."

Jane's thoughts stilled. Negotiating with God was never a good idea.

She opened her eyes and looked heavenward as tears streamed over her cheeks. "Father," Jane prayed through broken breath. "Please, please give me some clear direction. I don't know what I'm supposed to do. I'm feeling so guilty about the time I'm spending with Lindy. I know I should be evangelizing, but I just want to be with him. Is that so wrong?"

Not waiting for a response, Jane continued on her one-sided conversation. "You sent me this amazingly perfect man in Paul. Why can't I just do the right thing and focus my energy and my whole heart on him? Do I need to walk away from my friendship with Lindy to be completely with Paul? When will my heart and my head be in sync, Father? What am I supposed to do? What am I supposed to do?" Her prayer disintegrated into sorrowful repetition of the question.

She silenced herself, stubbornly intent on hearing God in the stillness of the space. Friendship with Lindy or relational commitment with Paul; the answer should be clear, but she felt as if she were looking through a foggy window. Jane's heart ached with the weight of the tears and the unanswered questions. Pulling her legs to her chest, she began to rock in her chair, waiting on God. "Please Father, please . . ." she whispered.

Laying her head back, she breathed deeply. She wiped her tearstained face, trying to push through her disappointment at God's silent response. "I thought just this once You might say just a little something," she muttered.

Unsure how long she sat staring at High Street, she was startled when the eerie quiet of her apartment was broken by the ringing of her telephone still in her hand.

"Hello," she answered in a voice hoarse from pleading with God.

"Jane? Are you okay?" Molly asked.

"Yeah, I'm fine, just watching the New Year roll in."

"Are you sure? Have you been crying over Paul leaving?"

"Something like that. What's up, Mol?"

"Well, your nieces and I thought you might be a little sad, and we wondered if you wanted to come over and watch some sappy movies, which might mean *The Little Mermaid*, if Lizzie is in charge, and eat chocolate and popcorn to ease your lonely heart."

Jane told her she needed to clean up but promised to come over in her sweats and no makeup, hoping the girls would fall asleep, and they could change from Disney melodrama to Cary Grant and *An Affair to Remember*. Jane hung up the phone and called Lindy to decline his invitation.

Thankfully, Anna answered the phone. Although Jane had a viable excuse, she could tell Anna was disappointed that she wouldn't be spending the evening with them.

"Dear, I'm going to be going home in a few days. Will I see you before I leave?" She asked.

"I'll make a point of it," Jane promised.

"I hope so. You're a friend of Linden's who I hope will be around for many years. You're a good influence on my son."

"Umm . . . thanks. I'm sorry, Anna, but I really must get moving. My sister is expecting me."

"Of course, dear. Happy New Year."

"Happy New Year to you, too. Good-bye, Anna." To Jane, the words sounded a little final as she hung up the phone.

She sat for a moment, taking in a deep breath before going to change. Walking down the hallway to her bedroom, she heard a soft whisper.

Patience.

Stopping in her tracks, she listened intently, wondering if she had only imagined the voice, but all she heard was the wind outside her windows. Shaking her head, she walked into her bedroom and pulled out her favorite lounging pants and OSU sweatshirt. As she dressed, she convinced herself that she'd completely imagined the voice.

After pulling on her socks and boots to brave the wintry cold, she made a quick check of her face in the bathroom mirror. Her eyes were a little puffy, but for her sister and her nieces, she would do. She ran ChapStick over her lips while she talked to herself in the mirror. "Patience? Seriously? Patience was the best you could imagine?"

She turned the light out in the bathroom, grabbed her coat, and opened the front door. In the hall she pulled her house key from her pocket and slid the metal bar into the lock shaft.

Wait.

Jane went completely still as a chill ran from the base of her spine to the top of her head. "Wait for what?" she whispered back.

Jane stood in that spot, with her house key frozen in the lock, for countless minutes, waiting for a response. "Wait for what?" she asked again, louder.

Silence enveloped the building. Jane continued to wait for further instruction from the voice she knew had to be God's, but no other sounds or voices came.

Locking the door completely, Jane shook her head and looked up. "I love *Field of Dreams* as much as the next girl, but do I have to go Kevin Costner crazy just to get an answer? Please don't make me build a baseball field in the middle of Daddy's corn. The family already thinks I'm a complete nut job. I don't want to give them any additional ammunition."

CHAPTER TWENTY-ONE

MOVIE NIGHT AT MOLLY'S WAS exactly the distraction Jane needed. They watched *The Little Mermaid*, as anticipated, but Lizzie and Chelsea fell asleep with the sniffles before Arial got her voice back, leaving the adults to cry their eyes out over Cary Grant and Deborah Kerr's ill-fated love affair. They curled up on Jake and Molly's tall king-sized bed, sharing a box of tissues and a container of Oreos as they watched the beautiful and tragic love story.

"How can he not know there's something wrong with her?" Molly sobbed as they watched Deborah Kerr say a simple hello to Cary Grant.

"Because he's too hurt by her betrayal," Jane blubbered.

"But she d-didn't betray him. She was hit by a car! Ugh! Why do I do this to myself?" Molly fell backward, throwing her arms across her tear-drenched face.

"Because 'If you can paint, I can walk,'" Jane said in her best Deborah Kerr imitation.

Molly giggled as she balanced herself on a bent arm. "Enough of the Hollywood-created drama, was there a tearful good-bye at Port Columbus today?"

"Not a tearful good-bye, just a good-bye," Jane said, sitting cross-legged on the bed.

"Did you at least kiss him?"

"Molly, why does that matter? All you and Millie ever care about is if I'm kissing or not. You both have an unhealthy obsession with my lips."

"Jane, it's important. Physical attraction is as important as anything in making a relationship work. And it's not sinful. God created us with a natural desire for each other. He gave us that gift so we would be bound together mentally, spiritually, and physically."

"Yes, Mrs. Snoopy-Pants. I did kiss him before he walked through security. And yes, we have kissed before. And yes, it's very nice."

"Nice?"

"What's wrong with nice?"

"Nothing is wrong with nice, but I don't know if I've ever described Jake's kisses as *nice*."

"Well, I like nice. Nice is safe. Nice is sweet. Nice is simple. Paul is very nice. I happen to want nice. I think it was on my list you made me write out all of those years ago," Jane retorted.

"Well, let's just see about that." Molly said, hopping off the bed as quickly as a pregnant woman could hop.

"What are you doing?" Jane asked as Molly disappeared into her walk-in closet.

"Just trying to see if you're right," Molly shouted.

Jane sat on the bed and waited for her sister for ten minutes while she absentmindedly watched Cary Grant realize that Deborah Kerr was paralyzed.

"Found it," Molly called as she trotted back into the bedroom with a crumpled piece of paper in her hand.

"Found what?"

"Your list," Molly said with a smile as she plopped back onto the bed.

"My list," Jane said with curiosity as she took the offered paper from her sister's outstretched hand.

"Your list for the perfect guy . . ."

"I remember," Jane whispered.

Jane remembered writing the list during Molly's bachelorette party. The list had been the idea of Molly's friend, Elaine, who'd said, "How can you be sure you haven't already met the right man, if you don't even know exactly what you want?"

Jane unfolded the aged piece of paper, trying to recall some of what her twenty-one-year-old self had desired in a mate. Before she undid the last crease, Molly snatched the paper from her fingers.

"Hey!" Jane yelled.

"Hey, nothing. If I let you read this, I'll never know what you wrote."

"Molly, you read it eleven years ago."

"Yes, but I've had two children. My brain has turned to Swiss cheese."

"Let's see . . . He must be a Christian." Looking over the top of the page, she smiled at Jane. "He should have a good sense of humor, that's a good one."

"I'm glad you approve." Jane pulled a pillow over her face to hide her rapidly reddening nose.

Ignoring her, Molly continued to read Jane's words. "He should be tall, because I'm tall. Have a good smile. Athletic would be nice, but at the very least know what ESPN stands for. What does ESPN stand for?" Molly asked.

"Excellence in Sports Performance Network," Jane muttered through the pillow.

"Huh. I wonder if Jake knows," Molly said before continuing to recite Jane's husband requirements.

"He should have good hair and take care of his mom. He should care about what I want and like me even when I'm clumsy or goofy."

"Molly, must you continue to read this? I think I'm embarrassed enough."

"Oh, shush up, Jane. This is fun and I'm pregnant, so we have to do what I want to do."

Jane pushed the pillow from her face. "When did that become an ob-gyn rule?"

"When I got pregnant for the third time. Jake is conforming to it, as shall you. Pregnancy gives you the right to make all the rules, even the silly ones." She returned her attention to the paper.

"Got it, Machiavelli."

"Okay, back to your list." Molly read in silence for a few more moments before she started to giggle.

Jane yanked the list out of her sister's hands. "What's so funny, Molls?"

Jane scanned the list. The attributes were pretty much what she had expected for twenty-one. Her ideal husband would have a good job, drive a nice car, and want to spend a year doing mission work in Mexico. For all of her superficiality, Jane had a desire to save the world, even at a self-centered twenty-one. Assuming that Molly found the mission work humorous, Jane looked up at her sister.

"What's funny about helping people in Mexico? I know I haven't done it yet, but it doesn't mean I didn't really want to then and maybe still do."

"That's not what I found funny. Did you read the last line?"

Jane turned the paper over and dropped her gaze to the bottom of the page and read, "My ideal husband is Lindy Barrett, if Lindy Barrett were a Christian." *Oh boy.*

Jane shrugged her shoulders, hoping that her sister hadn't suddenly acquired Anna's mom-mindreading abilities. "So what? I was twenty-one years old and living in a fantasy world. I had no reason to even hope that I would ever meet Lindy Barrett."

"But you have, haven't you?"

Jane's mind flashed to the night of Emory's party. She could feel Lindy's warm palm pressed to hers, and the memory shot a bullet of sensation ripping through her system. She shook her head in the negative, forcing the memory back into her box. "That doesn't change anything, Molly. Lindy and I are just friends. Who cares what I wrote on a stupid piece of paper over a decade ago?"

"Don't call my Hello Kitty stationary stupid. And you know exactly who would care."

"Who?"

"Paul. And based on everything you told me that happened during Emory's party? Lindy."

Jane squinted at Molly. *Is she a mom mind reader?*

Crumbling the paper into a tight wad, Jane threw it into the tiny trash can beside the nightstand. "Well, I guess we won't have to worry about either of them finding out, will we?"

"I guess not." Molly crossed her arms above her slightly swollen belly and gave Jane the all-knowing mom look.

"Okay, then." Jane ignored her sister's obvious censure and slid off of the bed. "I really need to get home. It's been a long couple of weeks, and I need to get a good night's sleep before I head into the office tomorrow." She pulled on her boots and smiled. "Thanks for having me, Molly. I really wasn't looking forward to being by myself tonight."

"You saved me from yet another round of bowl games. I can't believe Jake and his friends are still in his man cave in the basement. I think they've watched six full football games today."

"Well, you have to admire their endurance, even if it's couch sitting." Jane kissed her sister and turned to walk to the door, but Molly's voice stopped her.

"Janie, just one thing."

Jane turned to face her. "What is it?"

"If Lindy were a Christian, how would you feel about Paul?"

CHAPTER TWENTY-TWO

JANE'S COUGH SOUNDED LIKE the deep rumblings of a volcano ready to spew molten lava on the surrounding land mass. She was chilled to the bone, yet hot and crusty from twenty-four hours of flu fever. She was convinced God would soon put her out of her misery and call her home, because if she did survive this torture, she would surely kill her sweet little niece Lizzie for passing on the hellish flu bug.

She lay on the couch ensconced in a mountain of quilts and afghans, peppered with the remnants of several disgusting used tissues. Her body ached. Her head throbbed. Moreover, the best thing she could say about her stomach was that despite attempts to evict the afflicted organ from her body, the stupid thing had stuck with her. All of this, coupled with the seemingly unending RONCO infomercials for rotisseries, pasta makers, and super sealers, made her feel as if she had slipped from this life into a plane of existence solely dedicated to the Shop At Home network.

Lacking the energy to change the channels, she shifted deeper into the overstuffed couch, trying ineffectively to block out the hyperactive voices of Ron Popiel and his trusty infomercial sidekick. In her flu-induced coma, she barely comprehended the shrill sound of the intercom calling to her in the distance.

The buzzer sounded again, and she realized that her unwelcome guest wasn't going to leave without a fight, so she pushed herself off the couch and shuffled slowly to the door in her socked feet.

"Hello?" she croaked.

"Delivery for Jane Grey."

Ugh. "I'll be right down."

Grabbing her cardigan off the floor, she poured her aching body gingerly into the sweater. She trudged the rest of the way down the hallway of her apartment, opened her front door and began the trek down the three flights of stairs. As if she were descending Mt. Kilimanjaro and running low on oxygen in her tank, she took each stair as if her very life depended on a perfect descent. *Why don't I live in a building with an elevator?*

Reaching the foot of the stairs, she pulled open the apartment building door and stumbled back from the bright sunlight. Shielding her eyes, she tried to pretend she was still human as she stared at the twenty-year-old deliveryman.

"Jane Grey?" he asked.

"Yes."

"If you'll sign here," he said, thrusting a plastic tablet with an attached pen in her hands. Jane obliged, signing the paper, which could have given the young man rights to her firstborn for all she was aware. She desperately wanted to return to her couch and Ron Popiel.

"These are for you."

She looked up at him, and he seemed to pull a huge, artfully arranged bouquet of yellow long-stemmed roses from thin air.

Jane hazily focused on the flowers as the deliveryman placed the bouquet into her hands and continued to stand in front of her. Her mind was trying to figure out how she was going to carry the voluminous arrangement and herself back up the forty-five stairs to her apartment. After a few moments passed with her as still as a statue, simply staring at the flowers, he cleared his throat.

Finally registering that she needed to tip him, her thoughts slogged through the mud of her mind to her wallet, which was three flights up. She tried to communicate her dilemma, but words eluded her typically communicative mouth as she cocked her rather swollen head to the side in a mime version of an apology.

As she began to hand the flowers back to the deliveryman so she could re-ascend Kilimanjaro, a hand emerged from the sky with a five-dollar bill. Still holding the flowers out to the young man, she looked up at the body attached to the hand.

"Janesie," Lindy said in a concerned voice. "Let me take those. Let's get you back upstairs."

Lindy held open the door with his booted foot and gently nudged Jane forward with his free hand. But she couldn't muster the strength to walk. "Beautiful, you need to lift one leg and then the other. Unfortunately, your apartment is not going to come to you."

Looking up at Lindy with eyes full of fever, Jane hoped her face spoke words her lips couldn't.

"Since it doesn't appear that you will be addressing the stair situation on your own, I guess that leaves us with one alternative." Lindy set Jane's flowers down on the bottom step and proceeded to lift her over his shoulder like a sack of potatoes.

"Oh dear," her voice scratched out, as her stomach began to lurch on itself.

"Jane, I love you, kiddo, but if you throw up on me, I might have to whack you." As he spoke, Lindy leaned forward, picked up the enormous vase of roses, and began to hike up the three flights of ancient stairs. Each step Lindy took thrust his shoulder into Jane's stomach. With residual will-power she didn't know she possessed, she forced her evil stomach to remain in place, willing it to wait for its final eviction notice until she was on her own two feet or knees.

Lindy rushed out of the stairwell, asking, "Bed or couch?"

"Couch . . . bucket."

Even with his impaired knee, Lindy's naturally long stride took the narrow hall in four steps. He sat her down and kindly offered her the bucket with a full single second to spare. As her stomach tried to relieve itself of the alien in residence, Jane was vaguely aware of Lindy tenderly holding back her hair. With her head buried in the bucket, she even thought she might have heard the echo of a whispered prayer for her to stop.

She pushed away from the bucket and picked up a napkin to clean her mouth. Falling back on the couch, she whimpered, "Thanks," and promptly passed out.

⸻

Snuggling deep into the couch, Jane cautiously opened her eyes to try to gauge the time by the TV. Her living room was dark, and images of Stewart Scott floated into her consciousness. ESPN? What happened to RONCO?

Her mind began to come around, as she caught an unusual aroma: home-cooked food.

She tried to push herself to a sitting position, but she couldn't move her arms or her legs. Thinking herself paralyzed, she began to panic and yell, which in fact came out as a whimper for help.

Coming out of her kitchen, clad in a black sweater, jeans, and a green-and-white eyelet-trimmed 4-H apron, Lindy filled up her living room like a balloon in the Macy's Thanksgiving Day Parade. "Sleeping Beauty awakes."

"Can't move."

"Let me help you." Lindy pulled the blankets away from her sides, causing a series of tremors to roll through her body. She sat up and the chills she thought were long gone racked her body, followed by a series of coughs and sneezes. "Cold," she said, as her arms—now unhampered by the tightly tucked blanket—pulled it up to her chin.

"Aw, Beautiful, Millie was right, you have it but good, don't you?"

She nodded and allowed her three-hundred-pound head to fall back onto her pillow. "Smell?"

"Momma Barrett's chicken noodle: the cure for what ails you. Mom fixed me up a ton when she was here. I'm convinced it's why I'm walking without a limp today. Are you up to some soup?"

She smiled and shook her head in the affirmative, and Lindy returned to the kitchen. With her eyes shut, she could hear his soft humming coming from the kitchen. A few moments later, he lightly brushed Jane's shoulder, and her eyes fluttered open.

"Can you sit up?" he asked.

She slowly pushed up to a sitting position, as Lindy set the folding tray across her lap, and the soup's aromatic steam invited Jane's MIA appetite to awake.

"This looks wonderful," she said with a voice that sounded like she was Don Corleone and was ready to make him "an offer he couldn't refuse."

"Don't speak, just eat. Do you want me to feed you?" Lindy leaned down to tuck a napkin into her top.

Jane shook her head in the negative, lifting the soupspoon to her lips and tentatively taking in the warm liquid.

When she smiled at the taste, Lindy expelled a breath he had been unaware he was holding. He sat on the end of the couch, careful to avoid her blankets, and watched in silence as she ate her soup. Even two days into the flu, sitting in oversized pajamas, with a red nose from sneezing, she was adorable. Maybe someone should take his temperature; surely he was a sick man.

Jane took two more sips and laid the spoon on the tray. In the glow of the setting sun, she looked exhausted, as she laid her head back into her pillows. "How did you get to be so nice?"

The glimmer in her eyes made him feel like he had discovered the cure to cancer and slain a dragon. "Beautiful, some of us got it and some of us don't."

Her chuckle caused another round of coughing, and Lindy leaned down to remove her tray. "Drink some water."

She nodded and dutifully drank.

"Why don't you sleep a little more?" He lifted the tray from her lap and carried it toward the kitchen.

Before his feet hit the tile of the kitchen floor, he heard her heavy breathing and knew he would be entertaining himself for a few more hours. After cleaning the soup pan, he placed the leftovers in a disposable plastic container, thinking she may want to reheat the soup when she was feeling more alive. He continued to excel at his domestic chores, trying to ignore his thoughts as they wandered to his patient.

Jane. How did a clumsy old puck-handler wind up with a crush on a sweet girl like Jane? She definitely wasn't his normal type, not that he really had a type. He and Tess had been a couple so long, he never really thought about anyone beyond her.

He met Tess when he moved to Columbus. They clicked instantly. Within two months, she was practically living at his apartment, and he couldn't remember what the place had been like before she made the penthouse her domain. He had liked being part of a couple. She made his life a little easier. He could focus on his game, and when he needed a date, or a gift, or something needed to be organized, he never worried: Tess took care of it. She cheered for him at every home game, and early in their relationship, she had taken an occasional long weekend to the coast when the team was on a lengthy road trip.

Everyone told them what a perfect couple they made. She was fair and petite to his dark looks and oversized frame. She laughed at all of his jokes and encouraged him to spend time with "the boys" on his off days. For all intents and purposes, they were married, but their relationship had turned from her adoration of him to a business relationship with Tess acting more like a personal assistant than a girlfriend, or at least that's what she told Lindy when she left all those months ago.

Despite a lack of passion, Lindy was comfortable with Tess and liked that she wasn't overly demanding or clingy, and besides, he never really believed in all the until-death-do-us-part stuff. At least that's what he'd thought—until he met Jane.

In the past few weeks, he'd found his thoughts roaming toward her with greater frequency. Each thought of her face or the sound of her laughter brought a joy to his soul he had never before felt. He was starting to believe in that death-do-us-part number, and he didn't know quite when he had changed his attitude. He was smitten, he knew that for sure, but what could he do about it?

After their abbreviated discussion at her sister's party, he was afraid that they'd come to the crossroads between friends and something more, and chosen to be friends. Of course, the blame rested purely on Lindy's shoulders. When he first met Jane, he was wildly attracted to her but feared that his reaction was from a lack of Tess, not a true spark of interest. Now he knew that his feelings were more than a lack of a steady girlfriend. He wanted more, but more wasn't available. Jane was Paul's.

He knew he should be happy for her.

Paul was a good guy, even if he was like nails on Lindy's chalkboard. Paul had everything Jane could ever want. Until the party, Paul seemed to be one of Lindy's biggest supporters. Of course, the party was after the Chicago trip; after he had made a pretty big fool of himself. And, it was after he had heard her talking to God in the car, when she thought he was sleeping, and telling Him that she loved Lindy. Sure, she said she loved Paul, too, but she said she was having difficulty balancing the two men and her feelings.

Until that moment, Lindy had been totally satisfied—well, maybe not totally satisfied, but at least content—with being Jane's friend. As soon as she said she loved him, something innately competitive clicked in Lindy. He wasn't accustomed to giving up what he wanted, and he didn't figure he was about to change at thirty-four years old. He wanted to fight for her, but after seeing the monkey-in-the-middle routine she went through at her sister's engagement party, and again over Christmas, Lindy didn't think he could put her through any more stress. She seemed to want to make things work with Paul.

Lindy was happy for her. Really, he was. He just happened to be miserable for himself. He was dangerously close to losing the one person he cared about more than he was willing to admit, and he was uncertain how to win her. Life was so much easier when it was played on a thin sheet of ice, he thought; at least on the ice he knew how to win. *Pass. Shoot. Score. As simple as breathing.*

Putting away the last dish, he hung the silly apron back on the hook where he had discovered it and made his way from the kitchen to the makeshift hospital. He settled into the leather chair opposite Jane's couch. Watching her slight breaths as she slept, he once again wondered how anyone could be that unhealthy and continue to glow.

"Snap out of it, Barrett," Lindy said under his breath and clicked on the remote to drown his misery in another hour of *SportsCenter*.

———

He felt a tickle on his cheek and tried to swat the annoying notion from his face, but the irritation continued. Opening his eyes, he looked up at Jane, who was hovering over him and using a tissue to gently prod open his eyes.

Instinctively, Lindy pulled his face away from the tissue. "I hope that's clean."

"Yes, it is, and it's my last one, Rip Van Winkle. Do you think you could continue on your knight-in-shining-armor routine and run to the market for a couple more boxes?"

Sitting up, he wiped his mouth and tried to find his bearings. "I think I can handle that. You sound a little better. Is the soup kicking in?"

Unabashedly, she leaned into him, squeezing him in a bear hug. "You're the best! I think your mom's soup should be marketed as a cure-all."

She withdrew slightly, but without the support of his arms, she lost her balance and landed in his lap, coughing. "Sorry."

"Not a problem. This day just keeps getting better." He pulled her close. Ignoring the scarf twisted at her neck and the possibility of catching malaria, he slid his hands down her arms and cradled her against his chest. They sat cuddled in the chair until the end of *SportsCenter*, and Jane drifted back to sleep.

Lightly brushing her hair with his palm, Lindy watched more of her than he did the recounting of the Devils vs. Islanders Saturday afternoon matchup. He glanced at the clock and realized he should run to the market before the neighborhood became too busy with weekend-evening traffic. Trying to move as smoothly as possible, Lindy transferred Jane from his lap back to the couch, tucking endless blankets around her to ward off her chill. Pulling the final cover to her chin, he leaned down and gave into temptation, kissing her forehead before making his way out the door.

Thirty minutes later, Lindy cautiously opened Jane's front door, trying not to wake his patient. His arms laden with grocery sacks, he quietly closed the door with his foot. Quickly divesting himself of the groceries, he carried a box of tissues and the movies he'd impulsively rented to the living room, where Jane was sleeping peacefully. He set the tissue box on the distressed coffee table and gently nudged her awake.

"Hey, sleepyhead, you want to wipe that runny nose?"

Her eyes fluttered open. "You're fabulous, has anyone told you lately?"

"I don't think so . . . but I like it." He handed her a tissue and a cough drop.

"Thank you. I tried to walk to the store this morning, and it took me forty-five minutes to pull on jeans and a sweater. If I had to walk the whole way there, I imagine I would still be walking."

"I'm glad I could be of assistance." He gave her a slight smile. "You should go back to sleep. I'll put the groceries away and then I'll get out of your hair."

"You probably have some place else to be. I'm so sorry to have asked you to run my errands. I don't want to keep you."

He answered from the kitchen while he shelved the final box and folded the grocery sacks. "I don't have any place else to be tonight. I'm still on a stationary-bike-only regimen since the injury, so I'm at your beck and call."

He walked back into the living room and hovered over her. "Do you need something?"

"Just a friend to watch these great old movies with. What do you say?"

"That's the best offer I've had all year."

As she scanned the three cases, a smile crossed her face. All three were Cary Grant classics. "How did you know Cary Grant is the second great love of my life, behind Jesus, of course?"

"Of course. And I just had a feeling that you had a thing for Archie Leach."

"You know his real name?"

"Of course I do. And the fact that you have an eleven-by-fourteen framed picture in your hallway that has a plaque engraved with 'Most call me Cary Grant, but you can call me Archie Leach' may have been a clue."

Her face flushed deeper red, adding welcome color to her cheeks. "I guess I'm a little bit of a movie buff. Things seem simpler, romantically I mean, in the thirties and forties. Well, in any Cary Grant movie. When I was a kid I used to pretend . . . never mind."

Lindy sat on the edge of the coffee table, leaned forward, and pressed her to continue. "Go on. When you were a kid you used to pretend . . ."

"I used to pretend I was in the movie *Philadelphia Story* or *Bringing Up Baby*. I wanted to be as cool as Katherine Hepburn. It didn't matter that she was a tomboy or was often a bit off, Cary Grant always fell in love with her."

"How did you see so many old movies?"

"The theater downtown plays old movies a few nights a week. My grandma and grandpa Garrett, my mom's parents, would take me at least once a week. Molly wasn't interested, and Emory was a baby, so it was just my grandparents and me. I guess they knew I needed some special time, having been the baby for seven years before being thrust into middle-child land."

"Was it always Cary Grant?"

"Pretty much all Cary, at least until my grandpa took me to see *Seven Brides for Seven Brothers*, and I stopped wanting to be smart-talking Katherine Hepburn and longed to be Jane Powell and sing so beautifully that I would make Howard Keel fall in love with me, and he would whisk me away to his mountain cabin, sans the six smelly brothers, naturally."

"Naturally."

"Sorry, I tend to run off with myself when I talk about my make-believe life," she said with a cough, which seemed more out of embarrassment than actual sickness.

"It's nice to hear about your life . . . make-believe or not."

"Well, let's forget about my life and perpetually runny nose. Pop this one in the DVD player, and we'll watch Cary Grant win Myrna Loy's love while trying to avoid Shirley Temple's traps." She handed him the DVD box.

"What are you talking about?"

"That's the plot for *The Bachelor and the Bobby-Soxer*. Cary Grant plays this artist who gets in trouble, but I don't remember for what. Myrna Loy plays the judge who tries his case, and Shirley Temple plays her younger sister, who is a senior in high school. Shirley proceeds to fall in mad crush with Cary Grant, and who could blame her, and of course, he falls in mad crush with Myrna Loy—" A long coughing spell stopped her, and she tried to catch her breath.

"And who could blame him," Lindy added as he handed Jane a cold glass of water.

"Exactly. Thank you." She gave him a grateful look and drank deeply from the glass.

Lindy slid the disk into the DVD player and made his way to the over-stuffed chair. Maybe he was getting sick, because he was actually looking forward to watching this movie. He could count on one hand the number of movies he had watched in the last decade that didn't center on guns and an action-packed theme—and one of those was *Miracle*, about the 1980 gold medal winners—but watching Jane's face dance with delight as she described the movie made him willing to watch trees grow in the forest as long as he could be with her while he watched them.

"I can make room on the couch. I think my fever broke. It's hard to see the TV from that chair, and I would hate for you to miss out on any of the comedy high jinks." She pushed herself upright and rested her feet on the old coffee table.

"Are you sure?"

"If you aren't afraid of catching what I'm sure is a mix of the plague and malaria, pull up a cushion."

At that moment he would happily inject himself with the worst disease known to man if it meant he could sit near her. He plopped down on the couch beside her and pressed play on the remote control. "I'm a hockey player. Our only fears are a goalie's butterfly and ticking off the coach."

Lindy took in her red-nosed profile. "Are you comfortable? Do you want me to get you something to drink or some more medicine?"

"No, thank you. You've done more than enough."

"Well, let me know." He tried to relax into the couch, but his large frame didn't settle well in most furniture, particularly female furniture.

They watched the screen go from the colored warning labels to the grainy black-and-white synonymous with films of the thirties and forties. The movie theme was upbeat, and as Cary Grant's name splashed across the screen, he watched Jane's smile light up the room. He could definitely take a couple hours of discomfort for that smile.

Focusing back on the television screen, he asked, "Who were the flowers from?"

Jane's cheeks grew rosy, and she focused her attention on the tissue in her hand. "Paul. He called when I could barely speak yesterday and felt bad he couldn't be here to take care of me."

"Is that what the card said? 'Sorry I can't hold your puke bucket'?"

Jane let loose a series of hacking coughs. "No, Mr. Romantic. It says that he hopes I feel better soon and that he loves me."

"Hey, I'm just saying that holding someone's hair, when she's puking up a lung, as someone did in this room not so long ago, ought to be worth more than a couple dozen roses."

"Aww, the big hockey player can't handle a little vomit?"

Without thinking, Lindy draped his arm over her shoulders and pulled her tight to his side. "Beautiful, that wasn't a little vomit. That was Lake Erie you puked up."

"I really am sorry," she said, looking into his eyes. "I cannot thank you enough for coming to my rescue today. I know I wouldn't feel this good if you hadn't come to take care of me."

He drew her closer, enjoying the easy comfort her nearness evoked. "Jane, only for you would I clean out a puke bucket." For Jane, there was no telling what mountains he would climb or valleys he would crawl through.

CHAPTER TWENTY-THREE

"He cleaned up your puke?" Millie asked as she strutted through Jane's front door two days later.

"Hello, to you too, Millie," Jane said, closing the door behind Millie.

As Millie crossed the entrance into Jane's living room, she stopped and spun on her heel in an artful turn, allowing her long blonde locks to drape over her shoulder in a waterfall. "You aren't still contagious, are you?"

Jane shook her head. "Millie, how do you do that?"

"Do what?"

"Turn every space into your own personal stage."

"Janie, it's a gift. It took years of practice to hone that gift. Now it's a habit that I cannot break. Can we get back to the burly hockey player cleaning up your vomit?"

"I'm not sure I'm well enough to discuss it," Jane sat on her couch, drawing her pajama-encased legs to her chest.

Millie lowered herself onto Jane's favorite chair with the grace of a queen taking her throne. "Sweetie, I can see that red nose of yours, and I know it's not because you're still ill. Spill it—the story, not any remnant of the flu."

"There isn't much to tell. I'm not quite sure why Lindy showed up on Saturday, but he did, and I, for one, am extremely grateful. I don't think I would be feeling even a tenth as good as I feel if he hadn't. I couldn't do anything for myself."

"Well, isn't he a regular prince charming. What did hottie . . . Paul have to say about Lindy's servitude?" Millie asked.

"I fell asleep on the phone with him on Sunday, and he hasn't called today, so I haven't told him yet. But I will, so don't give me that wait-until-he-finds-out look. I'm sure he'll be thankful that Lindy was such a good friend in my time of need." *Yep, just two good friends falling asleep on the couch, watching a movie. Paul is going to be thrilled.*

"Hmm . . . I'm sure your gorgeous boyfriend will be ecstatic that an equally, if not more, buff and beautiful man came to your rescue when he was off in the wilderness."

"Millie, it really isn't that big of a deal. But I do think that Anna's soup is a miracle cure. Not only did I start to feel remarkably better within hours of eating it, I wasn't even worried that I was crusty and gross with Lindy in the house. It must have some sort of mental effects as well as physical."

Millie crossed her arms in front of her chest and slowly slid one leg over the other. "Okay . . ."

"I really should talk to someone at work, in R and D, and maybe try and find a distributor for her soup. I think she could make a killing."

"Don't you think it would be hard to sell, seeing as the real cure was more than likely the nurse who gave you the soup?"

"What?" Jane's cheeks grew warm as her traitorous mind flashed images of Lindy's tender ministrations, feeding the longings of her heart and fueling the internal war between guilt and desire.

Millie's eyes were like twin missiles honing in on their target. "You don't think you felt better because it was Lindy who was feeding you?"

"Of course not. Millie, you and Molly really need to put this whole there's-something-more-between-Lindy-and-me thing to rest. He's my friend. He was here almost all day on Saturday, and he didn't make one reference to his overtures at the party. He clearly does not have feelings for me, or he would have wanted to talk about them during one of the eight hours he was hanging out in my apartment." The more she spoke the truth, the more quickly her traitorous heart would come to accept it.

Millie's eyes sparkled with revelation. "My darling, you wanted to talk to him about his feelings for you, didn't you?"

"Don't be ridiculous, Millie. I don't want a confrontation anymore than he does, obviously. We're just friends." Jane stood up quickly, a little too quickly for her still-weakened state, and she stumbled as she made her way to the kitchen to escape Millie's questioning.

"Whatever," Millie called after her.

"Let's change the subject. What's new with you and Jason?" Jane asked as she pulled the teapot away from the running water and placed it on the stove to steam.

"Not much. He's pressuring me to take things to, you know, a deeper level, but I don't think I want to."

Jane emerged from the kitchen and stared at her free-love friend. Millie had always been open and permissive with her sexuality, something about which she and Jane agreed to disagree. "What are you saying?" Jane asked as she returned to her seat on the couch.

Millie laced her fingers together and focused her attention on the floor. "I'm not sure, really. Jason is different. And I don't want to mess this relationship up. I want it to matter. I want it to last." She lifted her gaze to Jane with a tearful grin. "Jane Eleanor Grey, I think you are right."

"About . . ."

"I don't know if that level of . . . intimacy is right between two people unless they've made a commitment to each other. Maybe even . . . a lifetime commitment. I'm still trying to figure it all out."

Jane was stunned by her friend's apparent altered perception, but she didn't want to make too big of a deal out of the change, for fear that Millie would run headlong in the opposite direction. "Millie, what changed your mind?"

"I guess it was the trip to visit his family. His parents are really wonderful, and so are his siblings. They treated me like someone special. Outside of the Grey family, I never had that. You know my own parents weren't much of an example, and I guess I always figured it was easier to keep my heart out of relationships. My body didn't really matter too much. I already sold it to the highest bidder as a model. But Jason makes me feel different. He actually makes me *feel*." Tears trickled down her perfect face.

"Oh, Millie, that's wonderful!" Jane exclaimed as she hugged her friend. *Thank You, God!*

"I think I want more from Jason. I want him . . . the inside him and the outside him. I love him, Jane, but I'm scared."

"I can understand. Loving someone is a big commitment. And being strong enough not to give in to your physical wants and desires is hard, especially if your heart is involved. But it will be worth the wait," Jane promised.

"What am I supposed to say to him? What if he doesn't want to be with me if I don't . . . ?"

"Then he isn't the guy I thought he was, and he isn't the right guy for you. If he loves you, or even thinks he's starting to fall in love with you, he'll be willing to wait until you're ready. And by ready, you know I mean married, right?"

Millie rolled her eyes and wiped her tears. "I know, O Pure One, I know. How do you do it? How do you push down all of those feelings that want to bubble to the service and make you forget that you need to be pure?"

"It isn't always easy, but the first step is setting the boundary. You have to tell him what you expect and don't put yourself in a position to tempt either of you."

"You make it sound easy." Millie sulked.

"It's not easy." The words sounded hollow to her as she thought of how effortlessly she had built a fort to keep Paul at a distance. And yet all Lindy had to do was touch her hand, and flames consumed the barrier. Despite her own confusion, Jane felt as if God wanted her to share His direction with Millie even though the once-clear message was muddled for Jane. "But I know that the reason God set marriage as the rule for physical intimacy is because it means so much to Him. If you think about it, sex is the most realistic place we, as human beings, get to participate in a God miracle. Even if you didn't think of it that way before, think about the children you and Jason may one day create. They're special gifts from God, which shouldn't be tainted by breaking God's rules, right?"

"Jane, you always know how to bring me down," Millie said.

"I'm proud of you, Millie, whether you like it or not." She felt like a hypocrite. Millie was becoming the woman Jane had always claimed to be.

"Yeah, I know. But you know I'm not going to go all churchy or anything."

"I know."

Jane's house phone rang at the same moment that the teapot, which she had managed to forget, whistled loudly from the kitchen.

Millie announced, "I'll get the tea. You answer your phone."

"Thanks, Mill." Jane reached over to the end table and picked up her phone. "Hello?"

"Hey, sweetheart." Paul's mellow voice came through the handheld.

She leaned into the couch, unsure how to deal with the trail mix of disappointment, joy, and guilt the sound of his voice stirred in her spirit. "Hi. I was wondering when you would call today."

"Well, I've been a bit stretched for time. I wanted to ask you a favor."

"What can I do for you?"

"I was wondering if you felt well enough to pick me up from the airport tonight."

"Tonight?" She wasn't sure she was ready to see Paul.

"Yeah, I've been flying most of the day and just landed in Chicago. Sorry this is so last minute. If you don't feel up to the drive, I can get a service to take me home."

"Of course I can pick you up." Jane's voice sounded steadier than she felt. Maybe once she saw Paul, her mixed emotions would dissipate. "I don't understand how I got so lucky to have you back so soon. Is the case over?"

"Not exactly. I'll explain when I get back to Columbus. Maybe we can have dinner at my place, if you're up to keeping food down."

"The food has stayed down since Saturday night. I might be able to eat a little something, as long as it's pretty mild and white rice-esque."

"I can handle white rice."

"What time will your flight get in?"

"In a little over an hour. I'm walking to my gate here in Chicago now."

"Wow . . . That's really fast. I guess I'll see you soon."

"Are you sure you're up to this? I don't want to inconvenience you."

"This is what girlfriends do. They pick up their boyfriends from the airport, and they bake chocolate chip cookies."

"So, you have cookies waiting for me?" His voice dropped, and Jane could hear the anticipation.

"Are you serious? I've been near death's door for four days. Unless you wanted me to bake a vial of typhoid in the brownie pan, I think my baking days are down the road a few weeks."

"I'll be counting the days."

"I'll see you in an hour." Jane said as she looked at her wall clock to estimate how long it would take her to go from crusty flu to presentable girlfriend.

"I'll be counting the minutes. I love you, Jane."

"I love you, too." The phone felt like a ten-pound weight as she tucked the receiver into the cradle. She rubbed her temples as her distant headache instantly grew to a throbbing pain.

Paul is coming home.

She rushed, as quickly as her weakened state would allow her, down the hall to the bathroom. She flipped on the faucet and pulled a washcloth from the linen closet, to scrub the funk off of her face.

"Was that Christian McHottie?" Millie said, folding her arms as she leaned against the bathroom doorframe.

"I'm too stressed to even correct you right now. Paul is coming home tonight. He's landing in about an hour, and he asked me to pick him up from the airport," Jane said through the terry cloth.

"Does he know you've been sick, for like a week? You can barely stand up." Millie pulled Jane's chair from her vanity and pushed her onto its seat.

"Yes, he asked me if I thought I was up to it. Millie, it's like, what, a ten mile round trip drive from here to the airport. I can totally handle that. Brushing my matted sickbed hair and looking somewhat presentable for him might be a completely different story." Jane's exhaustion caused her to drop the washcloth to her lap. How was she going to make it down the stairs let alone drive to the airport?

"Here's what we are going to do. I'm going to start your shower, and I'll pick out some clothes for you while you scrub off the stink. I'll work wonders on that fur you pass off as hair, and we'll put some shadow on your eyes and match your cheeks with that beautiful little button nose." Millie turned the water on in Jane's shower and walked out of the room to pick out clothes.

"Thanks for the vote of confidence, Mills. I'll just try and get my fur clean enough for you to do something with it," Jane called as she slipped out of her pajamas and stepped into the shower.

The water hurt as it hit each of her pores. The shower ran the fine line between pleasure and pain; pleasure from the sensation of being clean, and pain from the excruciating sting of each water droplet. She scrubbed her hair and skin, trying to rid herself of the remaining traces of the disease waging a war in her body. Revitalized after the first few minutes of the shower she began to feel she was actually human. She started to believe that she would be able to spend a nice night with Paul.

Paul was coming home. The thought made her smile as she washed her face. His visit over Christmas had been tense, with Lindy and all of the family drama, but maybe, if he was going to stay for a few days, they would have sometime to reconnect. Maybe the mix of emotions she had been experiencing was a result of her illness and Paul's distance. Maybe this was God's answer for her. "That would be . . . nice."

CHAPTER TWENTY-FOUR

"You're moving to Alaska?" Jane exclaimed an hour later, as she and Paul shared rice and vegetables at his apartment.

"Just for two years, maybe, three," he replied, with a mouthful of veggie rice.

"Two or three years," Jane repeated.

"It's a great opportunity." Paul wiped his mouth as he continued to ooze enthusiasm. "We're going to hire five or six additional attorneys, some paralegals, and an office staff. The firm wants to set up a satellite office in Juneau specifically for this case. My dad thinks the case will lead to several more, and he has the confidence to let me be the lead guy. I'll get to practice law, really help people, in my own way." Jane could sense how excited he was, and she wanted to be supportive and happy for him, but all she could manage was a weak smile.

"I have a couple weeks to wrap up my cases here and pack my place to have everything shipped to Alaska. It's all a little surreal." He stood up to take their bowls to the kitchen and kissed the top of her head.

"You can say that again," Jane muttered, following him into the kitchen. "So, what are you going to do with your apartment?"

"Probably sell it to the firm. They usually need housing when they bring in new attorneys or have people in town."

She pulled a glass down from the cabinet and poured herself water. Drinking the water gave her something to focus on rather than the fear rumbling along the edges of her mind as she felt Paul's arms enclose her waist, drawing her tightly against his chest.

"I missed you so much." He leaned forward and kissed her neck, leaving Jane feeling marked but hollow. She turned in his arms, hoping for even a subtle stirring, but all she felt was the burning heat of guilt as her memory taunted her with a vision of she and Lindy cuddled in her favorite chair.

"That is not playing fair." Was she censuring Paul or herself?

"All's fair in love and war," he said as he placed a feather-light kiss on her exposed collarbone.

"Paul," Jane said with a voice of tentative protest. "I thought we agreed we would be careful?"

"I'm being careful. One can only get so romantic in the middle of the kitchen." He lifted his hands to her face, lowering his lips to hers.

Jane's brain went into overdrive, but her body seemed to stall. The kiss was pleasant: warm, mellow and nice, just like Paul. But, she didn't feel the toe-curling sensation she felt she should.

You love this man. Come on, let's make it work, she cheered.

Jane stepped closer to Paul and wrapped her arms around his waist, kissing him with everything in her being, but she felt little more than a subtle wave of affection roll through her belly. With a sigh, she broke the connection between them, allowing her head to rest on Paul's solid chest.

"Wow," he said. And Jane knew his response was genuine, as she could feel the rapid beat of his heart and the shallow intake of his breath. "I guess I should have kissed you in the kitchen sooner."

He reached under her chin to lift her face to his once again.

She stepped into the kiss, allowing the tenderness she felt from his embrace envelop her. She wanted to make this work. Maybe they just needed more practice. She waited for the click, the moment when her mind would shut off and her emotions would take over, but the click never happened. With Paul, it seemed she was more than capable of maintaining complete control.

As the kiss ended, he pulled her tight to his chest. "I'm sorry. I know I should have stopped, sooner. I lose my head when I'm around you." He lightly kissed her brow.

"I should probably get home. I'm going to have to go in to the office tomorrow. I don't think Jasper believes I was as sick as I was," she said, delicately stepping out of his arms, trying to ignore the fresh guilt creeping at the corners of her conscience.

"Yeah, I need to get back on Columbus time, at least for the next few weeks. Are you free for dinner tomorrow? I want to spend as much time with you as possible," Paul said, lacing his fingers through hers.

"I think so. Can we talk about it tomorrow? My head is really starting to pound and I still need to drive home." She withdrew her hand from his, rubbing her forehead.

"I'm sorry I kept you so late. You're still recovering, and here I'm going on about my own stuff." He turned and walked the few steps to the coatrack to retrieve her coat.

"No, don't be silly. I really am happy for you, Paul."

He held open her coat as she slid into its down warmth. "I'm so happy to have you to share it with. Success isn't much fun if you're all alone. God is so good to me, to have sent you stumbling into my path way back in October."

"Stumbling has always been a gift. I guess God uses our strengths." She turned to face him.

"I love you from your beautiful face down to your clumsy feet, Jane Grey."

Jane smiled and stood on her tiptoes to place a kiss on his cheek. "We'll talk tomorrow."

"Until tomorrow," Paul said, returning her smile as he held open the door. She could feel his wistful gaze on her back the whole way down the hall.

CHAPTER TWENTY-FIVE

THREE DAYS LATER, Jane sat behind her desk, unable to focus on the laundry list of projects waiting for her. Paul was moving to Alaska. She couldn't wrap her mind around the reality. Three or four years in Alaska was permanent. Paul seemed to be thrilled about the move. What she couldn't determine was where the move put them as a couple.

If Paul wasn't coming back to Columbus, did that mean they were going to break up? Over the course of a few dinners and long talks, the subject of their future had not been discussed. Paul was as amorous as he had been over the holidays, wooing her with the entire arsenal of his romantic armory. She felt adored and cherished, yet she had a sinking feeling their courtship was running toward a brick wall. If someone had asked her two weeks ago what the barrier to her relationship with Paul was, she would have answered Lindy, at least in her mind. But now, as she thought about losing Paul to the frozen north, she became fearful. The person she had contemplated sharing the rest of her life with was slipping through her grasp.

Was she not supposed to be with Paul? Was this move God's way of separating them? Was He telling her that her focus was too much on herself, on her own personal drama, being torn between two men?

"Really, Jane," she mumbled to herself. "Are you really so self-centered that everything is about you?"

She tried to still the questions in her mind, focusing on her e-mail inbox, hoping to find at least one or two urgent messages. Although her project list was long, none of the items were pressing—not good for distraction purposes. She really needed something to take her mind off of Paul's move.

She answered her ringing phone. "Jane Grey."

"Hey, Beautiful, feeling better?"

Smiling, she swiveled her chair to take in the wintry scene below. "Much better, thanks to a secret Canadian recipe and a heck of a nurse. If you ever decide to give up hockey, you might want to look into nursing school, you know, as a backup plan."

"I'll keep that in mind, but for now, the doctor is giving me the go-ahead to start practicing again. Hopefully, I won't need to find a new career anytime soon."

"Lindy, that's wonderful. Are you sure your knee is up to it?"

"I guess we'll see. Every time it takes a knock, it seems to come back a little less agile than before. I'm hoping that with all the rehab this time, I'll at least be where I was before the hit. The good news is, I've been basically pain free for the last two days on the bike."

"Will you play on Saturday?"

"No. The team is in Detroit on Saturday, and as much as I would like to make it back for that game, Coach and Scottie both think waiting until next Tuesday's home game is a better option."

"Will you go up to Detroit with the team?"

"Naw. It's a quick trip, and traveling along to watch becomes more of a hassle than supportive."

"If you aren't busy, you should come with us to church."

"Church, on a Saturday? That sounds like you're bringing together people for a sacrifice or something."

"Don't be silly," she replied. "You remember that Christian group I'm a member of . . . we have those retreat-type weekends a few times a year? It's international . . . don't you remember?"

"I guess, kind of. . . . Janesie, you talk about a lot of church stuff. I'm not the best at keeping it all straight."

"Sorry," she apologized. "I tend to talk a lot about what's most important to me."

"Then I hope you talk about me nonstop."

Jane bit her lip and twirled the phone cord around her fingers. "Of course."

"So, you want me, your favorite conversation topic, to go to church with you?"

"Yes, I do. I think you would enjoy it. It's a pretty simple worship service. It usually only lasts about an hour. . . . I'll treat you to dinner after, if you go."

"Well, I'm a sucker for a free meal and a pretty face. I guess I can make it through anything."

Jane chuckled. "Thanks, don't sound so enthused."

"I would be delighted to go," Lindy replied brightly.

"Really?"

"Really. What time are you going to pick me up?"

"Is six thirty okay? We'll get there a little before the music starts, so there won't be as many, umm . . . distractions?"

"What kind of distractions?"

"Well, I don't want your worship time to be distracted with autograph seekers."

"Beautiful, don't worry. This is Columbus. The team will be in Detroit. No one will ever think it's me. And besides, I'm not an Ohio State football player. I'm not really that famous in this town."

"Well, if you think you'll be safe from detection, I'll pick you up around six, seeing as you're such a nobody in this town."

"You called it."

"Well, I guess I'll see you on Saturday."

"Sounds good," he said.

"Bye, Lindy."

"Bye, Beautiful."

Jane hung up the phone with a smile on her lips. She didn't realize how much she had come to appreciate his simple nickname for her. Being called Beautiful every time she spoke with him made her start to believe she really was beautiful. But then again, he could mean it ironically, like when a fat guy is called Slim. *Now that's a downer.*

Refocusing her attention on her work, she was able to remain attentive until lunchtime, when her phone rang again, interrupting her train of thought.

"Jane Grey," she answered in a distracted tone.

"Paul Wade," Paul responded.

"Hi, Paul, what's up?" she asked, without taking her focus off of her notes for her final presentation for the Johnson account the following week.

"I was wondering if you would mind staying in tonight instead of going out to dinner."

"Sure, I guess."

"Well, I thought we could talk easier if we were alone."

"Okay, that sounds good . . ."

"I would have an easier time ravishing your naked body."

Jane quickly sat tall in her chair. "What?"

"I didn't think you were paying attention." He chuckled.

"I'm sorry. I was on a roll, and it's taken me quite awhile this morning to get my rhythm in place. You want to eat at your place tonight?"

"That is what I was thinking. Or we could grab a pizza and eat at your apartment. I thought it would be a little quieter. This week has been a bit of a whirlwind for me, and I'm sure that you're still fighting tiredness."

"Staying in sounds good. Is seven okay? I need to be here most of the day. I have an appointment this afternoon and a meeting with a few people downtown."

"Let's make it seven thirty. That way neither of us will rush. I have plenty to do here. It's amazing how hard it is to transfer a caseload and pack up an office. Not to change the subject, but did you still want to go to church tomorrow night?"

"I was planning on it. I invited Lindy, too," she said.

"Oh." His voice sounded like she had just told him she had cancelled his subscription to the *Harvard Law Review*.

"Is that okay? I thought it would be a good way for him to attend church, when it wasn't so churchy."

"No, it's okay. I was thinking we could go to the new play at the Rife Center, but church is probably the better thing."

"Are you sure? I can call him and cancel. He didn't seem too thrilled to be going, anyway."

His sigh was loud and tangible. "No, if you got him to agree, you should follow through on it."

"Thanks for understanding. I know that there's some sort of guy tension between the two of you, but I would really like it if you could get along."

"I'll try for your sake."

"Thank you. That means a lot to me."

"How much?" he asked.

"Why don't you come to my apartment tonight, and I'll show you." Jane winced at the overture.

"Well, Miss Grey, I do believe you have learned how to flirt."

"I just might have." She giggled, but had she learned how from Lindy?

"I'll see you tonight. I love you."

"Love you, too," she said hanging up the phone.

She turned in her chair and caught her reflection in the window. Who was she? A woman who professed her love to one man while pining after another; this was not the Jane Grey she wanted to be. This Jane Grey was going in the box, and the real Jane Grey would be the only one present tomorrow night. Maybe if she was on her best behavior, Lindy and Paul would finally become friends. Maybe then the guilt threatening to consume her help would slink back to its dingy corner. A girl could dream.

CHAPTER TWENTY-SIX

"HERE WE ARE," Jane said as they pulled into her church parking lot Saturday evening. The car passengers remained silent, as they had for most of the thirty-minute journey from downtown.

When she and Paul picked up Lindy, Paul waited in the car. Lindy met Jane at the door to the lobby and pulled her into a massive hug. She must have lingered too long in his embrace, because by the time the two smiling friends returned to the oversized SUV, Paul's original good humor had vanished. He grew even more dour when she suggested Lindy take the front seat to accommodate his knee.

"I'm really excited about tonight's worship service," she said, trying to inject good cheer into the evening. "One of my friends is speaking tonight. I think you both will enjoy what he shares."

"Great, more men," Paul muttered loud enough for Jane to hear.

"Paul, are you okay?" she asked.

He flexed his hands against the steering wheel, not taking his eyes off of the road. "How's it going, Lindy?"

"I'm good, dude. And you?"

"Good."

That eloquent transaction of words was the extent of the discussion for the entire trip. Jane sat in the backseat, with sports talk radio humming on the edges of her ears, wondering how she was going to get through the church service.

By the time the trio was walking toward the worship center doors, Jane's mind was exhausted from prayer. She desperately wanted her friend and her boyfriend to feel anything other than antagonism toward each other, and she prayed for everything from a natural disaster, where the two would need to help each other survive, to a curable but timely illness, which would force the men to work together to find an answer. God quickly reminded her that she had recovered from such an illness only a week ago and that it had not made her guys friends.

"Jane?" A light hand touched her shoulder.

Turning, she pasted her best sorority girl smile on her face as she looked into the twinkling eyes of her ex-boyfriend. *Seriously, God. Could You not find any other entertainment tonight?*

"Hi, Brad."

"I didn't expect to see you, tonight. Molly said you were still pretty ill."

"I'm feeling much better. Brad, you remember Paul?"

"Hey, man, good to see you again. I thought you went back to Alaska after Christmas?" Brad said with a big smile, shaking Paul's hand.

"I had to come back to tie up a few loose ends. My firm is reassigning me to Juneau for the next couple years. I'm back to get my things in order." Paul put his arm around Jane's shoulders, pulling her possessively to his side.

"Really? Wow, talk about your long-distance relationships," Brad said.

"Umm, yeah," Jane said. "Brad, this is my friend Lindy."

"Nice to meet you." Lindy extended his hand.

"It's great to meet you," Brad said, with an ear-to-ear grin as he pumped Lindy's hand like an old-fashioned water pump. "Of course, I know all about you. Jane is your biggest fan and she never stops talking about how great you are."

"I think we should go find a seat," Jane said through clenched teeth.

"Jane used to drag me to all of the home hockey games, back when we were dating."

Jane tugged Paul's arm. "It looks like the service is going to be crowded. We really should go in, don't you think?"

"She knows everything about you. If you weren't so famous, I probably would've been pretty jealous of you. It's kind of crazy that you guys are friends, now."

Lindy lifted a single eyebrow and subtly shook his head. "I guess."

"We really need to get a seat. It was good seeing you, Brad." Jane stepped out of Paul's maniacal grip and inched toward the open doors of the worship center.

"Oh, sorry, didn't mean to keep you. I was just on my way up to my office. I'll see you after the service. Great meeting you, Lindy! Nice to see you again, Paul." Brad waved as he trotted down the hallway.

"Shall we go in," Jane said, trying to ignore her warm face.

Without a word, Paul grabbed Jane's hand and dragged her through the sanctuary doors, forcing Lindy to jog after them. Inside they found a seat near the back and listened to the opening music.

Jane wanted to sink into the carpeted floor out of sheer embarrassment. She should have expected Brad to run off at the mouth. *So much for pastoral confidentiality.*

The worship band had beautiful, soft harmonies, which helped to reduce Jane's anxiety. She tried to settle her spirit and focus her attention on God and off her impossibly sticky situation. Bowing her head, she cleared her mind and let the words of the worship music open her heart. She stayed in the passive position until her mind was free and wholly focused on God— so swept away in worship that she was oblivious to everything and everyone around her, except Jesus.

Watching Jane with her head thrown back, her gaze focused heavenward, and her hands raised in worship, Lindy was humbled. Her natural beauty was one thing to admire, but the ethereal quality she embodied as she worshiped, was otherworldly to him. She seemed to be awash in a special light, one that Lindy innately wanted. He glanced over to Paul. Although he wasn't as overt as Jane, he too appeared to have settled into a place of peace and joy.

Unable to take the intensity of the moment, Lindy shifted his gaze and stared out into the worship center. Hundreds of hands were lifted in praise to God, something that had always seemed false and slightly intimidating to Lindy. But now, standing beside his friend, who he knew didn't have a false bone in her body, he couldn't deny the exquisite beauty of the community in worship. Lindy didn't hear the words of the song—he barely heard the melody—but he could feel something waking inside him.

The music ended and the congregation lifted praise, clapping and welcoming the first speaker of the evening. Lindy took a seat beside Jane. His thigh touched hers, due to the close proximity, but she pulled away, crossing one leg over the other. Lindy couldn't help but feel a little hope in her obvious attempt to squelch the physical connection they shared.

As the first speaker, a young man in his early thirties, approached the podium to share, Jane leaned toward Lindy and whispered, "This is my friend Thomas. I think you'll like his story."

Lindy nodded, focusing his attention on the man, rather than the envy that was creeping through his body as Paul laced his fingers through Jane's.

"My name is Thomas Gibbons, and I attended Men's Walk number twenty-four, and I sat at the table of John." His strange introduction was greeted with applause.

When the applause ended, Thomas continued. "I was asked to speak tonight about what my Emmaus Walk meant to me. They want me to tell you how it changed my life. But I want to tell you, it not only changed my life, but it saved my life."

As Thomas continued, Lindy adjusted the collar of his shirt and glanced at the myriad of inserts distributed throughout the cubbies attached to the back of the pew in front of him. He picked up a card that had "LOST?" printed at the top and scanned a few Scriptures he vaguely remembered from vacation Bible school. Shoving the card in a hymnal, he found little else to distract him as he leaned back against the pew and crossed his arms over his chest.

Jane's friend had an easy smile, but Lindy could see the pain and sadness lingering in his eyes as he shared his story. Thomas disclosed excerpts of the wild life he had been living before his conversion of faith. Thomas's life had been a fairly common twenty-something experience, filled with drinking, excessive dating, and crazy work hours. He shared how his best friend, from high school had urged him to attend the Walk to Emmaus retreat for several years before he finally agreed just to get his friend to leave him alone. It was during his time on the retreat that Thomas was able to really see how far he was from God, even though he thought of himself as a good person. He realized how much he needed Jesus in his life. And, during the weekend, Thomas accepted Jesus into his heart and never looked back.

Thomas's voice rang loud in Lindy's ears, echoing through his mind, as he concluded his talk. "After years of trying to fill up the emptiness in my life with everything this world had to offer, I finally turned around and found my way back home to God. Today, five years later, my life isn't perfect, but it's a life centered on Jesus. And that best friend from high school is something a little bit more. She's my wife and soon to be the mother of my first child. Emmaus was more than a retreat to refuel my faith. Emmaus was God's love letter to me. He showed me His overwhelming love in so many different ways, it was impossible to deny Him. I pray that each of you find your way home to Jesus. Thank you."

Thomas nodded his head at the applause that followed him as he left the podium, but all Lindy could do was stare at the man. Thomas's words weren't anything exceptional or eloquent. He not was going to be quoted, like John F. Kennedy's inaugural speech, but the message behind the words touched Lindy.

His mom had been picking at Lindy to go back to church, to reconnect with God, but he didn't see the point. Lindy wasn't worthy to reconnect with the Lord. He was, after all, a murderer. His actions had led to someone's death, and he couldn't let that burden go.

Jamie Marcus was the kid's name. He was an awesome defenseman from Alberta, expected to go in the first round of the draft. He and Lindy had played with, or against, each other, since they were in mighty mites. They weren't friends, but they shared a mutual respect for each other's talent and work ethic.

The day of the accident started and ended like any hockey day. During the game, the opposition's coach made it a point to put his star defenseman against the star forward. He and Jamie played nearly every shift against each other. That night, Lindy was excited about the extra shifts and the level of game that Jamie brought out in him. Like in most sports, when the opponent is better, you get better, and Lindy played one of the best games of his junior career.

He had three points, a goal, and two assists, following through on nearly every checking opportunity. Jamie hadn't played as well as normal, and his frustration grew to a fevered pitch by the end of the second period.

As Lindy skated with the puck up ice, Jamie tagged him. He came up high on Lindy with a hip check. Lindy caught sight of the six-foot-two defender a split second before impact. Out of gut reaction, he leapt to avoid the brunt of the check. The two teenagers the size of linebackers broke the protective Plexiglas surrounding the rink with the force of the hit.

They landed in an awkward pile on the ice, but neither lost consciousness. Both teams' trainers insisted that the two players retire to the locker rooms for the remainder of the period. And the boys gingerly skated off the ice. As Lindy was ready to step over the safety rubber threshold leading to the locker room, he looked across the benches and caught sight of Jamie. The two hockey foes exchanged quick head nods and undetectable smiles. The hit had been clean, a part of what made hockey fun and exciting for the fans and the players. At that moment, Lindy looked forward to waiting with Jamie for their names to be announced at the draft. That day never came for Jamie.

Lindy could feel the nausea that always accompanied this particular trip down memory lane. He tried to settle his stomach and his mind, but he was losing the battle. He motioned to Jane that he needed to leave before he escaped the sanctuary.

Jane watched Lindy race toward the exit, feeling helpless. She'd sensed the anxiety rising in him throughout the worship service but had hoped tonight would lead to a breakthrough for him. Even if he didn't want to share with her the crisis of conscious she knew he was facing, she had hoped that Thomas, or even Pastor Luke, might say something that would give Lindy the window to reach out to someone.

After Anna shared the brief details of Lindy's struggle, Jane's greatest desire for Lindy was that he could release his burden. No one should carry that kind of guilt. Jane wanted to run after Lindy, to offer him the support and care their friendship demanded, but she knew she couldn't.

If she went after Lindy, she would be betraying a confidence—and she would hurt Paul. As much as she loved her friend, she was committed to Paul. Whatever mixed-up feelings she had for Lindy needed to stay buried. She needed to be cautious and guarded with Lindy, not only for the sake of their friendship, but also for the protection of her own heart.

Sitting in the pew, with Paul's hand gently caressing her arm, she continued to convince herself that she was where she needed to be. *We are not to yoke ourselves with unbelievers.*

Then why was her heart yearning to follow another?

Sitting in a high-backed chair just outside the worship center, Lindy waited for Jane and Paul to emerge. He was disgusted with his lack of control; running from the room like a little girl who'd lost her favorite toy. He wasn't behaving like the well-trained, controlled athlete he was paid to be.

Being in the church had triggered his slingshot into the past. He knew he shouldn't have come to the service with Jane, but he hadn't wanted to disappoint her. He loved her and wanted to be near her. Tonight his mental levee was destroyed with the hurricane of his memories, and he was too broken to lie to himself. He was in love with Jane. She was everything he knew he wanted, and so much more he never knew needed. And yet, she wasn't his. She would never be his, because he couldn't be God's.

Why did the one girl he could envision the rest of his life with have to come with so many regulations? Why couldn't she be easy, like other girls? He smiled sadly. If she were easy, if she were like other girls, she wouldn't be the one that Lindy wanted.

Lindy tried to still his mind, waiting for the conclusion of the service. He knew Jane had encouraged him to come tonight hoping Lindy would make some connection with God. Lindy found what he always found in church; a big ball of decade-old guilt. He also knew he had to walk away from Jane.

Lindy's heart was enmeshed with the beautiful brown-eyed girl who was at that moment with a man she professed to love. Lindy didn't want to be a stumbling block for her relationship with Paul, but if he allowed his life to continue to be intertwined with hers, he knew his selfishness would win. He would start to fight for Jane, and Lindy knew how to fight dirty.

With Paul moving to Alaska, Lindy had the perfect opportunity to wear Jane down. Lindy could make her fall in love with him, through very persuasive means—but in the end, he was missing the key ingredient. He wasn't a Christian and Paul was.

Jane often spoke of the need for spiritual leadership in a family and in a marriage. In a moment of complete transparency, she'd told him that if she ever married, her husband would love Jesus more than he loved her. Lindy didn't think he could love anyone or anything more than he loved Jane at that moment. He really didn't understand her complete devotion to a God who allowed the world to be in such disarray. Lindy wished he knew the God that Jane spoke of with such devotion, but God wouldn't want a guy like him.

Lindy wasn't worthy of the love of the God Jane spoke about, and he wasn't worthy to ask Jane for her love. He had to pull away, and he would start tonight.

Lying on the end table beside his chair was a small stack of postcards with the church's picture on the front. He picked up a card and pulled a pen from his pocket. Jotting a quick note to Jane, he stood to walk back into the sanctuary to hand it to her. But as he reached for the doors to reenter the worship center, he saw Brad shuffling down the hallway.

The young pastor raised his hand in a wave to Lindy, giving Lindy the perfect opportunity. With little regard to his manly hockey persona, Lindy explained that he was ill and needed to leave. He asked Brad to give Jane the note.

Brad readily agreed and asked Lindy how he was going to get home.

"I'll call a cab. Someone can be here in fifteen minutes or less, I'm sure."

"Why don't I give you a lift home?" Brad offered.

"I wouldn't want to put you out."

"No bother." He gave Lindy a knowing look. "I'm finished for the night, and I'm sure that if you're still sitting here when the service is over, Jane will insist on taking you home."

Lindy knew Brad was right. He didn't relish the idea of facing Jane with his feeble excuse. He needed physical distance in order to be the honorable man he was trying to be.

"If you really don't mind, I'm sure Jane and Paul would like some time alone." Lindy said, nearly choking on the words. His queasiness was returning, and it had nothing to do with Jamie Marcus.

"Trust me, man, I understand, better than most," Brad said, before disappearing into the worship center to pass Lindy's note to Jane.

The portly pastor returned with a smile and led Lindy out of the church to his car. The small hatchback was relatively new, and probably all that the pastor could afford, but Lindy's body screamed at the idea of being folded inside the tiny import.

"Sorry about the car. You're probably used to a Mercedes," Brad apologized.

"This is great. I really appreciate the ride home. This flu bug seemed to hit quick," Lindy covered.

"Maybe you picked it up from Jane. She was pretty sick, according to her sister. She might still be a carrier."

"Could be." Jane was definitely contagious.

Beyond the brief directions Lindy gave Brad to his building, the two men rode in relative silence, serenaded only by the hush of contemporary Christian music floating through the speakers. Lindy watched the freeway lights bounce off the newly fallen snow and tried to figure out how he was going to get over Jane.

He knew he could no longer call her or invite her to hockey games. To save himself, he was going to have to go cold turkey. Like an addict, he didn't have a choice. And like an addict, he could feel the withdrawal symptoms pulling at his mind and body.

Brad drove into the circle in front of Lindy's building and put the car in park. "Here we are."

"Thanks, man," Lindy said as he reached for the door handle to escape the car.

Brad reached out his hand to stop Lindy's hasty exit. Lindy turned and looked into a face filled with compassion. Brad definitely had the pastor thing down.

"Lindy, I know you probably don't want to talk about what's really going on in your mind, but whenever you do, I'm a good listener."

Lindy stared at the man who had once been at the center of Jane's world, and he recognized what she must have seen in him. Lindy responded to his offer with a simple nod of his head.

Reaching into the cup holder, Brad pulled out a business card. "Here are my numbers. I'm sure you have plenty of people to talk to, but sometimes it helps when the person doesn't know you, and you don't know him."

Lindy took the card and stared at the cream cardstock before whispering a thank-you to Brad. Unfolding himself from the car, Lindy stood on the sidewalk, slowly clicking the tiny red door closed.

Turning to walk the short distance to the lobby entrance, he heard the passenger window slide down, and Brad call after him. "Lindy, if you don't talk to me, please talk with Jane. She's your friend. I know she cares about you and wants you to be happy. Hope you feel better." Brad waved.

Lindy nodded as the car rolled out onto the main road. He braved the January wind for several minutes before heading inside the warmth of the luxury condominium building. Waiting for the elevator, he couldn't shake the cold that seemed to have seeped into every molecule of his body. But in his heart he knew that the warmth he sought would not return.

CHAPTER TWENTY-SEVEN

"THIS IS BARRETT, leave a message," Jane heard, for the tenth time, before closing her phone with a snap. She couldn't believe that Lindy had rushed out of the church without saying good-bye.

His note said he was feeling sick, and he didn't want to put his comeback in jeopardy. Afraid he had contracted her flu, she couldn't set her guilt aside to enjoy her dinner with Paul.

"He still isn't answering. Do you think I should go to his apartment to check on him?"

"Jane, Lindy is a big boy. I'm sure he has plenty of women and doctors to care for him. He was the one who left. If he wanted your help, he would have waited for you. I'm sure he called one of his women to come and pick him up. She's probably tending to his every need as we speak." Paul straightened his napkin with military precision, his face expressionless, but in his eyes Jane could see his cool facade cracking like a weathered oil painting.

Jane reached across the table and placed her hand on his. "Paul, Lindy is my friend. I'm concerned about his health, nothing more. I love you, remember."

Without breaking their connected gaze, he turned his hand over and clasped hers in a gentle squeeze. "I love you, too. I can't believe the jealousy you provoke in me," he confessed. "This is a new feeling, for me. Never in my life have I felt so protective or so possessive."

Jane smiled, hoping to mask the wariness she felt at his words.

"I know this has all happened quickly. We only met a few months ago, but it was as if the day we collided with each other at the office, my eyes and heart awoke from a deep sleep. Jane, you make me feel alive in ways I didn't think were possible outside of heaven."

At his words, Jane's heart began to sink, and the nausea she had fought only a week ago due to an illness rose like burning sulfur in her stomach.

"You're everything I always knew God would give me in a partner. I've known, since that first mixed-up date at the coffee shop, that you're the woman I've been praying to meet my entire adult life."

Waves of anxiety rolled through Jane's entire body.

"Jane Eleanor Grey," Paul said, as he stood from his chair and knelt on one knee before her. "I love you. I know this is sudden. I was hoping to wait a few more months, to ease you into the idea, but life happens, jobs change, and I can't imagine being apart from you for another week, let alone two years."

Paul pulled a small blue velvet box from his pocket. Opening on a tiny hinge, the box revealed a sparkling square-cut diamond in a vintage setting. "Jane, will you marry me?"

Jane sat in dumbfounded silence, staring at the ring. "I don't know what to say," she whispered.

"Well, I would like you to say yes." His low, smooth voice matched her own quiet tones.

"I'm just so surprised. Paul, I had no idea this was even in your thoughts." Looking into his face, she could see the pain her delayed answer was causing him, but what could she say?

He returned to his seat across from her, placing the ring box on the table between them as an overt centerpiece "I've known you were my one since practically the first moment we met. I was hoping to have more time to convince you that I was your one, but this Alaska thing isn't being cooperative. Jane, if I could woo you for six more months, or a year, or however long it took to completely make you fall in love with me, I would. But, unfortunately, I don't have the gift of time."

Taking hold of her hand, he tenderly caressed her fingers with his. "Jane, I love you. I want to spend the rest of my life loving you. I want to grow old with you and have children with you. I want to wake up beside you every morning and go to sleep every night holding you. You're a gift God has given to the world, and I'm the blessed one who gets to have you in his life, hopefully as his wife."

Overwhelmed by the sincerity and passion of Paul's words, Jane couldn't speak. His gentle touch was easing her apprehension and her fear, but the enemy of doubt crept its ugly way into the haven of love Paul had created.

"Paul, I love you, too, but this is so sudden. I'm not an impulsive person. I know it's not fair to you, but can I have a little time to think about it? To pray about it?"

Jane watched his hope-filled green eyes turn heavy with disappointment as he reluctantly nodded. She squeezed his hands before closing the ring box and sliding the box back to him to keep.

"No," he said with a shake of his head. "Please, wear it while you consider. I picked it out for you."

The reflection of authentic and raw love Jane saw on his face nearly broke her resolve. "Paul, that wouldn't be right."

"Wear it on your right hand, as a reminder of how much I love you." Paul lifted the ring from the box and slid the beautiful piece onto her right-hand ring finger.

The weight of platinum was light in comparison to the immensity of the symbolism the ring held. Jane admired the ring with a slight smile on her lips, unable to stop the feminine reaction to sparkly objects.

"Paul, it really is exquisite." Looking away from the ring and into Paul's eyes, she saw the hurt of her subtle rejection lingering behind his now composed passive expression. "I do love you. Please, know that. I need to make sure that I make the right decision. This is not one of those areas where I can renege at the last minute. I have to be sure. You only do this thing once."

He laced his right hand with her left, drawing her fingers to his lips. He kissed each one with a featherweight touch, but on the ring finger he lingered a moment longer, as if to imprint the empty spot with his mark. Even if his ring would not adorn the finger, he was making sure Jane knew his intentions.

Pulling her into an embrace with only his eyes, Paul rested his chin on their linked hands. "I know you love me, Jane. I just hope you're in love with me."

CHAPTER TWENTY-EIGHT

Driving home on I-270 South a week after the proposal, Jane was no closer to answering Paul. Her mind told her that marrying him was the right thing to do, but her heart was having doubts despite Paul's intense efforts to sway her decision. Paul had been pouring on the woo like tanning oil at the beach. In the past seven days, they'd had six dinners, followed by dancing, cuddly walks along the river, and late-night chats on the couch. He sent her flowers every other day and even wrote her a love letter, or at least a lawyer's typewritten, letterhead version of a love letter. He was trying to cram a year's worth of romance into a handful of days. He was pulling it off brilliantly.

Jane was beginning to envision their life together. She could see the two of them, with their curly-blonde-haired children, lined up in a pew at church or on the front porch, sipping iced tea on a rare warm evening in Alaska. She knew all of the elements for a happily-ever-after life were wrapped up in Paul's proposal. And yet she struggled. Her mind was bending to Paul's will, but each time she asked her heart to vote, Lindy was the unanimous candidate, even if he had become the vanishing Mr. Barrett.

She had left Lindy several messages, with no response. He had recovered from whatever bug he had the night of the church service. The paper reported Lindy was back to full-contact practices on Sunday, and he had played ten minutes in the previous night's game. Millie invited Jane to the game, but Paul had already made dinner reservations, giving her an easy excuse. Jane was reluctant to share with her friend her fear that Lindy would completely ignore her if he saw her, just as he had ignored her phone calls.

She knew she was being ridiculous. She was yearning for a man who obviously didn't care about her, at least not anymore. The passage from

Jeremiah about the heart being deceitful above all things was a touchstone as she struggled with her answer to Paul's proposal. Her mind wanted to say yes, but her heart held her back. The road between her head and her heart was like the worst freeway construction, and the two-way traffic was at a complete standstill.

Exiting the highway, Jane heard her phone ring. She answered the call with a push to the speakerphone button. "Hello."

"Hey, stranger, where have you been hiding my best friend?" Millie's voice filled Jane's BMW.

"Sorry, how was the game last night? It sounded like Jason was stellar."

"He was magnificent. Jane, I don't know how I ever doubted your enjoyment for the sport. What those boys do on the ice is like an artfully frozen ballet. Well, if ballerinas were two hundred pounds, wore twenty pounds of gear, and sweated like prostitutes in church."

"Mill, as always, you're always clever with a turn of phrase."

"Life is interesting. It deserves color commentary. Now, stop avoiding the reason I'm calling. Have you made a decision?"

"I don't know what to say," Jane honestly whined. "I do love Paul, but I feel like something is holding me back."

"Janesie, something is two hundred and thirty-five pounds, is the leading scorer for Columbus, and has been acting like someone shot his puppy for the last week."

"Lindy is not the problem."

"Dunderhead, you know he is. You have been in lust with that guy since you were twenty years old. Now, you know him, like him as a person, and if I had to bet every penny I made in Europe on it, I would say you're head over heels in love him."

Jane rolled into her parking space and turned off her car. Leaning her head back against the soft black leather of her driver's seat, she spoke. "Millie, I think I've read one too many Jane Austen books and seen one too many Cary Grant movies, because I'm turning myself into a tortured heroine. Who says, 'Let me think about it,' to a perfect guy like Paul? How can he love someone who is as indecisive as I am? I'm going to wind up like one of those Grey Manor ladies, in that whacked-out documentary, with like a thousand cats living with me, and only Lizzie to take care of me in my old age." Tears rolled down Jane's warm cheeks as the words erupted from her mouth.

"Well," Millie began in slow, deliberate speech. "First, the thought that Lizzie will be the one to take care of you is a stretch. Second, I don't think you're in any danger of winding up like one of those crazy ladies in the Hamptons, and the two-carat beast you're wearing on your right hand agrees. Third, you're the one making your life complicated, no one else."

"What do you mean?" She wiped the tears from her eyes.

"What I mean is, if you want to be married to Paul, hang up the phone and call him. If you want to be with Lindy, drive over to his place and tell him you love him. You're in total control of this whole situation."

"But Lindy doesn't like me anymore. I think I forced too much church on him, and he finally had enough. He left the worship service without saying good-bye. He won't return any of my phone calls. I'm starting to feel like a groupie and a little stalkerish. I think our friendship is over. And you want me to just blurt out that I love him when he had some girl I've never met pick him up at church?"

"Jane, Lindy didn't call a girl to come pick him up Saturday. Brad brought him back to his apartment. I guess the worship service struck a nerve in him. He didn't tell Jason much, but from what I could drag out of my rather uninformative boyfriend, Lindy didn't feel like he was good enough to be at the church."

"What?"

"That is all I know, friend, but I don't think you're going to get a response simply by leaving the guy messages. He's pretty disciplined, and if he's decided he's no good for God, he's probably decided he's no good for you, either," Millie concluded.

"Do you really think so?" Jane could feel her sixteen-year-old self twirling inside her, the glimmer of hope fueling her dance.

"Yes, I do. But Jane, at the end of the day, whether you accept Paul's proposal or take a leap of faith and profess your feelings to Lindy, you have to make sure the decision is right for you. I'll admit I've seen you and Lindy together more than I've seen you and Paul. Maybe. I'm missing something in regard to your relationship with Paul, I don't know. Maybe he really is the one. And all of my talk and prodding is only causing you to doubt your feelings for him because you're afraid he'll hurt you like Brad did. I don't have a Magic 8 Ball that can give you an answer. Only you can answer the question of who you really want to be with."

Silence filled Jane's car as Millie's voice went quiet. Jane knew Millie was giving her the time she needed to process her thoughts and to devise a plan.

"Millie, my whole life, I've been waiting to be loved the way Paul loves me. He cherishes me. I know it's an old-fashioned word, but that's how he makes me feel. And most of the time it feels good, if I can let my heart and mind be in the moment . . ."

"But . . ." Millie countered, forcing Jane to finish her thought.

"But keeping my heart and mind focused on Paul isn't easy. I feel like Paul the apostle—I do what I don't want to do and not what I know I should. I want to be in love with Paul. That should be enough, shouldn't it?"

"I don't know."

Jane was quiet for a few more minutes before she said good-bye to her walking-and-talking conscience, Millie.

Jane remained in her car for nearly twenty minutes after ending the call. She knew Millie was right. She had to make a decision. She wanted to make the safe choice, the bird-in-the-hand decision, giving her a soft, simple landing. However, Jane knew this wasn't a moment for fence-sitting or easy choices. This was the moment when she needed to leap off of the cliff and trust God would catch her.

She turned her key in the ignition, backed her car out of her parking space, pressed the gas pedal, and sped toward the cliff.

CHAPTER TWENTY-NINE

As Jane drove to Lindy's apartment, her mind raced through several conversations and possible outcomes. Maybe he would open the door and pull her into his arms, declaring his love for her. Or he would laugh at her as he turned to make out with the voluptuous blonde she secretly suspected would be draped over his couch.

Jane knew she had to talk to Lindy, even if she would be embarrassed to her core, need to change her name and enter the witness protection program. Regardless of her fears, she couldn't start a marriage with Paul without knowing that a start with Lindy was impossible.

Her BMW rolled to a stop in front of Lindy's building. Stepping from the car, she gave O'Connor her keys, asking him if she could leave the car parked in the circle. He squeezed her hand in affirmation, and she gave him an apprehensive smile before heading to the bank of elevators. The center elevator doors opened with soundless precision. She stepped across the small gap and pressed the button for the top floor. As the elevator ascended, her confidence in Lindy's feelings for her dropped like a counterweight.

With the exception of a little flirtation, Lindy had shown only the slightest interest in her romantically. She was braving utter humiliation based on a "feeling" from her best friend and the confession of his mother, who clearly wanted a nice girl for her son. The conviction she'd felt while leaving her parking lot fled her, and she began to hit all of the elevator's down keys to avert going to the penthouse floor and facing her fears.

The elevator was evil and adamantly set against her; the buttons lit up in an artful array akin to Christmas lights, but the steel box was undeterred from its initial mission. The bell, announcing her arrival on Lindy's floor, sounded like a gong as the doors opened and she stepped into the slick-floored hall.

She noticed that Lindy's door was cracked open, indicating that he must have visitors. Taking the unexpected guests as a stay to her appointment with the romantic firing squad, she turned on her heel back to the elevator, pressing the down button in a telegraphic rhythm. But the elevator, her nemesis, was having the last laugh, as she watched the numbers scroll on the computer screen above the door. The merciless object was stopping on every floor on its way back down to the lobby.

"You're just mean," she hissed.

Pacing in front of the elevator doors, she kept a close eye on Lindy's door, afraid she wouldn't make her escape before he came into the hall with his guests. What had she been thinking? Someone like her would never be able to have a romantic relationship with someone like Lindy Barrett.

Lindy Barrett. She would probably always use his full name. The famous, intelligent, gorgeous hockey player who could have any woman he wanted without any religious or ethical strings attached. He was out of her league, and she should be okay with that knowledge. She had a man, a godly man, who loved her and wanted to make a life with her. Why was she trying to mess things up over some romantic fantasy that should have ended the day she moved out of the dorm and threw her poster of him in the Dumpster?

She watched the numbers above the elevator grow larger; getting through those doors was paramount. She would drive directly to Paul's house, accept his proposal, and put her longing for Lindy in a scrapbook where it belonged.

She heard the ding before the doors opened wide. Stepping through, she pushed the button for the lobby and watched as the mirrored doors shut on the part of her life that included Lindy Barrett. Tears pooled in her eyes, threatening to spill down her cheeks, as she looked heavenward and yanked the ring from her right finger, jamming it onto her left.

God, please forgive me for doubting Your plan, she prayed as she rubbed her ring finger and its new adornment.

Sinking in a pit of shame over her misstep into lust, she was shocked to find the doors rip open with the strength of a single hand. Quickly, she wiped the fallen tears from her cheeks and looked up at the smiling face of the man she loved, but could not have.

"Jane, why didn't you come in?" Lindy asked, holding the door open with his arm. "O'Connor called up ten minutes ago to say you had arrived."

Jane stood resolute in her spot and pressed her back tightly against the elevator wall, fearing that her sixteen-year-old would take control.

"No, you have company. I wanted to check in on you and make sure you're okay."

"I'm sorry I haven't called you back. I've been . . . well, it's been a pretty big week, and I wasn't sure I could talk to anyone." He leaned against the elevator door frame.

"I understand," she lied. "Glad to see you're back on your feet. Well, I'll get going. I stopped on my way to Paul's." She pressed the lobby button.

"Oh." The smile in Lindy's eyes dimmed with the mention of Paul's name.

"I'll let you get back to your guest. I didn't mean to disturb you."

"Jane, can't you come in for a minute? There is so much I have to tell you."

"Really?" She stepped toward him, searching his face for some olive branch of hope. "I have a lot to tell you, too."

Smiling down at her, he brushed her cheek with the back of his hand, sending a tremor of heat through her body like melted honey, before taking both of her hands in his. "Jane, there's so much to say . . ."

He broke off abruptly as his large, calloused fingers rolled over Paul's ring. He dropped her hands as if the metal burned his skin. "But maybe you should start?"

Jane's cheeks burned with traitorous guilt. "Paul asked me to marry him."

"And I'm guessing you said yes? Congratulations." He stuffed his hands into his pockets, stepping way from her.

"Not yet," she said as walked out of the elevator, closing the space he had created. "But I was going to give him an answer tonight."

She looked up at the stunningly handsome, yet amazingly kindhearted gentleman before her, searching his face for an answer to the question she had been harboring in her heart. "Is there any reason I shouldn't say yes?" Her voice sounded weak and frail to her own ears, but at least she had enough bravery left in her belly to ask the question.

Lindy rocked onto his heels as he shoved his hands deeper into his jean pockets. "I was traded tonight."

Jane took a step back, shaking her head in confusion. "What?"

"The team traded me to the 'Canes. I'm leaving in the morning for a ten-day West Coast trip."

"But why," she asked, stunned by the news that Columbus would trade its marquee player.

"I'm on the last few months of my contract, and we couldn't come to an equitable agreement. By trading me, they clear some cap space and move me to the other conference."

"Are you okay with moving to North Carolina?"

He leaned back against the wall of the hallway "It's only for a few months, and I don't really have a choice. The team is good and should make a decent run in the playoffs, so hockey speaking, I'm okay with it."

She searched his face. Was he going to let her walk away? "I can't believe you won't be in Columbus anymore."

He shrugged his shoulders. "It doesn't sound like you will be, either."

"Huh? Oh, yeah, Paul," she said disjointedly.

"He's a great guy, Jane. I hope you both will be very happy."

"Umm . . . thanks." Jane was so confused. How had this conversation taken such a turn? This wasn't one of the rehearsed versions she had conducted during drive over.

"You'd better invite me," he said with a subtle grin. "Don't forget about your old dumb hockey-player friend once you're a Mrs. Somebody Smart."

She tried to smile up at him, but her mind was completely befuddled by his words. Had she misread those initial moments in the elevator? She thought she saw tenderness in his eyes as he had reached for her hands, but now he was talking about her wedding and confirming an invitation. She was definitely having a mental breakdown from the stress of the last month and would wake up in the OSU psych ward in the morning.

"You probably should get going. I know how jealous Paul is of your time." He leaned forward and pressed the button for the elevator.

Unable to speak, Jane merely nodded her head.

They waited in tense silence for the elevator to reach the top floor. Jane wondered if she should try again but decided against it. Lindy clearly seemed in favor of her marriage to Paul. If he had any feelings for her, he wouldn't let her go so easily.

The doors opened, signaling her exit. Silently, she stepped inside.

"Bye," she said, unable to turn and face him.

"Give your old friend a hug for the road, okay?"

Turning, she stepped into his open arms and breathed deeply in his embrace. Lindy's hug enveloped every inch of Jane, cocooning her in his welcoming warmth.

Their bodies fit perfectly together, as if God had created them from one piece of cloth. She didn't want him to let her go, but his hands loosened their grip, and his arms unwound their embrace.

He leaned his forehead against hers. "Good-bye, Beautiful."

She looked into his eyes, unable to stop the tears as they raced down her cheeks. "Bye, Lindy."

She slid away from him before she gave in to the temptation for one more hug, one last touch. She pushed the button inside the elevator for the lobby and watched through a watery haze as the doors smoothly shut without anyone to stop them.

—⁓—

Lindy jammed his hands in his pockets to keep himself from stopping her. He stood in the spot she'd left, hoping the doors would reopen on their own; hoping she would change her mind and the last few minutes had been a nightmare. He didn't know how long he stared at his muddled reflection before he heard the slight cough coming from the direction of his penthouse. Turning, he saw his new friend and spiritual mentor, Brad, standing in the doorway.

"I'm guessing you didn't tell her that you accepted Jesus this week or that you're in love with her?"

CHAPTER THIRTY

ONCE THE DOORS SHUT to Lindy's floor, Jane's tears exploded from her eyes like a tapped fire hydrant. In the lobby, O'Connor handed her keys to her car. She mumbled, "Thank you," before hastily exiting the building. She drove along the river and then stopped and parked by the Firefighters Memorial.

Drawing her coat tight across her chest, she braved the wind cutting a bitter path down Marconi Boulevard. She stared at the memorial, entranced by its flame, which continued to burn against the cold night air. Her internal flame was about as dim as a birthday candle, and she didn't know where she was going to find the energy to talk to Paul.

She knew she needed to turn down his proposal. How could she marry one man when her heart belonged to another? It wasn't like they were living in Victorian England and she needed a man to protect her from the wicked world. But the idea of spending her life alone was painful.

She loved Paul, but did she love him enough to offset the love she held for Lindy? She couldn't be sure she could give her whole heart to Paul. She knew she had to return his ring and turn down his proposal.

She turned from the memorial and the memories of the first night she and Lindy had met, walking with purpose to her car, knowing what she had to do. The cliff wasn't as tall as it had been earlier, but what lay beneath was still as unknown as she drove the short distance to Paul's apartment.

When Paul opened the door to her, she was overwhelmed with the look of love and adoration on his face.

"I thought you needed to be alone today. This is an unexpected surprise." He drew her into a tight embrace and kissed the top of her head.

Jane waited for the chaotic onslaught of sensation to spread through her as it had when Lindy had held her in his arms, but instead she found a gentle peace, akin to coming home after a long journey. Paul placed his hands on either side of her face and brushed his lips to hers in a tender kiss, which left her with a feeling of lukewarm contentment.

Applying a light pressure to his chest, Jane broke the kiss. "Can we talk?"

"Of course . . . I'm sorry. You didn't even make it through the front door, and here I am, ravishing you." He took her coat as she walked ahead to his open living room. Taking a seat on the couch, she tried to organize her thoughts amid the disorganization of packing boxes and newspaper around the room.

Paul was leaving. Lindy was leaving. Was Jane really ready to be entirely alone again? She'd spent most of her life single, and if she was honest with herself, she preferred being part of a unit, but was she willing to sacrifice complete happiness just to be "a part" rather than apart?

Paul walked into the room, and Jane took in his agile form. He didn't fill the room with his overwhelming physical presence, but rather with the stealth aura of a hawk. He was as handsome today as he had been the first day in the office lobby, but his face alone wasn't what kept drawing her to him. He was a man after God's own heart. He was one of the most gentle and kind men she had ever known. He was a little rigid at times, but she appreciated his discipline and his dedication to God. When she was with him, she felt as if she were pleasing God. What more could she ask from a man?

Paul took a seat beside her on the couch and stretched his arm along the back of the sofa. "Sorry about the mess. The official packers come on Monday, but there are some things I wanted to go through before they arrived."

"Don't worry."

He cupped her chin in his hand with a gentle caress. "What has that pretty face of yours looking so sad?"

She subtly pulled her chin from his touch. "I thought we should talk."

"Jane, sweetie, you're making me nervous." He reached for her hands, and his concerned expression quickly turned to joy as he examined her ring finger. "Well, this is good news."

Jane snatched her fingers out of his hands, quickly stood, and began pacing the room, searching for the right words as a squadron of butterflies took flight in her stomach. Turning to Paul, who sat silently on the couch, her words rushed from her lips like a runaway freight train. "I don't know if I can marry you, Paul. I want to. I want to be your wife and to have your babies. I want to grow old with you, and all that other stuff you talked about last Saturday, but I'm scared."

His smile dissipated as soon as she admitted her fear. He stood and rested his hands on her shoulders, stopping her nervous pacing. "Jane, I'm scared, too."

Jane's butterflies landed safely as she mentally clung to the comfort offered in his eyes. "Really?"

"Really." He brushed an errant lock of hair from her face and let out a soft sigh. "I'm scared that I'm not good enough for you and that I'll be a terrible husband. I'm scared that you'll hate Alaska and blame me for dragging you away from your family. I'm scared that you're settling for me, when someone better could come along."

Guilt reared its ugly two-faced head, dumping a two-hundred-thirty-five-pound weight on her heart. She dropped her gaze to Paul's chest and spoke to the floor.

"Paul, I have feelings for Lindy." Her words were a mere whisper, but she knew he heard her because his hands tightened on her arms before relaxing.

"I know you do, Jane."

She looked up into his green eyes, expecting accusation, but instead saw kindness tinged with melancholy.

"I know you care about Lindy." His eyes reflected the pain he must have felt with the words. "I know you have feelings for him. I'm just hoping, and praying, that the feelings you have for me are strong enough to overshadow the ones you have for him."

No human being could be so generous in spirit. "I don't deserve you in my life." She blinked away her tears. "I've cried more today than I did when Shelly Stivers tickled me until I peed my pants on the playground in the second grade."

He tugged her tightly against his chest and chuckled. "Jane, only you could come up with that memory at a time like this." But when he stepped back from her, his face held a serious expression as his gaze locked with hers. "Jane, do you love me?"

She could feel her cheeks warm under his intense scrutiny. "Yes."

"Jane, will you marry me?"

A sense of peace washed over her like a warm summer rain. This man was willing to look past her concerns and her unfaithful feelings, and generously offer to share his life with her. She could only give one answer.

"Yes."

CHAPTER THIRTY-ONE

THE WEEKS FOLLOWING JANE'S engagement flew by in a haze of organza and packing. Jane and Paul celebrated their newly confirmed commitment with calls to both their parents that same night. She talked her mother off the engagement-party-and-bridal-shower ledge by agreeing to a tented, flower-filled ceremony at the farm in late April for three hundred of Bitsy's closest friends.

She shared the announcement with Molly and Millie, asking the ladies to serve as matron and maid of honor at lunch the following afternoon. Molly excitedly ignored the pink elephant, squealing about how fat she would look in the bridesmaid dress. Millie could not be counted on for the same unspoken need for discretion.

"Did you chicken out with the hockey player?"

Looking from her menu, she gave Millie a look that clearly explained to her that the subject was closed.

Millie picked up her own menu and perused the entrées for a few minutes. "He does love you, whether he's in Columbus, Raleigh, or Timbuktu."

"Drop it, Millie."

"Nope." She studied Jane over the rim of her glass before taking a long drink.

"For your information, best friend, I did go see Lindy Barrett, and he didn't go all lovey-dovey on me. He actually congratulated me on my upcoming marriage to Paul. Your unrequited-love theory has now been debunked. Can we make the discussion of Lindy Barrett an unmentionable?"

Molly nodded her head, but Millie pressed. "But did you tell him you loved him?"

"I don't love him, Millie." The lie left an acid taste in her mouth, but she was committed to Paul. Lindy was in her past. "And, despite your all-knowing intuition, he doesn't love me. Please drop it."

After that lunch, the subject of Lindy Barrett was closed, and she went about closing her life in Columbus and forging a new life in Alaska.

The night she accepted Paul's proposal, they discussed Jane's various career options. Paul offered a myriad of suggestions, plans, and options. He had obviously thought through the obstacle of Jane's career, and the idea that he sought to put her needs to the forefront in the middle of changing his entire life reaffirmed Jane's decision. Ultimately, the couple decided that Jane should resign from her position at DLT and seek a new opportunity in Juneau.

When she thought about the move, she was filled with a mix of trepidation and drowning fear. With the exception of graduate school, she had not lived more than a forty-five-minute drive from her family her entire life. She wasn't only moving or changing jobs, but she was getting married. Life was moving faster than the methodical planner inside her could handle.

A week after she accepted Paul's proposal, he returned to Alaska, but he made her book her flight for Valentine's Day before he left. He said he wanted to pay for the ticket, but she secretly believed he was afraid that once he was gone, she would change her mind. His fear was unfounded. Despite the shaky ground on which her acceptance had been given, Jane felt more confident each day that she had made the right choice. And she was committed. Once she committed, there was no turning back for Jane.

January rolled into February—the shortest month on the calendar was undoubtedly the longest month for Ohio weather—and Jane turned in her resignation at DLT. Last summer, when she had her first moments of her premature midlife crisis with Millie, she'd known she needed a change. At the time, the two best friends decided that the change she needed was to leave DLT behind her. Little did she know that the change would be giving up DLT for MRS.

In her last days at the company, she was in the midst of completing her client transfers, when her office phone rang. "Hello, this is Jane Grey."

"Hi, Jane, this is Dr. Macintosh . . . Wilbur. We met at the Children's Hospital benefit last fall."

She smiled as she recognized the doctor's broken New England accent. "Dr. Macintosh, it's so good to hear from you. How have you been?"

"Oh, quite well, thank you, despite all of this wintry weather we can't seem to shake."

"Yes, it's a bit of a disaster these days. Doctor, to what do I owe this unexpected call?" Jane asked.

"Oh, yes, my call. Well, we here at the center are starting the preparations for a new fundraising campaign and thought you might be able to help us."

Jane stared at the phone, astonished by his request. Not since that horrible interview had Jane even thought about event planning as a career, and now, all these months later, the opportunity was being placed before her. "Dr. Macintosh, thank you so much for thinking of me. I'm truly honored and wish I could help you, but I'm getting married in a couple months, and I'll be moving to be with my future husband."

"Oh, that's too bad. I really thought you would be a good fit. Maybe you could do it from your new home? Kind of a long-distance thing?"

A tickle of excitement fluttered in Jane's belly. "Umm . . . I guess I'll have to give it a little thought. When do you need to know?"

"Oh, if you could let me know in the next couple of weeks, that would be just fine."

"Okay. I'll give you a call soon."

"Good. Good. I was sad to hear Lindy was traded away from our city. He was such a faithful giver to a variety of charities, but maybe if we keep his future wife in our loop, we'll get to keep him as well," Dr. Macintosh said.

Swift pain rocketed through Jane's heart. "Doctor, I think you're mistaken. I'm not marrying Lindy." She hoped her voice reflected a calm she didn't feel.

"Really, well then, whoever could you be marrying? The two of you looked so much on the verge of love last fall. It didn't surprise me in the least when you said you were to be married. Although I was a little surprised that Lindy hadn't told me himself when I called to get your phone number."

"Well, that would be because I'm not marrying Lindy." Jane tried to hold her temper as she responded to the doctor's rambling. "My fiancé's name is Paul. He's an attorney."

"Oh, well, I guess that's nice, too."

"Thanks." *Doctor, you are a wackadoodle.*

"I don't want to keep you any longer. I look forward to hearing your answer, but only if it's a yes, Miss Grey."

"I'll definitely consider it, Doctor."

After the call ended, she shook off the conversation and tried to ignore the boxed up-feelings the mention of Lindy's name had ripped open. She was marrying Paul, whom she loved, and she had the possibility of a future business in the making. She was on cloud nine, or at least she would be, as soon as she had those feelings shoved into a better-sealed box. She definitely needed a bigger box.

A few days after Dr. Macintosh's unexpected call, she turned in her badge and corporate credit card, saying her final good-byes to DLT. With the end of her DLT career, her mother went into full wedding-planner mode, treating Jane as her trusty assistant. In between fittings, tasting menus, band auditions and guest list approvals, Jane was able to sublet her apartment and put all her furniture in storage. She knew she'd be back one day, and she refused to say good-bye to her favorite yellow chair or her view of High Street.

By the time her Valentine's excursion to Alaska arrived, she was quite ready for a vacation from Hurricane Bitsy. Unfortunately, her trip to Alaska fell short of her romantic expectations. Instead of the cozy dinner Paul had planned at the hotel restaurant, they ate takeout Chinese food in her hotel room while he went over his notes.

Jane spent her week in Juneau looking for a place for the couple to share after their honeymoon. She wanted something that was bright and cheery, but in the middle of the long winter in a frozen rainforest, bright and cheery were the proverbial needles in the haystack. She was careful not to complain to Paul, who wanted her to love the wilderness as much as he did. When Jane boarded the plane to Columbus a week later, she called Millie to get a much-needed pep talk from her own personal cheerleader.

"Sweetie, you knew Alaska was all gray and gross before you left. Besides, you should be used to gray—you grew up in C-bus."

"Millie, that is not the kind of pep talk I was looking for," Jane replied as she found her seat on the plane.

"Okay, how about this: you're fabulous and you're marrying a man who loves you, so you'd better get used to Alaska because that's where he is. Is that better?"

Millie's pep talk made Jane feel as if she were sinking into a bottomless pit of gray. "Marginally."

"Hey, I'm a little bummed myself, what with the great days of winter bearing down on us like a grizzly looking for his next meal. It's hard to be peppy in the midst of the February doldrums."

"Did you try on the bridesmaid dress?"

"Jane Eleanor Grey," Millie shrieked, forcing Jane to hold her phone away from her ear. "It's only because of the years I've dedicated to this friendship that I'm willing to even think about wearing that awful excuse for a dress. Who decided to put Emory in charge of picking out the bridal attire?"

"Well, she was so hurt that you and Molly both had special titles, I had to make one up for her. I told her there was an old English tradition of the youngest sister being in charge of the dressmaking for the bride and her bridesmaids. Who knew she would think I was serious? It's going to say *bridesmaid dresser* instead of *bridesmaid* by her name in the program."

"I still cannot believe that child is going to graduate from law school. It's a good thing that Baylor is rich and she'll never have to actually practice law," Millie retorted.

"Well, regardless, it pacified her. I'm sorry your dresses are so, well, so pink."

"Did you know she wants us to wear gloves? We're going to look like what you throw up after you down a bottle of Pepto."

Jane couldn't stifle her laughter. She knew her friend was right. For all of her sister's desired fashion sense, she really was clueless. "Just be happy you don't have her picking out your wedding dress. For the rest of my life, I'll have to look at pictures of myself in that dress. To my someday children, I'll point out that I'm the one who looks like she should be on top of a lemon pie in the pictures." Jane could hear the instructions from the flight attendant and knew she only had a few more minutes before she would be forced to say good-bye to her friend.

Millie snorted. "I'll give you that. Emory is definitely not allowed to attend my dress-shopping excursions for my wedding this summer."

"Your what?" Jane ignored the angry stares from her fellow passengers as the flight attendant reminded them to stow all electronic devices before takeoff.

"My wedding. Jason proposed on Valentine's Day. I know it's super cheesy, but he's super cheesy. It was amazing and wonderful, and even though I know we don't know each other that well, I couldn't wait any longer. I love him, Janesie. I really love him. He's smart and sexy. He cares about me and what I want. He doesn't think I'm just another pretty face. And he was totally cool with the whole waiting-until-we're-married thing, which is so crazy, since he's a jock, but it just shows how special he is, right? Please be happy for me."

"Oh my goodness, I'm so happy for you. This is amazing! I can't believe we've been talking about ugly dresses and gross weather when we could've been talking about your proposal." Jane could feel the ominous stare before she looked up and saw the rather large flight attendant shaking her head and finger at her. "I have to go, friend, but you must write down every detail so you don't forget a single one between now and when I land in Columbus in twelve hours. I love you. Can you believe we're both getting married? God is so good."

"Yes, He is." Millie's voice was light and dreamy as the friends shared a final good-bye.

Jane's heart felt like it was filled with helium as a wide grin stretched across her face. She turned her phone off and rested her head against the seat. Closing her eyes, she could see the coming months unfolding before her and her light as air heart began to sink in her chest, slowly wiping the smile from her face.

Millie and I are both getting married. And Millie is in love. Isn't that nice?

Jane's eyes snapped open. *Nice . . .*

———

When Jane landed in Columbus, the pace of the wedding plans went from Saturday afternoon drive to the Indy 500. She barely had a moment to get settled into her old bedroom at the farm before her mother tangled her in the web of details. As March roared in like a lion, Jane was working full days orchestrating a wedding she was beginning to feel was for someone else.

Trying to keep her sanity, she agreed to sign on as Dr. Macintosh's event planner. He was thrilled and even mentioned that a few other non-profits in town were looking for event planning consultants. She spoke to all of the good doctor's contacts, and by the end of March she had five clients and a small business she was running from her high-school desk. Most of the coordination for the events could be managed via e-mail, teleconferencing, and Web links, giving Jane the freedom to move her business wherever she wanted. Her excitement over her new venture grew apace with her fear of the wedding.

Jane began giving herself daily, and then hourly, pep talks about the blessed event. The wedding had spun completely out of control. Between her mother's friends, her dad's buddies, and the lengthy list of associates Paul felt he had to invite, the guest list was teetering at close to five hundred people. Her parents' farm definitely had the space to accommodate the large crowd, but to Jane, the wedding was losing its meaning.

Curled up in her bed two weeks before the big day, she shared her concerns with Paul over the phone. "I want to make sure this is about God bringing us together as a couple, not about our parents throwing a killer party."

"Jane, it's about God being at the center of our marriage. But there are expectations that need to be met. A fancy party does not diminish God's importance in our lives."

"Doesn't it?"

"No, it doesn't. You need to stop worrying and start focusing on the fact that you're a beautiful bride-to-be who's about to make me the happiest man on the face of the planet."

She forced a smile into her voice as she said her good-byes, but her doubt over the ceremony and reception lingered. She knew that she and Paul had their focus on the Lord, but something didn't feel right. Perhaps it was the combination of the rushed wedding, the hideous dresses, and her growing envy over the simplicity of the Mediterranean ceremony Millie and Jason had planned for early May. With the Jackets out of playoff contention, the couple had decided to move their date forward. Millie wanted Jane to be there as her witness, but the timing didn't look like it was going to work with Jane's honeymoon. She was trying to convince Paul that the coast of Italy would make a nice detour for whatever secret honeymoon destination he had planned.

Millie's wedding was exactly what Jane had always dreamed her own wedding would be. Simple and authentic. No frills or fancy nuts; just her closest friends and family celebrating. Her wedding extravaganza was a compromise she was willing to make to please Paul and her mother. It was only a wedding, after all. The marriage was what was important.

Thrusting her worries into her box that night, she snuggled under the mound of covers, hiding her face in the pillows of her old canopy bed and began to pray herself to sleep. "God, my Holy and Wonderful Father, thank You for this day and for Your blessings that are so abundant in my life. Thank You for the health of my family and my friends. Lord God, please help to ease the anxiety I'm feeling over this party. It's really silly, actually. It shouldn't matter what I wear, or what food we're serving, as long as I'm marrying the man You have chosen for me."

Jane paused and in a whisper asked, "I am, aren't I?"

She waited for an answer, even a feeling of confirmation, but her room remained silent.

CHAPTER THIRTY-TWO

THREE DAYS BEFORE THE WEDDING, Jane leisurely made her way
down from her room to the breakfast nook. She'd been given a blessed
reprieve for the day. Her mother had scheduled herself an elaborate spa fes-
tival filled with peels, waxes, coloring, and exfoliating. The whole ordeal was
more than Jane could endure, and she begged off, claiming she needed to tie
up a few loose ends with her business before the honeymoon. She longed for
the two-week trip to escape the days bursting with Jordan Almonds, gravy
boats, and table assignments.

Padding into the kitchen in socked feet and pajama pants, Jane was
surprised to see her early-rising father still in the kitchen. "Hi, Daddy," Jane
said, kissing his clean-shaven cheek.

"Hi, peanut, there's fresh coffee in the pot, and your mom made some
blueberry muffins this morning that are out-of-this-world good," he said as
he refocused his attention on the sports pages.

Jane poured herself a much-needed cup of coffee and placed a muffin on a plate before settling in the seat across from her father. "Anything
interesting?"

"Not too much. The Reds started this season pretty much how they
ended last season, losing. I didn't think times could get worse then when
Marge was in charge, but I've been proven wrong."

"Any news on the Stanley Cup playoffs?" she asked nonchalantly.

"Well, with the Jackets out, I hadn't really been paying much attention.
But it looks like your friend Lindy was hurt last night."

"What?" Jane snatched the paper from her father's hands.

"I would have given it to you if you had only asked."

"Sorry, Daddy," she apologized half-heartedly as she scanned the headlines. "Former Jacket Sustains Season-Ending Injury in OT Loss."

Jane's stomach dropped to her toes as she skimmed the article. Lindy had collided with a Penguins defenseman driving the puck across the blue line. The article said that the injury was to his surgically repaired knee and that the Hurricane's organization wasn't releasing details about the treatment. Her heart twisted at the thought of another injury for Lindy. She knew that he was only one bad hit away from ending his career. She hoped this wasn't that hit.

The two friends had not spoken since they said their good-byes in Lindy's hallway. As she reflected on that moment, she knew she'd made the right decision saving her pride that night. Now that she was removed from the emotional intensity of those weeks, she realized a man like Lindy could never have returned her feelings. He was probably on to a new girl in Raleigh, or maybe many new girls in Raleigh. She doubted he'd ever thought of her as more than his good friend.

She had abided by Lindy's request and sent him a wedding invitation. In return, he sent his regrets and a lovely antique Bible for a wedding present. She understood she shouldn't have been impressed with the gift, but the thoughtfulness was touching, as was the card he'd written.

He told Jane and Paul that he admired their faith and the strength and righteousness that faith instilled in each of them. He hoped their marriage was blessed and happy. His message was simple, but as she'd read the words two weeks ago with the arrival of the gift, she broke down in a mass of tears alone in her room.

Her room, which once had been a refuge, was now her enemy. The memories of the night of Emory's party hammered at the edges of her mind each night as she tried to fall asleep. She could see Lindy, reclined on her bed, reaching out his hand to her. In the defenseless moments before dreams infiltrate, her mind would rage against her by creating a myriad of fantasies, ranging from Lindy kissing her lips to him pulling her into his strong embrace. Her imagination's power was potent, and in an effort to resist its seduction, she had taken to sleeping on the couch when her parents retired early. The wedding could not come soon enough for Jane. She believed that the reality of Paul would be far superior to the fantasy of Lindy.

Jane scanned the hockey articles, hoping to find additional information on Lindy, but the search was futile. What little was written she had already devoured. The news on the 'Canes' playoff run didn't look hopeful. Despite what was described as inspired play by Lindy during the previous night's multiple overtime game, the team was down 3–0 in the series against Pittsburgh. The final game would be Thursday night in Raleigh. She hoped, for Lindy's sake, that the team would lose. She knew he hated having the constant speculation about his injuries as fodder for the various beat reporters. If the 'Canes were knocked out of the playoffs, his injury would become a footnote until summer when free agency began.

Jane gave the paper back to her father and carefully drank her steaming-hot coffee. Her gaze floated out to the side lawn, where a large white tent was already assembled. "Did Mom rent that thing from the State Fair?"

Henry Grey looked up from his paper, slowly sipping his own coffee, as he admired the monstrosity gracing his backyard. "Well, it does look like you could show a pig or two under it. Maybe that's why your sister picked pink for your bridesmaid dresses?"

Jane and her father shared a wink and a smile.

"So, what did it say about your friend's injury?"

"Nothing much, but based on how bad he was in December, I'm not sure if he'll be able to bounce back for another season."

"That's too bad. He's a real nice fella. Between you and me, before Paul showed up at your sister's party, your mother and I thought there might be a little something between the two of you. You two seemed to have a spark, but I've been wrong before when it comes to that kind of thing. I should probably go out and make sure they're not destroying the new grass seed I planted last week." Her father stood and kissed the top of her head "I always love you, peanut. No matter what you decide to do in your life. Know that I'll, always love you."

The unprecedented emotion from her father caused tears to trickle down Jane's cheeks, and she stood, turning into his tight hug. In an instant, she was an eight-year-old little girl, no longer the baby, and too young to follow her older sister. Jane's father had pulled her aside and told her that he always loved her. Whether she was big enough or the baby or someone in between, his love would always be hers.

Jane smiled into his warm flannel shirt as the memory floated through her mind. She stepped back and looked up at her father's weathered face and salt-and-pepper hair. "I love you, too, Daddy. Can you believe I'm getting married on Saturday?"

"No, peanut, I can't. I still see you sitting on that old tire swing, waiting for someone to come and push you. I guess I always thought I would be the only one to do it. Now, you have a new man to push you along."

"Oh, Daddy, please stop or I'll never get my puffy eyes to go down by Saturday, and Mom will kill us both."

"You're right. I'll just be getting at those workers and making sure that my grass is safe." He pulled a handkerchief from his back pocket and wiped it over his eyes as he walked out the door.

Jane dropped back into the seat. Staring into her coffee, she tried to avoid thinking about what her dad had said about her and Lindy and the imagined spark he saw. She was sure it had been his fatherly imagination and hope. But her memory wouldn't let her forget that her father had said the same thing about the spark between Molly and Jake, and the spark between Emory and Baylor. He'd never said anything about a spark between Jane and Paul, but he could be right two out of three times. It was still a pretty good batting average.

CHAPTER THIRTY-THREE

JANE SLEPT POORLY the next two nights, blaming her nerves and her mother's unending lists for her inability to relax into blissful dreamland. Her mind rolled over every detail from the rehearsal dinner to the final exit from the reception. She knew her mother had everything under control, but years of being raised to put on Bitsy Gray bashes didn't allow Jane to let any detail go untouched.

Paul had arrived late Thursday night. His father picked him up at the airport, and Jane didn't see him until lunch on Friday. The meal was the first time they had been in each other's company since the uninspired Valentine's trip. Each time Paul had planned to come home, his trip was postponed due to new hearings, motions, or some other legal catastrophe. As they ordered their sandwiches, less than twenty-four hours before they were to say I do, Jane said a silent prayer of thanks that Paul hadn't let some lawyerly activity keep him from attending his own wedding.

As the waitress left their table to enter their orders, Paul reached his hand across the table and laced his fingers with Jane's. "I missed your face."

"I could have sent you a picture."

"But a picture doesn't have the smart mouth attached."

She snatched her hand from his. "Noted."

They sat in an awkward silence as the natural noise of the sandwich shop swirled around them. Jane tried to think of something, anything, to say, but her mind was blank. She hadn't seen her fiancé, her twenty-four-hours-and-counting husband-to-be, in two months, and she was at a loss for a discussion starter.

"How about those Reds," she threw out.

"Uh, I haven't really seen much ESPN, lately. I've been pretty engrossed in the case. If you want to talk about environmental dumping, I'm your man, but RBI's and homers . . . I'm completely lost."

"Sorry." She retreated back into the silence of their table.

Jane could sense Paul's discomfort as he retrieved his Blackberry from his pocket. Her heart deflated like a three-day-old Mylar balloon as she watched him return e-mails and text messages.

Unwilling to allow herself to wallow in self-pity or to force conversation with the supposed love of her life, she turned her head and focused her attention on the traffic outside the small café. Fear twisted in her as she saw flashes of her life in the next year, two years . . . ten years. Would she be waiting at home, alone, for a husband who would turn to work instead of to her? Would she never again feel the closeness that had first drawn them together?

A tear escaped her eye as her mind began to unravel the tapestry of the beautifully planned life she had created over the past few months.

"Sweetheart?" Paul nudged her hand.

Jane jerked her hand away from his gentle touch, quickly wiping her wet cheeks, but not before her previously obtuse fiancé noticed. "Jane, what's wrong?"

"Nothing," she said with a shake of her head.

"Sweetheart, you're crying. Something is obviously wrong."

"We should pray before we eat, don't you think?"

Paul nodded and bowed his head for the blessing. He thanked God for the meal, for bringing them together, and for safe travels for everyone as they made their way to Ohio.

With the blessing's conclusion, Jane went about dressing her sandwich and disregarding her lunch companion. She was halfway through her meal before she realized that Paul had not taken a single bite.

She lifted an eyebrow. "Is something wrong with your order?"

"Not my order, no. But something is definitely wrong with you, Jane. Do you mind telling me why you were crying and why you're now trying to consume your food in record time?"

She could feel anger boiling in her heart like lava inside Mt. Vesuvius as she set her sandwich back on her plate and focused her complete attention on Paul. "I'm not really sure why I was crying."

"Jane, you're the worst liar in the history of modern man. Try again."

She could feel the lava bubble hotter. "I don't know. I guess it just kind of freaked me out that we're getting married tomorrow, we haven't seen each other in two months, and we don't have anything to talk about."

"Jane, I think it's a good thing that we can be together and not feel a need to talk."

"Are you serious?"

"Okay, so maybe you don't agree."

"Paul, we're getting married. Tomorrow. We haven't been married for fifty years. We should have everything to talk about. We should be wearing ourselves out, we are talking so much. We should be in the Stanley Cup playoffs of talking." *Boom!* Jane could feel the lava oozing from the eruption ready to destroy everything and everyone in its path.

"Okay—"

"You think I'm crazy!" The lava was spewing out of her uncontrollably. She had officially become her worst nightmare. She was her mother.

"Jane, please calm down. You're being ridiculous."

"Ridiculous? Did you just call me ridiculous? Well, maybe you would rather marry someone else, bucko. Huh! I'll show you ridiculous!" She stood up from her chair, threw her napkin on her seat, grabbed her bag, and made a hasty exit to the door.

She continued to mutter to herself walking up High Street with little thought to where she would end up. Inundated with the blistering cold of mid-spring in Columbus, her temper started to waver. Paul was right. She was being ridiculous. She shouldn't have stormed out of the restaurant like she was Alexis Carrington in the shoulder-pad glory days of the eighties, but she couldn't take another minute.

Jane stopped and dropped onto a nearby bench, mentally trying to cap her internal Vesuvius. What was she doing? She was getting married to a man she barely knew, moving to the other side of the world, and giving up all semblance of her known life. She wasn't just ridiculous—she was crazy. These weren't the actions of the sensible, somewhat clumsy, Jane Grey she knew. She needed to get herself together. Paul deserved better. She deserved better.

She sat on the park bench for a few minutes, wallowing and mellowing, before she talked herself into returning to the restaurant. She stood up and walked with her head down to avoid the inevitable stumble on the sidewalk, mentally preparing her apology.

"Jane."

She turned at the memorable voice. And there he stood, all six feet four inches and two hundred and thirty-five pounds of beautifully muscled athlete named Lindy Barrett. Her heart flipped at the slight upturn of his full lips. His eyes were shielded behind sunglasses, but she knew their blue depths held warmth and welcoming.

"Lindy, what are you doing here?" Her feet had grown roots and were firmly planted into the ground. It was impossible for her to step away or to step closer to him.

"Getting my knee checked out."

She looked down at the ugly brace that engulfed his thick leg, and for the first time she noticed the crutches. Her legs uprooted and she went to him. "Oh, my goodness, you should be sitting."

"I'm okay. I'm a tough hockey player, remember?"

She smiled in response to his wide grin. "Good drugs, huh?"

"The best."

"It's really good to see you, Lindy."

"Not as good as it is to see you, Jane. I missed that face."

His words broke the spell, driving a knife of guilt through her heart at the echo of Paul's voice floated through her mind. "I'm sorry. I have to go. I need to get back to Paul."

"I'm sorry. I didn't mean to bug you. I saw you storm out of the restaurant and wanted to make sure you were okay. Are you okay, Jane?"

Listening to him stumble over his words, Jane sensed he was nervous, something quite rare for the famous athlete. "I'm okay, just pre-wedding jitters, I guess. You saw me run out of the restaurant?"

"Yeah. I'm not so fast on these things, but I can still keep a pretty decent pace against those crazy shoes you're wearing." He used his crutch to point to her three-inch heels. "Those cannot be good for your long-term foot care."

"No, but they're good for my short-term fashion sense." She looked back up High Street and wondered if Paul was still waiting for her. Knowing him, he was dutifully following the Boy Scout rule of staying put until your party returns to safety.

"I'm sorry, I have to get back. Do you need a ride anywhere?" she asked, moving toward the restaurant.

"No, I'm good." He leaned on his crutches.

"Okay, well, it was really good to see you." Jane leaned toward him, intending to kiss him lightly on the cheek, with the universal friendship kiss. But as her lips touched his skin, she felt as if she were physically burned from heat the simple touch radiated. Lindy pulled her close to his chest with one arm and without a moment for her to contemplate the consequences he dropped his lips to hers.

The kiss was electric. Jane felt lightning shoot through her body with the union of their lips. He drew her closer and she clung to him, trying to avoid drowning in the deep pool of sensation his tender kiss was creating. She was no match for the passion he poured into her. Her mind ceased to think; she could only feel. And in that moment, Lindy whisked Jane away to an island where it was just the two of them. Nothing else mattered. All she could do was cling to him, hoping he would safely guide her home.

She had no idea how long the kiss lasted, or even where she was as Lindy barely lifted his mouth from hers. She let out a soft sigh that mingled with his labored breath as she rested her head to his chest, content to be in his protective embrace. Caught in their own private bubble, on a busy Friday afternoon on High Street, Jane lifted her heavy-lidded gaze to Lindy's, expecting to sink a little deeper into the liquid blue of his eyes. Instead she felt an unseen bucket of ice water splash over her as her passion-laden eyes took in her own mussed reflection in Lindy's sunglasses.

What am I doing?

"You were kissing me," Lindy murmured as he raised his hand to gently brush the hair from her cheek.

Jane's confused expression caused Lindy to chuckle low and deep. "You said, 'What am I doing.'"

"I said that out loud?" She could feel her nose glow red as embarrassment and shame pounded through her body like waves on the beach during a hurricane.

"Yes, Beautiful, you spoke your thoughts. You do it more often then you realize." He chuckled as he continued to cuddle her in his embrace.

"I do?" Who would have thought that she didn't just over share from the mouth? *Great. One more thing to worry about.*

As Lindy's hand gently roamed up and down her spine, she realized they were still intimately entangled. Her conscious reminded her, loudly, that her fiancé was waiting for her to return from her eighties, *Dynasty*-esque fit.

Jane slowly stepped back and out of Lindy's arms, careful not to make the injured athlete lose his balance and fall. "I'm sorry, Lindy. I really need to get back."

His smile fell as he pushed his sunglasses back on his head. "To Paul?"

"Yes, to Paul."

"You're still going to marry him even after what just happened?" His voice shook with tightly leashed anger.

"Of course. I'm marrying, Paul. The wedding is tomorrow. I made a commitment to him, and I don't break my commitments." She took a further step away from his magnetic pull, afraid that if she was too close, she would slip and fall back into his arms.

"Jane, how can you even think about marrying another man when we share what we share?"

Her two-timing heart melted at Lindy's words, but her mind wouldn't listen to its passionate plea. "What do we share, Lindy?"

"Jane, you know I care about you, and we obviously have passion between us."

"You care about me?" Her voice was low and soft as she stared up at him, her arms crossed protectively across her chest. "You care about me? What is *that* supposed to mean? Paul and I are getting married tomorrow, and you expect me to . . . what? Cancel the wedding because you *care* about me?"

"Jane, you know it's more than that. Paul isn't the right guy for you."

"And you are?"

"I think I might be, but if you marry him, we'll never know."

"Then I guess we'll never know. Good-bye Lindy." Before she could allow her heart to argue with her mind, she turned and ran as quickly as her three-hundred-dollar shoes would take her. She could feel his eyes watching her, but she didn't let herself turn and look at the possibility she was leaving behind.

Jane ran the two blocks to the restaurant, ignoring the tears streaming down her face as she tried desperately to get back to the well-ordered life she'd planned. As she approached the café, she found that life waiting for her on the front step.

She stopped a few feet away from Paul and watched as he stood and closed the gap between them. "I'm sorry," he whispered.

She rushed into his hug and allowed the tears to continue to pour out of her heart and onto his chest—shedding all of the pent-up emotion of the past months, weeks, days, and hours.

She leaned back, remaining in the loose grip of his arms. "You don't need to apologize. I'm the one who had a minor freak-out. I'm sorry. I shouldn't have yelled or stormed out like that."

"Jane, you've been under an unbelievable amount of stress. You've made so many adjustments in the last few months. From the moment you agreed to marry me, you've given up everything in your life with no complaints. I'm amazed that you didn't yell at me sooner. I certainly deserve it." He drew her tightly into his arms, and Jane breathed his scent deeply, thankful for the ability to hide her shame from his eyes.

He smelled like clean air and fresh water. His scent was like him, uncomplicated and straightforward. And from this moment on, her life would be uncomplicated and straightforward.

She just had to get through the wedding.

CHAPTER THIRTY-FOUR

JANE HOOKED THE TINY EYEHOOK on the bedazzled ivory cocktail dress her mother had selected as her rehearsal dinner dress. The beaded contraption weighed as much as Jane's prize-winning rabbit in elementary school; wearing the thing had to count as a workout giving her a free pass to devour every bite of cake or cookie in the path of her shame-sparked appetite tonight.

Returning to her small cosmetic assortment, she put the finishing touches on her makeup, when a quiet knock interrupted her mascara wand. "Come in."

To Jane's surprise, Brad walked through the door decked out in his best suit and tie. "Brad, what are you doing up here? I'm not so late that the pastor has to come and get me?" Jane smiled as she walked to her old friend, who had offered to fill in when Paul's pastor had been admitted to the hospital two days earlier.

"No, I wanted a few minutes with the blushing bride," he said, a broad smile on his round face. "You look amazing, Jane. Not that you don't always, but you have truly outdone yourself tonight."

"Well, I guess I have to believe you, since you're a pastor and all."

His smile faded as he stepped further into her room and sat at the small table in the corner. "Can we talk for a few minutes?"

Jane nodded her head in agreement, joining him at the table, opting to use the tabletop as a seat for fear of damaging the delicate dress. "What do you want to talk about?"

Brad reached for her hand. "Jane, did you see Lindy today?"

She yanked her hand from his and quickly stood out of his reach. "Why?"

"I know you spoke with him. I want to know if, after you saw him, talked to him, you're still prepared to commit your life to Paul."

"What are you talking about?" Jane turned her back to Brad, afraid her face would betray her true feelings.

Brad stood and walked close behind her, placing his hand on her shoulder to turn her to face him. With her heels, she was a hair's breadth taller than him, enabling her to avoid his direct gaze as he spoke. "I talked with Lindy today, after he saw you, and what he shared with me gave me reason to doubt your sincerity in this marriage."

"Since when do you talk to Lindy Barrett?" Was the whole world conspiring against her happily ever after?

"Since the night I found him outside of the worship center. He seemed fairly distraught, so I offered him a ride. I waited for him to share what was weighing on him, but he remained quiet. Before he could make his less-than-speedy escape, I gave him my card and asked him to call me if he wanted to talk. I was a little surprised to find him waiting for me in my office the next day."

Jane listened as Brad recounted his meetings with Lindy. He told her how the tough hockey player had wept over the loss of his friend, and the struggles he was having releasing the guilt. Brad told her that he shared with Lindy the healing power that Jesus's love brings, if one only accepts it, and how two days later, Lindy had knelt on the floor of Brad's office and accepted Jesus as his Savior. Jane felt her tears pour down her cheeks as her breath came in shallow spurts as her heart experienced the story of Lindy's conversion.

Brad's own eyes were wet as he placed his hand on Jane's. "Lindy turned around and found God waiting behind him."

God You're so good! Thank You for answering this prayer. It was a big one. I love You so much!

Jane wiped her eyes as she stepped into Brad's hug. Her breathing slowed and she squeezed his shoulders, moving slightly back from him. Swiping her fingers under her eyes to rectify the damage her tears had caused, she dropped onto the edge of her bed. "Thank you for helping him, Brad. Why didn't he tell me?"

"He tried, well, sort of tried, the night you came to his apartment."

"No, he didn't . . ." She thought back to the heartbreaking memory. He'd wanted to tell her something.

"Yes, he did, Jane, but you trumped his moment with the announcement that you and Paul were getting married."

"I did?"

"Well, that's how he felt. He was so excited to share with you, but he was a little afraid you would think he did it to win you away from Paul, and he wanted to be sure you knew his faith was real. When you told him about the engagement, he didn't feel like it was fair to tell you."

"Not fair? I've been praying for him for months. I would have celebrated with him. He deserves a celebration." She could feel her tears burn in her throat as she pulled her worn teddy bear into her arms.

Brad walked to her. Sitting on the bed beside her and he draped his arm around her shoulders. "You're right, but the only person he wanted to celebrate with was you, and you were already taken."

Turning to face him, she lifted her eyes to his. "How did my life become a soap opera?"

"Just lucky, I guess. You always did have a flare for the dramatic." He chuckled.

Lindy was a Christian. That revelation changed her whole view of him—and their relationship.

"Jane," Brad interrupted her thoughts. "We do need to get downstairs. But before we go, I need to know . . . I need to know if you're in love with Lindy."

Jane stared at her crossed arms and the old teddy in their grasp. Her heart quickly answered yes to Brad's question, but her mind put on the brakes. In roughly eighteen hours, hundreds of friends and family would be descending upon this very house to see her wed her Prince Charming. She wasn't in a position to pull a Julia Roberts and find the nearest horse.

"Jane, honey, you have a unique and envied problem. You have two wonderful people who are in love with you. You need to decide which one you want to marry—and which one God wants you to marry." Brad kissed the top of her coiffed head and made his retreat from the room.

Her world had turned upside down on its axis yet again, and she longed to know which way was true north. How could this be happening the night before her wedding?

Better than the night after.

"Great, I'm officially having a breakdown. I'm hearing voices. And I'm once again talking to myself." Jane threw herself backward on the bed, dragged the teddy across her face, and screamed into it.

After a few moments, her frustration sated, she sat up, tossed the bear onto the bed and walked to her dressing table. Her reflection wasn't awful, considering her emotional outburst. Her eyes were shiny, but bright, making her appear happy. She powdered her nose and smoothed out the tear streaks on her face, thankful for the waterproof mascara she had invested in months ago. She patted her hair in place and straightened her dress. Ambling to the door, she shut out the light with a sullen resolve. It was too late for her and Lindy, regardless of the passion, the connection or the faith they now shared. Paul had proven himself steady and reliable. She was getting married to a Volvo and not a Ferrari. She'd made a commitment to Paul, and nothing short of an intervention from God was going to stop her.

CHAPTER THIRTY-FIVE

GOD HAS A PARTICULARLY STRANGE sense of humor.

She stepped away from her window and the view of the monsoon that was swelling outside. Her wedding day was going to be reduced to a giant mud pit.

Jane tugged the belt to her satin robe, tightening it at her waist as she made her way to the bathroom to apply her makeup. The hairdresser her mother hired had twisted and teased Jane's hair into an elaborate bundle at the base of her neck. As she surveyed his handiwork, she was surprisingly pleased with the simple style, which had taken nearly an hour and a half to complete. Bitsy had offered to bring in a makeup artist, but flashbacks to the sorority sister's wedding, whose mother *was* a makeup artist, convinced her that her own subtle hand would be the best choice to decorate her face.

The house was teaming with guests counting down the minutes until the ceremony. Paul and his father had arrived twenty minutes earlier, according to Emory, who had usurped the role of blushing bride, forcing the hairstylist to not only coif her blonde curls, but also give her an eyebrow wax. Jane was actually thankful for Emory's antics. She had focused the attention away from Jane, allowing her a necessary reprieve from the chaos.

As she completed lining her lips, the hall door to the shared bathroom opened with a flourish that only Millie could bring. Her friend sauntered into the tiny bathroom, filling the space with the gentle fragrance of her high-end perfume and her natural presence. Jane took in her friend's form, wrapped in the heavy pink satin gown, and was amazed that Millie managed to make the pink monstrosity look gorgeous. Jane said as much as she turned back to the mirror to apply her lipstick.

"Well, darling, even when you put me in a gunnysack, I can't help but look fantastic. It's the genes." Millie gave Jane a dramatic wink. "What can I do?"

"Not much. Mom is ordering people around downstairs. Emory has cornered the stylist and won't let him leave until she looks better than I do. Molly is taking a nap, because, well, she's nearly eight months pregnant and huge."

"And the bride . . ."

"I'm strangely calm, despite the fact that these April showers aren't so friendly. Everything is good."

"Everything . . ."

Jane turned from the mirror and faced her friend. "What are you trying to ask, not so subtly, Amelia?"

"I heard you saw Lindy yesterday."

"Was it in the flipping *Dispatch*?" Jane muttered.

"Jason met him out last night. Don't worry, your boy didn't drink anything."

"He's not my boy. Lindy is not my anything." Jane turned to the mirror as she raised her hand, which had become a shaking noodle.

"Whatever. Lindy mentioned that you seemed upset when he ran into you yesterday at lunch. I thought you had lunch with Paul yesterday?"

"I did. I had a little Bridezilla moment and freaked out in the restaurant. I went outside to cool off, and Lindy happened to be there."

"He just happened to be there?"

"Millie, must you repeat everything I say in the form of a question? When did you turn into Alex Trebek?"

"He gives answers. The contestants respond in the form of a question."

"Whatever."

"Jane, what happened yesterday with Lindy? He wouldn't tell Jason, but Jay thinks it was something that rattled the Hockey Stud but good."

Jane dropped her gaze to the floor and whispered, "He kissed me."

"What?" Millie screeched.

Jane slammed the bathroom door closed and grabbed Millie by the arm, hauling her into the bedroom. "Would you be quiet? There is a houseful of people here for my wedding."

"To a man you weren't macking on yesterday."

"I wasn't macking on Lindy. We kissed. It really isn't any big deal."

Millie plopped down onto Jane's bed. "Janesie, this is Millie you're talking to, not some hillbilly you picked up on the street corner. Kissing, to you, is the biggest deal. What was it like? Is he an awesome kisser?"

"Millie, please don't be crude right now. This is something I'm trying to forget even happened." Jane fell back on her bed and pulled her teddy bear over her face.

Millie curled up on the bed beside her. "Jane, why do you want to forget?"

"Because . . ."

"Because . . ." Millie prodded.

"Because it was wonderful," she replied into the teddy.

Pulling the bear from Jane's face, Millie smiled down at her. "Jane, it's okay to think a kiss was wonderful from another man. That doesn't make you a heathen, or a harlot, or anything else you imagined. You're still in love with Paul and are marrying him. You didn't break your marriage vows. I mean it's not like Lindy asked you to marry him."

Jane could feel the red stain burn through her layers of makeup.

Millie blinked. "He didn't propose, did he?"

"No, not exactly."

"Jane, please don't beat around the bush. You're getting married in exactly three hours. We don't have time for a game of ring around the hockey player. Get to the point."

Jane forced herself up and stared at her friend, unsure how to succinctly explain everything she had learned in the last eighteen hours. She started with the night in January, and the rest spilled out like gumballs from a broken machine.

"And Brad seems to think that Lindy is in love with me," she finished.

Millie sat in stunned silence for several minutes before she thrust herself off of the canopy bed and began to pace the floor.

Despite the relief she felt over baring her soul, Jane's butterfly squadron was revving its engines for flight as she watched Millie wearing a hole in the hardwood. Millie always knew how to handle every situation. If this one stumped her, they were in trouble with a capital *T*.

And then, as if a cartoon light bulb lit atop her head, Millie stopped mid-stride, turned and faced her. "Jane, you have to stop the wedding."

Jane could hear her butterflies sing, "Off We Go into the Wild Blue Yonder."

"Millie, you know I can't. Think of all of the people, my parents, Paul. I can't just cancel the wedding a few hours before on my ex-boyfriend's hunch that my friend is in love with me. It's crazy. I made a commitment to Paul."

"Jane." Millie stepped forward and reached for Jane's hands. "Do you love Lindy? First answer that pops in your head."

"Yes," Jane blurted. "Oh, no . . ."

"Oh, yes. Jane Grey. I love you more than anyone on this planet, even more than I love Jason, but I'll deny it if you tell him. You deserve everything your heart desires. You shouldn't have to transform your life to marry a nice, safe Christian man. What was the one thing always holding you back from pursuing a romantic relationship with Lindy?"

"His faith."

"And what is his faith like now?"

"I don't know for sure, but Brad thinks he's pretty sincere . . . Millie, this is ridiculous. I'm marrying Paul." Jane walked to her wedding gown. "Now, I need help getting into this concoction. Would you please help me?

"Jane . . ."

She whirled and faced her friend with tears threatening in her eyes. "Please, Millie," she whispered. "Please, let's not talk about it anymore. I've made a commitment and I'm sticking by it."

Millie pulled the dress from the high hook and laid it on Jane's bed. She gently squeezed her shoulders and kissed her cheek. "I'm going to run and find your mother and sisters."

"Thanks. I could use a minute or two before they descend upon me." Jane tried to smile but failed miserably. Her heart felt as fragile as a paper cut-out she had once made in elementary school. She hoped her real heart survived this storm better than the one from the first grade.

CHAPTER THIRTY-SIX

JANE'S MOTHER BUTTONED the final tiny button on the back of Jane's dress as Molly buckled her shoes. Despite her advanced pregnancy, Molly continued to be remarkably agile. Millie had not returned with her sisters and her mother, but sent an excuse through Emory, who couldn't remember the details. Jane decided not to worry about Millie or what she was doing. Her goal was to remain blissfully ignorant until she was on the plane with her husband. It was better than tormenting herself with thoughts of what could never be.

The women oohed and awed over Jane's dress, but when the bride made eye contact with her older sister, it took both women's complete self-control not to begin giggling.

"Oh, Jane dear, you just look like a vision." Her mother choked back tears.

"That's one way to describe it." Jane stared at herself. The dress was worse than she remembered. From the spaghetti straps that wouldn't lay flush to her shoulders to the fitted bodice covered in beading, nothing was Jane. At least she'd talked her sister out of the tiara she wanted Jane to sport. The sisters had compromised, and as Jane watched Emory over her shoulder, she thought that the tiny rhinestone tiara fit her sister perfectly.

A knock sounded, causing all four Grey women to swivel in unison as their father, and husband, walked through the door looking like a dashing older version of James Bond.

"Daddy, you look wonderful." Molly smiled, giving their father a hug.

"Not as good as you, sweet pea."

Emory pouted and crossed her arms.

"Princess, you look every bit the princess you are." He smiled and kissed his youngest daughter's forehead. She responded with a pacified grin as she turned to admire herself in the mirror.

Henry walked to Jane and pulled her into a tight hug. "Oh, but peanut, this truly will be your day to shine."

"Well, somebody better shine, since the Lord went and hid the sun." Jane tried to joke.

"Oh, Henry, stop smooshing the girl," Bitsy fussed. "You'll get her all wrinkled."

"Jane," her father whispered in her ear. "I know it's bad luck and all, but Paul would really like to see you."

Jane stood back from her father's embrace with a furrowed brow. "Now?"

Her dad simply nodded his head. Knowing that her mother would never allow such an illicit meeting, Henry generously created a diversion. "Bitsy, honey, the caterers seem to be confused on the table arrangements. I heard one of them say that the cookie table is to be set up on the back lawn regardless of the weather. Thought you would want to know . . ."

"Oh, for goodness' sake. I can't leave those people alone for a minute. Emory and Molly, I'm going to need your help."

"But who will stay with Jane?" Molly asked.

Bitsy looked back at her husband and gave him a conspiratorial wink. "Oh, I think your father will hold down the fort for us." She pulled the door shut behind her, leaving father and daughter alone.

"I'll send Paul along." He paused before leaving the room. "You aren't superstitious, are you?"

"No, Daddy. If Paul wants to talk to me, it must be important."

Jane watched her father leave the room, trying to ground the butterflies as she waited for Paul to come to her. She wondered what he wanted. Maybe he had some special token he wanted to give her as a remembrance of the day. Maybe he wanted to pray with her. *That would be nice.*

She heard the soft knock on the door as Paul walked into her room, looking breathtakingly handsome in his black tuxedo with a white bow tie. His hair had been trimmed from its normal unruly blond mass, but he retained most of the length, which made Jane smile. She walked to her husband-to-be with her hands outstretched, but he didn't take hers in return.

Her arms dropped awkwardly to her sides as she watched Paul shove his hand through his hair and begin to pace the room. She waited for him to start, but the dread that seemed to have been hovering around the edges of this wedding from the beginning crept up her spine.

"Paul, my Dad said you wanted to talk to me."

Paul stopped and turned to face her. "Jane, do you love me?"

A sigh rushed over her body. Paul was nervous. Mr. Calm, Cool, and Collected, Attorney at Law, was experiencing wedding nerves. She closed the gap between them and placed her arms around his neck. "Of course I love you. I wouldn't put on this awful dress for anyone else," she teased as she stood on her tiptoes to brush his lips with her own.

"What about Lindy?"

Jane stiffened at the accusation in his voice. She jerked her arms back to herself, resetting the distance between them.

"Jane, can you answer me, please?"

Her heart felt like she had just run the one-hundred-yard dash. "I'm trying to figure out where all the landmines are."

"Jane," he said, closing the space between them with two long steps. "Just tell me you don't love Lindy, and we can go down those stairs and have Brad marry us."

She stared at his shirtfront, waiting for words to fill her mouth, but she had no response to the gauntlet Paul threw down before her.

He turned from her as if he couldn't bear to look at her. "Why did you agree to marry me, if you're in love with someone else?"

Jane swallowed deeply, but her mouth was as dry as sandpaper. "I love you, Paul. You know I do. I made a commitment to you, and I don't break my commitments, not ever. I chose you."

Paul leaned against the window frame, appearing to be entranced by the rain. "Are you sure I wasn't a consolation prize?" His voice was low and layered with pain.

Jane's heart felt as if it was being crumpled like that paper cutout. "Paul, that is not fair."

He turned back to her; his face twisted in the agony of a breaking heart. "Isn't it fair, Jane? How would you feel, being someone's duty dance?"

Jane felt hot tears race down her cheeks as she stepped closer to him.

"Paul, you're not a duty dance. How many times do I have to tell you that I love you before you will believe me?"

"Jane." He lifted his hand to her face and tenderly wiped the tears from her cheek. "I know you love me. But I don't think you're in love with me. I don't think you have ever been *in* love with me. I think I pushed you, too hard and too fast, three months ago. It's my fault. I should have known better when you came to my house in January, but I wanted you so badly, I was willing to do anything to make the puzzle pieces fit. I was willing, until I heard you talking with Brad last night and Millie this morning."

"You eavesdropped on my private conversations?"

"Well, they had to do with me. Your parents' house is not exactly sound-proof. Your mom sent me to get you last night. I overheard Brad telling you about Lindy. And today, I just happened to get stuck by your bedroom as they were trucking flower arrangements up the stairs. I heard you tell Millie that Lindy kissed you."

"Paul, it was nothing. Really. It shouldn't have happened, and I'm sorry it did, but it doesn't mean anything."

"What about when you told her that you loved him? Did that mean nothing, too?" Paul shoved his hand in his hair and turned back to the window.

Jane stared at Paul's broad shoulders, sagging in defeat, and felt her little paper heart dissolve into dust. What was she doing? She loved this man, but was she willing to lie to herself for the rest of her life?

She closed the slight distance between them and watched their reflection in the rain-soaked window. Wrapping her arms around his waist, she placed her chin on his shoulder. "We look like Bedazzled Ken and Barbie. Emory always wanted life-size dolls."

He rested his cheek against hers. "Jane, I love you."

Jane swallowed against the lump in her throat. She unlinked her hands and withdrew her engagement ring from her ring finger. "Paul, I love you, too."

Pressing the ring into his hand, she met his gaze in the window. "I love you too much to give you anything less than everything. I can't marry you."

He glanced at the ring shining in his hand. "I thought God brought us together for a bigger purpose, but maybe we were only ever supposed to be friends. Maybe I wanted it to be something more, so badly that I couldn't see what God was telling us."

He placed the ring in his pocket and turned to face her. He pressed a kiss on her forehead. "Good-bye, Jane."

His footsteps echoed against the hardwood as Jane watched Paul walk out of her life. The door closed behind him, and she dropped to the floor in a mound of crinoline and tulle, waiting for the tears that had been her true companion during this journey, but they didn't come.

Jane sat on the floor for a few more moments, wallowing in the pity party for one she threw for herself, as she tried to summon the fortitude to walk down the stairs, out into the rain, and tell five hundred people, including her mother, there wouldn't be a wedding. And she was going to have to do it in this dress.

Pushing herself up, she walked to the door and began to laugh the deep, hearty laugh of enjoyment or the criminally insane. She lifted her head and winked toward heaven. "I hope You gave the folks up there a bowl of popcorn to watch this movie today, God. 'Cause this little dramedy is a doozy."

After she told everyone that she and Paul had decided not to get married, her mother, always the consummate hostess, invited all of the guests to eat, drink, and celebrate the decision to avoid a future divorce. Only her mother could turn a defunct wedding reception into an anti-divorce party.

About two hours into the party, after every guest was soaked, God stopped the rain and put on a beautiful display of rainbows in the sky. Jane knew she was probably a little conceited to think that God was reminding her of His covenant with her, but she liked to think those rainbows were just for her.

As the party wound down, Jane slipped out the back entrance of the tent. She yanked off her soiled shoes and let her mud-splattered dress drag through every bit of gunk she could find. She headed toward the tire swing, hoping the many happy memories from childhood it held would rub off on her mood.

Jane's dirty feet peeped out of the bottom of her voluminous skirts, but she still wasn't quite tall enough to reach the ground and push herself. The thought brought a little whimper to her lips. Once again, she was alone. She didn't have anyone to push her.

All day, she had been shoving down the self-pity that threatened to swallow her whole. She had been able to distract herself with dancing, friends, and platefuls of calorie-laden food. But now, all alone in the quietness of the setting sun, she couldn't run from the pity demons any longer.

The tears, absent most of the day, reestablished their territory. She cried for the way she'd hurt Paul. She cried for how she had been so misguided about Lindy. She cried for her parents and all of the money they'd spent on this elaborate party. She cried because she hadn't listened to God and sought patience. And she cried because she didn't have anyone to help her get out of this conundrum of a dress.

Awash in her pain, she felt strong hands push her forward, causing a smile to break through her tears.

"Hi, Daddy," she said quietly, knowing he was the one man she could always count on.

"Well, Beautiful, if you want to call me Daddy, we might need to play a different game." The sound of the deeply rough voice sent shivers down Jane's spine as she tried ineffectively to turn in the swing to see his face.

Lindy accommodated her wiggle by stopping the swing and slowly walking around to the front, using the sides of the tire for leverage.

Fresh tears rolled down her cheeks as she gazed into the warm blue of the eyes of the man she loved. Cupping her face in his palms, he brushed the wetness from her cheeks with his thumb. "Beautiful, don't you know there's no crying in baseball?"

"This isn't baseball, Lindy."

"No, but we've been playing a game with each other these past few months."

She nodded her head, afraid to speak.

"I don't want to play games with you anymore, Jane. In fact, I don't want to play anything with you, ever again."

The finality of his words caused Jane to sit as erect as the tire swing and her stiff corset would allow. He was leaving, too. The wave of sadness hit her harder than telling Paul she couldn't marry him.

"I see."

"I don't think you do. Jane, I want to stop the games between us, because I only want the real thing. Jane Eleanor Grey, I love you. I've loved you since the first moment you walked across that ballroom, pretending that you were some fierce woman. I love that your emotions are painted across your face like the watercolor shades of God's palette. I love the way you look when you're all gussied up, and I love the way you look when you're sick as a dog. I love the way you love God and put Him before everything in your life. I love the way you've loved me, even when you tried not to. Jane, I love you."

Jane lunged forward and wrapped her arms around Lindy's neck. The hard tire and the rough rope were between them, but she didn't mind. Lindy loved her. What else could matter?

Lindy placed his hands on either side of Jane's face and kissed her with the deep, pent-up passion she'd longed to feel for the last six months. She could feel him pour his heart filled with love into hers, and she in turn unlocked the tightly shut box filled with her feelings for him. They kissed as smoothly and intimately as they could with the tire swing as an impediment. For the first time since she'd met Lindy, she was free to be completely honest with herself, with him, and with God, and the release was like the opening of a dam.

Breaking their contact, she gently rested her head against his, idly stroking the soft fabric of his sweater. The day had been a roller coaster befitting the past few months.

"What are you thinking?" Lindy asked as he kissed her cheek.

"How crazy my sensible life has become? I've always tried to do the right thing, fulfill all of my responsibilities, wear the proper thing at the proper time . . . be the good girl. And here I am in this awful, overpriced wedding gown, kissing the man I adore, who is not the man I was supposed to marry, on my wedding day. I can remember sitting with Millie, wanting a nice, respectable change in my life . . . something manageable and proper. But despite of all of my efforts to be Plain Jane Grey, my life has been anything but plain and proper of late."

"Jane, you could never be plain." He kissed her again, and the sweetness of his touch sent tremors through her body and left her lungs gasping for air as he slowly pulled away.

Resting his forehead against hers, he gave her a lopsided grin. "Well, not to add to the disorder of your life, but would it be completely inappropriate to propose to a bride, who didn't actually get married, while she was still in her wedding dress, on her wedding day?"

Jane leaned back in the swing. She couldn't stop her lips from quivering as she fought tears. "I don't think Emily Post wrote a section on how to deal with that particular situation. I guess you're going to have to navigate that sea of propriety on your own."

Lindy reached into his pants pocket, retrieving a white leather box. "I hope you'll excuse my not getting down on my knee. Jane Eleanor Grey, will you do me the great honor of sharing your life with me and God?"

Jane nodded as he opened the box and revealed a simple platinum wedding band. She smiled and nodded profusely, unable to speak.

Lifting the ring from the box, he placed it on her left ring finger. "This was my father's ring for my mother. When she came at Christmas she brought it, specifically for you. She knew. She just knew."

Jane lost the control over the tears that flooded her eyes as she looked at her heart shining through Lindy's eyes. Caressing his rugged jaw, she whispered, "I always love you, Linden Barrett. I love you now. I will love you tomorrow. I loved you yesterday. I always love you."

Lindy pulled her tightly into his embrace, and she could feel his body shudder as he tried but failed to hold back his own tears. Jane held him with her own fierce grip as she lifted her eyes to the setting sun. She silently thanked God for His gifts and excellent timing, and in turn, she felt a sense of pleasure and contentment wash over her.

You're welcome.